My Ántonia

Willa Sibert Cather

WITH RELATED READINGS

THE EMC MASTERPIECE SERIES

Access Editions

EMC/Paradigm Publishing
St. Paul, Minnesota

Staff Credits

Laurie Skiba
Managing Editor

Brenda Owens
High School Editor

Becky Palmer
Associate Editor

Nichola Torbett
Associate Editor

Jennifer Anderson
Assistant Editor

Paul Spencer
Art and Photo Researcher

Valerie Murphy
Editorial Assistant

Lori Ann Coleman
Editorial Consultant

Shelley Clubb
Production Manager

Jennifer Wreisner
Senior Designer

Leslie Anderson
Senior Design and Production Specialist

Parkwood Composition
Compositor

Cover photo of Webster County, Nebraska: © Farrell Grehan/CORBIS
Cover Photo of Willa Cather: © Bettmann/CORBIS

Library of Congress Cataloging-in-Publication Data

Cather, Willa, 1873-1947.
My Ántonia / Willa Sibert Cather.
p. cm. – (The EMC Masterpiece Series Access Editions)
Contents: My Ántonia – Introduction to the 1926 edition / by Willa
Cather – Letter to Frances Samlund / by Anna Pavelka – [Excerpt] from
History of the State of Nebraska /
by William G. Cutter and A.T. Andreas – The Fir Tree / by Hans
Christian Andersen – Mint Snowball / Naomi Shihab Nye – The Prairie
Grass Dividing / by Walt Whitman –Riding into California / by Shirley
Geok-lin Lim – Plot analysis of My Ántonia – Creative writing activities
– Critical writing activities –Projects.
Summary: In the late nineteenth century, a fourteen-year-old immi-
grant girl from Bohemia and a ten-year-old orphan boy arrive in Black
Hawk, Nebraska, and in teaching each other, form a friendship that will
last a lifetime.
ISBN 0-8219-2509-1
1. Frontier and pioneer life—Fiction. 2. Farmers' spouses—Fiction. 3.
Women pioneers—Fiction. 4. Married women—Fiction. 5. Farm life—
Fiction. 6. Nebraska—Fiction. 7. Cather, Willa, 1873-1947. My Ántonia.
[1. Farm life—Nebraska—Fiction. 2. Frontier and pioneer life—
Nebraska—Fiction. 3. Friendship—Fiction. 4. Nebraska—Fiction.] I.
Title. II. Series.

PS3505.A87 M8 2002
813'.52 [Fic]—dc21

2001055669

ISBN 0-8219-2509-1

Copyright © 2003 by EMC Corporation

Published by EMC/Paradigm Publishing
875 Montreal Way
St. Paul, Minnesota 55102
800-328-1452
www.emcp.com
E-mail: educate@emcp.com

Printed in the United States of America.
   2 3 4 5 6 7 8 9 10 xxx 07 06 05 04 03 02

Table of Contents

THE LIFE AND WORKS OF

Willa Sibert Cather

The oldest of seven children, Willa Cather was born in 1873 in western Virginia. When she was ten years old, her family moved to rural Nebraska to live in Willa's grandparents' house. The landscape she encountered there, with its miles of waving red grasses, its few isolated trees, its openness to brutal weather, and its determined, lonely settlers, permeated Cather's imagination and became the source of and setting for many of her most significant literary works, including *My Ántonia*.

Willa Sibert Cather

In fact, many events from Cather's life following the move to Nebraska show up in the life of Jim Burden, the narrator of *My Ántonia*. Like Jim, Cather spent hours listening to immigrant neighbors tell stories of the old country and of their earliest years in Nebraska. Cather would never forget these stories, and many of them would later appear in her fiction.

Less than two years after arriving in Nebraska, the Cathers left the farm and moved into Red Cloud, a small prairie town where Willa attended school for the first time. Red Cloud appears in Cather's fiction under a number of names, including *My Ántonia*'s town of Black Hawk. It was in Red Cloud that Willa met Annie Sadilek, a Bohemian girl who worked for the neighboring Miner family. The character of Ántonia is based on Annie, whose difficult life and vibrant personality fascinated Cather. A letter from the real Annie is included in the back of this book as a related reading.

The adolescent Cather and the townspeople of Red Cloud had mixed feelings about each other. Cather was gifted at seeing beneath the surface of the people around her and uncovering their unique stories. Her eccentricities, however, did not mesh well with a relatively conformist town. A tomboy, Cather often dressed in boys' clothing and even signed her name as William or Willie Cather for most of her teenage years. She was out of place in Red Cloud and often found companionship among the older residents and in her beloved books.

After graduation from high school, Cather, like Jim, attended the University of Nebraska in Lincoln. While she was at the university, a professor submitted one of her essays to the Lincoln newspaper for publication, kindling Cather's desire to write and publish. She began reviewing books, plays, and music for the Lincoln newspaper before she finished college.

Soon after graduation, Cather's writing aspirations drew her toward the East coast, where most of the magazines and journals of the time were published. In the first years of the new century, Cather lived in Pittsburgh and published many short stories and poems, including collections of both. She later moved to New York City to serve as editor of *McClure's*, a popular and controversial magazine, known for muckraking journalism that exposed scandals in industry and politics. In New York, Cather soon met Edith Lewis, the woman who would be her roommate and closest companion for the rest of her life.

Cather continued to write up until her death in 1947. In twelve novels and several collections of short stories, Cather explored her fascination with pioneers both literal and figurative.

In some cases, Cather's pioneers were sodbusters in the American Midwest. Several of her most important works, including *O Pioneers!*, *My Ántonia*, and *One of Ours,* describe the hardships and rewards of life on the frontier. The values Cather associates with the Midwestern prairie are celebrated and contrasted with the values of an increasingly urban, industrialized East coast.

Other books, including *The Song of the Lark* and *Lucy Gayheart*, trace the lives of artists breaking new ground in a more figurative sense. These artistic pioneers are struggling to maintain a connection to their own heritage while seeking artistic fulfillment.

Woven throughout Cather's body of work are themes of love and friendship, longing for connection to home, and the difficult decisions faced by those who choose to leave their homes to pursue a career, an artistic life, or military glory.

Time Line of Cather's Life and Works

Willa Cather is born on December 7 in her grandparents' house, where her parents live and farm, in western Virginia. She is the first child of seven children in her family.	**1873**
Willa, her parents, and several other family members move to southwestern Nebraska, sixteen miles northwest of the town of Red Cloud. Cather is initially frightened by the vast expanses of nothing but waving red grass and the loneliness of the landscape. Soon, however, she begins to enjoy visiting the neighbors, many of whom are immigrants from Norway, Bohemia, and Germany, and listening to their stories of the Old World.	**1883**
The Cather family moves to Red Cloud, where Willa starts school. There, too, she meets Annie Sadilek, a "hired girl" from Bohemia who becomes the inspiration for *My Ántonia*.	**1884**
Cather graduates from high school in June, one of a class of three, and leaves in September for Lincoln, where she begins studies at the University of Nebraska.	**1890**
A professor has the essay Cather wrote for his class published in the *Nebraska State Journal*. From the moment she sees her initials in print, she knows she will be a writer.	**1891**
One of the first short stories Cather ever wrote, called simply "Peter," is published in a Boston literary weekly. "Peter" tells the story of Francis Sadilek's suicide, an event that later appears in *My Ántonia*.	**1892**
Cather is hired as a critic for the *Nebraska State Journal*. She reviews books, plays, and music for the paper while finishing her university coursework and continuing to write short stories and poetry.	**1894**
Cather graduates from the University of Nebraska.	**1895**
The publisher of *Home Monthly*, a new magazine based in Pittsburgh, offers Cather the editorship of the magazine. She accepts and moves to Pittsburgh, where she soon also begins writing reviews for the *Pittsburgh Leader*.	**1896**
Cather becomes a full-time critic for the *Pittsburgh Leader*.	**1897**
Cather resigns from the *Pittsburgh Leader* to accept a position teaching high school English and Latin.	**1901**
Cather's book of poetry, *April Twilights*, is published.	**1903**
The Troll Garden, a book of short stories, is published.	**1905**
Recruited by the popular magazine *McClure's*, Cather moves to New York City and begins work as a contributing editor. She will eventually become managing editor and will remain with the magazine until 1912. Shortly after moving to New York, Cather meets Edith Lewis, who becomes and remains her roommate and companion for the rest of her life.	**1906**
Cather publishes her first novel, *Alexander's Bridge*.	**1912**

1913	The first of Cather's Nebraska novels, *O Pioneers!*, is published.
1915	*The Song of the Lark* is published.
1918	*My Ántonia* is published.
1920	The short story collection *Youth and the Bright Medusa* is published.
1922	Dismayed by what she perceives as a decline in values in the country, Cather suffers a period of depression.
1923	Cather wins the Pulitzer Prize for her new novel, *One of Ours. A Lost Lady* is published.
1925	*The Professor's House* is published.
1926	*My Mortal Enemy* and *Death Comes for the Archbishop* are published.
1930	The novel *Death Comes for the Archbishop* receives the Howells Medal from the American Academy and Institute of Arts and Letters.
1931	*Shadows on the Rock* is published.
1935	*Lucy Gayheart* is published.
1936	The essay collection *Not Under Forty* is published.
1941	*Sapphira and the Slave Girl* is published.
1944	For her outstanding body of work, Cather receives the Gold Medal for Fiction from the National Institute and the American Academy of Arts and Letters.
1947	Cather dies on April 24 of a cerebral hemorrhage in her Park Avenue, New York City apartment. She was seventy-four years old.

THE HISTORICAL CONTEXT OF

My Ántonia

My Ántonia tells the story of a lifelong friendship between Jim Burden and Ántonia Shimerda. When Jim was ten years old, both of his parents died, and he was sent by train to live with his grandparents in Nebraska. Although he couldn't have known it at the time, the fourteen-year-old girl from Bohemia, traveling just a few train cars away, was to become one of the most important people in his life.

The novel chronicles this friendship from the late 1880s through the early 1900s. Most of the events take place in or near the fictional town of Black Hawk, Nebraska. Black Hawk is based on the real town of Red Cloud in south central Nebraska, which was Willa Cather's home for nearly ten years of her childhood and adolescence.

In the early nineteenth century, this part of the country had been called "The Great American Desert." Because the land lacked trees, it was presumed to be useless, and few people had settled there. All of that was changing, though, as this novel begins. Between the end of the Civil War and 1890, new settlers flocked to Nebraska, and the population of Red Cloud reached approximately 2,500. This influx of people into the area was the result of several factors.

The Opening of the Frontier

"Free land!" This was the message sent by passage of the Homestead Act of 1862. This act granted 160 acres of public land to anyone who agreed to pay the ten dollar filing fee and live on the land for five years. For the government, the Homestead Act ensured that land in the west would be developed and made more valuable. For adventurous individuals and families, it meant hope for a new start, a chance to make a successful living outside the cities of the East, where poverty was rampant. By the time the Civil War ended in 1865, more than fifteen thousand families and individuals had claimed land in the western states. Hundreds of thousands more filed claims in the years to come.

The railroad also contributed to the population boom, not only by providing easy passage to Nebraska—no more long, difficult trips by covered wagon—but by selling the land on either side of the tracks for the low price of $2.50 an acre. Railroad brochures advertised the land west of the Mississippi as a New World paradise, and people responded.

Life on the Nebraska homestead was not easy, however. Many settlers, used to the more forested landscapes of the East, were unnerved by the wide open spaces of nothing but long grasses. Loneliness was sometimes crippling. Winters were harsh, bringing extremely cold temperatures, heavy snows, and bitter winds that whipped across the prairie with nothing to break them. In the mid-1870s, locusts devoured several years' worth of crops. Drought also took its toll during those years.

Because trees were so scarce, few people could afford to build wood homes. Instead, they lived in cave-like dugouts and sod houses (see illustrations on page xxii). Composed of three-foot blocks from the tough upper layer of prairie soil, sod houses were held together by the tangled root systems in the sod. While the dense material provided insulation against cold, the same material made attractive homes for insects and mice.

The same dense root systems that held sod houses together made prairie ground extremely hard to plow. About the first farms in Nebraska, Willa Cather wrote, "The record of the plow was insignificant, like the feeble scratches on stone left by prehistoric races, so indeterminate that they may, after all, be only the markings of glaciers, and not a record of human strivings." In *My Ántonia* and other writings, Cather reflects her respect for this tough landscape as well as her love of its austere beauty.

Poor urban families who moved west hoping for a new start often lacked the money and knowledge they needed to farm successfully. Land speculators and money-lenders, like *My Ántonia's* Wick Cutter, were quick to take advantage of struggling families.

The most successful families were often large, like Ántonia's, with many children to help work the land.

Immigrants: Strangers in a Strange Land

My Ántonia celebrates the varied ethnic heritage of Nebraska, which became home to many immigrant families. When the Homestead Act was passed, land in the state was advertised not only in the eastern part of the United States, but also in Europe, which is presumably how Mrs. Shimerda, Ántonia's mother, came to think of the American West as the land of opportunity. The Shimerdas would have been among the approximately ten million people who immigrated to the United States between 1865 and 1890. Railway lines, which were built rapidly during this period, allowed these newcomers easy access to the western frontier.

Most of the immigrants settling in Nebraska during this time were from Norway, Germany, Russia, Moravia, and Bohemia.

The fictional characters of Ántonia and her family are reported to have come to Nebraska from Bohemia, which is now a part of the Czech Republic. When Ántonia and her family would have lived there, Bohemia was under the rule of the Austrian Hapsburg family and had been for more than three hundred years. The Hapsburgs were Catholic, and Catholicism proves very important to the Shimerda family even after they come to America. The Shimerdas also reflect the rich cultural life of Bohemia, where folk music and art was vital to community life. The Czech city of Prague, which lies in the Bohemian region, is still one of Europe's prime cultural centers.

In addition to the hardships faced by all settlers in the West, immigrants from Bohemia and elsewhere faced a language barrier, culture shock, and homesickness.

Go West, Young Man? Women's Roles in the West

Because the country was considered to be too dangerous and rugged for women, the first people to travel west were men. By the mid-1800s, however, plenty of women and families were moving west.

In the nineteenth century, women's roles were clearly differentiated from men's. The home, the family, and the church made up the woman's sphere. Her role was to "civilize" the family and the community by exhibiting virtues like gentleness, purity, and chastity. Women were to be sheltered from physical labor and the crass world of business and finance. Scholars today sometimes call this set of beliefs about women the "Cult of True Womanhood." They are quick to point out that these restrictive ideals had little to do with how real women lived their lives. In addition, these ideals obviously excluded all working class and slave women from "true womanhood."

Most of these ideas about women's roles originated in the wealthier, more populous East, but many women who moved west carried the ideals with them and thought it their duty to "civilize" the frontier. Once they founded a homestead, however, they were likely to find themselves working alongside their husbands and sharing the burden of homesteading more or less equally.

This tension between the roles women were supposed to assume and those they actually found themselves inhabiting is evident in *My Ántonia*. For example, Jim describes Ántonia as "working like a man." Her tasks—plowing, harvesting, etc.—belong to the man's sphere, even though a woman—Ántonia—is accomplishing them.

The women's suffrage movement, or the campaign for women's right to vote, was well underway by 1880. In fact, women first won the right to vote in 1869 in the Wyoming Territory and in 1870 in Utah. In Nebraska, however, women would not be allowed to vote until 1920, when Congress approved the 19th Amendment granting suffrage to all women. Cather was critical of many suffragists, whom she characterized as self-important and lacking in warmth. One such characterization is evident in the description of Jim's wife in *My Ántonia*.

Regionalism in Literature

As settlers rapidly pushed west, stories about the new, exotic communities they were building became very popular in the East. Out of this interest grew a literary movement called **Regionalism**. Regionalist literature documented life in various parts of the growing country. It included local color writing, which chronicled the adventures of various odd characters in an area, often in a humorous way. Well-known Regionalist and local color writers included Mark Twain, George Washington Cable, Joel Chandler Harris, Bret Harte, and James Whitcomb Riley. Regionalism also included a wealth of writing by women authors, including short stories and novellas by Kate Chopin, Mary Wilkins Freeman, Sarah Orne Jewett, Mary Austin, Alice Dunbar Nelson, and Zitkala-Sä. In addition to insight into a particular area, these women Regionalists also documented the daily life of nineteenth-century women. Regionalist writing celebrated both the region and the realm in which the author lived.

While Cather was clearly influenced by Regionalism, and indeed strove to celebrate Nebraska in much of her fiction, *My Ántonia* betrays some of her differences with Regionalist writing. The town of Black Hawk comes across as far from ideal. The values of community, usually celebrated by women Regionalists, are not strong enough in Black Hawk to sustain Mr. Shimerda. Eventually, even Jim Burden, the character most closely allied with Cather herself, has to leave Nebraska in order to complete his education. While he is drawn to Nebraska repeatedly, something does not allow him to live there as an adult. The same tension is apparent in Cather's life.

Although Cather used the specifics of a particular region in her fiction, her goal was to illustrate and express universal emotions and experiences.

Transcendentalism, Realism, and the Early Twentieth Century

In the mid-nineteenth century, a literary and philosophical movement called **Transcendentalism** evolved in the United States. Transcendentalism advocated a belief in spiritual, or transcendent, truths beyond sense perception and material existence. These truths were believed to be more easily accessible if one placed oneself in natural settings and turned inward in self-exploration. Transcendentalists like Ralph Waldo Emerson, Henry David Thoreau, and Margaret Fuller abhorred the materialism and drive for progress that they witnessed in their culture. Instead, they celebrated the individual and the spiritual life. Any authority outside the self was questioned, and each individual was thought to be capable of intuiting the most profound truths about the universe. Words like *self-reliance, self-expression*, and *self-realization* come directly from these writers and thinkers. Because the individual was considered so important, Transcendentalists also advocated tolerance of diverse viewpoints.

The Transcendentalist movement is most often associated with the mid-nineteenth century. As the twentieth century approached, literary tastes turned increasingly toward **Realism**. Realism is an attempt to render in art an accurate portrayal of reality. Realist writing is characterized by attention to the real, often grim, details of ordinary life. The increasing popularity of Realism is linked to increasing industrialization, materialism, and drive for progress. Far from celebrating the individual, this literature often views the individual as a cog in an industrial-materialist machine. In a late essay, Cather criticized Realism for its excessive emphasis on material details, comparing Realist novels to rooms with too much furniture.

The tension between Realism and Transcendentalism is evident in *My Ántonia*. The novel is based on real life in Nebraska as Cather experienced it as a child, yet it celebrates the natural landscape and the feelings the characters associate with that landscape. Cather strove to include only those details that contributed to the emotional impact of the novel. Ántonia, as an individual woman, is invested with almost mythical significance and is sharply contrasted with those characters who leave the prairie to pursue their fortunes in more industrialized or materialistic places. Writing the novel during World War I, Cather may have longed for earlier times and values that seemed simpler and more humane. In so doing, she prefigured writers like Ernest Hemingway, T. S. Eliot, and F. Scott Fitzgerald, who would lament the shift in the country's values as the twentieth century progressed.

Characters in
My Ántonia

Major Characters

Jim Burden. Orphaned at age ten, Jim travels across the country to live with his grandparents on the Nebraska prairie. Just days after he gets there, he meets Ántonia, a young girl who has just arrived with her family from Bohemia. Jim helps her learn English, and the two become friends, exploring the new landscape and absorbing the stories of their neighbors. The history of their friendship, and what it comes to mean to Jim, is the story of *My Ántonia*.

Josiah Burden. Jim's grandfather, Mr. Burden, is a successful farmer in Nebraska. A quiet, serious man, Mr. Burden is well-respected by the neighbors, with whom he is generous with advice, equipment, and help.

Emmaline Burden. Mrs. Burden, Jim's grandmother, is described as "a woman of unusual endurance." She gardens, cooks, and helps tend to the neighbors, many of whom have recently arrived from other countries.

Ántonia Shimerda. Ántonia, or Tony, as she is sometimes called, is fourteen when she arrives with her family from Bohemia. Curious, friendly, and smart, Ántonia quickly learns English from Jim. When tragedy strikes her family, she shoulders additional responsibility for the farm and her family. Although her responsibilities at home prevent her from going to school, much less the university, she has much to teach Jim.

Mr. Shimerda. When Jim first meets Ántonia's father, Mr. Shimerda, he notices the man's beautiful, refined hands and his dignified, sorrowful face. In Bohemia, Mr. Shimerda had worked with his hands as a talented weaver and violinist. In a new and rugged country, under pressure to learn a completely new way of life, he suffers terrible homesickness.

Mrs. Shimerda. Struggling to make a home for her family from a cave dug out of a hill, Ántonia's mother, Mrs. Shimerda, comes across as bitter and envious. She sometimes resents the fact that the Burdens have a comfortable home and a successful farm.

Lena Lingard. The daughter of Norwegian immigrants, Lena grew up having to work the fields in tattered clothing and care for her younger brothers and sisters. Determined to escape poverty and scornful of the farm woman's limited role, Lena moves to town to learn dressmaking. Soon she becomes a talented dressmaker, supporting herself first in Lincoln and then in San Francisco.

Wick Cutter. The predatory Mr. Cutter is Black Hawk's local money-lender. While he appears only a few times in the novel, he is responsible for the financial ruin of Russian Peter, and his actions one awful night force Jim to grow up in a hurry.

Minor Characters

Genevieve Burden. Genevieve becomes Jim Burden's wife. She is mentioned only in the introduction, but her character provides important contrast to some of the other women in the novel.

Jake Marpole. Jake, who had worked on Jim's father's farm in Virginia, travels with Jim to Nebraska to work for Jim's grandfather.

Otto Fuchs. Another hired hand at the Nebraska farm, Otto has worked as "a cowboy, a stage-driver, a bartender, a miner." On winter nights, he entertains the family with stories of his adventures in the Wild West. Otto is originally from Austria.

Ambrosch Shimerda. Ántonia's brother Ambrosch is a strong, broad-shouldered young man who works hard and insists that Ántonia do the same. He often seems more interested in becoming a successful farmer than maintaining good relationships with his neighbors.

Marek Shimerda. Marek, Ántonia's other brother, is a kind, affectionate boy with a developmental disability.

Yulka Shimerda. Yulka is Ántonia's younger sister who sometimes accompanies Jim and Ántonia on their adventures.

Peter Krajiek. Distantly related to Mrs. Shimerda, Krajiek sells the Shimerdas his farm and stays on to work for Mr. Shimerda. Many of the neighbors believe Krajiek is not entirely honest.

Russian Peter. Fleeing from a bloody incident in their past, the jovial Peter and his surly brother Pavel are trying to survive as farmers in Nebraska. They are deeply in debt to Wick Cutter.

Pavel. Late one night, sick with a fever, Pavel tells the horrific story of how he and Peter came to live in Nebraska.

Mrs. Harling. Mrs. Harling, originally from Norway, employs Ántonia to help her care for the Harling children and their house.

Mr. Harling. A successful grain and cattle dealer, Mr. Harling is one of the most important businessmen in Black Hawk. He is rarely home, but when he is, no one dares to cross him.

Frances Harling. Frances, the oldest of the Harling children, works with her father in their business. She is also beloved by the farm families in the area.

Nina Harling. The youngest of the Harling children, Nina is exceptionally sensitive.

Charlie Harling. Charlie is Ántonia's favorite among the Harling children.

Sally Harling. Sally is known for dressing and acting like a boy.

Anton Jelinek. Jelinek is another Bohemian homesteader in the Black Hawk area. Later, he opens a saloon in Black Hawk.

Tiny Soderball. Tiny comes to town to work at the hotel, where she, Jim, and the other hired girls meet many traveling businessmen. Her work at the hotel also prepares her to make her fortune in a most unexpected way....

Ole Benson. Much to the outrage of his wife, Norwegian farmer Ole Benson develops a crush on Lena while Lena is still working in her family's fields.

"Crazy Mary" Benson. Ole's wife Mary had been sent away to an asylum after she tried to set a neighbor's barn on fire. Home from the asylum and jealous of Ole's attentions to Lena, she regularly threatens to slit Lena's throat with a corn knife.

Mrs. Cutter. Wick Cutter's wife is also his sparring partner until one of their ongoing arguments turns tragic.

Molly Gardener. Mrs. Gardener is the owner of Black Hawk's Boys' Home, one of the finest hotels on the railroad line.

Johnnie Gardener. Johnnie, Molly Gardener's husband, works at the hotel and generally caters to his wife's wishes.

Norwegian Anna. Anna is another of the hired girls.

The Three Marys. Daughters of Bohemian families, the three Marys move to town to work as cooks and housekeepers.

Samson d'Arnault. D'Arnault is a blind, African-American pianist who gives an outstanding performance in the Boys' Home in Black Hawk.

Mr. Ordinsky. Lena's Polish neighbor in Lincoln, Mr. Ordinsky, believes the Nebraskans are hopelessly uncultured.

Gaston Cleric. Gaston, Jim's Latin professor at the University of Nebraska, plays an important role in the direction Jim's life takes.

Larry Donovan. Larry courts Ántonia and asks her to move to Denver to marry him. The relationship does not go as planned.

Widow Steavens. Mrs. Steavens moves, with her brother, into the Burdens' old farmhouse when the Burdens move to town.

Anton Cuzak, Sr. Ántonia eventually marries Anton Cuzak, another immigrant from Bohemia.

Anton Cuzak, Jr. Anton, Jr., is one of Ántonia's sons.

Anna Cuzak. Anna is the oldest of Ántonia's daughters living at home when Jim visits.

Rudolph Cuzak. Rudolph is Ántonia's oldest son.

Ambrosch Cuzak. Ambrosch is another of Ántonia's sons. He is named after her brother but is more thoughtful than his namesake.

Leo Cuzak. Leo, whom Ántonia identifies as the favorite among her children, plays Mr. Shimerda's violin and has Mrs. Shimerda's cynicism despite his young age.

Yulka Cuzak. Named after Ántonia's sister, Yulka is one of Ántonia's daughters.

Jan Cuzak. Jan is Ántonia's young son.

Lucie Cuzak Lucie is one of Ántonia's younger daughters.

Nina Cuzak. Named after Nina Harling, Nina is one of Ántonia's daughters.

Martha Shimerda. Martha is Ántonia's first child, born under less than ideal circumstances.

Echoes:

Quotations from Willa Cather

On Nebraska

"[A writer] may acquire a great many interesting and vivid impressions in his mature years, but his thematic material, he acquires under fifteen years of age."

"So the [Nebraska] country and I had it out together and by the end of the first autumn, that shaggy grass country had gripped me with a passion I have never been able to shake. It has been the happiness and the curse of my life."

On trees

"I like trees because they seem more resigned to the way they have to live than other things do."

On the origin of her characters

"The great characters in literature are born out of love, often out of some beautiful experience of the writer."

"One of the people who interested me most as a child was the Bohemian hired girl of one of our neighbors, who was so good to me. She is one of the truest artists I ever knew in the keenness and sensitiveness of her enjoyment, in her love of people and in her willingness to take pains."

"[A} writer…has a brain like Limbo, full of ghosts for which he has always tried to find bodies….All the lovely emotions that one has had some day appear with bodies…."

On art and everyday life

"Art is made out of the love of old and intimate things. We always underestimate the common things."

"Many people seem to think that art is a luxury to be imported and tacked on to life. Art springs out of the very stuff that life is made of."

"Unless you can see the beauty all around you everywhere, and enjoy it, you can never comprehend art."

"Art thrives best where the personal life is the richest, fullest, and warmest, from the kitchen up."

"After all, it is the little things that really matter most, the unfinished things, the things that never quite come to birth."

"Life is a struggle or a torpor. All art must be serious, and comedy is the most serious of all. Art and religion express the same thing in us—that hunger for beauty that we, of all animals, have."

Images of My Ántonia

The Burlington train station in Red Cloud, Nebraska.

An example of a sod house in Nebraska, 1886.

The home of Anna Pavelka, the inspiration for Ántonia's home in Book V of My Ántonia.

Main Street of present day Red Cloud, Nebraska, Willa Cather's childhood home and the basis for the fictional town of Black Hawk.

This 1872 poster enticed people to settle in the Nebraska territory.

Critical Viewing

1. Who is selling this land in Iowa and Nebraska?
2. What incentives are offered to persuade people to buy land in these areas?
3. Based on the image on the poster, how would you expect the Nebraska landscape to look?

TO CARRIE AND IRENE MINER

In memory of affections
old and true

Optima dies . . . prima fugit[1]
—Virgil

Introduction

Last summer I happened to be crossing the plains of Iowa in a season of intense heat, and it was my good fortune to have for a traveling companion James Quayle Burden—Jim Burden, as we still call him in the West. He and I are old friends—we grew up together in the same Nebraska town—and we had much to say to each other. While the train flashed through never-ending miles of ripe wheat, by country towns and bright-flowered pastures and oak groves wilting in the sun, we sat in the observation car, where the woodwork was hot to the touch and red dust lay deep over everything. The dust and heat, the burning wind, reminded us of many things. We were talking about what it is like to spend one's childhood in little towns like these, buried in wheat and corn, under stimulating extremes of climate: burning summers when the world lies green and billowy beneath a brilliant sky, when one is fairly stifled in vegetation, in the color and smell of strong weeds and heavy harvests; blustery winters with little snow, when the whole country is stripped bare and gray as sheet-iron. We agreed that no one who had not grown up in a little prairie town could know anything about it. It was a kind of freemasonry[2], we said.

◀ *What did the narrator and Jim discuss on the train? On what do they agree?*

Although Jim Burden and I both live in New York, and are old friends, I do not see much of him there. He is legal counsel for one of the great Western railways, and is sometimes away from his New York office for weeks together. That is one reason why we do not often meet. Another is that I do not like his wife.

◀ *What two reasons does the narrator give for not seeing Jim much in New York?*

When Jim was still an obscure young lawyer, struggling to make his way in New York, his career was suddenly advanced by a brilliant marriage. Genevieve Whitney was the only daughter of a distinguished man. Her marriage with young Burden was the subject of sharp comment at the time. It was said she had been brutally jilted by her cousin, Rutland Whitney, and that she married this unknown man from the West out of bravado. She was a restless, headstrong girl, even then, who liked to astonish her friends. Later, when I knew her, she was always doing something unexpected. She gave one of her town houses for a Suffrage headquarters, produced one of her own plays

◀ *What "unexpected things" does Genevieve Burden do?*

---

1. **Optima dies...prima fugit**. "The best days are the first to flee"
2. **freemasonry**. Natural fellowship based on some common experience

What words does the narrator use to describe Jim's wife?

at the Princess Theater, was arrested for picketing during a garment-makers' strike, etc. I am never able to believe that she has much feeling for the causes to which she lends her name and her fleeting interest. She is handsome, energetic, <u>executive</u>, but to me she seems unimpressionable and <u>temperamentally</u> incapable of enthusiasm. Her husband's quiet tastes irritate her, I think, and she finds it worth while to play the patroness[3] to a group of young poets and painters of advanced ideas and <u>mediocre</u> ability. She has her own fortune and lives her own life. For some reason, she wishes to remain Mrs. James Burden.

As for Jim, no disappointments have been severe enough to chill his naturally romantic and ardent <u>disposition</u>. This disposition, though it often made him seem very funny when he was a boy, has been one of the strongest elements in his success. He loves with a personal passion the great country through which his railway runs and branches. His faith in it and his knowledge of it have played an important part in its development. He is always able to raise capital for new enterprises in Wyoming or Montana, and has helped young men out there to do remarkable things in mines and timber and oil. If a young man with an idea can once get Jim Burden's attention, can manage to accompany him when he goes off into the wilds hunting for lost parks or exploring new canyons, then the money which means action is usually forthcoming. Jim is still able to lose himself in those big Western dreams. Though he is over forty now, he meets new people and new enterprises with the impulsiveness by which his boyhood friends remember him. He never seems to me to grow older. His fresh color and sandy hair and quick-changing blue eyes are those of a young man, and his sympathetic, solicitous interest in women is as youthful as it is Western and American.

In what dreams does Jim lose himself?

During that burning day when we were crossing Iowa, our talk kept returning to a central figure, a Bohemian girl whom we had known long ago and whom both of us

Whom do Jim and the narrator discuss at length on the train, and what does she mean to them?

---

3. **patroness.** Wealthy or influential woman who supports an artist or writer

words for everyday use

ex • ec • u • tive (ig ze′ k[y]ə tiv) adj., designed for carrying into effect. *Marcia's executive abilities make her an ideal person to coordinate the new project.*

tem • pera • men • tal • ly (tem prə men′ təl ē) adv., as a result of personality. *Because Jeff was so quiet, he was temperamentally unsuited for yelling.*

me • di • o • cre (mē dē ō′ kər) adj., average or low. *Although the restaurant was highly recommended by friends, Sue and Ann found the food only mediocre.*

dis • po • si • tion (dis pə zi′ shən) n., character, personality. *Her cheerful disposition made her well-liked.*

admired. More than any other person we remembered, this girl seemed to mean to us the country, the conditions, the whole adventure of our childhood. To speak her name was to call up pictures of people and places, to set a quiet drama going in one's brain. I had lost sight of her altogether, but Jim had found her again after long years, had renewed a friendship that meant a great deal to him, and out of his busy life had set apart time enough to enjoy that friendship. His mind was full of her that day. He made me see her again, feel her presence, revived all my old affection for her.

"I can't see," he said impetuously, "why you have never written anything about Ántonia."

I told him I had always felt that other people—he himself, for one—knew her much better than I. I was ready, however, to make an agreement with him; I would set down on paper all that I remembered of Ántonia if he would do the same. We might, in this way, get a picture of her.

◀ What agreement do the two friends make about Ántonia?

He rumpled his hair with a quick, excited gesture, which with him often announces a new determination, and I could see that my suggestion took hold of him. "Maybe I will, maybe I will!" he declared. He stared out of the window for a few moments, and when he turned to me again his eyes had the sudden clearness that comes from something the mind itself sees. "Of course," he said, "I should have to do it in a direct way, and say a great deal about myself. It's through myself that I knew and felt her, and I've had no practice in any other form of presentation."

◀ What warning does Jim give about how he would have to go about this writing?

I told him that how he knew her and felt her was exactly what I most wanted to know about Ántonia. He had had opportunities that I, as a little girl who watched her come and go, had not.

Months afterward Jim Burden arrived at my apartment one stormy winter afternoon, with a bulging legal portfolio sheltered under his fur overcoat. He brought it into the sitting-room with him and tapped it with some pride as he stood warming his hands.

"I finished it last night—the thing about Ántonia," he said. "Now, what about yours?"

I had to confess that mine had not gone beyond a few straggling notes.

"Notes? I didn't make any." He drank his tea all at once and put down the cup. "I didn't arrange or rearrange. I simply wrote down what of herself and myself and other people Ántonia's name recalls to me. I suppose it hasn't any form. It hasn't any title, either." He went into the next

◀What flaw does Jim identify in what he has written?

▶ What word does Jim add, at the last minute, to the title of his manuscript?

▶ What has become of Jim's manuscript?

room, sat down at my desk and wrote on the pinkish face of the portfolio the word, "Ántonia." He frowned at this a moment, then prefixed another word, making it "My Ántonia." That seemed to satisfy him.

"Read it as soon as you can," he said, rising, "but don't let it influence your own story."

My own story was never written, but the following narrative is Jim's manuscript, substantially as he brought it to me.

BOOK I

The Shimerdas

Chapter 1

I first heard of Ántonia[1] on what seemed to me an <u>interminable</u> journey across the great midland plain of North America. I was ten years old then; I had lost both my father and mother within a year, and my Virginia relatives were sending me out to my grandparents, who lived in Nebraska. I traveled in the care of a mountain boy, Jake Marpole, one of the "hands" on my father's old farm under the Blue Ridge, who was now going West to work for my grandfather. Jake's experience of the world was not much wider than mine. He had never been in a railway train until the morning when we set out together to try our fortunes in a new world.

We went all the way in day-coaches, becoming more sticky and grimy with each stage of the journey. Jake bought everything the newsboys offered him: candy, oranges, brass collar buttons, a watch-charm, and for me a "Life of Jesse James,"[2] which I remember as one of the most satisfactory books I have ever read. Beyond Chicago we were under the protection of a friendly passenger conductor, who knew all about the country to which we were going and gave us a great deal of advice in exchange for our <u>confidence</u>. He seemed to us an experienced and worldly man who had been almost everywhere; in his conversation he threw out lightly the names of distant states and cities. He wore the rings and pins and badges of different <u>fraternal</u> orders to which he belonged. Even his cuff-buttons were engraved with hieroglyphics, and he was more inscribed than an Egyptian obelisk. Once when he sat down to chat, he told us that in the immigrant car ahead there was a family from "across the water" whose destination was the same as ours.

"They can't any of them speak English, except one little girl, and all she can say is 'We go Black Hawk, Nebraska.' She's not much older than you, twelve or thirteen, maybe,

---

1. **Ántonia.** The Bohemian name *Ántonia* is strongly accented on the first syllable, like the English name *Anthony*, and the *i* is, of course, given the sound of long *e*. The name is pronounced An'-ton-ee-ah.

2. **"Life of Jesse James."** One of a series of novels written about the deeds of this famous outlaw

words for everyday use

in • ter • min • ab • le (in tərm′ nə bəl) adj., seeming to have no end. *Josh was so excited to return to school that the last weeks of summer vacation seemed <u>interminable</u>.*

con • fi • dence (kän′ fə dəns) n., relationship of trust or intimacy. *As the two friends became closer, Jim took Jeremiah into his <u>confidence</u>.*

fra • ter • nal (frə tər′ nəl) adj., belonging to a society or brotherhood. *Anyone inducted into the Order of the Elk learns the <u>fraternal</u> code.*

and she's as bright as a new dollar. Don't you want to go ahead and see her, Jimmy? She's got the pretty brown eyes, too!"

This last remark made me bashful, and I shook my head and settled down to "Jesse James." Jake nodded at me approvingly and said you were likely to get diseases from foreigners.

I do not remember crossing the Missouri River, or anything about the long day's journey through Nebraska. Probably by that time I had crossed so many rivers that I was dull to them. The only thing very noticeable about Nebraska was that it was still, all day long, Nebraska.

I had been sleeping, curled up in a red plush seat, for a long while when we reached Black Hawk. Jake roused me and took me by the hand. We stumbled down from the train to a wooden siding, where men were running about with lanterns. I couldn't see any town, or even distant lights; we were surrounded by utter darkness. The engine was panting heavily after its long run. In the red glow from the fire-box, a group of people stood huddled together on the platform, <u>encumbered</u> by bundles and boxes. I knew this must be the immigrant family the conductor had told us about. The woman wore a fringed shawl tied over her head, and she carried a little tin trunk in her arms, hugging it as if it were a baby. There was an old man, tall and stooped. Two half-grown boys and a girl stood holding oil-cloth bundles, and a little girl clung to her mother's skirts. Presently a man with a lantern approached them and began to talk, shouting and exclaiming. I pricked up my ears, for it was positively the first time I had ever heard a foreign tongue.

Another lantern came along. A <u>bantering</u> voice called out: "Hello, are you Mr. Burden's folks? If you are, it's me you're looking for. I'm Otto Fuchs. I'm Mr. Burden's hired man, and I'm to drive you out. Hello, Jimmy, ain't you scared to come so far west?"

I looked up with interest at the new face in the lantern light. He might have stepped out of the pages of "Jesse James." He wore a sombrero hat, with a wide leather band and a bright buckle, and the ends of his moustache were twisted up stiffly, like little horns. He looked lively and

▶ Why doesn't Jim go see the girl with the immigrant family? How does Jake reinforce Jim's decision?

---

words for everyday use

en • cum • bered (in kəm′ bərd) adj., weighed down, burdened. *Our car was so <u>encumbered</u> by luggage that the back bumper nearly dragged on the ground.*

ban • ter • ing (ban′ tər iŋ) adj., speaking in a playful, teasing manner. *Because each favored a different team, the men enjoyed <u>bantering</u> about who would win the upcoming basketball tournament.*

ferocious, I thought, and as if he had a history. A long scar ran across one cheek and drew the corner of his mouth up in a sinister curl. The top of his left ear was gone, and his skin was brown as an Indian's. Surely this was the face of a desperado. As he walked about the platform in his high-heeled boots, looking for our trunks, I saw that he was a rather slight man, quick and wiry, and light on his feet. He told us we had a long night drive ahead of us, and had better be on the hike. He led us to a hitching-bar where two farm wagons were tied, and I saw the foreign family crowding into one of them. The other was for us. Jake got on the front seat with Otto Fuchs, and I rode on the straw in the bottom of the wagon-box, covered up with a buffalo hide. The immigrants rumbled off into the empty darkness, and we followed them.

I tried to go to sleep, but the jolting made me bite my tongue, and I soon began to ache all over. When the straw settled down I had a hard bed. Cautiously I slipped from under the buffalo hide, got up on my knees and peered over the side of the wagon. There seemed to be nothing to see; no fences, no creeks or trees, no hills or fields. If there was a road, I could not make it out in the faint starlight. There was nothing but land: not a country at all, but the material out of which countries are made. No, there was nothing but land—slightly undulating, I knew, because often our wheels ground against the brake as we went down into a hollow and lurched up again on the other side. I had the feeling that the world was left behind, that we had got over the edge of it, and were outside man's jurisdiction. I had never before looked up at the sky when there was not a familiar mountain ridge against it. But this was the complete dome of heaven, all there was of it. I did not believe that my dead father and mother were watching me from up there; they would still be looking for me at the sheepfold down by the creek, or along the white road that led to the mountain pastures. I had left even their spirits behind me. The wagon jolted on, carrying me I knew not whither. I don't think I was homesick. If we never arrived anywhere, it did not matter. Between that earth and that sky I felt erased, blotted out. I did not say my prayers that night: here, I felt, what would be would be.

◀ What does Jim worry about regarding his parents?

◀ How does Jim feel about the new landscape? Why doesn't he say his prayers?

words for everyday use

jur • is • dic • tion (jŭr əs dik′ shən) n., the limits within which authority may be exercised. *The ban on burning leaves can only be enforced within the city's jurisdiction; outside the city limits, you can't be arrested for burning them.*

Chapter 2

I do not remember our arrival at my grandfather's farm sometime before daybreak, after a drive of nearly twenty miles with heavy work-horses. When I awoke, it was afternoon. I was lying in a little room, scarcely larger than the bed that held me, and the window-shade at my head was flapping softly in a warm wind. A tall woman, with wrinkled brown skin and black hair, stood looking down at me; I knew that she must be my grandmother. She had been crying, I could see, but when I opened my eyes she smiled, peered at me anxiously, and sat down on the foot of my bed.

"Had a good sleep, Jimmy?" she asked briskly. Then in a very different tone she said, as if to herself, "My, how you do look like your father!" I remembered that my father had been her little boy; she must often have come to wake him like this when he overslept. "Here are your clean clothes," she went on, stroking my coverlid with her brown hand as she talked. "But first you come down to the kitchen with me, and have a nice warm bath behind the stove. Bring your things; there's nobody about."

"Down to the kitchen" struck me as curious; it was always "out in the kitchen" at home. I picked up my shoes and stockings and followed her through the living-room and down a flight of stairs into a basement. This basement was divided into a dining-room at the right of the stairs and a kitchen at the left. Both rooms were plastered and whitewashed—the plaster laid directly upon the earth walls, as it used to be in dugouts.[1] The floor was of hard cement. Up under the wooden ceiling there were little half-windows with white curtains, and pots of geraniums and wandering Jew in the deep sills. As I entered the kitchen, I sniffed a pleasant smell of gingerbread baking. The stove was very large, with bright nickel trimmings, and behind it there was a long wooden bench against the wall, and a tin washtub, into which grandmother poured hot and cold water. When she brought the soap and towels, I told her that I was used to taking my bath without help.

"Can you do your ears, Jimmy? Are you sure? Well, now, I call you a right smart little boy."

It was pleasant there in the kitchen. The sun shone into my bath-water through the west half-window, and a big

---

1. **dugouts.** Cavelike homes literally dug out of the sides of hills

Maltese cat came up and rubbed himself against the tub, watching me curiously. While I scrubbed, my grandmother busied herself in the dining-room until I called anxiously, "Grandmother, I'm afraid the cakes are burning!" Then she came laughing, waving her apron before her as if she were shooing chickens.

She was a spare, tall woman, a little stooped, and she was apt to carry her head thrust forward in an attitude of attention, as if she were looking at something, or listening to something, far away. As I grew older, I came to believe that it was only because she was so often thinking of things that were far away. She was quick-footed and energetic in all her movements. Her voice was high and rather shrill, and she often spoke with an anxious inflection, for she was exceedingly desirous that everything should go with due order and <u>decorum</u>. Her laugh, too, was high, and perhaps a little strident, but there was a lively intelligence in it. She was then fifty-five years old, a strong woman, of unusual endurance.

◀ *Why, according to Jim, does his grandmother walk with her head thrust forward?*

After I was dressed, I explored the long cellar next the kitchen. It was dug out under the wing of the house, was plastered and cemented, with a stairway and an outside door by which the men came and went. Under one of the windows there was a place for them to wash when they came in from work.

While my grandmother was busy about supper I settled myself on the wooden bench behind the stove and got acquainted with the cat— he caught not only rats and mice, but gophers, I was told. The patch of yellow sunlight on the floor traveled back toward the stairway, and grandmother and I talked about my journey, and about the arrival of the new Bohemian family; she said they were to be our nearest neighbors. We did not talk about the farm in Virginia, which had been her home for so many years. But after the men came in from the fields, and we were all seated at the supper-table, then she asked Jake about the old place and about our friends and neighbors there.

My grandfather said little. When he first came in he kissed me and spoke kindly to me, but he was not <u>demonstrative</u>. I felt at once his deliberateness and personal dig-

◀ *What qualities does Jim sense in his grandfather?*

words for everyday use

de • cor • um (di kōr' əm) n., conventions of polite behavior. *The host expected all guests to behave with <u>decorum</u> at the elegant party.*

de • mon • stra • tive (di män' strə' tiv) adj., inclined to display feelings openly. *Some teenagers are embarrassed when their parents are <u>demonstrative</u> in public.*

nity, and was a little in awe of him. The thing one immediately noticed about him was his beautiful, crinkly, snow-white beard. I once heard a missionary say it was like the beard of an Arabian sheik. His bald crown only made it more impressive.

Grandfather's eyes were not at all like those of an old man; they were bright blue, and had a fresh, frosty sparkle. His teeth were white and regular—so sound that he had never been to a dentist in his life. He had a delicate skin, easily roughened by sun and wind. When he was a young man his hair and beard were red; his eyebrows were still coppery.

As we sat at the table, Otto Fuchs and I kept stealing covert glances at each other. Grandmother had told me while she was getting supper that he was an Austrian who came to this country a young boy and had led an adventurous life in the Far West among mining-camps and cow outfits. His iron constitution was somewhat broken by mountain pneumonia, and he had drifted back to live in a milder country for a while. He had relatives in Bismarck, a German settlement to the north of us, but for a year now he had been working for grandfather.

The minute supper was over, Otto took me into the kitchen to whisper to me about a pony down in the barn that had been bought for me at a sale; he had been riding him to find out whether he had any bad tricks, but he was a "perfect gentleman," and his name was Dude. Fuchs told me everything I wanted to know: how he had lost his ear in a Wyoming blizzard when he was a stage-driver, and how to throw a lasso. He promised to rope a steer for me before sundown next day. He got out his "chaps" and silver spurs to show them to Jake and me, and his best cowboy boots, with tops stitched in bold design— roses, and true-lover's knots, and undraped female figures. These, he solemnly explained, were angels.

Before we went to bed, Jake and Otto were called up to the living-room for prayers. Grandfather put on silver-rimmed spectacles and read several Psalms. His voice was so sympathetic and he read so interestingly that I wished he had chosen one of my favorite chapters in the Book of Kings. I was awed by his intonation of the word "Selah." *"He shall choose our inheritance for us, the excellency of Jacob whom He loved. Selah."* I had no idea what the word meant; perhaps he had not. But, as he uttered it, it became <u>oracular</u>, the most sacred of words.

◀ What impresses Jim about the way his grandfather reads?

Early the next morning I ran out of doors to look about me. I had been told that ours was the only wooden house west of Black Hawk—until you came to the Norwegian settlement, where there were several. Our neighbors lived in sod houses[2] and dugouts—comfortable, but not very roomy. Our white frame house, with a story and half-story above the basement, stood at the east end of what I might call the farmyard, with the windmill close by the kitchen door. From the windmill the ground sloped westward, down to the barns and granaries and pig-yards. This slope was trampled hard and bare, and washed out in winding <u>gullies</u> by the rain. Beyond the corncribs, at the bottom of the shallow draw, was a muddy little pond, with rusty willow bushes growing about it. The road from the post-office came directly by our door, crossed the farm-yard, and curved round this little pond, beyond which it began to climb the gentle swell of unbroken prairie to the west. There, along the western sky-line, it skirted a great cornfield, much larger than any field I had ever seen. This cornfield, and the sorghum patch behind the barn, were the only broken land in sight. Everywhere, as far as the eye could reach, there was nothing but rough, shaggy, red grass, most of it as tall as I.

North of the house, inside the ploughed fire-breaks, grew a thick-set strip of box-elder trees, low and bushy, their leaves already turning yellow. This hedge was nearly a quarter of a mile long, but I had to look very hard to see it at all. The little trees were insignificant against the grass. It seemed as if the grass were about to run over them, and over the plum-patch behind the sod chicken-house.

As I looked about me I felt that the grass was the country, as the water is the sea. The red of the grass made all the great prairie the color of wine-stains, or of certain seaweeds when they are first washed up. And there was so much motion in it; the whole country seemed, somehow, to be running.

◀ What is the effect of the waving grass on the look of the landscape?

---

2. **sod houses.** Houses made from blocks of prairie sod and held together by the dense, tangled root systems

words for everyday use

or • a • cu • lar (o ra′ kye lər) adj., wise and authoritative. *Politicians often consult voice coaches in order to cultivate an <u>oracular</u> tone that will make them sound trustworthy.*

gul • ly (gŭ′ lē) n., a trench created by running water. *We saw a muskrat swimming in the <u>gully</u>.*

I had almost forgotten that I had a grandmother, when she came out, her sunbonnet on her head, a grain-sack in her hand, and asked me if I did not want to go to the garden with her to dig potatoes for dinner. The garden, curiously enough, was a quarter of a mile from the house, and the way to it led up a shallow draw past the cattle corral. Grandmother called my attention to a stout hickory cane, tipped with copper, which hung by a leather thong from her belt. This, she said, was her rattlesnake cane. I must never go to the garden without a heavy stick or a corn-knife; she had killed a good many rattlers on her way back and forth. A little girl who lived on the Black Hawk road was bitten on the ankle and had been sick all summer.

I can remember exactly how the country looked to me as I walked beside my grandmother along the faint wagon-tracks on that early September morning. Perhaps the glide of long railway travel was still with me, for more than anything else I felt motion in the landscape; in the fresh, easy-blowing morning wind, and in the earth itself, as if the shaggy grass were a sort of loose hide, and underneath it herds of wild buffalo were galloping, galloping . . .

Alone, I should never have found the garden—except, perhaps, for the big yellow pumpkins that lay about unprotected by their withering vines—and I felt very little interest in it when I got there. I wanted to walk straight on through the red grass and over the edge of the world, which could not be very far away. The light air about me told me that the world ended here: only the ground and sun and sky were left, and if one went a little farther there would be only sun and sky, and one would float off into them, like the tawny hawks which sailed over our heads making slow shadows on the grass. While grandmother took the pitchfork we found standing in one of the rows and dug potatoes, while I picked them up out of the soft brown earth and put them into the bag, I kept looking up at the hawks that were doing what I might so easily do.

When grandmother was ready to go, I said I would like to stay up there in the garden awhile.

She peered down at me from under her sunbonnet. "Aren't you afraid of snakes?"

"A little," I admitted, "but I'd like to stay anyhow."

"Well, if you see one, don't have anything to do with him. The big yellow and brown ones won't hurt you; they're bull-snakes and help to keep the gophers down. Don't be scared if you see anything look out of that hole in the bank over there. That's a badger hole. He's about as

> ▶ *What does Jim think must not be far away?*

big as a big 'possum, and his face is striped, black and white. He takes a chicken once in a while, but I won't let the men harm him. In a new country a body feels friendly to the animals. I like to have him come out and watch me when I'm at work."

◄ Why won't Jim's grandmother let the men kill the badger?

Grandmother swung the bag of potatoes over her shoulder and went down the path, leaning forward a little. The road followed the windings of the draw; when she came to the first bend, she waved at me and disappeared. I was left alone with this new feeling of lightness and content.

I sat down in the middle of the garden, where snakes could scarcely approach unseen, and leaned my back against a warm yellow pumpkin. There were some ground-cherry bushes growing along the furrows, full of fruit. I turned back the papery triangular sheaths that protected the berries and ate a few. All about me giant grasshoppers, twice as big as any I had ever seen, were doing acrobatic feats among the dried vines. The gophers scurried up and down the ploughed ground. There in the sheltered draw-bottom the wind did not blow very hard, but I could hear it singing its humming tune up on the level, and I could see the tall grasses wave. The earth was warm under me, and warm as I crumbled it through my fingers. Queer little red bugs came out and moved in slow squadrons around me. Their backs were polished <u>vermilion</u>, with black spots. I kept as still as I could. Nothing happened. I did not expect anything to happen. I was something that lay under the sun and felt it, like the pumpkins, and I did not want to be anything more. I was entirely happy. Perhaps we feel like that when we die and become a part of something entire, whether it is sun and air, or goodness and knowledge. At any rate, that is happiness; to be dissolved into something complete and great. When it comes to one, it comes as naturally as sleep.

◄ How does Jim define happiness?

words for everyday use

ver • mil • ion (vər mil' yən) adj., bright reddish-orange. *The trees turned gold, brown, and <u>vermilion</u> in the fall.*

Chapter 3

On Sunday morning Otto Fuchs was to drive us over to make the acquaintance of our new Bohemian neighbors. We were taking them some provisions, as they had come to live on a wild place where there was no garden or chicken-house, and very little broken land. Fuchs brought up a sack of potatoes and a piece of cured pork from the cellar, and grandmother packed some loaves of Saturday's bread, a jar of butter, and several pumpkin pies in the straw of the wagon-box. We clambered up to the front seat and jolted off past the little pond and along the road that climbed to the big cornfield.

I could hardly wait to see what lay beyond that cornfield; but there was only red grass like ours, and nothing else, though from the high wagon-seat one could look off a long way. The road ran about like a wild thing, avoiding the deep draws, crossing them where they were wide and shallow. And all along it, wherever it looped or ran, the sunflowers grew; some of them were as big as little trees, with great rough leaves and many branches which bore dozens of blossoms. They made a gold ribbon across the prairie. Occasionally one of the horses would tear off with his teeth a plant full of blossoms, and walk along munching it, the flowers nodding in time to his bites as he ate down toward them.

The Bohemian family, grandmother told me as we drove along, had bought the homestead of a fellow countryman, Peter Krajiek, and had paid him more than it was worth. Their agreement with him was made before they left the old country, through a cousin of his, who was also a relative of Mrs. Shimerda. The Shimerdas were the first Bohemian family to come to this part of the country. Krajiek was their only interpreter, and could tell them anything he chose. They could not speak enough English to ask for advice, or even to make their most pressing wants known. One son, Fuchs said, was well-grown, and strong enough to work the land; but the father was old and frail and knew nothing about farming. He was a weaver by trade; had been a skilled workman on tapestries and upholstery materials. He had brought his fiddle with him, which wouldn't be of much use here, though he used to pick up money by it at home.

"If they're nice people, I hate to think of them spending the winter in that cave of Krajiek's," said grandmother. "It's no better than a badger hole; no proper dugout at all.

▶ Why are the Shimerdas so dependent on Krajiek?

▶ What supposedly useless item has Mr. Shimerda brought with him to America? What use had this item had in Bohemia?

And I hear he's made them pay twenty dollars for his old cookstove that ain't worth ten."

"Yes'm," said Otto; "and he's sold 'em his oxen and his two bony old horses for the price of good workteams. I'd have interfered about the horses—the old man can understand some German—if I'd 'a' thought it would do any good. But Bohemians has a natural distrust of Austrians."

Grandmother looked interested. "Now, why is that, Otto?"

Fuchs wrinkled his brow and nose. "Well, ma'm, it's politics. It would take me a long while to explain."

The land was growing rougher; I was told that we were approaching Squaw Creek, which cut up the west half of the Shimerdas' place and made the land of little value for farming. Soon we could see the broken, grassy clay cliffs which indicated the windings of the stream, and the glittering tops of the cottonwoods and ash trees that grew down in the ravine. Some of the cottonwoods had already turned, and the yellow leaves and shining white bark made them look like the gold and silver trees in fairy tales.

As we approached the Shimerdas' dwelling, I could still see nothing but rough red hillocks, and draws with shelving banks and long roots hanging out where the earth had crumbled away. Presently, against one of those banks, I saw a sort of shed, thatched with the same wine-colored grass that grew everywhere. Near it tilted a shattered windmill-frame, that had no wheel. We drove up to this skeleton to tie our horses, and then I saw a door and window sunk deep in the draw-bank. The door stood open, and a woman and a girl of fourteen ran out and looked up at us hopefully. A little girl trailed along behind them. The woman had on her head the same embroidered shawl with silk fringes that she wore when she had alighted from the train at Black Hawk. She was not old, but she was certainly not young. Her face was alert and lively, with a sharp chin and shrewd little eyes. She shook grandmother's hand energetically.

"Very glad, very glad!" she ejaculated. Immediately she pointed to the bank out of which she had emerged and said, "House no good, house no good!"

◄ *What does Mrs. Shimerda immediately say about her house?*

Grandmother nodded consolingly. "You'll get fixed up comfortable after while, Mrs. Shimerda; make good house."

My grandmother always spoke in a very loud tone to foreigners, as if they were deaf. She made Mrs. Shimerda understand the friendly intention of our visit, and the

Bohemian woman handled the loaves of bread and even smelled them, and examined the pies with lively curiosity, exclaiming, "Much good, much thank!"—and again she wrung grandmother's hand.

The oldest son, Ambrŏz—they called it Ambrosch—came out of the cave and stood beside his mother. He was nineteen years old, short and broad-backed, with a close-cropped, flat head, and a wide, flat face. His hazel eyes were little and shrewd, like his mother's, but more sly and suspicious; they fairly snapped at the food. The family had been living on corncakes and sorghum molasses for three days.

The little girl was pretty, but Án-tonia—they accented the name thus, strongly, when they spoke to her—was still prettier. I remembered what the conductor had said about her eyes. They were big and warm and full of light, like the sun shining on brown pools in the wood. Her skin was brown, too, and in her cheeks she had a glow of rich, dark color. Her brown hair was curly and wild-looking. The little sister, whom they called Yulka (Julka), was fair, and seemed mild and obedient. While I stood awkwardly confronting the two girls, Krajiek came up from the barn to see what was going on. With him was another Shimerda son. Even from a distance one could see that there was something strange about this boy. As he approached us, he began to make <u>uncouth</u> noises, and held up his hands to show us his fingers, which were webbed to the first knuckle, like a duck's foot. When he saw me draw back, he began to crow delightedly, "Hoo, hoo-hoo, hoo-hoo!" like a rooster. His mother scowled and said sternly, "Marek!" then spoke rapidly to Krajiek in Bohemian.

"She wants me to tell you he won't hurt nobody, Mrs. Burden. He was born like that. The others are smart. Ambrosch, he make good farmer." He struck Ambrosch on the back, and the boy smiled knowingly.

At that moment the father came out of the hole in the bank. He wore no hat, and his thick, iron-gray hair was brushed straight back from his forehead. It was so long that it bushed out behind his ears, and made him look like the old portraits I remembered in Virginia. He was tall and slender, and his thin shoulders stooped. He looked at us understandingly, then took grandmother's hand and bent over it. I noticed how white and well-shaped his own hands were. They looked calm, somehow, and skilled. His eyes were melancholy, and were set back deep under his brow. His face was ruggedly formed, but it looked like ashes—like something from which all the warmth and light had died out. Everything about this old man was in keeping with his dignified manner. He was neatly dressed. Under his coat he wore a knitted gray vest, and, instead of a collar, a silk scarf of a dark bronze-green, carefully crossed and held together by a red coral pin. While Krajiek was translating for Mr. Shimerda, Ántonia came up to me and held out her hand coaxingly. In a moment we were running up the steep drawside together, Yulka trotting after us.

◀ What does Jim note about Mr. Shimerda's hands?

When we reached the level and could see the gold tree-tops, I pointed toward them, and Ántonia laughed and squeezed my hand as if to tell me how glad she was I had come. We raced off toward Squaw Creek and did not stop until the ground itself stopped— fell away before us so abruptly that the next step would have been out into the tree-tops. We stood panting on the edge of the ravine, looking down at the trees and bushes that grew below us. The wind was so strong that I had to hold my hat on, and the girls' skirts were blown out before them. Ántonia seemed to like it; she held her little sister by the hand and chattered away in that language which seemed to me spoken so much more rapidly than mine. She looked at me, her eyes fairly blazing with things she could not say.

"Name? What name?" she asked, touching me on the shoulder. I told her my name, and she repeated it after me and made Yulka say it. She pointed into the gold cotton-wood tree behind whose top we stood and said again, "What name?"

We sat down and made a nest in the long red grass. Yulka curled up like a baby rabbit and played with a grasshopper. Ántonia pointed up to the sky and questioned me with her glance. I gave her the word, but she was not satisfied and pointed to my eyes. I told her, and she repeated the word, making it sound like "ice." She pointed up to the sky, then to my eyes, then back to the sky, with movements so quick and impulsive that she distracted me, and I had no idea what she wanted. She got up on her knees and wrung her hands. She pointed to her own eyes and shook her head, then to mine and to the sky, nodding violently.

"Oh," I exclaimed, "blue; blue sky."

She clapped her hands and murmured, "Blue sky, blue eyes," as if it amused her. While we snuggled down there out of the wind, she learned a score of words. She was alive, and very eager. We were so deep in the grass that we could see nothing but the blue sky over us and the gold tree in front of us. It was wonderfully pleasant. After Ántonia had said the new words over and over, she wanted to give me a little chased silver ring she wore on her middle finger. When she coaxed and insisted, I repulsed her quite sternly. I didn't want her ring, and I felt there was something reckless and extravagant about her wishing to give it away to a boy she had never seen before. No wonder Krajiek got the better of these people, if this was how they behaved.

While we were disputing about the ring, I heard a mournful voice calling, "Ántonia, Ántonia!" She sprang up like a hare. *"Tatinek! Tatinek!"*[1] she shouted, and we ran to meet the old man who was coming toward us. Ántonia reached him first, took his hand and kissed it. When I came up, he touched my shoulder and looked searchingly down into my face for several seconds. I became somewhat embarrassed, for I was used to being taken for granted by my elders.

▶ *What does Mr. Shimerda do that embarrasses Jim? Why does it embarrass him?*

We went with Mr. Shimerda back to the dugout, where grandmother was waiting for me. Before I got into the wagon, he took a book out of his pocket, opened it, and showed me a page with two alphabets, one English and the other Bohemian. He placed this book in my grandmother's hands, looked at her entreatingly, and said, with an earnestness which I shall never forget, "Te-e-ach, te-e-ach my Án-tonia!"

▶ *What request does Mr. Shimerda make of the Burdens?*

---

1. *Tatinek.* Bohemian word for *daddy*

Chapter 4

On the afternoon of that same Sunday I took my first long ride on my pony, under Otto's direction. After that Dude and I went twice a week to the post-office, six miles east of us, and I saved the men a good deal of time by riding on errands to our neighbors. When we had to borrow anything, or to send about word that there would be preaching at the sod schoolhouse, I was always the messenger. Formerly Fuchs attended to such things after working hours.

All the years that have passed have not dimmed my memory of that first glorious autumn. The new country lay open before me: there were no fences in those days, and I could choose my own way over the grass uplands, trusting the pony to get me home again. Sometimes I followed the sunflower-bordered roads. Fuchs told me that the sunflowers were introduced into that country by the Mormons; that at the time of the persecution, when they left Missouri and struck out into the wilderness to find a place where they could worship God in their own way, the members of the first exploring party, crossing the plains to Utah, scattered sunflower seed as they went. The next summer, when the long trains of wagons came through with all the women and children, they had the sunflower trail to follow. I believe that botanists do not confirm Fuchs's story, but insist that the sunflower was native to those plains. Nevertheless, that legend has stuck in my mind, and sunflower-bordered roads always seem to me the roads to freedom.

I used to love to drift along the pale-yellow cornfields, looking for the damp spots one sometimes found at their edges, where the smartweed[1] soon turned a rich copper color and the narrow brown leaves hung curled like cocoons about the swollen joints of the stem. Sometimes I went south to visit our German neighbors and to admire their catalpa[2] grove, or to see the big elm tree that grew up out of a deep crack in the earth and had a hawk's nest in its branches. Trees were so rare in that country, and they had to make such a hard fight to grow, that we used to feel anxious about them, and visit them as if they were persons. It must have been the scarcity of detail in that tawny landscape that made detail so precious.

◀ *Why does Jim visit the trees?*

---

1. **smartweed.** Flowering weed with fuzzy leaves and greenish-pink flowers
2. **catalpa.** Large flowering tree

Sometimes I rode north to the big prairie-dog town to watch the brown earth-owls fly home in the late afternoon and go down to their nests underground with the dogs. Ántonia Shimerda liked to go with me, and we used to wonder a great deal about these birds of <u>subterranean</u> habit. We had to be on our guard there, for rattlesnakes were always lurking about. They came to pick up an easy living among the dogs and owls, which were quite defenseless against them; took possession of their comfortable houses and ate the eggs and puppies. We felt sorry for the owls. It was always mournful to see them come flying home at sunset and disappear under the earth. But, after all, we felt, winged things who would live like that must be rather <u>degraded</u> creatures. The dog-town was a long way from any pond or creek. Otto Fuchs said he had seen populous dog-towns in the desert where there was no surface water for fifty miles; he insisted that some of the holes must go down to water—nearly two hundred feet, hereabouts. Ántonia said she didn't believe it; that the dogs probably lapped up the dew in the early morning, like the rabbits.

Ántonia had opinions about everything, and she was soon able to make them known. Almost every day she came running across the prairie to have her reading lesson with me. Mrs. Shimerda grumbled, but realized it was important that one member of the family should learn English. When the lesson was over, we used to go up to the watermelon patch behind the garden. I split the melons with an old corn-knife, and we lifted out the hearts and ate them with the juice trickling through our fingers. The white Christmas melons we did not touch, but we watched them with curiosity. They were to be picked late, when the hard frosts had set in, and put away for winter use. After weeks on the ocean, the Shimerdas were <u>famished</u> for fruit. The two girls would wander for miles along the edge of the cornfields, hunting for ground-cherries.

Ántonia loved to help grandmother in the kitchen and to learn about cooking and housekeeping. She would stand beside her, watching her every movement. We were willing to believe that Mrs. Shimerda was a good housewife in her

words for everyday use

sub • ter • ra • nean (səb tə rā′ nē ən) adj., underground. *Wells are used to collect <u>subterranean</u> water for human use.*

de • gra • ded (di grād′ əd) adj., reduced far below ordinary standards of civilized life. *Having lived alone, far from human society, for* so many years, her manners were <u>degraded</u>, and she had to relearn social customs.

fa • mished (fa′ misht) adj., intensely hungry. *After moving all of the furniture into their new apartment, the roommates were <u>famished</u> and had to order two large pizzas.*

own country, but she managed poorly under new conditions: the conditions were bad enough, certainly!

I remember how horrified we were at the sour, ashy-gray bread she gave her family to eat. She mixed her dough, we discovered, in an old tin peck-measure that Krajiek had used about the barn. When she took the paste out to bake it, she left smears of dough sticking to the sides of the measure, put the measure on the shelf behind the stove, and let this residue ferment. The next time she made bread, she scraped this sour stuff down into the fresh dough to serve as yeast.

During those first months the Shimerdas never went to town. Krajiek encouraged them in the belief that in Black Hawk they would somehow be mysteriously separated from their money. They hated Krajiek, but they clung to him because he was the only human being with whom they could talk or from whom they could get information. He slept with the old man and the two boys in the dugout barn, along with the oxen. They kept him in their hole and fed him for the same reason that the prairie dogs and the brown owls housed the rattlesnakes— because they did not know how to get rid of him.

◄ *Why don't the Shimerdas ever go to town?*

Chapter 5

We knew that things were hard for our Bohemian neighbors, but the two girls were light-hearted and never complained. They were always ready to forget their troubles at home, and to run away with me over the prairie, scaring rabbits or starting up flocks of quail.

I remember Ántonia's excitement when she came into our kitchen one afternoon and announced: "My papa find friends up north, with Russian mans. Last night he take me for see, and I can understand very much talk. Nice mans, Mrs. Burden. One is fat and all the time laugh. Everybody laugh. The first time I see my papa laugh in this kawn-tree. Oh, very nice!"

I asked her if she meant the two Russians who lived up by the big dog-town. I had often been tempted to go to see them when I was riding in that direction, but one of them was a wild-looking fellow and I was a little afraid of him. Russia seemed to me more remote than any other country— farther away than China, almost as far as the North Pole. Of all the strange, uprooted people among the first settlers, those two men were the strangest and the most aloof. Their last names were unpronounceable, so they were called Pavel and Peter. They went about making signs to people, and until the Shimerdas came they had no friends. Krajiek could understand them a little, but he had cheated them in a trade, so they avoided him. Pavel, the tall one, was said to be an <u>anarchist</u>; since he had no means of imparting his opinions, probably his wild <u>gesticulations</u> and his generally excited and rebellious manner gave rise to this supposition. He must once have been a very strong man, but now his great frame, with big, knotty joints, had a wasted look, and the skin was drawn tight over his high cheek-bones. His breathing was hoarse, and he always had a cough.

Peter, his companion, was a very different sort of fellow; short, bow-legged, and as fat as butter. He always seemed pleased when he met people on the road, smiled and took off his cap to everyone, men as well as women. At a distance, on his wagon, he looked like an old man; his hair

▶ Why do the residents of Black Hawk think Pavel is an anarchist?

and beard were of such a pale flaxen color that they seemed white in the sun. They were as thick and curly as carded wool. His rosy face, with its snub nose, set in this fleece, was like a melon among its leaves. He was usually called "Curly Peter," or "Rooshian Peter."

The two Russians made good farmhands, and in summer they worked out together. I had heard our neighbors laughing when they told how Peter always had to go home at night to milk his cow. Other bachelor homesteaders used canned milk, to save trouble. Sometimes Peter came to church at the sod schoolhouse. It was there I first saw him, sitting on a low bench by the door, his plush cap in his hands, his bare feet tucked apologetically under the seat.

After Mr. Shimerda discovered the Russians, he went to see them almost every evening, and sometimes took Ántonia with him. She said they came from a part of Russia where the language was not very different from Bohemian, and if I wanted to go to their place, she could talk to them for me. One afternoon, before the heavy frosts began, we rode up there together on my pony.

The Russians had a neat log house built on a grassy slope, with a windlass well beside the door. As we rode up the draw, we skirted a big melon patch, and a garden where squashes and yellow cucumbers lay about on the sod. We found Peter out behind his kitchen, bending over a washtub. He was working so hard that he did not hear us coming. His whole body moved up and down as he rubbed, and he was a funny sight from the rear, with his shaggy head and bandy legs. When he straightened himself up to greet us, drops of perspiration were rolling from his thick nose down onto his curly beard. Peter dried his hands and seemed glad to leave his washing. He took us down to see his chickens, and his cow that was grazing on the hillside. He told Ántonia that in his country only rich people had cows, but here any man could have one who would take care of her. The milk was good for Pavel, who was often sick, and he could make butter by beating sour cream with a wooden spoon. Peter was very fond of his cow. He patted her flanks and talked to her in Russian while he pulled up her lariat pin[1] and set it in a new place.

After he had shown us his garden, Peter trundled a load of watermelons up the hill in his wheelbarrow. Pavel was not at home. He was off somewhere helping to dig a well.

◀ What is different about owning cows in America?

---

1. **lariat pin.** Stake used to tether grazing animals

The house I thought very comfortable for two men who were "batching." Besides the kitchen, there was a living-room, with a wide double bed built against the wall, properly made up with blue gingham sheets and pillows. There was a little storeroom, too, with a window, where they kept guns and saddles and tools, and old coats and boots. That day the floor was covered with garden things, drying for winter; corn and beans and fat yellow cucumbers. There were no screens or window-blinds in the house, and all the doors and windows stood wide open, letting in flies and sunshine alike.

Peter put the melons in a row on the oilcloth-covered table and stood over them, <u>brandishing</u> a butcher knife. Before the blade got fairly into them, they split of their own ripeness, with a delicious sound. He gave us knives, but no plates, and the top of the table was soon swimming with juice and seeds. I had never seen anyone eat so many melons as Peter ate. He assured us that they were good for one—better than medicine; in his country people lived on them at this time of year. He was very hospitable and jolly. Once, while he was looking at Ántonia, he sighed and told us that if he had stayed at home in Russia perhaps by this time he would have had a pretty daughter of his own to cook and keep house for him. He said he had left his country because of a "great trouble."

▶ What does Peter do when Jim and Ántonia get up to leave?

When we got up to go, Peter looked about in perplexity for something that would entertain us. He ran into the storeroom and brought out a <u>gaudily</u> painted harmonica, sat down on a bench, and spreading his fat legs apart began to play like a whole band. The tunes were either very lively or very <u>doleful</u>, and he sang words to some of them.

Before we left, Peter put ripe cucumbers into a sack for Mrs. Shimerda and gave us a lard-pail full of milk to cook them in. I had never heard of cooking cucumbers, but Ántonia assured me they were very good. We had to walk the pony all the way home to keep from spilling the milk.

words for everyday use

bran • dish • ing (bran' dish iŋ) v., shaking or waving menacingly or aggressively. *Never approach someone who is <u>brandish</u>ing a weapon.*

gau • di • ly (gó' dəl ē) adv., Showily, tastelessly. *The room, with its many gold and purple accents, was <u>gaudily</u> decorated.*

dole • ful (dōl' fəl) adj., expressing grief. *When she was getting ready for a trip, she couldn't bear to look at her beagle's <u>doleful</u> face begging her to stay.*

Chapter 6

One afternoon we were having our reading lesson on the warm, grassy bank where the badger lived. It was a day of amber sunlight, but there was a shiver of coming winter in the air. I had seen ice on the little horse-pond that morning, and as we went through the garden we found the tall asparagus, with its red berries, lying on the ground, a mass of slimy green.

Tony was barefooted, and she shivered in her cotton dress and was comfortable only when we were tucked down on the baked earth, in the full blaze of the sun. She could talk to me about almost anything by this time. That afternoon she was telling me how highly esteemed our friend the badger was in her part of the world, and how men kept a special kind of dog, with very short legs, to hunt him. Those dogs, she said, went down into the hole after the badger and killed him there in a terrific struggle underground; you could hear the barks and yelps outside. Then the dog dragged himself back, covered with bites and scratches, to be rewarded and petted by his master. She knew a dog who had a star on his collar for every badger he had killed.

The rabbits were unusually <u>spry</u> that afternoon. They kept starting up all about us, and dashing off down the draw as if they were playing a game of some kind. But the little buzzing things that lived in the grass were all dead— all but one. While we were lying there against the warm bank, a little insect of the palest, frailest green hopped painfully out of the buffalo grass and tried to leap into a bunch of bluestem. He missed it, fell back, and sat with his head sunk between his long legs, his antennae quivering, as if he were waiting for something to come and finish him. Tony made a warm nest for him in her hands; talked to him gaily and indulgently in Bohemian. Presently he began to sing for us—a thin, rusty little chirp. She held him close to her ear and laughed, but a moment afterward I saw there were tears in her eyes. She told me that in her village at home there was an old beggar woman who went about selling herbs and roots she had dug up in the forest. If you took her in and gave her a warm place by the fire,

◄ What memory does the chirping insect bring to Ántonia's mind?

she sang old songs to the children in a cracked voice, like this. Old Hata, she was called, and the children loved to see her coming and saved their cakes and sweets for her.

When the bank on the other side of the draw began to throw a narrow shelf of shadow, we knew we ought to be starting homeward; the chill came on quickly when the sun got low, and Ántonia's dress was thin. What were we to do with the frail little creature we had lured back to life by false pretenses? I offered my pockets, but Tony shook her head and carefully put the green insect in her hair, tying her big handkerchief down loosely over her curls. I said I would go with her until we could see Squaw Creek, and then turn and run home. We drifted along lazily, very happy, through the magical light of the late afternoon.

All those fall afternoons were the same, but I never got used to them. As far as we could see, the miles of copper-red grass were drenched in sunlight that was stronger and fiercer than at any other time of the day. The blond corn-fields were red gold, the haystacks turned rosy and threw long shadows. The whole prairie was like the bush that burned with fire and was not consumed. That hour always had the <u>exultation</u> of victory, of triumphant ending, like a hero's death—heroes who died young and gloriously. It was a sudden <u>transfiguration</u>, a lifting-up of day.

How many an afternoon Ántonia and I have trailed along the prairie under that magnificence! And always two long black shadows flitted before us or followed after, dark spots on the ruddy grass.

We had been silent a long time, and the edge of the sun sank nearer and nearer the prairie floor, when we saw a figure moving on the edge of the upland, a gun over his shoulder. He was walking slowly, dragging his feet along as if he had no purpose. We broke into a run to overtake him.

"My papa sick all the time," Tony panted as we flew. "He not look good, Jim."

As we neared Mr. Shimerda she shouted, and he lifted his head and peered about. Tony ran up to him, caught his hand and pressed it against her cheek. She was the only one of his family who could rouse the old man from the

▶ *What does Ántonia say about her father?*

torpor in which he seemed to live. He took the bag from his belt and showed us three rabbits he had shot, looked at Ántonia with a wintry flicker of a smile and began to tell her something. She turned to me.

"My *tatinek* make me little hat with the skins, little hat for win-ter!" she exclaimed joyfully. "Meat for eat, skin for hat"—she told off these benefits on her fingers.

Her father put his hand on her hair, but she caught his wrist and lifted it carefully away, talking to him rapidly. I heard the name of old Hata. He untied the handkerchief, separated her hair with his fingers, and stood looking down at the green insect. When it began to chirp faintly, he listened as if it were a beautiful sound.

I picked up the gun he had dropped; a queer piece from the old country, short and heavy, with a stag's head on the cock. When he saw me examining it, he turned to me with his far-away look that always made me feel as if I were down at the bottom of a well. He spoke kindly and gravely, and Ántonia translated:—

"My *tatinek* say when you are big boy, he give you his gun. Very fine, from Bohemie. It was belong to a great man, very rich, like what you not got here; many fields, many forests, many big house. My papa play for his wedding, and he give my papa fine gun, and my papa give you."

I was glad that this project was one of <u>futurity</u>. There never were such people as the Shimerdas for wanting to give away everything they had. Even the mother was always offering me things, though I knew she expected substantial presents in return. We stood there in friendly silence, while the feeble minstrel[1] sheltered in Ántonia's hair went on with its scratchy chirp. The old man's smile, as he listened, was so full of sadness, of pity for things, that I never afterward forgot it. As the sun sank there came a sudden coolness and the strong smell of earth and drying grass. Ántonia and her father went off hand in hand, and I buttoned up my jacket and raced my shadow home.

◄ What will Jim never forget about Mr. Shimerda's response to the insect?

---

1. **minstrel.** Musician, especially a singer of verses to the accompaniment of a harp

| **words for everyday use** | **tor • por** (tor' pər) n., a state of extreme sluggishness or stagnation, lethargy. *After eating the huge turkey dinner, the family fell into a <u>torpor</u>, staring mindlessly at the television or napping in their rooms.* | **fu • tur • i • ty** (fyù tur' ə tē) n., the quality or state of being in the future. *Although the family wanted to move to California, the actual relocation was definitely a case of <u>futurity</u>.* |

Chapter 7

▶ *What does Jim resent about Ántonia?*

Much as I liked Ántonia, I hated a superior tone that she sometimes took with me. She was four years older than I, to be sure, and had seen more of the world; but I was a boy and she was a girl, and I resented her protecting manner. Before the autumn was over, she began to treat me more like an equal and to defer to me in other things than reading lessons. This change came about from an adventure we had together.

One day when I rode over to the Shimerdas' I found Ántonia starting off on foot for Russian Peter's house, to borrow a spade Ambrosch needed. I offered to take her on the pony, and she got up behind me. There had been another black frost the night before, and the air was clear and heady as wine. Within a week all the blooming roads had been <u>despoiled</u>, hundreds of miles of yellow sunflowers had been transformed into brown, rattling, burry stalks.

We found Russian Peter digging his potatoes. We were glad to go in and get warm by his kitchen stove and to see his squashes and Christmas melons, heaped in the storeroom for winter. As we rode away with the spade, Ántonia suggested that we stop at the prairie-dog town and dig into one of the holes. We could find out whether they ran straight down, or were horizontal, like mole-holes; whether they had underground connections; whether the owls had nests down there, lined with feathers. We might get some puppies, or owl eggs, or snake-skins.

The dog-town was spread out over perhaps ten acres. The grass had been nibbled short and even, so this stretch was not shaggy and red like the surrounding country, but gray and velvety. The holes were several yards apart, and were disposed with a good deal of regularity, almost as if the town had been laid out in streets and avenues. One always felt that an orderly and very sociable kind of life was going on there. I picketed Dude down in a draw, and we went wandering about, looking for a hole that would be easy to dig. The dogs were out, as usual, dozens of them, sitting up on their hind legs over the doors of their houses. As we approached, they barked, shook their tails at us, and

---

words for everyday use   de • spoil • ed (di spoild') adj., stripped of belongings, possessions, or value. *Soldiers not only drove villagers away but <u>despoiled</u> the entire village before moving on.*

scurried underground. Before the mouths of the holes were little patches of sand and gravel, scratched up, we supposed, from a long way below the surface. Here and there, in the town, we came on larger gravel patches, several yards away from any hole. If the dogs had scratched the sand up in excavating, how had they carried it so far? It was on one of these gravel beds that I met my adventure.

We were examining a big hole with two entrances. The burrow sloped into the ground at a gentle angle, so that we could see where the two corridors united, and the floor was dusty from use, like a little highway over which much travel went. I was walking backward, in a crouching position, when I heard Ántonia scream. She was standing opposite me, pointing behind me and shouting something in Bohemian. I whirled round, and there, on one of those dry gravel beds, was the biggest snake I had ever seen. He was sunning himself, after the cold night, and he must have been asleep when Ántonia screamed. When I turned, he was lying in long loose waves, like a letter "W." He twitched and began to coil slowly. He was not merely a big snake, I thought—he was a circus monstrosity. His abominable muscularity, his loathsome, fluid motion, somehow made me sick. He was as thick as my leg, and looked as if millstones couldn't crush the disgusting vitality out of him. He lifted his hideous little head, and rattled. I didn't run because I didn't think of it—if my back had been against a stone wall I couldn't have felt more cornered. I saw his coils tighten—now he would spring, spring his length, I remembered. I ran up and drove at his head with my spade, struck him fairly across the neck, and in a minute he was all about my feet in wavy loops. I struck now from hate. Ántonia, barefooted as she was, ran up behind me. Even after I had pounded his ugly head flat, his body kept on coiling and winding, doubling and falling back on itself. I walked away and turned my back. I felt seasick. Ántonia came after me, crying, "O Jimmy, he not bite you? You sure? Why you not run when I say?"

◀ What do Jim and Ántonia discover in the dog-town?

◀ How does Jim react to the snake?

words for everyday use

a • bom • in • a • ble (e bäm′ nə bəl) adj., worthy of disgust or hatred, detestable. *Kim's mother demanded that Kim clean up the abominable mess.*

loath • some (lōth′ səm) adj., giving rise to dislike, disgust, or hatred. *The peace activists declared all forms of violence to be loathsome.*

vi • tal • i • ty (vī ta′ lə tē), n., the peculiarity distinguishing the living from the nonliving. *Not wanting to be stung, I carefully checked for vitality before picking up the wasp's body to throw it away.*

"What did you jabber Bohunk for? You might have told me there was a snake behind me!" I said <u>petulantly</u>.

"I know I am just awful, Jim, I was so scared." She took my handkerchief from my pocket and tried to wipe my face with it, but I snatched it away from her. I suppose I looked as sick as I felt.

"I never know you was so brave, Jim," she went on comfortingly. "You is just like big mans; you wait for him lift his head and then you go for him. Ain't you feel scared a bit? Now we take that snake home and show everybody. Nobody ain't seen in this kawn-tree so big snake like you kill."

She went on in this strain until I began to think that I had longed for this opportunity, and had hailed it with joy. Cautiously we went back to the snake; he was still groping with his tail, turning up his ugly belly in the light. A faint, <u>fetid</u> smell came from him, and a thread of green liquid oozed from his crushed head.

"Look, Tony, that's his poison," I said.

I took a long piece of string from my pocket, and she lifted his head with the spade while I tied a noose around it. We pulled him out straight and measured him by my riding-quirt; he was about five and a half feet long. He had twelve rattles, but they were broken off before they began to taper, so I insisted that he must once have had twenty-four. I explained to Ántonia how this meant that he was twenty-four years old, that he must have been there when white men first came, left on from buffalo and Indian times. As I turned him over, I began to feel proud of him, to have a kind of respect for his age and size. He seemed like the ancient, eldest Evil. Certainly his kind have left horrible unconscious memories in all warm-blooded life. When we dragged him down into the draw, Dude sprang off to the end of his tether and shivered all over— wouldn't let us come near him.

We decided that Ántonia should ride Dude home, and I would walk. As she rode along slowly, her bare legs swinging against the pony's sides, she kept shouting back to me about how astonished everybody would be. I followed with the spade over my shoulder, dragging my snake. Her

▶ *How does Ántonia's impression of Jim change as a result of this incident?*

▶ *What greater significance does Jim attribute to the snake?*

---

words for everyday use

pet • u • lant • ly (pe′ chə lənt lē), adv., with temporary ill humor, peevishly. *Angry at her mother, the five year old refused to answer and looked away <u>petulantly</u>.*

fe • tid (fe′ təd), adj., having a heavy, offensive smell. *Investigating the source of the <u>fetid</u> smell in the attic, the girls found a dead mouse.*

32 MY ÁNTONIA

exultation was contagious. The great land had never looked to me so big and free. If the red grass were full of rattlers, I was equal to them all. Nevertheless, I stole <u>furtive</u> glances behind me now and then to see that no avenging mate, older and bigger than my quarry, was racing up from the rear.

The sun had set when we reached our garden and went down the draw toward the house. Otto Fuchs was the first one we met. He was sitting on the edge of the cattle-pond, having a quiet pipe before supper. Ántonia called him to come quick and look. He did not say anything for a minute, but scratched his head and turned the snake over with his boot.

"Where did you run onto that beauty, Jim?"

"Up at the dog-town," I answered <u>laconically</u>.

"Kill him yourself? How come you to have a weepon?"

"We'd been up to Russian Peter's, to borrow a spade for Ambrosch."

Otto shook the ashes out of his pipe and squatted down to count the rattles. "It was just luck you had a tool," he said cautiously. "Gosh! I wouldn't want to do any business with that fellow myself, unless I had a fence-post along. Your grandmother's snake-cane wouldn't more than tickle him. He could stand right up and talk to you, he could. Did he fight hard?"

Ántonia broke in: "He fight something awful! He is all over Jimmy's boots. I scream for him to run, but he just hit and hit that snake like he was crazy."

Otto winked at me. After Ántonia rode on he said: "Got him in the head first crack, didn't you? That was just as well."

We hung him up to the windmill, and when I went down to the kitchen, I found Ántonia standing in the middle of the floor, telling the story with a great deal of color.

<u>Subsequent</u> experiences with rattlesnakes taught me that my first encounter was fortunate in circumstance. My big rattler was old, and had led too easy a life; there was not much fight in him. He had probably lived there for years, with a fat prairie dog for breakfast whenever he felt like it, a sheltered home, even an owl-feather bed, perhaps,

◀ How does Jim's interpretation of this event change as he continues to live in Nebraska?

words for everyday use	**fur • tive** (fər' tiv) adj., expressive of stealth, sly. *The child took the cookies from the cookie jar with a quick, <u>furtive</u> glance.* **la • con • i • cal • ly** (lə kä' nik lē) adv., concisely, even to the point of being rude. *"Hey," Shelley said <u>laconically</u> in response to*	*her mother's request that she say "hello."* **sub • se • quent** (səb' si kw[a]nt) adj., following in time, order, or place. *The editor published the controversial editorial with the intention of printing opposing viewpoints in <u>subsequent</u> issues.*

and he had forgot that the world doesn't owe rattlers a living. A snake of his size, in fighting trim, would be more than any boy could handle. So in reality it was a mock adventure; the game was fixed for me by chance, as it probably was for many a dragon-slayer. I had been adequately armed by Russian Peter; the snake was old and lazy; and I had Ántonia beside me, to appreciate and admire.

That snake hung on our corral fence for several days; some of the neighbors came to see it and agreed that it was the biggest rattler ever killed in those parts. This was enough for Ántonia. She liked me better from that time on, and she never took a <u>supercilious</u> air with me again. I had killed a big snake—I was now a big fellow.

words for everyday use

sup • er • cil • i • ous (sü pər si′ le əs) adj., coolly and patronizingly haughty, proud. *The woman's icy tone made her compliments sound <u>supercilious</u>.*

Chapter 8

While the autumn color was growing pale on the grass and cornfields, things went badly with our friends the Russians. Peter told his troubles to Mr. Shimerda: he was unable to meet a note which fell due on the first of November; had to pay an <u>exorbitant</u> bonus on renewing it, and to give a mortgage on his pigs and horses and even his milk cow. His creditor was Wick Cutter, the merciless Black Hawk money-lender, a man of evil name throughout the county, of whom I shall have more to say later. Peter could give no very clear account of his transactions with Cutter. He only knew that he had first borrowed two hundred dollars, then another hundred, then fifty—that each time a bonus was added to the principal, and the debt grew faster than any crop he planted. Now everything was plastered with mortgages.

◀ What financial trouble are Peter and Pavel in?

Soon after Peter renewed his note, Pavel strained himself lifting timbers for a new barn, and fell over among the shavings with such a gush of blood from the lungs that his fellow-workmen thought he would die on the spot. They hauled him home and put him into his bed, and there he lay, very ill indeed. Misfortune seemed to settle like an evil bird on the roof of the log house, and to flap its wings there, warning human beings away. The Russians had such bad luck that people were afraid of them and liked to put them out of mind.

◀ Why didn't people want to think about the two Russians?

One afternoon Ántonia and her father came over to our house to get buttermilk, and lingered, as they usually did, until the sun was low. Just as they were leaving, Russian Peter drove up. Pavel was very bad, he said, and wanted to talk to Mr. Shimerda and his daughter; he had come to fetch them. When Ántonia and her father got into the wagon, I entreated grandmother to let me go with them: I would gladly go without my supper, I would sleep in the Shimerdas' barn and run home in the morning. My plan must have seemed very foolish to her, but she was often large-minded about humoring the desires of other people. She asked Peter to wait a moment, and when she came back from the kitchen she brought a bag of sandwiches and doughnuts for us.

---

words for everyday use   ex • or • bi • tant (ig zôr′ bə tənt) adj., excessive, exceeding the customary limits. *Don't you think spending five hours each night on homework is <u>exorbitant</u>?*

Mr. Shimerda and Peter were on the front seat; Ántonia and I sat in the straw behind and ate our lunch as we bumped along. After the sun sank, a cold wind sprang up and moaned over the prairie. If this turn in the weather had come sooner, I should not have got away. We burrowed down in the straw and curled up close together, watching the angry red die out of the west and the stars begin to shine in the clear, windy sky. Peter kept sighing and groaning. Tony whispered to me that he was afraid Pavel would never get well. We lay still and did not talk. Up there the stars grew magnificently bright. Though we had come from such different parts of the world, in both of us there was some dusky superstition that those shining groups have their influence upon what is and what is not to be. Perhaps Russian Peter, come from farther away than any of us, had brought from his land, too, some such belief.

▶ What significance do Ántonia and Jim attribute to the stars?

The little house on the hillside was so much the color of the night that we could not see it as we came up the draw. The ruddy windows guided us—the light from the kitchen stove, for there was no lamp burning.

We entered softly. The man in the wide bed seemed to be asleep. Tony and I sat down on the bench by the wall and leaned our arms on the table in front of us. The firelight flickered on the hewn logs that supported the thatch overhead. Pavel made a rasping sound when he breathed, and he kept moaning. We waited. The wind shook the doors and windows impatiently, then swept on again, singing through the big spaces. Each gust, as it bore down, rattled the panes, and swelled off like the others. They made me think of defeated armies, retreating; or of ghosts who were trying desperately to get in for shelter, and then went moaning on. Presently, in one of those sobbing intervals between the blasts, the coyotes tuned up with their whining howl; one, two, three, then all together—to tell us that winter was coming. This sound brought an answer from the bed— a long complaining cry,—as if Pavel were having bad dreams or were waking to some old misery. Peter listened, but did not stir. He was sitting on the floor by the kitchen stove. The coyotes broke out again; yap, yap, yap—then the high whine. Pavel called for something and struggled up on his elbow.

▶ What makes Pavel so agitated?

"He is scared of the wolves," Ántonia whispered to me. "In his country there are very many, and they eat men and women." We slid closer together along the bench.

I could not take my eyes off the man in the bed. His

shirt was hanging open, and his <u>emaciated</u> chest, covered with yellow bristle, rose and fell horribly. He began to cough. Peter shuffled to his feet, caught up the tea-kettle and mixed him some hot water and whiskey. The sharp smell of spirits went through the room.

Pavel snatched the cup and drank, then made Peter give him the bottle and slipped it under his pillow, grinning disagreeably, as if he had outwitted someone. His eyes followed Peter about the room with a <u>contemptuous</u>, unfriendly expression. It seemed to me that he despised him for being so simple and <u>docile</u>.

Presently Pavel began to talk to Mr. Shimerda, scarcely above a whisper. He was telling a long story, and as he went on, Ántonia took my hand under the table and held it tight. She leaned forward and strained her ears to hear him. He grew more and more excited, and kept pointing all around his bed, as if there were things there and he wanted Mr. Shimerda to see them.

"It's wolves, Jimmy," Ántonia whispered. "It's awful, what he says!"

The sick man raged and shook his fist. He seemed to be cursing people who had wronged him. Mr. Shimerda caught him by the shoulders, but could hardly hold him in bed. At last he was shut off by a coughing fit which fairly choked him. He pulled a cloth from under his pillow and held it to his mouth. Quickly it was covered with bright red spots—I thought I had never seen any blood so bright. When he lay down and turned his face to the wall, all the rage had gone out of him. He lay patiently fighting for breath, like a child with croup. Ántonia's father uncovered one of his long bony legs and rubbed it rhythmically. From our bench we could see what a hollow case his body was. His spine and shoulder-blades stood out like the bones under the hide of a dead steer left in the fields. That sharp backbone must have hurt him when he lay on it.

Gradually, relief came to all of us. Whatever it was, the worst was over. Mr. Shimerda signed to us that Pavel was asleep. Without a word Peter got up and lit his lantern. He was going out to get his team to drive us home. Mr.

---

words for everyday use

e • ma • ci • a • ted (i mā′ shē āt əd) adj., wasted away physically, enfeebled. *In an effort to meet popular standards of attractiveness, some teenagers starve themselves until they become* <u>emaciated</u>.

con • temp • tu • ous (kən tem′ chə wəs) adj., manifesting, expressing, or feeling disdain. *By refusing to acknowledge their younger brothers, the fifteen-year-olds showed that they were* <u>contemptuous</u> *of anyone who still played with toy trucks.*

do • cile (dä′ səl) adj., easily led or managed. *The cows were so* <u>docile</u> *that the herding dogs hardly had to work at all to bring them into the paddock.*

Shimerda went with him. We sat and watched the long bowed back under the blue sheet, scarcely daring to breathe.

On the way home, when we were lying in the straw, under the jolting and rattling Ántonia told me as much of the story as she could. What she did not tell me then, she told later; we talked of nothing else for days afterward.

When Pavel and Peter were young men, living at home in Russia, they were asked to be groomsmen for a friend who was to marry the belle of another village. It was in the dead of winter and the groom's party went over to the wedding in sledges. Peter and Pavel drove in the groom's sledge, and six sledges followed with all his relatives and friends.

After the ceremony at the church, the party went to a dinner given by the parents of the bride. The dinner lasted all afternoon; then it became a supper and continued far into the night. There was much dancing and drinking. At midnight the parents of the bride said good-bye to her and blessed her. The groom took her up in his arms and carried her out to his sledge and tucked her under the blankets. He sprang in beside her, and Pavel and Peter (our Pavel and Peter!) took the front seat. Pavel drove. The party set out with singing and the jingle of sleigh-bells, the groom's sledge going first. All the drivers were more or less the worse for merry-making, and the groom was absorbed in his bride.

The wolves were bad that winter, and every one knew it, yet when they heard the first wolf-cry, the drivers were not much alarmed. They had too much good food and drink inside them. The first howls were taken up and echoed and with quickening repetitions. The wolves were coming together. There was no moon, but the starlight was clear on the snow. A black drove came up over the hill behind the wedding party. The wolves ran like streaks of shadow; they looked no bigger than dogs, but there were hundreds of them.

Something happened to the hindmost sledge: the driver lost control,— he was probably very drunk,—the horses left the road, the sledge was caught in a clump of trees, and overturned. The occupants rolled out over the snow, and the fleetest of the wolves sprang upon them. The shrieks that followed made everybody sober. The drivers stood up and lashed their horses. The groom had the best team and his sledge was lightest— all the others carried from six to a dozen people.

▶ *Who was driving the bride and groom home?*

Another driver lost control. The screams of the horses were more terrible to hear than the cries of the men and women. Nothing seemed to check the wolves. It was hard to tell what was happening in the rear; the people who were falling behind shrieked as piteously as those who were already lost. The little bride hid her face on the groom's shoulder and sobbed. Pavel sat still and watched his horses. The road was clear and white, and the groom's three blacks went like the wind. It was only necessary to be calm and to guide them carefully.

At length, as they breasted a long hill, Peter rose cautiously and looked back. "There are only three sledges left," he whispered.

"And the wolves?" Pavel asked.

"Enough! Enough for all of us."

Pavel reached the brow of the hill, but only two sledges followed him down the other side. In that moment on the hilltop, they saw behind them a whirling black group on the snow. Presently the groom screamed. He saw his father's sledge overturned, with his mother and sisters. He sprang up as if he meant to jump, but the girl shrieked and held him back. It was even then too late. The black ground-shadows were already crowding over the heap in the road, and one horse ran out across the fields, his harness hanging to him, wolves at his heels. But the groom's movement had given Pavel an idea.

◀ *What did the bride and groom see from the hilltop?*

They were within a few miles of their village now. The only sledge left out of six was not very far behind them, and Pavel's middle horse was failing. Beside a frozen pond something happened to the other sledge; Peter saw it plainly. Three big wolves got abreast of the horses, and the horses went crazy. They tried to jump over each other, got tangled up in the harness, and overturned the sledge.

When the shrieking behind them died away, Pavel realized that he was alone upon the familiar road. "They still come?" he asked Peter.

"Yes."

"How many?"

"Twenty, thirty—enough."

Now his middle horse was being almost dragged by the other two. Pavel gave Peter the reins and stepped carefully into the back of the sledge. He called to the groom that they must lighten— and pointed to the bride. The young man cursed him and held her tighter. Pavel tried to drag her away. In the struggle, the groom rose. Pavel knocked him over the side of the sledge and threw the girl after

◀ *How did Pavel lighten the load on his sledge?*

him. He said he never remembered exactly how he did it, or what happened afterward. Peter, crouching in the front seat, saw nothing. The first thing either of them noticed was a new sound that broke into the clear air, louder than they had ever heard it before—the bell of the monastery of their own village, ringing for early prayers.

▶ What happened to Pavel and Peter as a result?

Pavel and Peter drove into the village alone, and they had been alone ever since. They were run out of their village. Pavel's own mother would not look at him. They went away to strange towns, but when people learned where they came from, they were always asked if they knew the two men who had fed the bride to the wolves. Wherever they went, the story followed them. It took them five years to save money enough to come to America. They worked in Chicago, Des Moines, Fort Wayne, but they were always unfortunate. When Pavel's health grew so bad, they decided to try farming.

Pavel died a few days after he unburdened his mind to Mr. Shimerda, and was buried in the Norwegian graveyard. Peter sold off everything, and left the country—went to be cook in a railway construction camp where gangs of Russians were employed.

At his sale we bought Peter's wheelbarrow and some of his harness. During the auction he went about with his head down, and never lifted his eyes. He seemed not to care about anything. The Black Hawk money-lender who held mortgages on Peter's livestock was there, and he bought in the sale notes at about fifty cents on the dollar. Every one said Peter kissed the cow before she was led away by her new owner. I did not see him do it, but this I know: after all his furniture and his cookstove and pots and pans had been hauled off by the purchasers, when his house was stripped and bare, he sat down on the floor with his clasp-knife and ate all the melons that he had put away for winter. When Mr. Shimerda and Krajiek drove up in their wagon to take Peter to the train, they found him with a dripping beard, surrounded by heaps of melon rinds.

▶ How did the loss of Pavel and Peter affect Mr. Shimerda?

The loss of his two friends had a depressing effect upon old Mr. Shimerda. When he was out hunting, he used to go into the empty log house and sit there, brooding. This cabin was his hermitage until the winter snows penned him in his cave. For Ántonia and me, the story of the wedding party was never at an end. We did not tell Pavel's secret to anyone, but guarded it jealously—as if the wolves of the Ukraine had gathered that night long ago, and the wedding party been sacrificed, to give us a painful and peculiar pleasure. At night, before I went to sleep, I often found myself in a sledge drawn by three horses, dashing through a country that looked something like Nebraska and something like Virginia.

Chapter 9

The first snowfall came early in December. I remember how the world looked from our sitting-room window as I dressed behind the stove that morning: the low sky was like a sheet of metal; the blond cornfields had faded out into ghostliness at last; the little pond was frozen under its stiff willow bushes. Big white flakes were whirling over everything and disappearing in the red grass.

Beyond the pond, on the slope that climbed to the cornfield, there was, faintly marked in the grass, a great circle where the Indians used to ride. Jake and Otto were sure that when they galloped round that ring the Indians tortured prisoners, bound to a stake in the center; but grandfather thought they merely ran races or trained horses there. Whenever one looked at this slope against the setting sun, the circle showed like a pattern in the grass; and this morning, when the first light spray of snow lay over it, it came out with wonderful distinctness, like strokes of Chinese white on canvas. The old figure stirred me as it had never done before and seemed a good omen for the winter.

As soon as the snow had packed hard I began to drive about the country in a clumsy sleigh that Otto Fuchs made for me by fastening a wooden goods-box on bobs.[1] Fuchs had been apprenticed to a cabinet-maker in the old country and was very handy with tools. He would have done a better job if I hadn't hurried him. My first trip was to the post-office, and the next day I went over to take Yulka and Ántonia for a sleigh-ride.

It was a bright, cold day. I piled straw and buffalo robes into the box, and took two hot bricks wrapped in old blankets. When I got to the Shimerdas' I did not go up to the house, but sat in my sleigh at the bottom of the draw and called. Ántonia and Yulka came running out, wearing little rabbit-skin hats their father had made for them. They had heard about my sledge from Ambrosch and knew why I had come. They tumbled in beside me and we set off toward the north, along a road that happened to be broken.

The sky was brilliantly blue, and the sunlight on the glittering white stretches of prairie was almost blinding. As Ántonia said, the whole world was changed by the

> ▶ What significance does Jim attribute to the sight of the Indian circle coated in snow?

---

1. **goods box on bobs.** Supply box that has been placed on runners

snow; we kept looking in vain for familiar landmarks. The deep <u>arroyo</u> through which Squaw Creek wound was now only a cleft between snowdrifts—very blue when one looked down into it. The tree-tops that had been gold all the autumn were dwarfed and twisted, as if they would never have any life in them again. The few little cedars, which were so dull and dingy before, now stood out a strong, dusky green. The wind had the burning taste of fresh snow; my throat and nostrils smarted as if someone had opened a hartshorn bottle. The cold stung, and at the same time delighted one. My horse's breath rose like steam, and whenever we stopped he smoked all over. The cornfields got back a little of their color under the dazzling light, and stood the palest possible gold in the sun and snow. All about us the snow was crusted in shallow terraces, with tracings like ripple-marks at the edges, curly waves that were the actual impression of the stinging lash in the wind.

The girls had on cotton dresses under their shawls; they kept shivering beneath the buffalo robes and hugging each other for warmth. But they were so glad to get away from their ugly cave and their mother's scolding that they begged me to go on and on, as far as Russian Peter's house. The great fresh open, after the <u>stupefying</u> warmth indoors, made them behave like wild things. They laughed and shouted, and said they never wanted to go home again. Couldn't we settle down and live in Russian Peter's house, Yulka asked, and couldn't I go to town and buy things for us to keep house with?

◀ *Why are the girls so happy to be out?*

All the way to Russian Peter's we were extravagantly happy, but when we turned back,—it must have been about four o'clock,— the east wind grew stronger and began to howl; the sun lost its heartening power and the sky became gray and somber. I took off my long woolen comforter and wound it around Yulka's throat. She got so cold that we made her hide her head under the buffalo robe. Ántonia and I sat erect, but I held the reins clumsily, and my eyes were blinded by the wind a good deal of the time. It was growing dark when we got to their house, but I refused to go in with them and get warm. I knew my

| words for everyday use | **ar • roy • o** (ə roiʹ ō) n., a water-carved gully or channel. *The presence of this arroyo indicates that a stream once flowed through the valley.* | **stu • pe • fy** (stüʹ pə fī) vt., to make stupid, groggy, or insensible. *When panelists speak in monotonous voices and show little enthusiasm, they stupefy their audience and even cause some to fall asleep.* |

hands would ache terribly if I went near a fire. Yulka forgot to give me back my comforter, and I had to drive home directly against the wind. The next day I came down with an attack of quinsy, which kept me in the house for nearly two weeks.

The basement kitchen seemed heavenly safe and warm in those days— like a tight little boat in a winter sea. The men were out in the fields all day, husking corn, and when they came in at noon, with long caps pulled down over their ears and their feet in red-lined overshoes, I used to think they were like Arctic explorers. In the afternoons, when grandmother sat upstairs darning, or making husking-gloves, I read *The Swiss Family Robinson*[2] aloud to her, and I felt that the Swiss family had no advantages over us in the way of an adventurous life. I was convinced that man's strongest <u>antagonist</u> is the cold. I admired the cheerful zest with which grandmother went about keeping us warm and comfortable and well-fed. She often reminded me, when she was preparing for the return of the hungry men, that this country was not like Virginia; and that here a cook had, as she said, "very little to do with." On Sundays she gave us as much chicken as we could eat, and on other days we had ham or bacon or sausage meat. She baked either pies or cake for us every day, unless, for a change, she made my favorite pudding, striped with currants and boiled in a bag.

Next to getting warm and keeping warm, dinner and supper were the most interesting things we had to think about. Our lives centered around warmth and food and the return of the men at nightfall. I used to wonder, when they came in tired from the fields, their feet numb and their hands cracked and sore, how they could do all the chores so <u>conscientiously</u>: feed and water and bed the horses, milk the cows, and look after the pigs. When supper was over, it took them a long while to get the cold out of their bones. While grandmother and I washed the dishes and grandfather read his paper upstairs, Jake and Otto sat on

2. *The Swiss Family Robinson.* Nineteenth-century novel about a ship-wrecked Swiss family

| **words for everyday use** | an • tag • o • nist (an ta' gə nist) n., adversary, opponent. *Since Chris and Melanie were friends, it was hard for each of them to think of the other as an <u>antagonist</u>, even though they were playing each other in the final round of the chess tournament.* | con • sci • en • tious • ly (kän shē en' shəs lē) adv., meticulously, carefully. *Hoping to impress the supervisor, Meg completed each of the closing tasks <u>conscientiously</u> before leaving the store.* |

the long bench behind the stove, "easing" their inside boots, or rubbing mutton tallow into their cracked hands.

Every Saturday night we popped corn or made taffy, and Otto Fuchs used to sing, "For I Am a Cowboy and Know I've Done Wrong," or, "Bury Me Not on the Lone Prairee." He had a good baritone voice and always led the singing when we went to church services at the sod schoolhouse.

I can still see those two men sitting on the bench; Otto's close-clipped head and Jake's shaggy hair slicked flat in front by a wet comb. I can see the sag of their tired shoulders against the whitewashed wall. What good fellows they were, how much they knew, and how many things they had kept faith with!

Fuchs had been a cowboy, a stage-driver, a bartender, a miner; had wandered all over that great Western country and done hard work everywhere, though, as grandmother said, he had nothing to show for it. Jake was duller than Otto. He could scarcely read, wrote even his name with difficulty, and he had a violent temper which sometimes made him behave like a crazy man—tore him all to pieces and actually made him ill. But he was so soft-hearted that anyone could impose upon him. If he, as he said, "forgot himself" and swore before grandmother, he went about depressed and shamefaced all day. They were both of them jovial about the cold in winter and the heat in summer, always ready to work overtime and to meet emergencies. It was a matter of pride with them not to spare themselves. Yet they were the sort of men who never get on, somehow, or do anything but work hard for a dollar or two a day.

◀ What sort of men does Jim say Jake and Otto are?

On those bitter, starlit nights, as we sat around the old stove that fed us and warmed us and kept us cheerful, we could hear the coyotes howling down by the corrals, and their hungry, wintry cry used to remind the boys of wonderful animal stories; about gray wolves and bears in the Rockies, wildcats and panthers in the Virginia mountains. Sometimes Fuchs could be persuaded to talk about the outlaws and desperate characters he had known. I remember one funny story about himself that made grandmother, who was working her bread on the bread-board, laugh until she wiped her eyes with her bare arm, her hands being floury. It was like this:—

When Otto left Austria to come to America, he was asked by one of his relatives to look after a woman who was crossing on the same boat, to join her husband in Chicago. The woman started off with two children, but it was clear that her family might grow larger on the journey.

Fuchs said he "got on fine with the kids," and liked the mother, though she played a sorry trick on him. In mid-ocean she proceeded to have not one baby, but three! This event made Fuchs the object of undeserved <u>notoriety</u>, since he was traveling with her. The steerage stewardess was indignant with him, the doctor regarded him with suspicion. The first-cabin passengers, who made up a purse for the woman, took an embarrassing interest in Otto, and often inquired of him about his charge. When the triplets were taken ashore at New York, he had, as he said, "to carry some of them." The trip to Chicago was even worse than the ocean voyage. On the train it was very difficult to get milk for the babies and to keep their bottles clean. The mother did her best, but no woman, out of her natural resources, could feed three babies. The husband, in Chicago, was working in a furniture factory for modest wages, and when he met his family at the station he was rather crushed by the size of it. He, too, seemed to consider Fuchs in some fashion to blame. "I was sure glad," Otto concluded, "that he didn't take his hard feeling out on that poor woman; but he had a sullen eye for me, all right! Now, did you ever hear of a young feller's having such hard luck, Mrs. Burden?"

Grandmother told him she was sure the Lord had remembered these things to his credit, and had helped him out of many a scrape when he didn't realize that he was being protected by Providence.[3]

▶ *What dismayed the father in Chicago?*

▶ *How did the father feel about Otto?*

---

3. **Providence.** God, thought of as the power sustaining and guiding human destiny

words for everyday use

no • tor • i • et • y (nō tə rī' ə tē) n., a state of being widely and unfavorably known. *Even before she was suspended, that student had achieved <u>notoriety</u> for her bullying of younger students.*

Chapter 10

For several weeks after my sleigh-ride, we heard nothing from the Shimerdas. My sore throat kept me indoors, and grandmother had a cold which made the housework heavy for her. When Sunday came she was glad to have a day of rest. One night at supper Fuchs told us he had seen Mr. Shimerda out hunting.

"He's made himself a rabbit-skin cap, Jim, and a rabbit-skin collar that he buttons on outside his coat. They ain't got but one overcoat among 'em over there, and they take turns wearing it. They seem awful scared of cold, and stick in that hole in the bank like badgers."

"All but the crazy boy," Jake put in. "He never wears the coat. Krajiek says he's turrible strong and can stand anything. I guess rabbits must be getting scarce in this locality. Ambrosch come along by the cornfield yesterday where I was at work and showed me three prairie dogs he'd shot. He asked me if they was good to eat. I spit and made a face and took on, to scare him, but he just looked like he was smarter'n me and put 'em back in his sack and walked off."

Grandmother looked up in alarm and spoke to grandfather. "Josiah, you don't suppose Krajiek would let them poor creatures eat prairie dogs, do you?"

"You had better go over and see our neighbors tomorrow, Emmaline," he replied gravely.

Fuchs put in a cheerful word and said prairie dogs were clean beasts and ought to be good for food, but their family connections were against them. I asked what he meant, and he grinned and said they belonged to the rat family.

When I went downstairs in the morning, I found grandmother and Jake packing a hamper basket in the kitchen.

"Now, Jake," grandmother was saying, "if you can find that old rooster that got his comb froze, just give his neck a twist, and we'll take him along. There's no good reason why Mrs. Shimerda couldn't have got hens from her neighbors last fall and had a henhouse going by now. I reckon she was confused and didn't know where to begin. I've come strange to a new country myself, but I never forgot hens are a good thing to have, no matter what you don't have."

"Just as you say, ma'm," said Jake, "but I hate to think of Krajiek getting a leg of that old rooster." He tramped out through the long cellar and dropped the heavy door behind him.

After breakfast grandmother and Jake and I bundled ourselves up and climbed into the cold front wagon-seat.

As we approached the Shimerdas' we heard the frosty whine of the pump and saw Ántonia, her head tied up and her cotton dress blown about her, throwing all her weight on the pump-handle as it went up and down. She heard our wagon, looked back over her shoulder, and catching up her pail of water, started at a run for the hole in the bank.

Jake helped grandmother to the ground, saying he would bring the provisions after he had blanketed his horses. We went slowly up the icy path toward the door sunk in the drawside. Blue puffs of smoke came from the stovepipe that stuck out through the grass and snow, but the wind whisked them roughly away.

▶ What does Mrs. Shimerda do as soon as she opens the door?

Mrs. Shimerda opened the door before we knocked and seized grandmother's hand. She did not say "How do!" as usual, but at once began to cry, talking very fast in her own language, pointing to her feet which were tied up in rags, and looking about accusingly at every one.

The old man was sitting on a stump behind the stove, crouching over as if he were trying to hide from us. Yulka was on the floor at his feet, her kitten in her lap. She peeped out at me and smiled, but, glancing up at her mother, hid again. Ántonia was washing pans and dishes in a dark corner. The crazy boy lay under the only window, stretched on a gunnysack stuffed with straw. As soon as we entered, he threw a grainsack over the crack at the bottom of the door. The air in the cave was stifling, and it was very dark, too. A lighted lantern, hung over the stove, threw out a feeble yellow glimmer.

Mrs. Shimerda snatched off the covers of two barrels behind the door, and made us look into them. In one there were some potatoes that had been frozen and were rotting, in the other was a little pile of flour. Grandmother murmured something in embarrassment, but the Bohemian woman laughed scornfully, a kind of whinny-laugh, and catching up an empty coffee-pot from the shelf, shook it at us with a look positively <u>vindictive</u>.

▶ Which subjects does Grandmother avoid?

Grandmother went on talking in her polite Virginia way, not admitting their <u>stark</u> need or her own remissness[1], until Jake arrived with the hamper, as if in direct

---

1. **remissness.** Negligence in the performance of work or duty

---

| words for everyday use | **vin • dic • tive** (vin dik′ tiv) adj., spiteful, intended to cause anguish or hurt. *The woman was upset by her ex-husband's <u>vindictive</u> words.* | **stark** (stärk) adj., utter, sheer. *The tour group was saddened by the <u>stark</u> poverty they witnessed in much of Cuba.* |

answer to Mrs. Shimerda's reproaches. Then the poor woman broke down. She dropped on the floor beside her crazy son, hid her face on her knees, and sat crying bitterly. Grandmother paid no heed to her, but called Ántonia to come and help empty the basket. Tony left her corner reluctantly. I had never seen her crushed like this before.

"You not mind my poor *maminka*,[2] Mrs. Burden. She is so sad," she whispered, as she wiped her wet hands on her skirt and took the things grandmother handed her.

The crazy boy, seeing the food, began to make soft, gurgling noises and stroked his stomach. Jake came in again, this time with a sack of potatoes. Grandmother looked about in perplexity.

"Haven't you got any sort of cave or cellar outside, Ántonia? This is no place to keep vegetables. How did your potatoes get frozen?"

"We get from Mr. Bushy, at the post-office,—what he throw out. We got no potatoes, Mrs. Burden," Tony admitted mournfully.

When Jake went out, Marek crawled along the floor and stuffed up the door-crack again. Then, quietly as a shadow, Mr. Shimerda came out from behind the stove. He stood brushing his hand over his smooth gray hair, as if he were trying to clear away a fog about his head. He was clean and neat as usual, with his green neckcloth and his coral pin. He took grandmother's arm and led her behind the stove, to the back of the room. In the rear wall was another little cave; a round hole, not much bigger than an oil barrel, scooped out in the black earth. When I got up on one of the stools and peered into it, I saw some quilts and a pile of straw. The old man held the lantern. "Yulka," he said in a low, despairing voice, "Yulka; my Ántonia!"

Grandmother drew back. "You mean they sleep in there,—your girls?" He bowed his head.

Tony slipped under his arm. "It is very cold on the floor, and this is warm like the badger hole. I like for sleep there," she insisted eagerly. "My *maminka* have nice bed, with pillows from our own geese in Bohemie. See, Jim?" She pointed to the narrow bunk which Krajiek had built against the wall for himself before the Shimerdas came.

Grandmother sighed. "Sure enough, where *would* you sleep, dear! I don't doubt you're warm there. You'll have a better house after while, Ántonia, and then you will forget these hard times."

---

2. *maminka.* Bohemian word for *mama*

Mr. Shimerda made grandmother sit down on the only chair and pointed his wife to a stool beside her. Standing before them with his hand on Ántonia's shoulder, he talked in a low tone, and his daughter translated. He wanted us to know that they were not beggars in the old country; he made good wages, and his family were respected there. He left Bohemia with more than a thousand dollars in savings, after their passage money was paid. He had in some way lost on exchange in New York, and the railway fare to Nebraska was more than they had expected. By the time they paid Krajiek for the land, and bought his horses and oxen and some old farm machinery, they had very little money left. He wished grandmother to know, however, that he still had some money. If they could get through until spring came, they would buy a cow and chickens and plant a garden, and would then do very well. Ambrosch and Ántonia were both old enough to work in the fields, and they were willing to work. But the snow and the bitter weather had disheartened them all.

▶ What has happened to the Shimerdas' money?

Ántonia explained that her father meant to build a new house for them in the spring; he and Ambrosch had already split the logs for it, but the logs were all buried in the snow, along the creek where they had been felled.

While grandmother encouraged and gave them advice, I sat down on the floor with Yulka and let her show me her kitten. Marek slid cautiously toward us and began to exhibit his webbed fingers. I knew he wanted to make his queer noises for me—to bark like a dog or whinny like a horse,—but he did not dare in the presence of his elders. Marek was always trying to be agreeable, poor fellow, as if he had it on his mind that he must make up for his deficiencies.

Mrs. Shimerda grew more calm and reasonable before our visit was over, and, while Ántonia translated, put in a word now and then on her own account. The woman had a quick ear, and caught up phrases whenever she heard English spoken. As we rose to go, she opened her wooden chest and brought out a bag made of bed-ticking, about as long as a flour sack and half as wide, stuffed full of something. At sight of it, the crazy boy began to smack his lips. When Mrs. Shimerda opened the bag and stirred the contents with her hand, it gave out a salty, earthy smell, very pungent, even among the other odors of that cave. She measured a teacup full, tied it up in a bit of sacking, and presented it ceremoniously to grandmother.

"For cook," she announced. "Little now; be very much

when cook," spreading out her hands as if to indicate that the pint would swell to a gallon. "Very good. You no have in this country. All things for eat better in my country."

"Maybe so, Mrs. Shimerda," grandmother said dryly. "I can't say but I prefer our bread to yours, myself."

Ántonia undertook to explain. "This very good, Mrs. Burden,"—she clasped her hands as if she could not express how good,—"it make very much when you cook, like what my mama say. Cook with rabbit, cook with chicken, in the gravy,—oh, so good!"

All the way home grandmother and Jake talked about how easily good Christian people could forget they were their brothers' keepers.

◀ What do Jim's grandmother and Jake talk about on the way home?

"I will say, Jake, some of our brothers and sisters are hard to keep. Where's a body to begin, with these people? They're wanting in everything, and most of all in horse-sense. Nobody can give 'em that, I guess. Jimmy, here, is about as able to take over a homestead as they are. Do you reckon that boy Ambrosch has any real push in him?"

"He's a worker, all right, ma'm, and he's got some ketch-on[3] about him; but he's a mean one. Folks can be mean enough to get on in this world; and then, ag'in, they can be too mean."

That night, while grandmother was getting supper, we opened the package Mrs. Shimerda had given her. It was full of little brown chips that looked like the shavings of some root. They were as light as feathers, and the most noticeable thing about them was their penetrating, earthy odor. We could not determine whether they were animal or vegetable.

"They might be dried meat from some queer beast, Jim. They ain't dried fish, and they never grew on stalk or vine. I'm afraid of 'em. Anyhow, I shouldn't want to eat anything that had been shut up for months with old clothes and goose pillows."

She threw the package into the stove, but I bit off a corner of one of the chips I held in my hand, and chewed it tentatively. I never forgot the strange taste; though it was many years before I knew that those little brown shavings, which the Shimerdas had brought so far and treasured so jealously, were dried mushrooms. They had been gathered, probably, in some deep Bohemian forest. . . .

◀ What has Mrs. Shimerda given the Burdens?

---

3. **ketch-on.** Ability to "catch on" and succeed

Chapter 11

During the week before Christmas, Jake was the most important person of our household, for he was to go to town and do all our Christmas shopping. But on the 21st of December, the snow began to fall. The flakes came down so thickly that from the sitting-room windows I could not see beyond the windmill— its frame looked dim and gray, unsubstantial like a shadow. The snow did not stop falling all day, or during the night that followed. The cold was not severe, but the storm was quiet and resistless. The men could not go farther than the barns and corral. They sat about the house most of the day as if it were Sunday; greasing their boots, mending their suspenders, plaiting whiplashes.

On the morning of the 22d, grandfather announced at breakfast that it would be impossible to go to Black Hawk for Christmas purchases. Jake was sure he could get through on horseback, and bring home our things in saddle-bags; but grandfather told him the roads would be <u>obliterated</u>, and a newcomer in the country would be lost ten times over. Anyway, he would never allow one of his horses to be put to such a strain.

We decided to have a country Christmas, without any help from town. I had wanted to get some picture-books for Yulka and Ántonia; even Yulka was able to read a little now. Grandmother took me into the ice-cold storeroom, where she had some bolts of gingham and sheeting. She cut squares of cotton cloth and we sewed them together into a book. We bound it between pasteboards, which I covered with brilliant calico, representing scenes from a circus. For two days I sat at the dining-room table, pasting this book full of pictures for Yulka. We had files of those good old family magazines which used to publish colored lithographs of popular paintings, and I was allowed to use some of these. I took "Napoleon Announcing the Divorce to Josephine" for my frontispiece. On the white pages I grouped Sunday-School cards and advertising cards which I had brought from my "old country." Fuchs got out the old candle-moulds and made tallow candles. Grandmother hunted up her fancy cake-cutters and baked gingerbread

▶ *What prevents Jake from doing the Christmas shopping?*

men and roosters, which we decorated with burnt sugar and red cinnamon drops.

On the day before Christmas, Jake packed the things we were sending to the Shimerdas in his saddle-bags and set off on grandfather's gray gelding. When he mounted his horse at the door, I saw that he had a hatchet slung to his belt, and he gave grandmother a meaning look which told me he was planning a surprise for me. That afternoon I watched long and eagerly from the sitting-room window. At last I saw a dark spot moving on the west hill, beside the half-buried cornfield, where the sky was taking on a coppery flush from the sun that did not quite break through. I put on my cap and ran out to meet Jake. When I got to the pond I could see that he was bringing in a little cedar tree across his pommel. He used to help my father cut Christmas trees for me in Virginia, and he had not forgotten how much I liked them.

By the time we had placed the cold, fresh-smelling little tree in a corner of the sitting-room, it was already Christmas Eve. After supper we all gathered there, and even grandfather, reading his paper by the table, looked up with friendly interest now and then. The cedar was about five feet high and very shapely. We hung it with the gingerbread animals, strings of popcorn, and bits of candle which Fuchs had fitted into pasteboard sockets. Its real splendors, however, came from the most unlikely place in the world—from Otto's cowboy trunk. I had never seen anything in that trunk but old boots and spurs and pistols, and a fascinating mixture of yellow leather thongs, cartridges, and shoemaker's wax. From under the lining he now produced a collection of brilliantly colored paper figures, several inches high and stiff enough to stand alone. They had been sent to him year after year, by his old mother in Austria. There was a bleeding heart,[1] in tufts of paper lace; there were the three kings, gorgeously appareled, and the ox and the ass and the shepherds; there was the Baby in the manger, and a group of angels, singing; there were camels and leopards, held by the black slaves of the three kings. Our tree became the talking tree of the fairy tale[2]; legends and stories nestled like birds in its

---

1. **bleeding heart.** Image of Christ's heart literally bleeding because of love for humanity

2. **...the talking tree of the fairy tale.** Reference to Hans Christian Andersen's "The Fir Tree," a story about a small fir that is transformed into a Christmas tree and is enchanted by the children's stories it hears in the house. See the related reading at the end of this book.

branches. Grandmother said it reminded her of the Tree of Knowledge. We put sheets of cotton wool under it for a snow-field, and Jake's pocket-mirror for a frozen lake.

I can see them now, exactly as they looked, working about the table in the lamplight: Jake with his heavy features, so rudely moulded that his face seemed, somehow, unfinished; Otto with his half-ear and the savage scar that made his upper lip curl so ferociously under his twisted moustache. As I remember them, what unprotected faces they were; their very roughness and violence made them defenseless. These boys had no practiced manner behind which they could retreat and hold people at a distance. They had only their hard fists to batter at the world with. Otto was already one of those drifting, case-hardened laborers who never marry or have children of their own. Yet he was so fond of children!

▶ *What do Jake and Otto lack?*

Chapter 12

On Christmas morning, when I got down to the kitchen, the men were just coming in from their morning chores— the horses and pigs always had their breakfast before we did. Jake and Otto shouted "Merry Christmas!" to me, and winked at each other when they saw the waffle-irons on the stove. Grandfather came down, wearing a white shirt and his Sunday coat. Morning prayers were longer than usual. He read the chapters from St. Matthew about the birth of Christ, and as we listened, it all seemed like something that had happened lately, and near at hand. In his prayer he thanked the Lord for the first Christmas, and for all that it had meant to the world ever since. He gave thanks for our food and comfort, and prayed for the poor and destitute in great cities, where the struggle for life was harder than it was here with us. Grandfather's prayers were often very interesting. He had the gift of simple and moving expression. Because he talked so little, his words had a peculiar force; they were not worn dull from constant use. His prayers reflected what he was thinking about at the time, and it was chiefly through them that we got to know his feelings and his views about things.

◄ *Why were Grandfather's prayers particularly moving?*

After we sat down to our waffles and sausage, Jake told us how pleased the Shimerdas had been with their presents; even Ambrosch was friendly and went to the creek with him to cut the Christmas tree. It was a soft gray day outside, with heavy clouds working across the sky, and occasional squalls of snow. There were always odd jobs to be done about the barn on holidays, and the men were busy until afternoon. Then Jake and I played dominoes, while Otto wrote a long letter home to his mother. He always wrote to her on Christmas Day, he said, no matter where he was, and no matter how long it had been since his last letter. All afternoon he sat in the dining-room. He would write for a while, then sit idle, his clenched fist lying on the table, his eyes following the pattern of the oil-cloth. He spoke and wrote his own language so seldom that it came to him awkwardly. His effort to remember entirely absorbed him.

At about four o'clock a visitor appeared: Mr. Shimerda, wearing his rabbit-skin cap and collar, and new mittens his wife had knitted. He had come to thank us for the presents, and for all grandmother's kindness to his family. Jake and Otto joined us from the basement and we sat

▶ What explanation does Jim give for Mr. Shimerda's pleasure in the Burdens' house?

about the stove, enjoying the deepening gray of the winter afternoon and the atmosphere of comfort and security in my grandfather's house. This feeling seemed completely to take possession of Mr. Shimerda. I suppose, in the crowded clutter of their cave, the old man had come to believe that peace and order had vanished from the earth, or existed only in the old world he had left so far behind. He sat still and passive, his head resting against the back of the wooden rocking-chair, his hands relaxed upon the arms. His face had a look of weariness and pleasure, like that of sick people when they feel relief from pain. Grandmother insisted on his drinking a glass of Virginia apple-brandy after his long walk in the cold, and when a faint flush came up in his cheeks, his features might have been cut out of a shell, they were so transparent. He said almost nothing, and smiled rarely; but as he rested there we all had a sense of his utter content.

As it grew dark, I asked whether I might light the Christmas tree before the lamp was brought. When the candle ends sent up their conical yellow flames, all the colored figures from Austria stood out clear and full of meaning against the green boughs. Mr. Shimerda rose, crossed himself[1], and quietly knelt down before the tree, his head sunk forward. His long body formed a letter "S." I saw grandmother look apprehensively at grandfather. He was rather narrow in religious matters, and sometimes spoke out and hurt people's feelings. There had been nothing strange about the tree before, but now, with some one kneeling before it,—images, candles, . . . Grandfather merely put his finger-tips to his brow and bowed his venerable head, thus Protestantizing the atmosphere.

▶ What does Mr. Shimerda do before leaving?

We persuaded our guest to stay for supper with us. He needed little urging. As we sat down to the table, it occurred to me that he liked to look at us, and that our faces were open books to him. When his deep-seeing eyes rested on me, I felt as if he were looking far ahead into the future for me, down the road I would have to travel.

At nine o'clock Mr. Shimerda lighted one of our lanterns and put on his overcoat and fur collar. He stood in the little entry hall, the lantern and his fur cap under his arm, shaking hands with us. When he took grandmother's hand, he bent over it as he always did, and said slowly, "Good wo-man!" He made the sign of the cross over me,

---

1. **crossed himself.** Catholic gesture that involves making the shape of the cross over the head and chest

put on his cap and went off in the dark. As we turned back to the sitting-room, grandfather looked at me searchingly. "The prayers of all good people are good," he said quietly.

◀ *How does Grandfather react to Mr. Shimerda's religious gestures?*

Chapter 13

The week following Christmas brought in a thaw, and by New Year's Day all the world about us was a broth of gray slush, and the guttered slope between the windmill and the barn was running black water. The soft black earth stood out in patches along the roadsides. I resumed all my chores, carried in the cobs and wood and water, and spent the afternoons at the barn, watching Jake shell corn with a hand-sheller.

One morning, during this <u>interval</u> of fine weather, Ántonia and her mother rode over on one of their shaggy old horses to pay us a visit. It was the first time Mrs. Shimerda had been to our house, and she ran about examining our carpets and curtains and furniture, all the while commenting upon them to her daughter in an envious, complaining tone. In the kitchen she caught up an iron pot that stood on the back of the stove and said: "You got many, Shimerdas no got." I thought it weak-minded of grandmother to give the pot to her.

▶ What does Jim think about his grandmother's giving her pot away?

After dinner, when she was helping to wash the dishes, she said, tossing her head: "You got many things for cook. If I got all things like you, I make much better."

She was a conceited, boastful old thing, and even misfortune could not humble her. I was so annoyed that I felt coldly even toward Ántonia and listened unsympathetically when she told me her father was not well.

▶ How does Ántonia know her father is sad?

"My papa sad for the old country. He not look good. He never make music any more. At home he play violin all the time; for weddings and for dance. Here never. When I beg him for play, he shake his head no. Some days he take his violin out of his box and make with his fingers on the strings, like this, but never he make the music. He don't like this kawn-tree."

"People who don't like this country ought to stay at home," I said severely. "We don't make them come here."

▶ How did Mr. Shimerda's feelings about coming to America differ from his wife's feelings?

"He not want to come, nev-er!" she burst out. "My *maminka* make him come. All the time she say: "America big country; much money, much land for my boys, much husband for my girls." My papa, he cry for leave his old friends what make music with him. He love very much the

words for everyday use

in • ter • val (in′ tər vəl) n., space of time between events or states. *In the <u>interval</u> between hearing the urgent buzzing and recognizing that it was the fire alarm, the class was completely silent.*

58   MY ÁNTONIA

man what play the long horn like this"— she indicated a slide trombone. "They go to school together and are friends from boys. But my mama, she want Ambrosch for be rich, with many cattle."

"Your mama," I said angrily, "wants other people's things."

"Your grandfather is rich," she retorted fiercely. "Why he not help my papa? Ambrosch be rich, too, after while, and he pay back. He is very smart boy. For Ambrosch my mama come here."

Ambrosch was considered the important person in the family. Mrs. Shimerda and Ántonia always <u>deferred</u> to him, though he was often <u>surly</u> with them and contemptuous toward his father. Ambrosch and his mother had everything their own way. Though Ántonia loved her father more than she did any one else, she stood in awe of her elder brother.

After I watched Ántonia and her mother go over the hill on their miserable horse, carrying our iron pot with them, I turned to grandmother, who had taken up her darning, and said I hoped that snooping old woman wouldn't come to see us any more.

Grandmother chuckled and drove her bright needle across a hole in Otto's sock. "She's not old, Jim, though I expect she seems old to you. No, I wouldn't mourn if she never came again. But, you see, a body never knows what traits poverty might bring out in 'em. It makes a woman grasping to see her children want for things. Now read me a chapter in *The Prince of the House of David.*[1] Let's forget the Bohemians."

We had three weeks of this mild, open weather. The cattle in the corral ate corn almost as fast as the men could shell it for them, and we hoped they would be ready for an early market. One morning the two big bulls, Gladstone and Brigham Young, thought spring had come, and they began to tease and butt at each other across the barbed wire that separated them. Soon they got angry. They bel-

◀ What accusation does Ántonia make against Jim's family?

◀ What explanation does Jim's grandmother give for Mrs. Shimerda's behavior?

◀ What effect does the mild weather have on the bulls?

---

1. ***The Prince of the House of David.*** Story written in the mid-nineteenth century about the life of Jesus

---

words for everyday use

de • fer (di fər') vt., submit to another's wishes, opinion, or governance. *Sue deferred to Lee whenever they chose movies to see, which meant that she had to sit through countless action-adventure movies.*

sur • ly (sər' le) adj., irritably sullen and difficult in mood. *I won't go back to that bookstore after the owner was so surly with me, merely grunting in response to my greeting and failing to say "thank you" after I paid.*

lowed and pawed up the soft earth with their hoofs, rolling their eyes and tossing their heads. Each withdrew to a far corner of his own corral, and then they made for each other at a gallop. Thud, thud, we could hear the impact of their great heads, and their bellowing shook the pans on the kitchen shelves. Had they not been dehorned, they would have torn each other to pieces. Pretty soon the fat steers took it up and began butting and horning each other. Clearly, the affair had to be stopped. We all stood by and watched admiringly while Fuchs rode into the corral with a pitchfork and prodded the bulls again and again, finally driving them apart.

The big storm of the winter began on my eleventh birthday, the 20th of January. When I went down to breakfast that morning, Jake and Otto came in white as snowmen, beating their hands and stamping their feet. They began to laugh <u>boisterously</u> when they saw me, calling:—

"You've got a birthday present this time, Jim, and no mistake. They was a full-grown blizzard ordered for you."

All day the storm went on. The snow did not fall this time, it simply spilled out of heaven, like thousands of featherbeds being emptied. That afternoon the kitchen was a carpenter-shop; the men brought in their tools and made two great wooden shovels with long handles. Neither grandmother nor I could go out in the storm, so Jake fed the chickens and brought in a pitiful contribution of eggs.

Next day our men had to shovel until noon to reach the barn— and the snow was still falling! There had not been such a storm in the ten years my grandfather had lived in Nebraska. He said at dinner that we would not try to reach the cattle— they were fat enough to go without their corn for a day or two; but tomorrow we must feed them and thaw out their water-tap so that they could drink. We could not so much as see the corrals, but we knew the steers were over there, huddled together under the north bank. Our ferocious bulls, subdued enough by this time, were probably warming each other's backs. "This'll take the bile out of 'em!" Fuchs remarked gleefully.

At noon that day the hens had not been heard from.

▶ How has the weather caused the behavior of the bulls to change?

After dinner Jake and Otto, their damp clothes now dried on them, stretched their stiff arms and plunged again into the drifts. They made a tunnel under the snow to the hen-house, with walls so solid that grandmother and I could walk back and forth in it. We found the chickens asleep; perhaps they thought night had come to stay. One old rooster was stirring about, pecking at the solid lump of ice in their water-tin. When we flashed the lantern in their eyes, the hens set up a great cackling and flew about clumsily, scattering down-feathers. The mottled, pin-headed guinea-hens, always resentful of captivity, ran screeching out into the tunnel and tried to poke their ugly, painted faces through the snow walls. By five o'clock the chores were done—just when it was time to begin them all over again! That was a strange, unnatural sort of day.

Chapter 14

On the morning of the 22d I wakened with a start. Before I opened my eyes, I seemed to know that something had happened. I heard excited voices in the kitchen— grandmother's was so shrill that I knew she must be almost beside herself. I looked forward to any new crisis with delight. What could it be, I wondered, as I hurried into my clothes. Perhaps the barn had burned; perhaps the cattle had frozen to death; perhaps a neighbor was lost in the storm.

Down in the kitchen grandfather was standing before the stove with his hands behind him. Jake and Otto had taken off their boots and were rubbing their woolen socks. Their clothes and boots were steaming, and they both looked exhausted. On the bench behind the stove lay a man, covered up with a blanket. Grandmother motioned me to the dining-room. I obeyed reluctantly. I watched her as she came and went, carrying dishes. Her lips were tightly compressed and she kept whispering to herself: "Oh, dear Saviour!" "Lord, Thou knowest!"

Presently grandfather came in and spoke to me: "Jimmy, we will not have prayers this morning, because we have a great deal to do. Old Mr. Shimerda is dead, and his family are in great distress. Ambrosch came over here in the middle of the night, and Jake and Otto went back with him. The boys have had a hard night, and you must not bother them with questions. That is Ambrosch, asleep on the bench. Come in to breakfast, boys."

After Jake and Otto had swallowed their first cup of coffee, they began to talk excitedly, disregarding grandmother's warning glances. I held my tongue, but I listened with all my ears.

"No, sir," Fuchs said in answer to a question from grandfather, "nobody heard the gun go off. Ambrosch was out with the ox team, trying to break a road, and the women folks was shut up tight in their cave. When Ambrosch come in it was dark and he didn't see nothing, but the oxen acted kind of queer. One of 'em ripped around and got away from him— bolted clean out of the stable. His hands is blistered where the rope run through. He got a lantern and went back and found the old man, just as we seen him."

"Poor soul, poor soul!" grandmother groaned. "I'd like to think he never done it. He was always considerate and un-wishful to give trouble. How could he forget himself and bring this on us!"

"I don't think he was out of his head for a minute, Mrs. Burden," Fuchs declared. "He done everything natural. You know he was always sort of fixy[1], and fixy he was to the last. He shaved after dinner, and washed hisself all over after the girls had done the dishes. Ántonia heated the water for him. Then he put on a clean shirt and clean socks, and after he was dressed he kissed her and the little one and took his gun and said he was going out to hunt rabbits. He must have gone right down to the barn and done it then. He layed down on that bunk-bed, close to the ox stalls, where he always slept. When we found him, everything was decent except,"—Fuchs wrinkled his brow and hesitated,—"except what he couldn't nowise foresee. His coat was hung on a peg, and his boots was under the bed. He'd took off that silk neckcloth he always wore, and folded it smooth and stuck his pin through it. He turned back his shirt at the neck and rolled up his sleeves."

"I don't see how he could do it!" grandmother kept saying.

Otto misunderstood her. "Why, ma'am, it was simple enough; he pulled the trigger with his big toe. He layed over on his side and put the end of the barrel in his mouth, then he drew up one foot and felt for the trigger. He found it all right!"

◀ *How did Mr. Shimerda die?*

"Maybe he did," said Jake grimly. "There's something mighty queer about it."

"Now what do you mean, Jake?" grandmother asked sharply.

"Well, ma'm, I found Krajiek's axe under the manger, and I picks it up and carries it over to the corpse, and I take my oath it just fit the gash in the front of the old man's face. That there Krajiek had been sneakin' round, pale and quiet, and when he seen me examinin' the axe, he begun whimperin', 'My God, man, don't do that!' 'I reckon I'm a-goin' to look into this,' says I. Then he begun to squeal like a rat and run about wringin' his hands. 'They'll hang me!' says he. 'My God, they'll hang me sure!'"

Fuchs spoke up impatiently. "Krajiek's gone silly, Jake, and so have you. The old man wouldn't have made all them preparations for Krajiek to murder him, would he? It don't hang together. The gun was right beside him when Ambrosch found him."

"Krajiek could 'a' put it there, couldn't he?" Jake demanded.

---

1. **Fixy.** Showing careful attention to details, fastidious

Grandmother broke in excitedly: "See here, Jake Marpole, don't you go trying to add murder to suicide. We're deep enough in trouble. Otto reads you too many of them detective stories."

"It will be easy to decide all that, Emmaline," said grandfather quietly. "If he shot himself in the way they think, the gash will be torn from the inside outward."

"Just so it is, Mr. Burden," Otto affirmed. "I seen bunches of hair and stuff sticking to the poles and straw along the roof. They was blown up there by gunshot, no question."

Grandmother told grandfather she meant to go over to the Shimerdas' with him.

"There is nothing you can do," he said doubtfully. "The body can't be touched until we get the coroner here from Black Hawk, and that will be a matter of several days, this weather."

▶ What does Jim's grandmother say about Ántonia's situation now?

"Well, I can take them some victuals, anyway, and say a word of comfort to them poor little girls. The oldest one was his darling, and was like a right hand to him. He might have thought of her. He's left her alone in a hard world." She glanced distrustfully at Ambrosch, who was now eating his breakfast at the kitchen table.

Fuchs, although he had been up in the cold nearly all night, was going to make the long ride to Black Hawk to fetch the priest and the coroner. On the gray gelding, our best horse, he would try to pick his way across the country with no roads to guide him.

"Don't you worry about me, Mrs. Burden," he said cheerfully, as he put on a second pair of socks. "I've got a good nose for directions, and I never did need much sleep. It's the gray I'm worried about. I'll save him what I can, but it'll strain him, as sure as I'm telling you!"

"This is no time to be over-considerate of animals, Otto; do the best you can for yourself. Stop at the Widow Steavens's for dinner. She's a good woman, and she'll do well by you."

After Fuchs rode away, I was left with Ambrosch. I saw a side of him I had not seen before. He was deeply, even <u>slavishly</u>, devout. He did not say a word all morning, but sat with his rosary[2] in his hands, praying, now silently, now

---

2. **rosary.** String of beads sometimes used by Catholics to count prayers

words for everyday use   slav • ish • ly (slā′ vish lē) adj., like a slave, basely or abjectly servile. *She waited slavishly on her husband's every desire.*

aloud. He never looked away from his beads, nor lifted his hands except to cross himself. Several times the poor boy fell asleep where he sat, wakened with a start, and began to pray again.

No wagon could be got to the Shimerdas' until a road was broken, and that would be a day's job. Grandfather came from the barn on one of our big black horses, and Jake lifted grandmother up behind him. She wore her black hood and was bundled up in shawls. Grandfather tucked his bushy white beard inside his overcoat. They looked very Biblical as they set off, I thought. Jake and Ambrosch followed them, riding the other black and my pony, carrying bundles of clothes that we had got together for Mrs. Shimerda. I watched them go past the pond and over the hill by the drifted cornfield. Then, for the first time, I realized that I was alone in the house.

I felt a considerable extension of power and authority, and was anxious to <u>acquit</u> myself <u>creditably</u>. I carried in cobs and wood from the long cellar, and filled both the stoves. I remembered that in the hurry and excitement of the morning nobody had thought of the chickens, and the eggs had not been gathered. Going out through the tunnel, I gave the hens their corn, emptied the ice from their drinking-pan, and filled it with water. After the cat had had his milk, I could think of nothing else to do, and I sat down to get warm. The quiet was delightful, and the ticking clock was the most pleasant of companions. I got *Robinson Crusoe*[3] and tried to read, but his life on the island seemed dull compared with ours. Presently, as I looked with satisfaction about our comfortable sitting-room, it flashed upon me that if Mr. Shimerda's soul were lingering about in this world at all, it would be here, in our house, which had been more to his liking than any other in the neighborhood. I remembered his contented face when he was with us on Christmas Day. If he could have lived with us, this terrible thing would never have happened.

◀ How does Jim react to being left alone in the house?

◀ Where does Jim think Mr. Shimerda's soul is?

---

3. *Robinson Crusoe.* Eighteenth-century novel about a shipwreck on a deserted island

words for everyday use

a • cquit (ə kwit') vt., to conduct oneself, behave. *Knights in the Middle Ages were expected to <u>acquit</u> themselves with honor.*

cred • i • tab • ly (kre' di tə blē) adv., sufficiently well to bring esteem or praise. *The children were rewarded for having behaved <u>creditably</u> even during especially stressful times.*

▶ What does Jim believe killed Mr. Shimerda?

I knew it was homesickness that had killed Mr. Shimerda, and I wondered whether his released spirit would not eventually find its way back to his own country. I thought of how far it was to Chicago, and then to Virginia, to Baltimore,—and then the great wintry ocean. No, he would not at once set out upon that long journey. Surely, his exhausted spirit, so tired of cold and crowding and the struggle with the ever-falling snow, was resting now in this quiet house.

I was not frightened, but I made no noise. I did not wish to disturb him. I went softly down to the kitchen which, tucked away so snugly underground, always seemed to me the heart and center of the house. There, on the bench behind the stove, I thought and thought about Mr. Shimerda. Outside I could hear the wind singing over hundreds of miles of snow. It was as if I had let the old man in out of the tormenting winter, and were sitting there with him. I went over all that Ántonia had ever told me about his life before he came to this country; how he used to play the fiddle at weddings and dances. I thought about the friends he had mourned to leave, the trombone-player, the great forest full of game,—belonging, as Ántonia said, to the "nobles,"— from which she and her mother used to steal wood on moonlight nights. There was a white hart that lived in that forest, and if anyone killed it, he would be hanged, she said. Such vivid pictures came to me that they might have been Mr. Shimerda's memories, not yet faded out from the air in which they had haunted him.

▶ Whose memories have come to Jim?

It had begun to grow dark when my household returned, and grandmother was so tired that she went at once to bed. Jake and I got supper, and while we were washing the dishes he told me in loud whispers about the state of things over at the Shimerdas'. Nobody could touch the body until the coroner came. If anyone did, something terrible would happen, apparently. The dead man was frozen through, "just as stiff as a dressed turkey you hang out to freeze," Jake said. The horses and oxen would not go into the barn until he was frozen so hard that there was no longer any smell of blood. They were stabled there now, with the dead man, because there was no other place to keep them. A lighted lantern was kept hanging over Mr. Shimerda's head. Ántonia and Ambrosch and the mother took turns going down to pray beside him. The crazy boy went with them, because he did not feel the cold. I believed he felt cold as much as anyone else, but he liked to be thought <u>insensible</u> to it. He was always <u>coveting</u> distinction, poor Marek!

Ambrosch, Jake said, showed more human feeling than he would have supposed him capable of; but he was chiefly concerned about getting a priest, and about his father's soul, which he believed was in a place of torment and would remain there until his family and the priest had prayed a great deal for him. "As I understand it," Jake concluded, "it will be a matter of years to pray his soul out of Purgatory[4], and right now he's in torment."

"I don't believe it," I said <u>stoutly</u>. "I almost know it isn't true." I did not, of course, say that I believed he had been in that very kitchen all afternoon, on his way back to his own country. Nevertheless, after I went to bed, this idea of punishment and Purgatory came back on me crushingly. I remembered the account of Dives[5] in torment, and shuddered. But Mr. Shimerda had not been rich and selfish: he had only been so unhappy that he could not live any longer.

◀ What is Ambrosch's chief concern?

---

4. **Purgatory.** According to Catholic tradition, a transitional realm in which souls are purified before entering Heaven

5. **Dives.** Rich man whose excruciating torment in Hell is described in the Gospel of Luke 16: 19-31. (Jim is confusing Purgatory with Hell here.)

words for everyday use

in • sen • si • ble (in sen' sə bəl) adj., lacking sensory perception or ability to react. *Men and boys sometimes feel pressured to behave as if they are <u>insensible</u> to pain.*

co • vet (kə' vət) vt., wish for enviously, desire inordinately. *Even though Andrea didn't know Jill had been <u>coveting</u> her gold bracelet, she gave her one just like it for her birthday.*

stout • ly (staut' lē) adv., firmly, with determination. *When her mother asked her if she had seen the green sweater, Latisha <u>stoutly</u> denied any knowledge of its whereabouts.*

Chapter 15

Otto Fuchs got back from Black Hawk at noon the next day. He reported that the coroner would reach the Shimerdas' sometime that afternoon, but the missionary priest was at the other end of his parish, a hundred miles away, and the trains were not running. Fuchs had got a few hours' sleep at the livery barn in town, but he was afraid the gray gelding had strained himself. Indeed, he was never the same horse afterward. That long trip through the deep snow had taken all the endurance out of him.

Fuchs brought home with him a stranger, a young Bohemian who had taken a homestead near Black Hawk, and who came on his only horse to help his fellow-countrymen in their trouble. That was the first time I ever saw Anton Jelinek. He was a strapping young fellow in the early twenties then, handsome, warm-hearted, and full of life, and he came to us like a miracle in the midst of that grim business. I remember exactly how he strode into our kitchen in his felt boots and long wolfskin coat, his eyes and cheeks bright with the cold. At sight of grandmother, he snatched off his fur cap, greeting her in a deep, rolling voice which seemed older than he.

"I want to thank you very much, Mrs. Burden, for that you are so kind to poor strangers from my kawn-tree."

He did not hesitate like a farmer boy, but looked one eagerly in the eye when he spoke. Everything about him was warm and spontaneous. He said he would have come to see the Shimerdas before, but he had hired out to husk corn all the fall, and since winter began he had been going to the school by the mill, to learn English, along with the little children. He told me he had a nice "lady-teacher" and that he liked to go to school.

At dinner grandfather talked to Jelinek more than he usually did to strangers.

"Will they be much disappointed because we cannot get a priest?" he asked.

Jelinek looked serious. "Yes, sir, that is very bad for them. Their father has done a great sin,"—he looked straight at grandfather. "Our Lord has said that."

Grandfather seemed to like his frankness. "We believe that, too, Jelinek. But we believe that Mr. Shimerda's soul will come to its Creator as well off

> ▶ Why, according to Jelinek, will the family be greatly disappointed if they cannot find a priest?

without a priest. We believe that Christ is our only intercessor."

The young man shook his head. "I know how you think. My teacher at the school has explain. But I have seen too much. I believe in prayer for the dead. I have seen too much."

We asked him what he meant.

He glanced around the table. "You want I shall tell you? When I was a little boy like this one, I begin to help the priest at the altar. I make my first communion very young; what the Church teach seem plain to me. By 'n' by war-times come, when the Prussians fight us. We have very many soldiers in camp near my village, and the cholera break out in that camp, and the men die like flies. All day long our priest go about there to give the Sacrament to dying men, and I go with him to carry the vessels with the Holy Sacrament. Everybody that go near that camp catch the sickness but me and the priest. But we have no sickness, we have no fear, because we carry that blood and that body of Christ, and it preserve us." He paused, looking at grandfather. "That I know, Mr. Burden, for it happened to myself. All the soldiers know, too. When we walk along the road, the old priest and me, we meet all the time soldiers marching and officers on horse. All those officers, when they see what I carry under the cloth, pull up their horses and kneel down on the ground in the road until we pass. So I feel very bad for my kawntree-man to die without the Sacrament, and to die in a bad way for his soul, and I feel sad for his family."

◀ Why, according to Jelinek, did he not get sick?

We had listened attentively. It was impossible not to admire his frank, manly faith.

"I am always glad to meet a young man who thinks seriously about these things," said grandfather, "and I would never be the one to say you were not in God's care when you were among the soldiers." After dinner it was decided that young Jelinek should hook our two strong black farmhorses to the scraper and break a road through to the Shimerdas', so that a wagon could go when it was necessary. Fuchs, who was the only cabinet-maker in the neighborhood, was set to work on a coffin.

words for everyday use

in • ter • ces • sor (in tər se' sər) n., one who prays, petitions, or entreats in favor of another. *Because Sagar was afraid to approach his father directly, he asked his brother to be his intercessor.*

Jelinek put on his long wolfskin coat, and when we admired it, he told us that he had shot and skinned the coyotes, and the young man who "batched" with him, Jan Bouska, who had been a fur-worker in Vienna, made the coat. From the windmill I watched Jelinek come out of the barn with the blacks, and work his way up the hillside toward the cornfield. Sometimes he was completely hidden by the clouds of snow that rose about him; then he and the horses would emerge black and shining.

Our heavy carpenter's bench had to be brought from the barn and carried down into the kitchen. Fuchs selected boards from a pile of planks grandfather had hauled out from town in the fall to make a new floor for the oats bin. When at last the lumber and tools were assembled, and the doors were closed again and the cold draughts shut out, grandfather rode away to meet the coroner at the Shimerdas', and Fuchs took off his coat and settled down to work. I sat on his work-table and watched him. He did not touch his tools at first, but figured for a long while on a piece of paper, and measured the planks and made marks on them. While he was thus engaged, he whistled softly to himself, or teasingly pulled at his half-ear. Grandmother moved about quietly, so as not to disturb him. At last he folded his ruler and turned a cheerful face to us.

"The hardest part of my job's done," he announced. "It's the head end of it that comes hard with me, especially when I'm out of practice. The last time I made one of these, Mrs. Burden," he continued, as he sorted and tried his chisels, "was for a fellow in the Black Tiger mine, up above Silverton, Colorado. The mouth of that mine goes right into the face of the cliff, and they used to put us in a bucket and run us over on a trolley and shoot us into the shaft. The bucket traveled across a box cañon three hundred feet deep, and about a third full of water. Two Swedes had fell out of that bucket once, and hit the water, feet down. If you'll believe it, they went to work the next day. You can't kill a Swede. But in my time a little Eyetalian tried the high dive, and it turned out different with him. We was snowed in then, like we are now, and I happened to be the only man in camp that could make a coffin for him. It's a handy thing to know, when you knock about like I've done."

"We'd be hard put to it now, if you didn't know, Otto," grandmother said.

"Yes, 'm," Fuchs admitted with modest pride. "So few folks does know how to make a good tight box that'll turn water. I sometimes wonder if there'll be anybody about to do it for me. However, I'm not at all particular that way."

All afternoon, wherever one went in the house, one could hear the panting wheeze of the saw or the pleasant purring of the plane. They were such cheerful noises, seeming to promise new things for living people: it was a pity that those freshly planed pine boards were to be put underground so soon. The lumber was hard to work because it was full of frost, and the boards gave off a sweet smell of pine woods, as the heap of yellow shavings grew higher and higher. I wondered why Fuchs had not stuck to cabinet-work, he settled down to it with such ease and content. He handled the tools as if he liked the feel of them; and when he planed, his hands went back and forth over the boards in an eager, <u>beneficent</u> way as if he were blessing them. He broke out now and then into German hymns, as if this occupation brought back old times to him.

◀ What is ironic about the noises of the saw?

At four o'clock Mr. Bushy, the postmaster, with another neighbor who lived east of us, stopped in to get warm. They were on their way to the Shimerdas'. The news of what had happened over there had somehow got abroad through the snow-blocked country. Grandmother gave the visitors sugar-cakes and hot coffee. Before these callers were gone, the brother of the Widow Steavens, who lived on the Black Hawk road, drew up at our door, and after him came the father of the German family, our nearest neighbors on the south. They dismounted and joined us in the dining-room. They were all eager for any details about the suicide, and they were greatly concerned as to where Mr. Shimerda would be buried. The nearest Catholic cemetery was at Black Hawk, and it might be weeks before a wagon could get so far. Besides, Mr. Bushy and grandmother were sure that a man who had killed himself could not be buried in a Catholic graveyard. There was a burying-ground over by the Norwegian church, west of Squaw Creek; perhaps the Norwegians would take Mr. Shimerda in.

◀ Why might Mr. Shimerda not be permitted to be buried in the Catholic cemetery?

After our visitors rode away in single file over the hill, we returned to the kitchen. Grandmother began to make

---

words for everyday use

be • ne • fi • cent (bə ne′ fə sənt) adj., doing or producing good. *The volunteers at the homeless shelter were recognized for their <u>beneficent</u> deeds at an annual volunteer appreciation dinner.*

the icing for a chocolate cake, and Otto again filled the house with the exciting, expectant song of the plane. One pleasant thing about this time was that everybody talked more than usual. I had never heard the postmaster say anything but "Only papers, to-day," or, "I've got a sackful of mail for ye," until this afternoon. Grandmother always talked, dear woman: to herself or to the Lord, if there was no one else to listen; but grandfather was naturally <u>taciturn</u>, and Jake and Otto were often so tired after supper that I used to feel as if I were surrounded by a wall of silence. Now every one seemed eager to talk. That afternoon Fuchs told me story after story; about the Black Tiger mine, and about violent deaths and casual buryings, and the queer fancies of dying men. You never really knew a man, he said, until you saw him die. Most men were game, and went without a grudge.

The postmaster, going home, stopped to say that grandfather would bring the coroner back with him to spend the night. The officers of the Norwegian church, he told us, had held a meeting and decided that the Norwegian graveyard could not extend its hospitality to Mr. Shimerda.

Grandmother was indignant. "If these foreigners are so clannish, Mr. Bushy, we'll have to have an American graveyard that will be more liberal-minded. I'll get right after Josiah to start one in the spring. If anything was to happen to me, I don't want the Norwegians holding <u>inquisitions</u> over me to see whether I'm good enough to be laid amongst 'em."

Soon grandfather returned, bringing with him Anton Jelinek, and that important person, the coroner. He was a mild, flurried old man, a Civil War veteran, with one sleeve hanging empty. He seemed to find this case very perplexing, and said if it had not been for grandfather he would have sworn out a warrant against Krajiek. "The way he acted, and the way his axe fit the wound, was enough to convict any man."

Although it was perfectly clear that Mr. Shimerda had killed himself, Jake and the coroner thought something ought to be done to Krajiek because he behaved like a

▶ *What, according to Mrs. Burden, would an "American graveyard" be like?*

tac • i • turn (ta' sə tərn) adj., temperamentally disinclined to talk, quiet. *Michelle is so <u>taciturn</u> that she is very hard to get to know.*

in • qui • si • tion (in kwə zi' shən) n., an official, often severe inquiry. *When Steve came home after his curfew, he was subject to an <u>inquisition</u> from his parents.*

guilty man. He was badly frightened, certainly, and perhaps he even felt some stirrings of remorse for his indifference to the old man's misery and loneliness.

At supper the men ate like vikings, and the chocolate cake, which I had hoped would linger on until tomorrow in a mutilated condition, disappeared on the second round. They talked excitedly about where they should bury Mr. Shimerda; I gathered that the neighbors were all disturbed and shocked about something. It developed that Mrs. Shimerda and Ambrosch wanted the old man buried on the southwest corner of their own land; indeed, under the very stake that marked the corner. Grandfather had explained to Ambrosch that some day, when the country was put under fence and the roads were confined to section lines, two roads would cross exactly on that corner. But Ambrosch only said, "It makes no matter."

◄ Where do Mrs. Shimerda and Ambrosch want to bury Mr. Shimerda? What caution does grandfather urge about this burial site?

Grandfather asked Jelinek whether in the old country there was some superstition to the effect that a suicide must be buried at the cross-roads.

Jelinek said he didn't know; he seemed to remember hearing there had once been such a custom in Bohemia.[1] "Mrs. Shimerda is made up her mind," he added. "I try to persuade her, and say it looks bad for her to all the neighbors; but she say so it must be. "There I will bury him, if I dig the grave myself," she say. I have to promise her I help Ambrosch make the grave to-morrow."

◄ What custom governs the placement of Mr. Shimerda's grave?

Grandfather smoothed his beard and looked judicial. "I don't know whose wish should decide the matter, if not hers. But if she thinks she will live to see the people of this country ride over that old man's head, she is mistaken."

---

1. **such a custom in Bohemia.** Custom of burying the bodies of suicides and other sinners, who could not be buried on sacred ground, at a crossroads

Chapter 16

Mr. Shimerda lay dead in the barn four days, and on the fifth they buried him. All day Friday Jelinek was off with Ambrosch digging the grave, chopping out the frozen earth with old axes. On Saturday we breakfasted before daylight and got into the wagon with the coffin. Jake and Jelinek went ahead on horseback to cut the body loose from the pool of blood in which it was frozen fast to the ground.

When grandmother and I went into the Shimerdas' house, we found the women-folk alone; Ambrosch and Marek were at the barn. Mrs. Shimerda sat crouching by the stove, Ántonia was washing dishes. When she saw me, she ran out of her dark corner and threw her arms around me. "Oh, Jimmy," she sobbed, "what you tink for my lovely papa!" It seemed to me that I could feel her heart breaking as she clung to me.

Mrs. Shimerda, sitting on the stump by the stove, kept looking over her shoulder toward the door while the neighbors were arriving. They came on horseback, all except the postmaster, who brought his family in a wagon over the only broken wagon-trail. The Widow Steavens rode up from her farm eight miles down the Black Hawk road. The cold drove the women into the cave-house, and it was soon crowded. A fine, sleety snow was beginning to fall, and everyone was afraid of another storm and anxious to have the burial over with.

Grandfather and Jelinek came to tell Mrs. Shimerda that it was time to start. After bundling her mother up in clothes the neighbors had brought, Ántonia put on an old cape from our house and the rabbit-skin hat her father had made for her. Four men carried Mr. Shimerda's box up the hill; Krajiek slunk along behind them. The coffin was too wide for the door, so it was put down on the slope outside. I slipped out from the cave and looked at Mr. Shimerda. He was lying on his side, with his knees drawn up. His body was draped in a black shawl, and his head was bandaged in white muslin, like a mummy's; one of his long, shapely hands lay out on the black cloth; that was all one could see of him.

Mrs. Shimerda came out and placed an open prayer-book against the body, making the sign of the cross on the bandaged head with her fingers. Ambrosch knelt down and made the same gesture, and after him Ántonia and Marek. Yulka hung back. Her mother pushed her forward, and kept saying something to her over and over. Yulka knelt down, shut her eyes, and put out her hand a little way, but she drew it back and began to cry wildly. She was afraid to touch the bandage. Mrs. Shimerda caught her by the shoulders and pushed her toward the coffin, but grandmother interfered.

"No, Mrs. Shimerda," she said firmly, "I won't stand by and see that child frightened into spasms. She is too little to understand what you want of her. Let her alone."

At a look from grandfather, Fuchs and Jelinek placed the lid on the box, and began to nail it down over Mr. Shimerda. I was afraid to look at Ántonia. She put her arms round Yulka and held the little girl close to her.

The coffin was put into the wagon. We drove slowly away, against the fine, icy snow which cut our faces like a sand-blast. When we reached the grave, it looked a very little spot in that snow-covered waste. The men took the coffin to the edge of the hole and lowered it with ropes. We stood about watching them, and the powdery snow lay without melting on the caps and shoulders of the men and the shawls of the women. Jelinek spoke in a persuasive tone to Mrs. Shimerda, and then turned to grandfather.

"She says, Mr. Burden, she is very glad if you can make some prayer for him here in English, for the neighbors to understand."

Grandmother looked anxiously at grandfather. He took off his hat, and the other men did likewise. I thought his prayer remarkable. I still remember it. He began, "Oh, great and just God, no man among us knows what the sleeper knows, nor is it for us to judge what lies between him and Thee." He prayed that if any man there had been remiss toward the stranger come to a far country, God would forgive him and soften his heart. He recalled the promises to the widow and the fatherless, and asked God to smooth the way before this widow and her children, and to "incline the hearts of men to deal justly with her." In closing, he said we were leaving Mr. Shimerda at "Thy judgment seat, which is also Thy mercy seat."

◀ For what does Grandfather ask God's forgiveness?

All the time he was praying, grandmother watched him through the black fingers of her glove, and when he said "Amen," I thought she looked satisfied with him. She turned to Otto and whispered, "Can't you start a hymn, Fuchs? It would seem less heathenish."

Fuchs glanced about to see if there was general approval of her suggestion, then began, "Jesus, Lover of my Soul," and all the men and women took it up after him.

Whenever I have heard the hymn since, it has made me remember that white waste and the little group of people; and the bluish air, full of fine, eddying snow, like long veils flying:—

> "While the nearer waters roll,
> While the tempest still is high."

Years afterward, when the open-grazing days were over, and the red grass had been ploughed under and under until it had almost disappeared from the prairie; when all the fields were under fence, and the roads no longer ran about like wild things, but followed the surveyed section-lines, Mr. Shimerda's grave was still there, with a sagging wire fence around it, and an unpainted wooden cross. As grandfather had predicted, Mrs. Shimerda never saw the roads going over his head. The road from the north curved a little to the east just there, and the road from the west swung out a little to the south; so that the grave, with its tall red grass that was never mowed, was like a little island; and at twilight, under a new moon or the clear evening star, the dusty roads used to look like soft gray rivers flowing past it. I never came upon the place without emotion, and in all that country it was the spot most dear to me. I loved the dim superstition, the <u>propitiatory</u> intent, that had put the grave there; and still more I loved the spirit that could not carry out the sentence— the error from the surveyed lines, the <u>clemency</u> of the soft earth roads along which the home-coming wagons rattled after sunset. Never a tired driver passed the wooden cross, I am sure, without wishing well to the sleeper.

▶ What two things does Jim love about this spot?

words for everyday use

pro • pi • ti • a • tory (prō pi' shē ə tor ē) adj., intended to appease or satisfy. *After their initial anger had subsided, both friends' words were more <u>propitiatory</u>, and they quickly settled the argument.*

cle • men • cy (kle' mən sē) n., desire to be merciful or lenient. *Under special circumstances, the president of the United States might grant <u>clemency</u> to people who have broken laws.*

76   MY ÁNTONIA

Chapter 17

When spring came, after that hard winter, one could not get enough of the nimble air. Every morning I wakened with a fresh consciousness that winter was over. There were none of the signs of spring for which I used to watch in Virginia, no budding woods or blooming gardens. There was only—spring itself; the throb of it, the light restlessness, the vital essence of it everywhere; in the sky, in the swift clouds, in the pale sunshine, and in the warm, high wind—rising suddenly, sinking suddenly, impulsive and playful like a big puppy that pawed you and then lay down to be petted. If I had been tossed down blindfold on that red prairie, I should have known that it was spring.

Everywhere now there was the smell of burning grass. Our neighbors burned off their pasture before the new grass made a start, so that the fresh growth would not be mixed with the dead stand of last year. Those light, swift fires, running about the country, seemed a part of the same kindling that was in the air.

The Shimerdas were in their new log house by then. The neighbors had helped them to build it in March. It stood directly in front of their old cave, which they used as a cellar. The family were now fairly equipped to begin their struggle with the soil. They had four comfortable rooms to live in, a new windmill,—bought on credit,— a chicken-house and poultry. Mrs. Shimerda had paid grandfather ten dollars for a milk cow, and was to give him fifteen more as soon as they harvested their first crop.

When I rode up to the Shimerdas' one bright windy afternoon in April, Yulka ran out to meet me. It was to her, now, that I gave reading lessons; Ántonia was busy with other things. I tied my pony and went into the kitchen where Mrs. Shimerda was baking bread, chewing poppy seeds as she worked. By this time she could speak enough English to ask me a great many questions about what our men were doing in the fields. She seemed to think that my elders withheld helpful information, and that from me she might get valuable secrets. On this occasion she asked me very craftily when grandfather expected to begin planting corn. I told her, adding that he thought we should have a dry spring and that the corn would not be held back by too much rain, as it had been last year.

She gave me a <u>shrewd</u> glance. "He not Jesus," she blustered; "he not know about the wet and the dry."

I did not answer her; what was the use? As I sat waiting for the hour when Ambrosch and Ántonia would return from the fields, I watched Mrs. Shimerda at her work. She took from the oven a coffee-cake which she wanted to keep warm for supper, and wrapped it in a quilt stuffed with feathers. I have seen her put even a roast goose in this quilt to keep it hot. When the neighbors were there building the new house, they saw her do this, and the story got abroad that the Shimerdas kept their food in their feather beds.

When the sun was dropping low, Ántonia came up the big south draw with her team. How much older she had grown in eight months! She had come to us a child, and now she was a tall, strong young girl, although her fifteenth birthday had just slipped by. I ran out and met her as she brought her horses up to the windmill to water them. She wore the boots her father had so thoughtfully taken off before he shot himself, and his old fur cap. Her outgrown cotton dress switched about her calves, over the boot-tops. She kept her sleeves rolled up all day, and her arms and throat were burned as brown as a sailor's. Her neck came up strongly out of her shoulders, like the bole of a tree out of the turf. One sees that draught-horse neck among the peasant women in all old countries.

▶ What does Jim notice about Ántonia's body?

She greeted me gaily, and began at once to tell me how much ploughing she had done that day. Ambrosch, she said, was on the north quarter, breaking sod with the oxen.

"Jim, you ask Jake how much he ploughed to-day. I don't want that Jake get more done in one day than me. I want we have very much corn this fall."

While the horses drew in the water, and nosed each other, and then drank again, Ántonia sat down on the windmill step and rested her head on her hand. "You see the big prairie fire from your place last night? I hope your grandpa ain't lose no stacks?"

"No, we didn't. I came to ask you something, Tony. Grandmother wants to know if you can't go to the term of school that begins next week over at the sod schoolhouse. She says there's a good teacher, and you'd learn a lot."

---

words for everyday use

shrewd (shrüd) adj., clever, discerning. *Because Mr. Harling is such a <u>shrewd</u> businessperson, no one ever succeeds in overcharging or cheating him.*

Ántonia stood up, lifting and dropping her shoulders as if they were stiff. "I ain't got time to learn. I can work like mans now. My mother can't say no more how Ambrosch do all and nobody to help him. I can work as much as him. School is all right for little boys. I help make this land one good farm."

She clucked to her team and started for the barn. I walked beside her, feeling vexed. Was she going to grow up boastful like her mother, I wondered? Before we reached the stable, I felt something tense in her silence, and glancing up I saw that she was crying. She turned her face from me and looked off at the red streak of dying light, over the dark prairie.

I climbed up into the loft and threw down the hay for her, while she unharnessed her team. We walked slowly back toward the house. Ambrosch had come in from the north quarter, and was watering his oxen at the tank.

Ántonia took my hand. "Sometime you will tell me all those nice things you learn at the school, won't you, Jimmy?" she asked with a sudden rush of feeling in her voice. "My father, he went much to school. He know a great deal; how to make the fine cloth like what you not got here. He play horn and violin, and he read so many books that the priests in Bohemie come to talk to him. You won't forget my father, Jim?"

"No," I said, "I will never forget him."

Mrs. Shimerda asked me to stay for supper. After Ambrosch and Ántonia had washed the field dust from their hands and faces at the wash-basin by the kitchen door, we sat down at the oilcloth-covered table. Mrs. Shimerda ladled meal mush out of an iron pot and poured milk on it. After the mush we had fresh bread and sorghum molasses, and coffee with the cake that had been kept warm in the feathers. Ántonia and Ambrosch were talking in Bohemian; disputing about which of them had done more ploughing that day. Mrs. Shimerda egged them on, chuckling while she gobbled her food.

Presently Ambrosch said sullenly in English: "You take them ox to-morrow and try the sod plough. Then you not be so smart."

His sister laughed. "Don't be mad. I know it's awful hard work for break sod. I milk the cow for you to-morrow, if you want."

Mrs. Shimerda turned quickly to me. "That cow not give so much milk like what your grandpa say. If he make talk about fifteen dollars, I send him back the cow."

◀ Why can't Ántonia go to school with Jim? For whom does Ántonia say school is okay?

"He doesn't talk about the fifteen dollars," I exclaimed indignantly. "He doesn't find fault with people."

"He say I break his saw when we build, and I never," grumbled Ambrosch.

▶ Why does Jim wish he hadn't stayed for dinner? How does Jim describe the way Ántonia eats now?

I knew he had broken the saw, and then hid it and lied about it. I began to wish I had not stayed for supper. Everything was disagreeable to me. Ántonia ate so noisily now, like a man, and she yawned often at the table and kept stretching her arms over her head, as if they ached. Grandmother had said, "Heavy field work'll spoil that girl. She'll lose all her nice ways and get rough ones." She had lost them already.

After supper I rode home through the sad, soft spring twilight. Since winter I had seen very little of Ántonia. She was out in the fields from sun-up until sun-down. If I rode over to see her where she was ploughing, she stopped at the end of a row to chat for a moment, then gripped her plough-handles, clucked to her team, and waded on down the furrow, making me feel that she was now grown up and had no time for me. On Sundays she helped her mother make garden or sewed all day. Grandfather was pleased with Ántonia. When we complained of her, he only smiled and said, "She will help some fellow get ahead in the world."

▶ Of what has Ántonia grown proud?

▶ What does Jim remember when he sees Ántonia in the fields?

Nowadays Tony could talk of nothing but the prices of things, or how much she could lift and endure. She was too proud of her strength. I knew, too, that Ambrosch put upon her some chores a girl ought not to do, and that the farmhands around the country joked in a nasty way about it. Whenever I saw her come up the furrow, shouting to her beasts, sunburned, sweaty, her dress open at the neck, and her throat and chest dust-plastered, I used to think of the tone in which poor Mr. Shimerda, who could say so little, yet managed to say so much when he exclaimed, "My Án-tonia!"

Chapter 18

After I began to go to the country school, I saw less of the Bohemians. We were sixteen pupils at the sod schoolhouse, and we all came on horseback and brought our dinner. My schoolmates were none of them very interesting, but I somehow felt that, by making comrades of them I was getting even with Ántonia for her indifference. Since the father's death, Ambrosch was more than ever the head of the house, and he seemed to direct the feelings as well as the fortunes of his womenfolk. Ántonia often quoted his opinions to me, and she let me see that she admired him, while she thought of me only as a little boy. Before the spring was over, there was a distinct coldness between us and the Shimerdas. It came about in this way.

One Sunday I rode over there with Jake to get a horse-collar which Ambrosch had borrowed from him and had not returned. It was a beautiful blue morning. The buffalo-peas were blooming in pink and purple masses along the roadside, and the larks, perched on last year's dried sun-flower stalks, were singing straight at the sun, their heads thrown back and their yellow breasts a-quiver. The wind blew about us in warm, sweet gusts. We rode slowly, with a pleasant sense of Sunday <u>indolence</u>.

We found the Shimerdas working just as if it were a week-day. Marek was cleaning out the stable, and Ántonia and her mother were making garden, off across the pond in the draw-head. Ambrosch was up on the windmill tower, oiling the wheel. He came down, not very <u>cordially</u>. When Jake asked for the collar, he grunted and scratched his head. The collar belonged to grandfather, of course, and Jake, feeling responsible for it, flared up.

"Now, don't you say you haven't got it, Ambrosch, because I know you have, and if you ain't a-going to look for it, I will."

Ambrosch shrugged his shoulders and sauntered down the hill toward the stable. I could see that it was one of his mean days. Presently he returned, carrying a collar that had been badly used— trampled in the dirt and gnawed by rats until the hair was sticking out of it.

---

words for everyday use

in • do • lence (in' də ləns) n., laziness, sloth. *Kelly was afraid her own <u>indolence</u>, manifested in an urge to spend all her time sleeping or watching television, would keep her from succeeding in a career.*

cor • dial • ly (korj' lē) adv., sincerely, warmly. *The host of the party <u>cordially</u> welcomed each guest as he or she came through the door.*

▶ About what do Jake and Ambrosch fight?

"This what you want?" he asked surlily.

Jake jumped off his horse. I saw a wave of red come up under the rough stubble on his face. "That ain't the piece of harness I loaned you, Ambrosch; or, if it is, you've used it shameful. I ain't a-going to carry such a looking thing back to Mr. Burden."

Ambrosch dropped the collar on the ground. "All right," he said coolly, took up his oil-can, and began to climb the mill. Jake caught him by the belt of his trousers and yanked him back. Ambrosch's feet had scarcely touched the ground when he lunged out with a vicious kick at Jake's stomach. Fortunately, Jake was in such a position that he could dodge it. This was not the sort of thing country boys did when they played at fisticuffs, and Jake was furious. He landed Ambrosch a blow on the head—it sounded like the crack of an axe on a cow-pumpkin. Ambrosch dropped over, stunned.

We heard squeals, and looking up saw Ántonia and her mother coming on the run. They did not take the path around the pond, but plunged through the muddy water, without even lifting their skirts. They came on, screaming and clawing the air. By this time Ambrosch had come to his senses and was sputtering with nosebleed. Jake sprang into his saddle. "Let's get out of this, Jim," he called.

Mrs. Shimerda threw her hands over her head and clutched as if she were going to pull down lightning. "Law, law!" she shrieked after us. "Law for knock my Ambrosch down!"

"I never like you no more, Jake and Jim Burden," Ántonia panted. "No friends any more!"

Jake stopped and turned his horse for a second. "Well, you're a damned ungrateful lot, the whole pack of you," he shouted back. "I guess the Burdens can get along without you. You've been a sight of trouble to them, anyhow!"

We rode away, feeling so outraged that the fine morning was spoiled for us. I hadn't a word to say, and poor Jake was white as paper and trembling all over. It made him sick to get so angry. "They ain't the same, Jimmy," he kept saying in a hurt tone. "These foreigners ain't the same. You can't trust 'em to be fair. It's dirty to kick a feller. You heard how the women turned on you— and after all we went through on account of 'em last winter! They ain't to be trusted. I don't want to see you get too thick with any of 'em."

▶ What does Jake say about foreigners?

"I'll never be friends with them again, Jake," I declared hotly. "I believe they are all like Krajiek and Ambrosch underneath."

Grandfather heard our story with a twinkle in his eye. He advised Jake to ride to town to-morrow, go to a justice of the peace, tell him he had knocked young Shimerda down, and pay his fine. Then if Mrs. Shimerda was inclined to make trouble— her son was still under age— she would be <u>forestalled</u>. Jake said he might as well take the wagon and haul to market the pig he had been fattening. On Monday, about an hour after Jake had started, we saw Mrs. Shimerda and her Ambrosch proudly driving by, looking neither to the right nor left. As they rattled out of sight down the Black Hawk road, grandfather chuckled, saying he had rather expected she would follow the matter up.

Jake paid his fine with a ten-dollar bill grandfather had given him for that purpose. But when the Shimerdas found that Jake sold his pig in town that day, Ambrosch worked it out in his shrewd head that Jake had to sell his pig to pay his fine. This theory afforded the Shimerdas great satisfaction, apparently. For weeks afterward, whenever Jake and I met Ántonia on her way to the post-office, or going along the road with her work-team, she would clap her hands and call to us in a spiteful, crowing voice:—

"Jake-y, Jake-y, sell the pig and pay the slap!"

Otto pretended not to be surprised at Ántonia's behavior. He only lifted his brows and said, "You can't tell me anything new about a Czech; I'm an Austrian."

Grandfather was never a party to what Jake called our feud with the Shimerdas. Ambrosch and Ántonia always greeted him respectfully, and he asked them about their affairs and gave them advice as usual. He thought the future looked hopeful for them. Ambrosch was a far-seeing fellow; he soon realized that his oxen were too heavy for any work except breaking sod, and he succeeded in selling them to a newly arrived German. With the money he bought another team of horses, which grandfather selected for him. Marek was strong, and Ambrosch worked him hard; but he could never teach him to cultivate corn, I remember. The one idea that had ever got through poor Marek's thick head was that all exertion was <u>meritorious</u>.

<table>
<tr><td rowspan="4">words
for
everyday
use</td><td>fore • stall (fōr stȯl′) vt., prevent, hinder. The investigators carefully documented each finding to <u>forestall</u> any questions later.</td><td>mer • i • tor • i • ous (mer ə tōr′ ē əs) adj., deserving of honor or esteem. The heroic efforts of firefighters and rescue crews following the destruction of the World Trade Center's Twin Towers were <u>meritorious</u> in the extreme.</td></tr>
</table>

He always bore down on the handles of the cultivator and drove the blades so deep into the earth that the horses were soon exhausted.

In June Ambrosch went to work at Mr. Bushy's for a week, and took Marek with him at full wages. Mrs. Shimerda then drove the second cultivator; she and Ántonia worked in the fields all day and did the chores at night. While the two women were running the place alone, one of the new horses got colic and gave them a terrible fright.

Ántonia had gone down to the barn one night to see that all was well before she went to bed, and she noticed that one of the roans was swollen about the middle and stood with its head hanging. She mounted another horse, without waiting to saddle him, and hammered on our door just as we were going to bed. Grandfather answered her knock. He did not send one of his men, but rode back with her himself, taking a syringe and an old piece of carpet he kept for hot applications when our horses were sick. He found Mrs. Shimerda sitting by the horse with her lantern, groaning and wringing her hands. It took but a few moments to release the gases pent up in the poor beast, and the two women heard the rush of wind and saw the roan visibly diminish in girth.

▶ What does Ántonia threaten to do if the horse dies?

"If I lose that horse, Mr. Burden," Ántonia exclaimed, "I never stay here till Ambrosch come home! I go drown myself in the pond before morning."

When Ambrosch came back from Mr. Bushy's, we learned that he had given Marek's wages to the priest at Black Hawk, for masses for their father's soul. Grandmother thought Ántonia needed shoes more than Mr. Shimerda needed prayers, but grandfather said tolerantly, "If he can spare six dollars, pinched as he is, it shows he believes what he professes."

▶ How does Jim's grandfather bring about a reconciliation with the Shimerdas?

It was grandfather who brought about a <u>reconciliation</u> with the Shimerdas. One morning he told us that the small grain was coming on so well, he thought he would begin to cut his wheat on the first of July. He would need more men, and if it were agreeable to everyone he would engage Ambrosch for the reaping and threshing, as the Shimerdas had no small grain of their own.

---

words for everyday use
re • con • cil • i • a • tion (re kən si lē ā' shən) n., restoration of friendship or harmony. *A mediator was called in to help the two neighborhood groups achieve a <u>reconciliation</u>.*

"I think, Emmaline," he concluded, "I will ask Ántonia to come over and help you in the kitchen. She will be glad to earn something, and it will be a good time to end misunderstandings. I may as well ride over this morning and make arrangements. Do you want to go with me, Jim?" His tone told me that he had already decided for me.

After breakfast we set off together. When Mrs. Shimerda saw us coming, she ran from her door down into the draw behind the stable, as if she did not want to meet us. Grandfather smiled to himself while he tied his horse, and we followed her.

Behind the barn we came upon a funny sight. The cow had evidently been grazing somewhere in the draw. Mrs. Shimerda had run to the animal, pulled up the lariat pin, and, when we came upon her, she was trying to hide the cow in an old cave in the bank. As the hole was narrow and dark, the cow held back, and the old woman was slapping and pushing at her hind quarters, trying to spank her into the draw-side.

Grandfather ignored her <u>singular</u> occupation and greeted her politely. "Good-morning, Mrs. Shimerda. Can you tell me where I will find Ambrosch? Which field?"

"He with the sod corn." She pointed toward the north, still standing in front of the cow as if she hoped to conceal it.

"His sod corn will be good for fodder this winter," said grandfather encouragingly. "And where is Ántonia?"

"She go with." Mrs. Shimerda kept wiggling her bare feet about nervously in the dust.

"Very well. I will ride up there. I want them to come over and help me cut my oats and wheat next month. I will pay them wages. Good morning. By the way, Mrs. Shimerda," he said as he turned up the path, "I think we may as well call it square about the cow."

She started and clutched the rope tighter. Seeing that she did not understand, grandfather turned back. "You need not pay me anything more; no more money. The cow is yours."

"Pay no more, keep cow?" she asked in a bewildered tone, her narrow eyes snapping at us in the sunlight.

words for everyday use

sin • gu • lar (siŋ′ gyə lər) adj., unusual, out of the ordinary. *The old man had such a <u>singular</u> way of speaking that his speech was immediately recognizable to most people in town.*

▶ What brings the
Old World so close to
the new?

"Exactly. Pay no more, keep cow." He nodded.

Mrs. Shimerda dropped the rope, ran after us, and, crouching down beside grandfather, she took his hand and kissed it. I doubt if he had ever been so much embarrassed before. I was a little startled, too. Somehow, that seemed to bring the Old World very close.

We rode away laughing, and grandfather said: "I expect she thought we had come to take the cow away for certain, Jim. I wonder if she wouldn't have scratched a little if we'd laid hold of that lariat rope!"

Our neighbors seemed glad to make peace with us. The next Sunday Mrs. Shimerda came over and brought Jake a pair of socks she had knitted. She presented them with an air of great magnanimity, saying, "Now you not come any more for knock my Ambrosch down?"

Jake laughed sheepishly. "I don't want to have no trouble with Ambrosch. If he'll let me alone, I'll let him alone."

"If he slap you, we ain't got no pig for pay the fine," she said <u>insinuatingly</u>.

Jake was not at all <u>disconcerted</u>. "Have the last word ma'm," he said cheerfully. "It's a lady's privilege."

---

words for everyday use

in • sin • u • a • ting (in sin' yə wāt iŋ) adj., subtly causing doubt or distrust. *Politicians sometimes make <u>insinuating</u> remarks about each other's characters and abilities.*

dis • con • cert • ed (dis kən sərt' id) adj., disturbed, bothered. *After listening to all his girlfriend's accusations against him, Jeff appeared <u>disconcerted</u> and stumbled when he tried to respond.*

Chapter 19

July came on with that breathless, brilliant heat which makes the plains of Kansas and Nebraska the best corn country in the world. It seemed as if we could hear the corn growing in the night; under the stars one caught a faint crackling in the dewy, heavy-odored cornfields where the feathered stalks stood so juicy and green. If all the great plain from the Missouri to the Rocky Mountains had been under glass, and the heat regulated by a thermometer, it could not have been better for the yellow tassels that were ripening and fertilizing the silk day by day. The cornfields were far apart in those times, with miles of wild grazing land between. It took a clear, meditative eye like my grandfather's to foresee that they would enlarge and multiply until they would be, not the Shimerdas' cornfields, or Mr. Bushy's, but the world's cornfields; that their yield would be one of the great economic facts, like the wheat crop of Russia, which underlie all the activities of men, in peace or war.

◄ *What was Jim's grandfather able to foresee?*

The burning sun of those few weeks, with occasional rains at night, secured the corn. After the milky ears were once formed, we had little to fear from dry weather. The men were working so hard in the wheatfields that they did not notice the heat,—though I was kept busy carrying water for them,—and grandmother and Ántonia had so much to do in the kitchen that they could not have told whether one day was hotter than another. Each morning, while the dew was still on the grass, Ántonia went with me up to the garden to get early vegetables for dinner. Grandmother made her wear a sunbonnet, but as soon as we reached the garden she threw it on the grass and let her hair fly in the breeze. I remember how, as we bent over the pea-vines, beads of perspiration used to gather on her upper lip like a little moustache.

"Oh, better I like to work out of doors than in a house!" she used to sing joyfully. "I not care that your grandmother say it makes me like a man. I like to be like a man." She would toss her head and ask me to feel the muscles swell in her brown arm.

◄ *How does Ántonia feel about "working like a man"?*

We were glad to have her in the house. She was so gay and responsive that one did not mind her heavy, running step, or her clattery way with pans. Grandmother was in high spirits during the weeks that Ántonia worked for us.

All the nights were close and hot during that harvest season. The harvesters slept in the hayloft because it was cooler there than in the house. I used to lie in my bed by the open window, watching the heat lightning play softly along the horizon, or looking up at the <u>gaunt</u> frame of the windmill against the blue night sky. One night there was a beautiful electric storm, though not enough rain fell to damage the cut grain. The men went down to the barn immediately after supper, and when the dishes were washed, Ántonia and I climbed up on the slanting roof of the chicken-house to watch the clouds. The thunder was loud and metallic, like the rattle of sheet iron, and the lightning broke in great zigzags across the heavens, making everything stand out and come close to us for a moment. Half the sky was checkered with black thunderheads, but all the west was <u>luminous</u> and clear: in the lightning-flashes it looked like deep blue water, with the sheen of moonlight on it; and the mottled part of the sky was like marble pavement, like the <u>quay</u> of some splendid sea-coast city, doomed to destruction. Great warm splashes of rain fell on our upturned faces. One black cloud, no bigger than a little boat, drifted out into the clear space unattended, and kept moving westward. All about us we could hear the felty beat of the raindrops on the soft dust of the farmyard. Grandmother came to the door and said it was late, and we would get wet out there.

"In a minute we come," Ántonia called back to her. "I like your grandmother, and all things here," she sighed. "I wish my papa live to see this summer. I wish no winter ever come again."

"It will be summer a long while yet," I reassured her. "Why aren't you always nice like this, Tony?"

"How nice?"

"Why, just like this; like yourself. Why do you all the time try to be like Ambrosch?"

She put her arms under her head and lay back, looking up at the sky. "If I live here, like you, that is different. Things will be easy for you. But they will be hard for us."

▶ What prediction does Ántonia make?

Respond to the Selection

My Ántonia begins with Jim traveling back to Nebraska as an adult. Imagine that you are Jim on the train, going back to visit the place where you lived as a child. What memories come to your mind? Are they happy memories or sad? Are you excited to go back to your old home?

Investigate, Inquire, and Imagine

Recall: GATHERING FACTS

Interpret: FINDING MEANING

1a. From where, according to the Introduction, did the manuscript for this book come? What word is added to the title of the manuscript at the last minute?

1b. How does the word that is added change the meaning of the title?

2a. How old is Ántonia at the beginning and end of Book I? Why doesn't she go to school with Jim?

2b. Why does Ántonia seem so much older to Jim by the end of Book I? How does Jim's going to school highlight the differences between Ántonia and him?

3a. Who are Pavel and Peter, and where are they from? What story does Pavel tell before he dies? How did they come to live near Black Hawk?

3b. Why does Pavel tell this story before he dies? Why does the story fascinate Ántonia and Jim? Do you see any common themes in the story Pavel tells and the story of *My Ántonia* so far?

4a. What surprising gesture does Mr. Shimerda make in front of the Christmas tree on Christmas Day? What does Jim's grandfather say about this gesture as Mr. Shimerda leaves?

4b. Why does Mr. Shimerda's action make Jim uncomfortable? What does Jim's grandfather's comment indicate about his character?

5a. How does Mr. Shimerda die? What does Jim, left alone in the house, sense about Mr. Shimerda?

5b. What factors contribute to Mr. Shimerda's death? Why does Jim identify with Mr. Shimerda?

Analyze: TAKING THINGS APART

6a. Analyze what it means to be a boy or a girl on the Nebraska prairie. In what ways do Jim and Ántonia take on traditional gender roles? In what ways do they defy those roles?

Synthesize: BRINGING THINGS TOGETHER

➤ 6b. Jim asks Ántonia, "Why aren't you always nice like this, Tony?...Why do you all the time try to be like Ambrosch?" Ántonia answers, "Things will be easy for you. But they will be hard for us." Explain what Ántonia means. Has she answered Jim's question? If so, how? If not, how do you think she would answer it?

Evaluate: MAKING JUDGMENTS

7a. When Jim first arrives in Nebraska, he thinks to himself: "Perhaps we feel like [this] when we die and become a part of something entire, whether it is sun and air, or goodness and knowledge. At any rate: that is happiness; to be dissolved into something complete and great." What makes Jim so happy in this scene? What do you think of his definition of happiness?

Extend: CONNECTING IDEAS

➤ 7b. Do all people have the same access as Jim to this kind of happiness? What about the Shimerdas? What challenges do the Shimerdas face as newcomers to the prairie? Predict how Ántonia's life will differ from Jim's as they both grow older.

Understanding Literature

Narrator. A **narrator** is one who tells a story. Who is the narrator of *My Ántonia*? Consider how the narrator describes the scene when Jim and Ántonia first meet. How would this scene be different if it were narrated by Ántonia? by Jim's grandmother? As you read the rest of the novel, consider why Cather chose this narrator to tell the story.

Frame narrative. A **frame narrative** is a narrative, or story, that provides a vehicle for telling another story. *My Ántonia* begins with a frame narrative in which an unnamed narrator meets Jim Burden on a train. Both Jim and the first narrator are going back, as adults, to visit the place where they grew up. Why do you think Cather uses a frame narrative for this story? What does the frame narrative add?

Setting. The **setting** of a literary work is the time and place in which it occurs, together with all the details used to create a sense of a particular time and place. Describe the setting of *My Ántonia*. Some critics have suggested that the setting of this novel is actually a character in itself. What do you think this statement means? What demands does the setting of this novel make on the characters?

Conflict. A **conflict** is a struggle between two forces in a literary work. A plot involves the introduction, development, and eventual resolution of a conflict. One side of the central conflict in a story or drama is usually taken by the main character. That character may struggle against another character, against the forces of nature, against society or social norms, against fate, or against some element within himself or herself. What examples of conflict can you find in book 1 of *My Ántonia*? Which of these do you expect to be the central conflict, and why?

BOOK II

The Hired Girls

Chapter 1

I had been living with my grandfather for nearly three years when he decided to move to Black Hawk. He and grandmother were getting old for the heavy work of a farm, and as I was now thirteen they thought I ought to be going to school. Accordingly our homestead was rented to "that good woman, the Widow Steavens," and her bachelor brother, and we bought Preacher White's house, at the north end of Black Hawk. This was the first town house one passed driving in from the farm, a landmark which told country people their long ride was over.

◀ Who moves into the Burdens' homestead?

We were to move to Black Hawk in March, and as soon as grandfather had fixed the date he let Jake and Otto know of his intention. Otto said he would not be likely to find another place that suited him so well; that he was tired of farming and thought he would go back to what he called the "wild West." Jake Marpole, lured by Otto's stories of adventure, decided to go with him. We did our best to <u>dissuade</u> Jake. He was so handicapped by illiteracy and by his trusting disposition that he would be an easy prey to sharpers. Grandmother begged him to stay among kindly, Christian people, where he was known; but there was no reasoning with him. He wanted to be a prospector. He thought a silver mine was waiting for him in Colorado.

Jake and Otto served us to the last. They moved us into town, put down the carpets in our new house, made shelves and cupboards for grandmother's kitchen, and seemed <u>loath</u> to leave us. But at last they went, without warning. Those two fellows had been faithful to us through sun and storm, had given us things that cannot be bought in any market in the world. With me they had been like older brothers; had restrained their speech and manners out of care for me, and given me so much good comradeship. Now they got on the westbound train one morning, in their Sunday clothes, with their oilcloth valises—and I never saw them again. Months afterward we got a card from Otto, saying that Jake had been down with mountain fever, but now they were both working in the Yankee Girl mine, and were doing well. I wrote to them at that address, but my letter was returned to me, "unclaimed." After that we never heard from them.

words for everyday use

dis • suade (di swād') vt., advise a person against something. *Worried about his safety, Jason's parents tried to <u>dissuade</u> him from climbing that particular bluff.*

loath (lōth) adj., reluctant, unwilling to do something contrary to one's way of thinking. *Because she believes in nonviolence, Maria was <u>loath</u> to support the war effort in any way.*

Black Hawk, the new world in which we had come to live, was a clean, well-planted little prairie town, with white fences and good green yards about the dwellings, wide, dusty streets, and shapely little trees growing along the wooden sidewalks. In the center of the town there were two rows of new brick "store" buildings, a brick school-house, the courthouse, and four white churches. Our own house looked down over the town, and from our upstairs windows we could see the winding line of the river bluffs, two miles south of us. That river was to be my compensation for the lost freedom of the farming country.

We came to Black Hawk in March, and by the end of April we felt like town people. Grandfather was a deacon in the new Baptist Church, grandmother was busy with church suppers and missionary societies, and I was quite another boy, or thought I was. Suddenly put down among boys of my own age, I found I had a great deal to learn. Before the spring term of school was over, I could fight, play "keeps,"[1] tease the little girls, and use forbidden words as well as any boy in my class. I was restrained from utter savagery only by the fact that Mrs. Harling, our nearest neighbor, kept an eye on me, and if my behavior went beyond certain bounds I was not permitted to come into her yard or to play with her jolly children.

▶ What things does Jim learn from other boys?

We saw more of our country neighbors now than when we lived on the farm. Our house was a convenient stopping-place for them. We had a big barn where the farmers could put up their teams, and their women-folk more often accompanied them, now that they could stay with us for dinner, and rest and set their bonnets right before they went shopping. The more our house was like a country hotel, the better I liked it. I was glad, when I came home from school at noon, to see a farm wagon standing in the back yard, and I was always ready to run downtown to get beefsteak or baker's bread for unexpected company. All through that first spring and summer I kept hoping that Ambrosch would bring Ántonia and Yulka to see our new house. I wanted to show them our red plush furniture, and the trumpet-blowing cherubs the German paper-hanger had put on our parlor ceiling.

When Ambrosch came to town, however, he came alone, and though he put his horses in our barn, he would never stay for dinner, or tell us anything about his mother

---

1. "keeps." Game of marbles in which the winner gets to keep certain of the losers' marbles

and sisters. If we ran out and questioned him as he was slipping through the yard, he would merely work his shoulders about in his coat and say, "They all right, I guess."

Mrs. Steavens, who now lived on our farm, grew as fond of Ántonia as we had been, and always brought us news of her. All through the wheat season, she told us, Ambrosch hired his sister out like a man, and she went from farm to farm, binding sheaves or working with the threshers. The farmers liked her and were kind to her; said they would rather have her for a hand than Ambrosch. When fall came she was to husk corn for the neighbors until Christmas, as she had done the year before; but grandmother saved her from this by getting her a place to work with our neighbors, the Harlings.

◀ *How does Ántonia spend the wheat season?*

Chapter 2

Grandmother often said that if she had to live in town, she thanked God she lived next the Harlings. They had been farming people, like ourselves, and their place was like a little farm, with a big barn and a garden, and an orchard and grazing lots,—even a windmill. The Harlings were Norwegians, and Mrs. Harling had lived in Christiania until she was ten years old. Her husband was born in Minnesota. He was a grain merchant and cattle buyer, and was generally considered the most <u>enterprising</u> business man in our county. He controlled a line of grain elevators in the little towns along the railroad to the west of us, and was away from home a great deal. In his absence his wife was the head of the household.

Mrs. Harling was short and square and sturdy-looking, like her house. Every inch of her was charged with an energy that made itself felt the moment she entered a room. Her face was rosy and solid, with bright, twinkling eyes and a stubborn little chin. She was quick to anger, quick to laughter, and jolly from the depths of her soul. How well I remember her laugh; it had in it the same sudden recognition that flashed into her eyes, was a burst of humor, short and intelligent. Her rapid footsteps shook her own floors, and she <u>routed</u> <u>lassitude</u> and indifference wherever she came. She could not be negative or <u>perfunctory</u> about anything. Her enthusiasm, and her violent likes and dislikes, asserted themselves in all the every-day occupations of life. Wash-day was interesting, never dreary, at the Harlings'. Preserving-time was a prolonged festival, and house-cleaning was like a revolution. When Mrs. Harling made garden that spring, we could feel the stir of her undertaking through the willow hedge that separated our place from hers.

Three of the Harling children were near me in age. Charley, the only son,— they had lost an older boy,—was sixteen; Julia, who was known as the musical one, was fourteen when I was; and Sally, the tomboy with short hair, was a year younger. She was nearly as strong as I, and uncannily clever at all boys' sports. Sally was a wild thing, with sunburned yellow hair, bobbed about her ears, and a brown skin, for she never wore a hat. She raced all over town on one roller skate, often cheated at "keeps," but was such a quick shot one couldn't catch her at it.

The grown-up daughter, Frances, was a very important person in our world. She was her father's chief clerk, and virtually managed his Black Hawk office during his frequent absences. Because of her unusual business ability, he was stern and exacting with her. He paid her a good salary, but she had few holidays and never got away from her responsibilities. Even on Sundays she went to the office to open the mail and read the markets. With Charley, who was not interested in business, but was already preparing for Annapolis, Mr. Harling was very indulgent; bought him guns and tools and electric batteries, and never asked what he did with them.

Frances was dark, like her father, and quite as tall. In winter she wore a sealskin coat and cap, and she and Mr. Harling used to walk home together in the evening, talking about grain-cars and cattle, like two men. Sometimes she came over to see grandfather after supper, and her visits flattered him. More than once they put their wits together to rescue some unfortunate farmer from the clutches of Wick Cutter, the Black Hawk money-lender. Grandfather said Frances Harling was as good a judge of credits as any banker in the county. The two or three men who had tried to take advantage of her in a deal acquired celebrity by their defeat. She knew every farmer for miles about: how much land he had under cultivation, how many cattle he was feeding, what his <u>liabilities</u> were. Her interest in these people was more than a business interest. She carried them all in her mind as if they were characters in a book or a play.

When Frances drove out into the country on business, she would go miles out of her way to call on some of the old people, or to see the women who seldom got to town. She was quick at understanding the grandmothers who spoke no English, and the most <u>reticent</u> and distrustful of them would tell her their story without realizing they were doing so. She went to country funerals and weddings in all

◀ Who is Wick Cutter?

◀ In what ways does Frances express her interest in the country people?

words for everyday use

li • a • bil • i • ty (lī ə bil′ lə tē) n., something for which one is financially responsible, debt. *Jennifer was still paying off college loans and didn't feel that she could take on the additional <u>liability</u> of an auto loan.*

re • ti • cent (re′ tə sənt) adj., inclined to be silent or uncommunicative in speech, reserved. *The police tried to get the girl to explain what had happened, but she remained <u>reticent</u>.*

weathers. A farmer's daughter who was to be married could count on a wedding present from Frances Harling.

In August the Harlings' Danish cook had to leave them. Grandmother <u>entreated</u> them to try Ántonia. She cornered Ambrosch the next time he came to town, and pointed out to him that any connection with Christian Harling would strengthen his credit and be of advantage to him. One Sunday Mrs. Harling took the long ride out to the Shimerdas' with Frances. She said she wanted to see "what the girl came from" and to have a clear understanding with her mother. I was in our yard when they came driving home, just before sunset. They laughed and waved to me as they passed, and I could see they were in great good humor. After supper, when grandfather set off to church, grandmother and I took my short cut through the willow hedge and went over to hear about the visit to the Shimerdas'.

▶ What suggestion does Jim's grandmother make to Mrs. Harling?

We found Mrs. Harling with Charley and Sally on the front porch, resting after her hard drive. Julia was in the hammock— she was fond of <u>repose</u>—and Frances was at the piano, playing without a light and talking to her mother through the open window.

Mrs. Harling laughed when she saw us coming. "I expect you left your dishes on the table tonight, Mrs. Burden," she called. Frances shut the piano and came out to join us.

They had liked Ántonia from their first glimpse of her; felt they knew exactly what kind of girl she was. As for Mrs. Shimerda, they found her very amusing. Mrs. Harling chuckled whenever she spoke of her. "I expect I am more at home with that sort of bird than you are, Mrs. Burden. They're a pair, Ambrosch and that old woman!"

▶ What disagreement do Ambrosch and Mrs. Harling have, and how do they resolve it?

They had had a long argument with Ambrosch about Ántonia's allowance for clothes and pocket-money. It was his plan that every cent of his sister's wages should be paid over to him each month, and he would provide her with such clothing as he thought necessary. When Mrs. Harling told him firmly that she would keep fifty dollars a year for Ántonia's own use, he declared they wanted to take his sister to town and dress her up and make a fool of her. Mrs.

---

words for everyday use

en • treat (in trēt') vt., make an earnest request, plead. *Knowing that her father would overreact, she <u>entreated</u> her mother not to talk to him about the problem.*

re • pose (ri pōz') n., a state of resting after exertion or strain. *After the long football season and the thrill of winning the state title, the team wanted first a victory celebration and then a period of <u>repose</u>.*

Harling gave us a lively account of Ambrosch's behavior throughout the interview; how he kept jumping up and putting on his cap as if he were through with the whole business, and how his mother tweaked his coat-tail and prompted him in Bohemian. Mrs. Harling finally agreed to pay three dollars a week for Ántonia's services—good wages in those days—and to keep her in shoes. There had been hot dispute about the shoes, Mrs. Shimerda finally saying persuasively that she would send Mrs. Harling three fat geese every year to "make even." Ambrosch was to bring his sister to town next Saturday.

"She'll be awkward and rough at first, like enough," grandmother said anxiously, "but unless she's been spoiled by the hard life she's led, she has it in her to be a real helpful girl."

Mrs. Harling laughed her quick, decided laugh. "Oh, I'm not worrying, Mrs. Burden! I can bring something out of that girl. She's barely seventeen, not too old to learn new ways. She's good-looking, too!" she added warmly.

Frances turned to grandmother. "Oh, yes, Mrs. Burden, you didn't tell us that! She was working in the garden when we got there, barefoot and ragged. But she has such fine brown legs and arms, and splendid color in her cheeks—like those big dark red plums."

We were pleased at this praise. Grandmother spoke feelingly. "When she first came to this country, Frances, and had that <u>genteel</u> old man to watch over her, she was as pretty a girl as ever I saw. But, dear me, what a life she's led, out in the fields with those rough threshers! Things would have been very different with poor Ántonia if her father had lived."

The Harlings begged us to tell them about Mr. Shimerda's death and the big snowstorm. By the time we saw grandfather coming home from church, we had told them pretty much all we knew of the Shimerdas.

"The girl will be happy here, and she'll forget those things," said Mrs. Harling confidently, as we rose to take our leave.

---

words for everyday use

gen • teel (jen tēl') adj., free from vulgarity or rudeness, polite. *The admissions committee was impressed by the student's poise and <u>genteel</u> manner.*

Chapter 3

On Saturday Ambrosch drove up to the back gate, and Ántonia jumped down from the wagon and ran into our kitchen just as she used to do. She was wearing shoes and stockings, and was breathless and excited. She gave me a playful shake by the shoulders. "You ain't forget about me, Jim?"

Grandmother kissed her. "God bless you, child! Now you've come, you must try to do right and be a credit to us."

▶ What is Ántonia's hope in coming to town?

Ántonia looked eagerly about the house and admired everything. "Maybe I be the kind of girl you like better; now I come to town," she suggested hopefully.

How good it was to have Ántonia near us again; to see her every day and almost every night! Her greatest fault, Mrs. Harling found, was that she so often stopped her work and fell to playing with the children. She would race about the orchard with us, or take sides in our hay-fights in the barn, or be the old bear that came down from the mountain and carried off Nina. Tony learned English so quickly that by the time school began she could speak as well as any of us.

I was jealous of Tony's admiration for Charley Harling. Because he was always first in his classes at school, and could mend the water-pipes or the door-bell and take the clock to pieces, she seemed to think him a sort of prince. Nothing that Charley wanted was too much trouble for her. She loved to put up lunches for him when he went hunting, to mend his ball-gloves and sew buttons on his shooting-coat, baked the kind of nut-cake he liked, and fed his setter dog when he was away on trips with his father. Ántonia had made herself cloth working-slippers out of Mr. Harling's old coats, and in these she went padding about after Charley, fairly panting with eagerness to please him.

Next to Charley, I think she loved Nina best. Nina was only six, and she was rather more complex than the other children. She was fanciful, had all sorts of unspoken preferences, and was easily offended. At the slightest disappointment or displeasure her velvety brown eyes filled with tears, and she would lift her chin and walk silently away. If we ran after her and tried to <u>appease</u> her, it did no good. She walked on <u>unmollified</u>. I used to think that no

---

words for everyday use

ap • pease (ə pēz') vt., bring to a state of peace or quiet, calm. *The event organizers tried to appease the crowd, which was becoming increasingly restless as the start of the concert got later and later.*

un • mol • li • fied (ən mäl' lə fīd) adj., not soothed. *The environmentalists are unmollified by the explanations of why the trees must be cut down to allow for the new highway.*

eyes in the world could grow so large or hold so many tears as Nina's. Mrs. Harling and Ántonia invariably took her part. We were never given a chance to explain. The charge was simply: "You have made Nina cry. Now, Jimmy can go home, and Sally must get her arithmetic." I liked Nina, too; she was so quaint and unexpected, and her eyes were lovely; but I often wanted to shake her.

We had jolly evenings at the Harlings' when the father was away. If he was at home, the children had to go to bed early, or they came over to my house to play. Mr. Harling not only demanded a quiet house, he demanded all his wife's attention. He used to take her away to their room in the west ell[1], and talk over his business with her all evening. Though we did not realize it then, Mrs. Harling was our audience when we played, and we always looked to her for suggestions. Nothing flattered one like her quick laugh.

◀ How are things different when Mr. Harling is at home?

Mr. Harling had a desk in his bedroom, and his own easy-chair by the window, in which no one else ever sat. On the nights when he was at home, I could see his shadow on the blind, and it seemed to me an arrogant shadow. Mrs. Harling paid no heed to anyone else if he was there. Before he went to bed she always got him a lunch of smoked salmon or anchovies and beer. He kept an alcohol lamp in his room, and a French coffee-pot, and his wife made coffee for him at any hour of the night he happened to want it.

Most Black Hawk fathers had no personal habits outside their <u>domestic</u> ones; they paid the bills, pushed the baby carriage after office hours, moved the sprinkler about over the lawn, and took the family driving on Sunday. Mr. Harling, therefore, seemed to me <u>autocratic</u> and <u>imperial</u> in his ways. He walked, talked, put on his gloves, shook hands, like a man who felt that he had power. He was not tall, but he carried his head so haughtily that he looked a commanding figure, and there was something daring and challenging in his eyes. I used to imagine that the "nobles"

◀ What makes Mr. Harling unusual among Black Hawk fathers?

---

1. **ell**. Extension at right angles to the length of a building

words for everyday use

do • mes • tic (də mes' tik) adj., relating to the household or family. *The "Cult of True Womanhood" in the nineteenth century emphasized women's work as <u>domestic</u>—raising children and keeping house.*

au • to • cra • tic (ȯ tə kra' tik) adj., resembling one who has undisputed power. *This candidate for executive director might be too <u>autocratic</u> for our organization, which makes decisions by consensus.*

im • per • i • al (im pir' ē əl) adj., befitting an emperor. *Karen had an <u>imperial</u> air about her, with her way of holding her head slightly lifted and walking with confidence and purpose.*

of whom Ántonia was always talking probably looked very much like Christian Harling, wore caped overcoats like his, and just such a glittering diamond upon the little finger.

Except when the father was at home, the Harling house was never quiet. Mrs. Harling and Nina and Ántonia made as much noise as a houseful of children, and there was usually somebody at the piano. Julia was the only one who was held down to regular hours of practicing, but they all played. When Frances came home at noon, she played until dinner was ready. When Sally got back from school, she sat down in her hat and coat and drummed the plantation melodies that negro minstrel troupes brought to town. Even Nina played the Swedish Wedding March.

Mrs. Harling had studied the piano under a good teacher, and somehow she managed to practice every day. I soon learned that if I were sent over on an errand and found Mrs. Harling at the piano, I must sit down and wait quietly until she turned to me. I can see her at this moment: her short, square person planted firmly on the stool, her little fat hands moving quickly and neatly over the keys, her eyes fixed on the music with intelligent concentration.

Chapter 4

"I won't have none of your weevily wheat,
    and I won't have none of your barley,
But I'll take a measure of fine white
    flour, to make a cake for Charley."

We were singing rhymes to tease Ántonia while she was beating up one of Charley's favorite cakes in her big mixing-bowl. It was a crisp autumn evening, just cold enough to make one glad to quit playing tag in the yard, and retreat into the kitchen. We had begun to roll popcorn balls with syrup when we heard a knock at the back door, and Tony dropped her spoon and went to open it. A plump, fair-skinned girl was standing in the doorway. She looked <u>demure</u> and pretty, and made a graceful picture in her blue cashmere dress and little blue hat, with a plaid shawl drawn neatly about her shoulders and a clumsy pocketbook in her hand.

"Hello, Tony. Don't you know me?" she asked in a smooth, low voice, looking in at us <u>archly</u>.

Ántonia gasped and stepped back. "Why, it's Lena! Of course I didn't know you, so dressed up!"

Lena Lingard laughed, as if this pleased her. I had not recognized her for a moment, either. I had never seen her before with a hat on her head—or with shoes and stockings on her feet, for that matter. And here she was, brushed and smoothed and dressed like a town girl, smiling at us with perfect composure.

"Hello, Jim," she said carelessly as she walked into the kitchen and looked about her. "I've come to town to work, too, Tony."

"Have you, now? Well, ain't that funny!" Ántonia stood ill at ease, and didn't seem to know just what to do with her visitor.

The door was open into the dining-room, where Mrs. Harling sat crocheting and Frances was reading. Frances asked Lena to come in and join them.

"You are Lena Lingard, aren't you? I've been to see your mother, but you were off herding cattle that day. Mama, this is Chris Lingard's oldest girl."

words for everyday use

de • mure (di myur') adj., reserved, modest. *Her accomplishments were impressive, but she was so <u>demure</u> that she never mentioned them.*

arch • ly (ärch' lē) adv., mischievously. *He grinned <u>archly</u> as Neiti searched for her keys, which he had hidden in his backpack.*

BOOK II   CHAPTER 4   **105**

Mrs. Harling dropped her worsted and examined the visitor with quick, keen eyes. Lena was not at all disconcerted. She sat down in the chair Frances pointed out, carefully arranging her pocketbook and gray cotton gloves on her lap. We followed with our popcorn, but Ántonia hung back— said she had to get her cake into the oven.

"So you have come to town," said Mrs. Harling, her eyes still fixed on Lena. "Where are you working?"

▶ Where will Lena be working?

"For Mrs. Thomas, the dressmaker. She is going to teach me to sew. She says I have quite a knack. I'm through with the farm. There ain't any end to the work on a farm, and always so much trouble happens. I'm going to be a dressmaker."

"Well, there have to be dressmakers. It's a good trade. But I wouldn't run down the farm, if I were you," said Mrs. Harling rather severely. "How is your mother?"

"Oh, mother's never very well; she has too much to do. She'd get away from the farm, too, if she could. She was willing for me to come. After I learn to do sewing, I can make money and help her."

"See that you don't forget to," said Mrs. Harling skeptically, as she took up her crocheting again and sent the hook in and out with nimble fingers.

"No, 'm, I won't," said Lena blandly. She took a few grains of the popcorn we pressed upon her, eating them discreetly and taking care not to get her fingers sticky.

Frances drew her chair up nearer to the visitor. "I thought you were going to be married, Lena," she said teasingly. "Didn't I hear that Nick Svendsen was rushing you pretty hard?"

Lena looked up with her curiously innocent smile. "He did go with me quite a while. But his father made a fuss about it and said he wouldn't give Nick any land if he married me, so he's going to marry Annie Iverson. I wouldn't like to be her; Nick's awful sullen, and he'll take it out on her. He ain't spoke to his father since he promised."

Frances laughed. "And how do you feel about it?"

▶ How does Lena feel about not marrying Nick?

"I don't want to marry Nick, or any other man," Lena murmured. "I've seen a good deal of married life, and I don't care for it. I want to be so I can help my mother and the children at home, and not have to ask lief of anybody."

"That's right," said Frances. "And Mrs. Thomas thinks you can learn dressmaking?"

"Yes, 'm. I've always liked to sew, but I never had much to do with. Mrs. Thomas makes lovely things for all the town ladies. Did you know Mrs. Gardener is having a purple velvet made? The velvet came from Omaha. My, but it's lovely!" Lena sighed softly and stroked her cashmere folds. "Tony knows I never did like out-of-door work," she added.

Mrs. Harling glanced at her. "I expect you'll learn to sew all right, Lena, if you'll only keep your head and not go gadding about to dances all the time and neglect your work, the way some country girls do."

"Yes, 'm. Tiny Soderball is coming to town, too. She's going to work at the Boys' Home Hotel. She'll see lots of strangers," Lena added wistfully.

◀ Where will Tiny be working?

"Too many, like enough," said Mrs. Harling. "I don't think a hotel is a good place for a girl; though I guess Mrs. Gardener keeps an eye on her waitresses."

Lena's candid eyes, that always looked a little sleepy under their long lashes, kept straying about the cheerful rooms with naïve admiration. Presently she drew on her cotton gloves. "I guess I must be leaving," she said irresolutely.

Frances told her to come again, whenever she was lonesome or wanted advice about anything. Lena replied that she didn't believe she would ever get lonesome in Black Hawk.

She lingered at the kitchen door and begged Ántonia to come and see her often. "I've got a room of my own at Mrs. Thomas's, with a carpet."

Tony shuffled uneasily in her cloth slippers. "I'll come sometime, but Mrs. Harling don't like to have me run much," she said evasively.

"You can do what you please when you go out, can't you?" Lena asked in a guarded whisper. "Ain't you crazy about town, Tony? I don't care what anybody says, I'm done with the farm!" She glanced back over her shoulder toward the dining-room, where Mrs. Harling sat.

When Lena was gone, Frances asked Ántonia why she hadn't been a little more cordial to her.

"I didn't know if your mother would like her coming here," said Ántonia, looking troubled. "She was kind of talked about, out there."

"Yes, I know. But mother won't hold it against her if she behaves well here. You needn't say anything about that to the children. I guess Jim has heard all that gossip?"

---

words for everyday use

e • va • sive • ly (i vā′ siv lē) adv., in a way intended to avoid answering directly. *When Beth asked where her chocolate had gone, her sister answered evasively, "Hm, I haven't seen it lately."*

When I nodded, she pulled my hair and told me I knew too much, anyhow. We were good friends, Frances and I.

I ran home to tell grandmother that Lena Lingard had come to town. We were glad of it, for she had a hard life on the farm.

Lena lived in the Norwegian settlement west of Squaw Creek, and she used to herd her father's cattle in the open country between his place and the Shimerdas'. Whenever we rode over in that direction we saw her out among her cattle, bareheaded and barefooted, scantily dressed in tattered clothing, always knitting as she watched her herd. Before I knew Lena, I thought of her as something wild, that always lived on the prairie, because I had never seen her under a roof. Her yellow hair was burned to a ruddy thatch on her head; but her legs and arms, curiously enough, in spite of constant exposure to the sun, kept a miraculous whiteness which somehow made her seem more undressed than other girls who went scantily clad. The first time I stopped to talk to her, I was astonished at her soft voice and easy, gentle ways. The girls out there usually got rough and mannish after they went to herding. But Lena asked Jake and me to get off our horses and stay awhile, and behaved exactly as if she were in a house and were accustomed to having visitors. She was not embarrassed by her ragged clothes, and treated us as if we were old acquaintances. Even then I noticed the unusual color of her eyes— a shade of deep violet—and their soft, confiding expression.

Chris Lingard was not a very successful farmer, and he had a large family. Lena was always knitting stockings for little brothers and sisters, and even the Norwegian women, who disapproved of her, admitted that she was a good daughter to her mother. As Tony said, she had been talked about. She was accused of making Ole Benson lose the little sense he had— and that at an age when she should still have been in pinafores.

Ole lived in a leaky dugout somewhere at the edge of the settlement. He was fat and lazy and discouraged, and bad luck had become a habit with him. After he had had every other kind of misfortune, his wife, "Crazy Mary," tried to set a neighbor's barn on fire, and was sent to the asylum at Lincoln. She was kept there for a few months, then escaped and walked all the way home, nearly two hundred miles, traveling by night and hiding in barns and haystacks by day. When she got back to the Norwegian settlement, her poor feet were as hard as hoofs. She promised

▶ What were Jim's first impressions of Lena?

▶ How was Jim forced to change his first impressions?

to be good, and was allowed to stay at home—though everyone realized she was as crazy as ever, and she still ran about barefooted through the snow, telling her domestic troubles to her neighbors.

Not long after Mary came back from the asylum, I heard a young Dane, who was helping us to thresh, tell Jake and Otto that Chris Lingard's oldest girl had put Ole Benson out of his head, until he had no more sense than his crazy wife. When Ole was cultivating his corn that summer, he used to get discouraged in the field, tie up his team, and wander off to wherever Lena Lingard was herding. There he would sit down on the draw-side and help her watch her cattle. All the settlement was talking about it. The Norwegian preacher's wife went to Lena and told her she ought not to allow this; she begged Lena to come to church on Sundays. Lena said she hadn't a dress in the world any less ragged than the one on her back. Then the minister's wife went through her old trunks and found some things she had worn before her marriage.

The next Sunday Lena appeared at church, a little late, with her hair done up neatly on her head, like a young woman, wearing shoes and stockings, and the new dress, which she had made over for herself very becomingly. The congregation stared at her. Until that morning no one—unless it were Ole—had realized how pretty she was, or that she was growing up. The swelling lines of her figure had been hidden under the shapeless rags she wore in the fields. After the last hymn had been sung, and the congregation was dismissed, Ole slipped out to the hitch-bar and lifted Lena on her horse. That, in itself, was shocking; a married man was not expected to do such things. But it was nothing to the scene that followed. Crazy Mary darted out from the group of women at the church door, and ran down the road after Lena, shouting horrible threats.

"Look out, you Lena Lingard, look out! I'll come over with a corn-knife one day and trim some of that shape off you. Then you won't sail round so fine, making eyes at the men! . . ."

◀ How did Crazy Mary threaten Lena, and why?

The Norwegian women didn't know where to look. They were formal housewives, most of them, with a severe sense of decorum. But Lena Lingard only laughed her lazy, good-natured laugh and rode on, gazing back over her shoulder at Ole's infuriated wife.

The time came, however, when Lena didn't laugh. More than once Crazy Mary chased her across the prairie and round and round the Shimerdas' cornfield. Lena never told

▶ Why didn't Lena tell her father?

her father; perhaps she was ashamed; perhaps she was more afraid of his anger than of the corn-knife. I was at the Shimerdas' one afternoon when Lena came bounding through the red grass as fast as her white legs could carry her. She ran straight into the house and hid in Ántonia's feather-bed. Mary was not far behind: she came right up to the door and made us feel how sharp her blade was, showing us very graphically just what she meant to do to Lena. Mrs. Shimerda, leaning out of the window, enjoyed the situation keenly, and was sorry when Ántonia sent Mary away, mollified by an apronful of bottle-tomatoes. Lena came out from Tony's room behind the kitchen, very pink from the heat of the feathers, but otherwise calm. She begged Ántonia and me to go with her, and help get her cattle together; they were scattered and might be gorging themselves in somebody's cornfield.

"Maybe you lose a steer and learn not to make somethings with your eyes at married men," Mrs. Shimerda told her hectoringly.

▶ How does Lena respond to Mrs. Shimerda's criticism?

Lena only smiled her sleepy smile. "I never made anything to him with my eyes. I can't help it if he hangs around, and I can't order him off. It ain't my prairie."

---

words for everyday use

mol • li • fied (mä' lə fid) adj., soothed in temper or disposition, appeased. *The crying baby was mollified by its pacifier.*

gorg • ing (gorj iŋ) vi., to eat greedily. *It's Halloween night, and kids around the country are gorging themselves on candy.*

hec • tor • ing • ly (hək' tə riŋ lē) adv., in a manner intended to intimidate or harass by bluster or personal pressure. *The school bully often followed younger children around the playground, calling out to them hectoringly to give him their lunch money.*

Chapter 5

After Lena came to Black Hawk I often met her down-town, where she would be matching sewing silk or buying "findings"[1] for Mrs. Thomas. If I happened to walk home with her, she told me all about the dresses she was helping to make, or about what she saw and heard when she was with Tiny Soderball at the hotel on Saturday nights.

The Boys' Home was the best hotel on our branch of the Burlington, and all the commercial travelers in that terri-tory tried to get into Black Hawk for Sunday. They used to assemble in the parlor after supper on Saturday nights. Marshall Field's man, Anson Kirkpatrick, played the piano and sang all the latest sentimental songs. After Tiny had helped the cook wash the dishes, she and Lena sat on the other side of the double doors between the parlor and the dining-room, listening to the music and giggling at the jokes and stories. Lena often said she hoped I would be a traveling man when I grew up. They had a gay life of it; nothing to do but ride about on trains all day and go to theaters when they were in big cities. Behind the hotel there was an old store building, where the salesmen opened their big trunks and spread out their samples on the counters. The Black Hawk merchants went to look at these things and order goods, and Mrs. Thomas, though she was "retail trade," was permitted to see them and to "get ideas." They were all generous, these traveling men; they gave Tiny Soderball handkerchiefs and gloves and rib-bons and striped stockings, and so many bottles of per-fume and cakes of scented soap that she bestowed some of them on Lena.

◀ *In Lena's imagination, what is the life of a traveling man like?*

One afternoon in the week before Christmas I came upon Lena and her funny, square-headed little brother Chris, standing before the drug-store, gazing in at the wax dolls and blocks and Noah's arks arranged in the frosty show window. The boy had come to town with a neighbor to do his Christmas shopping, for he had money of his own this year. He was only twelve, but that winter he had got the job of sweeping out the Norwegian church and making the fire in it every Sunday morning. A cold job it must have been, too!

We went into Duckford's dry-goods store, and Chris unwrapped all his presents and showed them to me—something for each of the six younger than himself, even

---

1. **"findings."** Supplies

a rubber pig for the baby. Lena had given him one of Tiny Soderball's bottles of perfume for his mother, and he thought he would get some handkerchiefs to go with it. They were cheap, and he hadn't much money left. We found a tableful of handkerchiefs spread out for view at Duckford's. Chris wanted those with initial letters in the corner, because he had never seen any before. He studied them seriously, while Lena looked over his shoulder, telling him she thought the red letters would hold their color best. He seemed so perplexed that I thought perhaps he hadn't enough money, after all. Presently he said gravely,—

"Sister, you know mother's name is Berthe. I don't know if I ought to get B for Berthe, or M for Mother."

▶ Why does Lena think it will especially please Mrs. Lingard to get the handkerchiefs embroidered with the initial B?

Lena patted his bristly head. "I'd get the B, Chrissy. It will please her for you to think about her name. Nobody ever calls her by it now."

That satisfied him. His face cleared at once, and he took three reds and three blues. When the neighbor came in to say that it was time to start, Lena wound Chris's comforter about his neck and turned up his jacket collar—he had no overcoat— and we watched him climb into the wagon and start on his long, cold drive. As we walked together up the windy street, Lena wiped her eyes with the back of her woolen glove. "I get awful homesick for them, all the same," she murmured, as if she were answering some remembered reproach.

Chapter 6

Winter comes down savagely over a little town on the prairie. The wind that sweeps in from the open country strips away all the leafy screens that hide one yard from another in summer, and the houses seem to draw closer together. The roofs, that looked so far away across the green tree-tops, now stare you in the face, and they are so much uglier than when their angles were softened by vines and shrubs.

In the morning, when I was fighting my way to school against the wind, I couldn't see anything but the road in front of me; but in the late afternoon, when I was coming home, the town looked bleak and <u>desolate</u> to me. The pale, cold light of the winter sunset did not beautify—it was like the light of truth itself. When the smoky clouds hung low in the west and the red sun went down behind them, leaving a pink flush on the snowy roofs and the blue drifts, then the wind sprang up afresh, with a kind of bitter song, as if it said: "This is reality, whether you like it or not. All those frivolities of summer, the light and shadow, the living mask of green that trembled over everything, they were lies, and this is what was underneath. This is the truth." It was as if we were being punished for loving the loveliness of summer.

◀ *What is the message of the winter wind?*

If I loitered on the playground after school, or went to the post-office for the mail and lingered to hear the gossip about the cigar-stand, it would be growing dark by the time I came home. The sun was gone; the frozen streets stretched long and blue before me; the lights were shining pale in kitchen windows, and I could smell the suppers cooking as I passed. Few people were abroad, and each one of them was hurrying toward a fire. The glowing stoves in the houses were like magnets. When one passed an old man, one could see nothing of his face but a red nose sticking out between a frosted beard and a long plush cap. The young men <u>capered</u> along with their hands in their pockets, and sometimes tried a slide on the icy sidewalk. The children, in their bright hoods and comforters, never walked, but always ran from the moment they left their

words for everyday use

de • so • late (de′ sə lət) adj., barren, lifeless. *The population in the Dakotas is so scarce that vast stretches of the landscape appear <u>desolate</u>.*

ca • per (kā′ pər) vi., leap or prance about in a playful manner. *Excited by the arrival of their owner, the cats <u>capered</u> around the apartment, knocking things off windowsills and tables.*

▶ For what are the
Nebraskans hungry
in the winter?

door, beating their mittens against their sides. When I got as far as the Methodist Church, I was about halfway home. I can remember how glad I was when there happened to be a light in the church, and the painted glass window shone out at us as we came along the frozen street. In the winter bleakness a hunger for color came over people, like the Laplander's craving for fats and sugar. Without knowing why, we used to linger on the sidewalk outside the church when the lamps were lighted early for choir practice or prayer-meeting, shivering and talking until our feet were like lumps of ice. The crude reds and greens and blues of that colored glass held us there.

On winter nights, the lights in the Harlings' windows drew me like the painted glass. Inside that warm, roomy house there was color, too. After supper I used to catch up my cap, stick my hands in my pockets, and dive through the willow hedge as if witches were after me. Of course, if Mr. Harling was at home, if his shadow stood out on the blind of the west room, I did not go in, but turned and walked home by the long way, through the street, wondering what book I should read as I sat down with the two old people.

Such disappointments only gave greater zest to the nights when we acted charades, or had a costume ball in the back parlor, with Sally always dressed like a boy. Frances taught us to dance that winter, and she said, from the first lesson, that Ántonia would make the best dancer among us. On Saturday nights, Mrs. Harling used to play the old operas for us,—"Martha," "Norma," "Rigoletto,"— telling us the story while she played. Every Saturday night was like a party. The parlor, the back parlor, and the dining-room were warm and brightly lighted, with comfortable chairs and sofas, and gay pictures on the walls. One always felt at ease there. Ántonia brought her sewing and sat with us—she was already beginning to make pretty clothes for herself. After the long winter evenings on the prairie, with Ambrosch's sullen silences and her mother's complaints, the Harlings' house seemed, as she said, "like Heaven" to her. She was never too tired to make taffy or chocolate cookies for us. If Sally whispered in her ear, or Charley gave her three winks, Tony would rush into the kitchen and build a fire in the range on which she had already cooked three meals that day.

While we sat in the kitchen waiting for the cookies to bake or the taffy to cool, Nina used to coax Ántonia to tell her stories—about the calf that broke its leg, or how Yulka saved her little turkeys from drowning in the freshet, or about old Christmases and weddings in Bohemia. Nina interpreted the stories about the crêche fancifully, and in spite of our <u>derision</u> she cherished a belief that Christ was born in Bohemia a short time before the Shimerdas left that country. We all liked Tony's stories. Her voice had a peculiarly engaging quality; it was deep, a little husky, and one always heard the breath vibrating behind it. Everything she said seemed to come right out of her heart.

◀ From where did Ántonia's words seem to come?

One evening when we were picking out kernels for walnut taffy, Tony told us a new story.

"Mrs. Harling, did you ever hear about what happened up in the Norwegian settlement last summer, when I was threshing there? We were at Iversons', and I was driving one of the grain wagons."

Mrs. Harling came out and sat down among us. "Could you throw the wheat into the bin yourself, Tony?" She knew what heavy work it was.

"Yes, ma'm, I did. I could shovel just as fast as that fat Andern boy that drove the other wagon. One day it was just awful hot. When we got back to the field from dinner, we took things kind of easy. The men put in the horses and got the machine going, and Ole Iverson was up on the deck, cutting bands. I was sitting against a straw stack, trying to get some shade. My wagon wasn't going out first, and somehow I felt the heat awful that day. The sun was so hot like it was going to burn the world up. After a while I see a man coming across the stubble, and when he got close I see it was a tramp. His toes stuck out of his shoes, and he hadn't shaved for a long while, and his eyes was awful red and wild, like he had some sickness. He comes right up and begins to talk like he knows me already. He says: 'The ponds in this country is done got so low a man couldn't drownd himself in one of 'em.'

"I told him nobody wanted to drownd themselves, but if we didn't have rain soon we'd have to pump water for the cattle.

"'Oh, cattle,' he says, "you'll all take care of your cattle! Ain't you got no beer here?' I told him he'd have to go to the Bohemians for beer; the Norwegians didn't have none

words for everyday use

der • i • sion (di ri' zhən) n., the use of ridicule or scorn to show contempt. *The debater's derision of his opponent's case was evident not only in his word choices but in his sarcastic tone.*

when they threshed. 'My God!' he says, 'so it's Norwegians now, is it? I thought this was Americy.'

"Then he goes up to the machine and yells out to Ole Iverson, 'Hello, partner, let me up there. I can cut bands, and I'm tired of trampin'. I won't go no farther.'

"I tried to make signs to Ole, 'cause I thought that man was crazy and might get the machine stopped up. But Ole, he was glad to get down out of the sun and chaff— it gets down your neck and sticks to you something awful when it's hot like that. So Ole jumped down and crawled under one of the wagons for shade, and the tramp got on the machine. He cut bands all right for a few minutes, and then, Mrs. Harling, he waved his hand to me and jumped head-first right into the threshing machine after the wheat.

"I begun to scream, and the men run to stop the horses, but the belt had sucked him down, and by the time they got her stopped, he was all beat and cut to pieces. He was wedged in so tight it was a hard job to get him out, and the machine ain't never worked right since."

"Was he clear dead, Tony?" we cried.

"Was he dead? Well, I guess so! There, now, Nina's all upset. We won't talk about it. Don't you cry, Nina. No old tramp won't get you while Tony's here."

Mrs. Harling spoke up sternly. "Stop crying, Nina, or I'll always send you upstairs when Ántonia tells us about the country. Did they never find out where he came from, Ántonia?"

"Never, ma'm. He hadn't been seen nowhere except in a little town they call Conway. He tried to get beer there, but there wasn't any saloon. Maybe he came in on a freight, but the brakeman hadn't seen him. They couldn't find no letters nor nothing on him; nothing but an old penknife in his pocket and the wishbone of a chicken wrapped up in a piece of paper, and some poetry."

"Some poetry?" we exclaimed.

"I remember," said Frances. "It was 'The Old Oaken Bucket,' cut out of a newspaper and nearly worn out. Ole Iverson brought it into the office and showed it to me."

"Now, wasn't that strange, Miss Frances?" Tony asked thoughtfully. "What would anybody want to kill themselves in summer for? In threshing time, too! It's nice everywhere then."

"So it is, Ántonia," said Mrs. Harling heartily. "Maybe I'll go home and help you thresh next summer. Isn't that taffy nearly ready to eat? I've been smelling it a long while."

► *What happened to the old tramp?*

There was a basic harmony between Ántonia and her mistress. They had strong, independent natures, both of them. They knew what they liked, and were not always trying to imitate other people. They loved children and animals and music, and rough play and digging in the earth. They liked to prepare rich, hearty food and to see people eat it; to make up soft white beds and to see youngsters asleep in them. They ridiculed conceited people and were quick to help unfortunate ones. Deep down in each of them there was a kind of hearty <u>joviality</u>, a relish of life, not over-delicate, but very invigorating. I never tried to define it, but I was distinctly conscious of it. I could not imagine Ántonia's living for a week in any other house in Black Hawk than the Harlings'.

◀ In what ways are Ántonia and Mrs. Harling alike? What did both of them possess deep down?

words for everyday use
jo • vi • al • i • ty (jō vē a' lə tē) n., good humor. *Peter's <u>joviality</u> made him well-liked in the community despite his difficulty with English.*

Chapter 7

▶ How is winter different in town than in the country?

Winter lies too long in country towns; hangs on until it is stale and shabby, old and sullen. On the farm the weather was the great fact, and men's affairs went on underneath it, as the streams creep under the ice. But in Black Hawk the scene of human life was spread out shrunken and pinched, frozen down to the bare stalk.

Through January and February I went to the river with the Harlings on clear nights, and we skated up to the big island and made bonfires on the frozen sand. But by March the ice was rough and choppy, and the snow on the river bluffs was gray and mournful-looking. I was tired of school, tired of winter clothes, of the rutted streets, of the dirty drifts and the piles of cinders that had lain in the yards so long. There was only one break in the dreary monotony of that month; when Blind d'Arnault[1], the negro pianist, came to town. He gave a concert at the Opera House on Monday night, and he and his manager spent Saturday and Sunday at our comfortable hotel. Mrs. Harling had known d'Arnault for years. She told Ántonia she had better go to see Tiny that Saturday evening, as there would certainly be music at the Boys' Home.

Saturday night after supper I ran downtown to the hotel and slipped quietly into the parlor. The chairs and sofas were already occupied, and the air smelled pleasantly of cigar smoke. The parlor had once been two rooms, and the floor was sway-backed where the partition had been cut away. The wind from without made waves in the long carpet. A coal stove glowed at either end of the room, and the grand piano in the middle stood open.

There was an atmosphere of unusual freedom about the house that night, for Mrs. Gardener had gone to Omaha for a week. Johnnie had been having drinks with the guests until he was rather absent-minded. It was Mrs. Gardener who ran the business and looked after everything. Her husband stood at the desk and welcomed incoming travelers. He was a popular fellow, but no manager.

Mrs. Gardener was admittedly the best-dressed woman in Black Hawk, drove the best horse, and had a smart trap and a little white-and-gold sleigh. She seemed indifferent

---

1. **Blind d'Arnault.** Character based on two blind musicians who toured through Nebraska while Cather lived there: Thomas "Blind Tom" Bethune and John William "Blind" Boone

to her possessions, was not half so <u>solicitous</u> about them as her friends were. She was tall, dark, severe, with something Indian-like in the rigid immobility of her face. Her manner was cold, and she talked little. Guests felt that they were receiving, not <u>conferring</u>, a favor when they stayed at her house. Even the smartest traveling men were flattered when Mrs. Gardener stopped to chat with them for a moment. The patrons of the hotel were divided into two classes; those who had seen Mrs. Gardener's diamonds, and those who had not.

When I stole into the parlor Anson Kirkpatrick, Marshall Field's man, was at the piano, playing airs from a musical comedy then running in Chicago. He was a dapper little Irishman, very vain, homely as a monkey, with friends everywhere, and a sweetheart in every port, like a sailor. I did not know all the men who were sitting about, but I recognized a furniture salesman from Kansas City, a drug man, and Willy O'Reilly, who traveled for a jewelery house and sold musical instruments. The talk was all about good and bad hotels, actors and actresses and musical prodigies. I learned that Mrs. Gardener had gone to Omaha to hear Booth and Barrett[2], who were to play there next week, and that Mary Anderson[3] was having a great success in "A Winter's Tale," in London.

The door from the office opened, and Johnnie Gardener came in, directing Blind d'Arnault,—he would never consent to be led. He was a heavy, bulky mulatto[4], on short legs, and he came tapping the floor in front of him with his gold-headed cane. His yellow face was lifted in the light, with a show of white teeth, all grinning, and his shrunken, papery eyelids lay motionless over his blind eyes.

"Good-evening, gentlemen. No ladies here? Good evening, gentlemen. We going to have a little music? Some of you gentlemen going to play for me this evening?" It was the soft, <u>amiable</u> negro voice, like those I remembered

---

2. **Booth and Barrett.** Edwin Booth and Lawrence Barrett, two famous Shakespearean actors of the time
3. **Mary Anderson.** Another famous Shakespearean actor
4. **mulatto.** Person of mixed white and black ancestry

words for everyday use

so • li • ci • tous (sə li' sə təs) adj., full of concerns or fears, apprehensive. *The sisters were <u>solicitous</u> of their mother's health because she had already had two small strokes.*

con • fer (kən fər') vt., bestow, grant. *The National Institute and the American Academy of Arts and Letters <u>conferred</u> on Willa Cather the Gold Medal for Fiction.*

am • i • a • ble (ā' mē ə bəl) adj., friendly, sociable, and congenial. *Zach is so <u>amiable</u> that it's hard to imagine anyone saying anything negative about him.*

from early childhood, with the note of docile <u>subservience</u> in it. He had the negro head, too; almost no head at all; nothing behind the ears but folds of neck under close-clipped wool. He would have been <u>repulsive</u> if his face had not been so kindly and happy. It was the happiest face I had seen since I left Virginia.

He felt his way directly to the piano. The moment he sat down, I noticed the nervous <u>infirmity</u> of which Mrs. Harling had told me. When he was sitting, or standing still, he swayed back and forth incessantly, like a rocking toy. At the piano, he swayed in time to the music, and when he was not playing, his body kept up this motion, like an empty mill grinding on. He found the pedals and tried them, ran his yellow hands up and down the keys a few times, tinkling off scales, then turned to the company.

"She seems all right, gentlemen. Nothing happened to her since the last time I was here. Mrs. Gardener, she always has this piano tuned up before I come. Now gentlemen, I expect you've all got grand voices. Seems like we might have some good old plantation songs tonight."

The men gathered round him, as he began to play "My Old Kentucky Home." They sang one negro melody after another, while the mulatto sat rocking himself, his head thrown back, his yellow face lifted, his shriveled eyelids never fluttering.

He was born in the Far South, on the d'Arnault plantation, where the spirit if not the fact of slavery persisted. When he was three weeks old, he had an illness which left him totally blind. As soon as he was old enough to sit up alone and toddle about, another <u>affliction</u>, the nervous motion of his body, became apparent. His mother, a buxom young negro wench who was laundress for the d'Arnaults, concluded that her blind baby was "not right" in his head, and she was ashamed of him. She loved him devotedly, but he was so ugly, with his sunken eyes and his "fidgets," that she hid him away from people. All the dainties she brought down from the "Big House" were for the blind child, and she beat and cuffed her other children whenever she found them teasing him or trying to get his chicken-bone away from him. He began to talk early, remembered everything he heard, and his mammy said he "wasn't all wrong." She named him Samson, because he was blind, but on the plantation he was known as "yellow Martha's simple child." He was docile and obedient, but when he was six years old he began to run away from home, always taking the same direction. He felt his way through the lilacs, along the boxwood hedge, up to the south wing of the "Big House," where Miss Nellie d'Arnault practiced the piano every morning. This angered his mother more than anything else he could have done; she was so ashamed of his ugliness that she couldn't bear to have white folks see him. Whenever she caught him slipping away from the cabin, she whipped him unmercifully, and told him what dreadful things old Mr. d'Arnault would do to him if he ever found him near the "Big House." But the next time Samson had a chance, he ran away again. If Miss d'Arnault stopped practicing for a moment and went toward the window, she saw this hideous little pickaninny, dressed in an old piece of sacking, standing in the open space between the hollyhock rows, his body rocking automatically, his blind face lifted to the sun and wearing an expression of idiotic rapture. Often she was tempted to tell Martha that the child must be kept at home, but somehow the memory of his foolish, happy face deterred her. She remembered that his sense of hearing was nearly all he had,— though it did not occur to her that he might have more of it than other children.

One day Samson was standing thus while Miss Nellie was playing her lesson to her music-master. The windows were open. He heard them get up from the piano, talk a little while, and then leave the room. He heard the door close after them. He crept up to the front windows and stuck his head in: there was no one there. He could always detect the presence of anyone in a room. He put one foot over the window sill and straddled it. His mother had told him over and over how his master would give him to the big mastiff if he ever found him "meddling." Samson had got too near the mastiff's kennel once, and had felt his terrible breath in his face. He thought about that, but he pulled in his other foot.

Through the dark he found his way to the Thing, to its mouth. He touched it softly, and it answered softly, kindly. He shivered and stood still. Then he began to feel it all over, ran his finger tips along the slippery sides, embraced the carved legs, tried to get some conception

◀ *Where did Samson go when he ran away?*

of its shape and size, of the space it occupied in <u>primeval</u> night. It was cold and hard, and like nothing else in his black universe. He went back to its mouth, began at one end of the keyboard and felt his way down into the mellow thunder, as far as he could go. He seemed to know that it must be done with the fingers, not with the fists or the feet. He approached this highly artificial instrument through a mere instinct, and coupled himself to it, as if he knew it was to piece him out and make a whole creature of him. After he had tried over all the sounds, he began to finger out passages from things Miss Nellie had been practicing, passages that were already his, that lay under the bone of his pinched, conical little skull, definite as animal desires. The door opened; Miss Nellie and her music-master stood behind it, but blind Samson, who was so sensitive to presences, did not know they were there. He was feeling out the pattern that lay all ready-made on the big and little keys. When he paused for a moment, because the sound was wrong and he wanted another, Miss Nellie spoke softly. He whirled about in a spasm of terror, leaped forward in the dark, struck his head on the open window, and fell screaming and bleeding to the floor. He had what his mother called a fit. The doctor came and gave him opium.

When Samson was well again, his young mistress led him back to the piano. Several teachers experimented with him. They found he had absolute pitch, and a remarkable memory. As a very young child he could repeat, after a fashion, any composition that was played for him. No matter how many wrong notes he struck, he never lost the intention of a passage, he brought the substance of it across by irregular and astonishing means. He wore his teachers out. He could never learn like other people, never acquired any finish. He was always a negro prodigy who played <u>barbarously</u> and wonderfully. As piano playing, it was perhaps abominable, but as music it was something real, <u>vitalized</u> by a sense of rhythm that was stronger than his other physical senses,—that not

▶ *How did Samson know songs to play when he sat down at the piano for the first time?*

▶ *What makes Samson's piano-playing extraordinary?*

---

words for everyday use

pri • me • val (prī mē′vəl) adj., of or relating to the earliest ages, ancient, primitive. *Dinosaurs roamed the <u>primeval</u> forests.*

bar • bar • ous • ly (bär′ bə rəs lē) adv., in a way lacking culture or refinement. *He ate <u>barbarously</u>, tearing the meat from its bones.*

vi • tal • ize (vī′ təl īz) vt., endow with life, animate. *In an attempt to <u>vitalize</u> the class, the English teacher brought in chocolate chip cookies.*

only filled his dark mind, but worried his body <u>inces-</u><u>santly</u>. To hear him, to watch him, was to see a negro enjoying himself as only a negro can. It was as if all the agreeable sensations possible to creatures of flesh and blood were heaped up on those black and white keys, and he were gloating over them and trickling them through his yellow fingers.

In the middle of a crashing waltz d'Arnault suddenly began to play softly, and, turning to one of the men who stood behind him, whispered, "Somebody dancing in there." He jerked his bullet head toward the dining-room. "I hear little feet,—girls, I 'spect."

Anson Kirkpatrick mounted a chair and peeped over the transom. Springing down, he wrenched open the doors and ran out into the dining-room. Tiny and Lena, Ántonia and Mary Dusak, were waltzing in the middle of the floor. They separated and fled toward the kitchen, giggling.

Kirkpatrick caught Tiny by the elbows. "What's the matter with you girls? Dancing out here by yourselves, when there's a roomful of lonesome men on the other side of the partition! Introduce me to your friends, Tiny."

The girls, still laughing, were trying to escape. Tiny looked alarmed. "Mrs. Gardener wouldn't like it," she protested. "She'd be awful mad if you was to come out here and dance with us."

"Mrs. Gardener's in Omaha, girl. Now, you're Lena, are you?— and you're Tony and you're Mary. Have I got you all straight?"

O'Reilly and the others began to pile the chairs on the tables. Johnnie Gardener ran in from the office.

"Easy, boys, easy!" he entreated them. "You'll wake the cook, and there'll be the devil to pay for me. She won't hear the music, but she'll be down the minute anything's moved in the dining-room."

"Oh, what do you care, Johnnie? Fire the cook and wire Molly to bring another. Come along, nobody'll tell tales."

Johnnie shook his head. "'S a fact, boys," he said confidentially. "If I take a drink in Black Hawk, Molly knows it in Omaha!"

words for everyday use

in • ces • sant • ly (in se' sənt lē) adv., without interruption, continually. *The three-year-old prattled on incessantly about the dump truck they passed as they pulled out of the driveway.*

His guests laughed and slapped him on the shoulder. "Oh, we'll make it all right with Molly. Get your back up, Johnnie."

Molly was Mrs. Gardener's name, of course. "Molly Bawn" was painted in large blue letters on the glossy white sides of the hotel bus, and "Molly" was engraved inside Johnnie's ring and on his watch-case— doubtless on his heart, too. He was an affectionate little man, and he thought his wife a wonderful woman; he knew that without her he would hardly be more than a clerk in some other man's hotel.

▶ For what is Johnnie indebted to Molly?

At a word from Kirkpatrick, d'Arnault spread himself out over the piano, and began to draw the dance music out of it, while the perspiration shone on his short wool and on his uplifted face. He looked like some glistening African god of pleasure, full of strong, savage blood. Whenever the dancers paused to change partners or to catch breath, he would boom out softly, "Who's that goin' back on me? One of these city gentlemen, I bet! Now, you girls, you ain't goin' to let that floor get cold?"

Ántonia seemed frightened at first, and kept looking questioningly at Lena and Tiny over Willy O'Reilly's shoulder. Tiny Soderball was trim and slender, with lively little feet and pretty ankles—she wore her dresses very short. She was quicker in speech, lighter in movement and manner than the other girls. Mary Dusak was broad and brown of <u>countenance</u>, slightly marked by smallpox, but handsome for all that. She had beautiful chestnut hair, coils of it; her forehead was low and smooth, and her commanding dark eyes regarded the world indifferently and fearlessly. She looked bold and resourceful and <u>unscrupulous</u>, and she was all of these. They were handsome girls, had the fresh color of their country upbringing, and in their eyes that brilliancy which is called,— by no metaphor, alas!—"the light of youth."

D'Arnault played until his manager came and shut the piano. Before he left us, he showed us his gold watch which struck the hours, and a topaz ring, given him by some Russian nobleman who delighted in negro melodies, and had heard d'Arnault play in New Orleans. At last he

---

words for everyday use

coun • te • nance (kaun' tən əns) n., face. *Her countenance—especially her gleaming eyes and broad grin—revealed her happiness.*

un • scrup • u • lous (ən skrü' pyə ləs) adj., lacking in morality, unprincipled. *The con man's underscored unscrupulous business deals earned him a bad reputation.*

tapped his way upstairs, after bowing to everybody, docile and happy. I walked home with Ántonia. We were so excited that we dreaded to go to bed. We lingered a long while at the Harlings' gate, whispering in the cold until the restlessness was slowly chilled out of us.

◀ How do Jim and Ántonia feel after the performance?

Chapter 8

The Harling children and I were never happier, never felt more contented and secure, than in the weeks of spring which broke that long winter. We were out all day in the thin sunshine, helping Mrs. Harling and Tony break the ground and plant the garden, dig around the orchard trees, tie up vines and clip the hedges. Every morning, before I was up, I could hear Tony singing in the garden rows. After the apple and cherry trees broke into bloom, we ran about under them, hunting for the new nests the birds were building, throwing clods at each other, and playing hide-and-seek with Nina. Yet the summer which was to change everything was coming nearer every day. When boys and girls are growing up, life can't stand still, not even in the quietest of country towns; and they have to grow up, whether they will or no. That is what their elders are always forgetting.

▶ What are parents always forgetting?

It must have been in June, for Mrs. Harling and Ántonia were preserving cherries, when I stopped one morning to tell them that a dancing pavilion had come to town. I had seen two drays hauling the canvas and painted poles up from the depot.

▶ What strangers arrive in Black Hawk in June?

That afternoon three cheerful-looking Italians strolled about Black Hawk, looking at everything, and with them was a dark, stout woman who wore a long gold watch chain about her neck and carried a black lace parasol. They seemed especially interested in children and vacant lots. When I overtook them and stopped to say a word, I found them <u>affable</u> and confiding. They told me they worked in Kansas City in the winter, and in summer they went out among the farming towns with their tent and taught dancing. When business fell off in one place, they moved on to another.

The dancing pavilion was put up near the Danish laundry, on a vacant lot surrounded by tall, arched cottonwood trees. It was very much like a merry-go-round tent, with open sides and gay flags flying from the poles. Before the week was over, all the ambitious mothers were sending their children to the afternoon dancing class. At three o'clock one met little girls in white dresses and little boys

---

words for everyday use

af • fa • ble (a′ fə bəl) adj., characterized by ease and friendliness. *Christine worried that Lara might hold a grudge against her, but their conversation turned out to be completely* <u>*affable*</u>.

in the round-collared shirts of the time, hurrying along the sidewalk on their way to the tent. Mrs. Vanni received them at the entrance, always dressed in lavender with a great deal of black lace, her important watch chain lying on her bosom. She wore her hair on the top of her head, built up in a black tower, with red coral combs. When she smiled, she showed two rows of strong, crooked yellow teeth. She taught the little children herself, and her husband, the harpist, taught the older ones.

Often the mothers brought their fancy-work and sat on the shady side of the tent during the lesson. The popcorn man wheeled his glass wagon under the big cottonwood by the door, and lounged in the sun, sure of a good trade when the dancing was over. Mr. Jensen, the Danish laundryman, used to bring a chair from his porch and sit out in the grass plot. Some ragged little boys from the depot sold pop and iced lemonade under a white umbrella at the corner, and made faces at the spruce[1] youngsters who came to dance. That vacant lot soon became the most cheerful place in town. Even on the hottest afternoons the cottonwoods made a rustling shade, and the air smelled of popcorn and melted butter, and Bouncing Bets[2] wilting in the sun. Those hardy flowers had run away from the laundryman's garden, and the grass in the middle of the lot was pink with them.

The Vannis kept <u>exemplary</u> order, and closed every evening at the hour suggested by the City Council. When Mrs. Vanni gave the signal, and the harp struck up "Home, Sweet Home," all Black Hawk knew it was ten o'clock. You could set your watch by that tune as confidently as by the Round House whistle.

At last there was something to do in those long, empty summer evenings, when the married people sat like images on their front porches, and the boys and girls tramped and tramped the board sidewalks— northward to the edge of the open prairie, south to the depot, then back again to the post-office, the ice-cream parlor, the butcher shop. Now there was a place where the girls could wear their new

◀ Before the dancing pavilion came to town, what had the people of Black Hawk done on summer nights?

---

1. **spruce.** Neat in appearance, trim
2. **Bouncing Bets.** Whitish-pink flowers used for soap

words for everyday use ex • em • plar • y (ig zem′ plə rē) adj., deserving imitation, commendable. *Her willingness to be honest even when it's difficult is certainly <u>exemplary</u>.*

dresses, and where one could laugh aloud without being <u>reproved</u> by the ensuing silence. That silence seemed to ooze out of the ground, to hang under the foliage of the black maple trees with the bats and shadows. Now it was broken by light-hearted sounds. First the deep purring of Mr. Vanni's harp came in silvery ripples through the blackness of the dusty-smelling night; then the violins fell in— one of them was almost like a flute. They called so archly, so seductively, that our feet hurried toward the tent of themselves. Why hadn't we had a tent before?

Dancing became popular now, just as roller skating had been the summer before. The Progressive Euchre Club arranged with the Vannis for the exclusive use of the floor on Tuesday and Friday nights. At other times anyone could dance who paid his money and was orderly; the railroad men, the Round House mechanics, the delivery boys, the iceman, the farmhands who lived near enough to ride into town after their day's work was over.

I never missed a Saturday night dance. The tent was open until midnight then. The country boys came in from farms eight and ten miles away, and all the country girls were on the floor,—Ántonia and Lena and Tiny, and the Danish laundry girls and their friends. I was not the only boy who found these dances gayer than the others. The young men who belonged to the Progressive Euchre Club used to drop in late and risk a tiff with their sweethearts and general condemnation for a waltz with "the hired girls."

▶ For what reward were young men willing to risk their reputations?

words for everyday use

re • prove (ri prüv') vt., to scold or correct, usually gently or with kindly intent. *When the toddler continued to reach for the fragile figurines, she <u>reproved</u> him by telling him firmly "no" and asking him to go into the other room.*

Chapter 9

There was a curious social situation in Black Hawk. All the young men felt the attraction of the fine, well-set-up country girls who had come to town to earn a living, and, in nearly every case, to help the father struggle out of debt, or to make it possible for the younger children of the family to go to school.

Those girls had grown up in the first bitter-hard times, and had got little schooling themselves. But the younger brothers and sisters, for whom they made such sacrifices and who have had "advantages," never seem to me, when I meet them now, half as interesting or as well educated. The older girls, who helped to break up the wild sod, learned so much from life, from poverty, from their mothers and grandmothers; they had all, like Ántonia, been early awakened and made observant by coming at a tender age from an old country to a new. I can remember a <u>score</u> of these country girls who were in service in Black Hawk during the few years I lived there, and I can remember something unusual and engaging about each of them. Physically they were almost a race apart, and out-of-door work had given them a vigor which, when they got over their first shyness on coming to town, developed into a positive carriage and freedom of movement, and made them conspicuous among Black Hawk women.

◄ What makes the older immigrant girls more interesting than their younger siblings?

That was before the day of High-School athletics. Girls who had to walk more than half a mile to school were pitied. There was not a tennis court in the town; physical exercise was thought rather inelegant for the daughters of well-to-do families. Some of the High-School girls were jolly and pretty, but they stayed indoors in winter because of the cold, and in summer because of the heat. When one danced with them, their bodies never moved inside their clothes; their muscles seemed to ask but one thing—not to be disturbed. I remember those girls merely as faces in the schoolroom, gay and rosy, or listless and dull, cut off below the shoulders, like cherubs, by the ink-smeared tops of the high desks that were surely put there to make us round-shouldered and hollow-chested.

◄ Why are the town girls less distinctive than those from the country?

words for everyday use   **score** (skōr) n., twenty. *"Four <u>score</u> and seven years ago" means eighty-seven years ago.*

The daughters of Black Hawk merchants had a confident, uninquiring belief that they were "refined," and that the country girls, who "worked out," were not. The American farmers in our county were quite as hard-pressed as their neighbors from other countries. All alike had come to Nebraska with little capital and no knowledge of the soil they must subdue. All had borrowed money on their land. But no matter in what straits[1] the Pennsylvanian or Virginian found himself, he would not let his daughters go out into service. Unless his girls could teach a country school, they sat at home in poverty. The Bohemian and Scandinavian girls could not get positions as teachers, because they had had no opportunity to learn the language. Determined to help in the struggle to clear the homestead from debt, they had no alternative but to go into service. Some of them, after they came to town, remained as serious and as discreet in behavior as they had been when they ploughed and herded on their father's farm. Others, like the three Bohemian Marys, tried to make up for the years of youth they had lost. But every one of them did what she had set out to do, and sent home those hard-earned dollars. The girls I knew were always helping to pay for ploughs and reapers, brood-sows, or steers to fatten.

One result of this family <u>solidarity</u> was that the foreign farmers in our county were the first to become prosperous. After the fathers were out of debt, the daughters married the sons of neighbors,—usually of like nationality,— and the girls who once worked in Black Hawk kitchens are to-day managing big farms and fine families of their own; their children are better off than the children of the town women they used to serve.

I thought the attitude of the town people toward these girls very stupid. If I told my schoolmates that Lena Lingard's grandfather was a clergyman, and much respected in Norway, they looked at me blankly. What did it matter? All foreigners were ignorant people who couldn't speak English. There was not a man in Black Hawk who had the intelligence or <u>cultivation</u>, much less the personal distinction, of Ántonia's father. Yet people saw no difference

▶ How do the lives of many of the immigrant girls turn out?

---

1. **straits**. Situation of uncertainty or distress

words for everyday use

sol • i • dar • i • ty (sä lə dar′ ə tē) n., unity based on community interests, objectives, or values. *Many hospital employees expressed <u>solidarity</u> with the striking nurses by wearing buttons or refusing to work.*

cul • tiv • a • tion (kəl tə vā′ shən) n., culture, refinement. *Having studied in several different countries and paid close attention to the manners of her hosts, Sarah was known for her <u>cultivation</u>.*

between her and the three Marys; they were all Bohemians, all "hired girls."

I always knew I should live long enough to see my country girls come into their own, and I have. To-day the best that a harassed Black Hawk merchant can hope for is to sell provisions and farm machinery and automobiles to the rich farms where that first crop of stalwart Bohemian and Scandinavian girls are now the mistresses.

The Black Hawk boys looked forward to marrying Black Hawk girls, and living in a brand-new little house with best chairs that must not be sat upon, and hand-painted china that must not be used. But sometimes a young fellow would look up from his ledger, or out through the grating of his father's bank, and let his eyes follow Lena Lingard, as she passed the window with her slow, undulating walk, or Tiny Soderball, tripping by in her short skirt and striped stockings.

The country girls were considered a menace to the social order. Their beauty shone out too boldly against a conventional background. But anxious mothers need have felt no alarm. They mistook the <u>mettle</u> of their sons. The respect for respectability was stronger than any desire in Black Hawk youth.

◀ Why are the hired girls considered a menace to the town's social order?

◀ Why do the town mothers not need to worry about their sons?

Our young man of position was like the son of a royal house; the boy who swept out his office or drove his delivery wagon might frolic with the jolly country girls, but he himself must sit all evening in a plush parlor where conversation dragged so perceptibly that the father often came in and made blundering efforts to warm up the atmosphere. On his way home from his dull call, he would perhaps meet Tony and Lena, coming along the sidewalk whispering to each other, or the three Bohemian Marys in their long plush coats and caps, comporting themselves with a dignity that only made their eventful histories the more <u>piquant</u>. If he went to the hotel to see a traveling man on business, there was Tiny, arching her shoulders at him like a kitten. If he went into the laundry to get his collars, there were the four Danish girls, smiling up from their ironing-boards, with their white throats and their pink cheeks.

---

words for everyday use

met • tle (me′ təl) n., vigor or strength of spirit or temperament. *The coaches tested the team's <u>mettle</u> by making the players practice every day, including weekends, for several weeks.*

pi • quant (pē′ kənt) adj., having a lively, mischievous charm. *While some people found the behavior of the young women brash and unpleasant, those who appreciated their sense of playfulness found it <u>piquant</u>.*

The three Marys were the heroines of a cycle of scandalous stories, which the old men were fond of relating as they sat about the cigar-stand in the drugstore. Mary Dusak had been housekeeper for a bachelor rancher from Boston, and after several years in his service she was forced to retire from the world for a short time. Later she came back to town to take the place of her friend, Mary Svoboda, who was similarly embarrassed. The three Marys were considered as dangerous as high explosives to have about the kitchen, yet they were such good cooks and such admirable housekeepers that they never had to look for a place.

The Vannis' tent brought the town boys and the country girls together on neutral ground. Sylvester Lovett, who was cashier in his father's bank, always found his way to the tent on Saturday night. He took all the dances Lena Lingard would give him, and even grew bold enough to walk home with her. If his sisters or their friends happened to be among the onlookers on "popular nights," Sylvester stood back in the shadow under the cottonwood trees, smoking and watching Lena with a harassed expression. Several times I stumbled upon him there in the dark, and I felt rather sorry for him. He reminded me of Ole Benson, who used to sit on the draw-side and watch Lena herd her cattle. Later in the summer, when Lena went home for a week to visit her mother, I heard from Ántonia that young Lovett drove all the way out there to see her, and took her buggy-riding. In my <u>ingenuousness</u> I hoped that Sylvester would marry Lena, and thus give all the country girls a better position in the town.

Sylvester dallied about Lena until he began to make mistakes in his work; had to stay at the bank until after dark to make his books balance. He was daft about her, and everyone knew it. To escape from his predicament he ran away with a widow six years older than himself, who owned a half-section. This remedy worked, apparently. He never looked at Lena again, nor lifted his eyes as he ceremoniously tipped his hat when he happened to meet her on the sidewalk.

▶ What effect does Jim imagine a marriage between Lena and Sylvester would have?

▶ How did the relationship between Sylvester and Lena turn out?

---

words for everyday use

in • gen • u • ous • ness (in jen' yə wəs nəs) n., quality of innocent or childlike simplicity and candidness. *There was a kind of sweet <u>ingenuousness</u> in his belief that those around him had only good intentions.*

So that was what they were like, I thought, these white-handed, high-collared clerks and bookkeepers! I used to glare at young Lovett from a distance and only wished I had some way of showing my contempt for him.

Chapter 10

It was at the Vannis' tent that Ántonia was discovered. Hitherto she had been looked upon more as a ward of the Harlings than as one of the "hired girls." She had lived in their house and yard and garden; her thoughts never seemed to stray outside that little kingdom. But after the tent came to town she began to go about with Tiny and Lena and their friends. The Vannis often said that Ántonia was the best dancer of them all. I sometimes heard murmurs in the crowd outside the pavilion that Mrs. Harling would soon have her hands full with that girl. The young men began to joke with each other about "the Harlings' Tony" as they did about "the Marshalls' Anna" or "the Gardeners' Tiny."

Ántonia talked and thought of nothing but the tent. She hummed the dance tunes all day. When supper was late, she hurried with her dishes, dropped and smashed them in her excitement. At the first call of the music, she became irresponsible. If she hadn't time to dress, she merely flung off her apron and shot out of the kitchen door. Sometimes I went with her; the moment the lighted tent came into view she would break into a run, like a boy. There were always partners waiting for her; she began to dance before she got her breath.

▶ *What factors make a crisis inevitable at the Harlings'?*

Ántonia's success at the tent had its consequences. The iceman lingered too long now, when he came into the covered porch to fill the refrigerator. The delivery boys hung about the kitchen when they brought the groceries. Young farmers who were in town for Saturday came tramping through the yard to the back door to engage dances, or to invite Tony to parties and picnics. Lena and Norwegian Anna dropped in to help her with her work, so that she could get away early. The boys who brought her home after the dances sometimes laughed at the back gate and wakened Mr. Harling from his first sleep. A crisis was inevitable.

One Saturday night Mr. Harling had gone down to the cellar for beer. As he came up the stairs in the dark, he heard scuffling on the back porch, and then the sound of a vigorous slap. He looked out through the side door in time to see a pair of long legs vaulting over the picket fence. Ántonia was standing there, angry and excited. Young Harry Paine, who was to marry his employer's daughter on Monday, had come to the tent with a crowd of friends and danced all evening. Afterward, he begged

Ántonia to let him walk home with her. She said she supposed he was a nice young man, as he was one of Miss Frances's friends, and she didn't mind. On the back porch he tried to kiss her, and when she protested,— because he was going to be married on Monday,—he caught her and kissed her until she got one hand free and slapped him.

Mr. Harling put his beer bottles down on the table. "This is what I've been expecting, Ántonia. You've been going with girls who have a reputation for being free and easy, and now you've got the same reputation. I won't have this and that fellow tramping about my back yard all the time. This is the end of it, tonight. It stops, short. You can quit going to these dances, or you can hunt another place. Think it over."

The next morning when Mrs. Harling and Frances tried to reason with Ántonia, they found her agitated but determined. "Stop going to the tent?" she panted. "I wouldn't think of it for a minute! My own father couldn't make me stop! Mr. Harling ain't my boss outside my work. I won't give up my friends, either. The boys I go with are nice fellows. I thought Mr. Paine was all right, too, because he used to come here. I guess I gave him a red face for his wedding, all right!" she blazed out indignantly.

"You'll have to do one thing or the other, Ántonia," Mrs. Harling told her decidedly. "I can't go back on what Mr. Harling has said. This is his house."

◀ Why can't Mrs. Harling keep Ántonia in her employment?

"Then I'll just leave, Mrs. Harling. Lena's been wanting me to get a place closer to her for a long while. Mary Svoboda's going away from the Cutters' to work at the hotel, and I can have her place."

Mrs. Harling rose from her chair. "Ántonia, if you go to the Cutters' to work, you cannot come back to this house again. You know what that man is. It will be the ruin of you."

Tony snatched up the tea-kettle and began to pour boiling water over the glasses, laughing excitedly. "Oh, I can take care of myself! I'm a lot stronger than Cutter is. They pay four dollars there, and there's no children. The work's nothing; I can have every evening, and be out a lot in the afternoons."

"I thought you liked children. Tony, what's come over you?"

"I don't know, something has." Ántonia tossed her head and set her jaw. "A girl like me has got to take her good times when she can. Maybe there won't be any tent next year. I guess I want to have my fling, like the other girls."

◀ What does Ántonia suggest has come over her?

Mrs. Harling gave a short, harsh laugh. "If you go to work for the Cutters, you're likely to have a fling that you won't get up from in a hurry."

Frances said, when she told grandmother and me about this scene, that every pan and plate and cup on the shelves trembled when her mother walked out of the kitchen. Mrs. Harling declared bitterly that she wished she had never let herself get fond of Ántonia.

Chapter 11

Wick Cutter was the money-lender who had fleeced poor Russian Peter. When a farmer once got into the habit of going to Cutter, it was like gambling or the lottery; in an hour of discouragement he went back.

Cutter's first name was Wycliffe, and he liked to talk about his pious bringing-up. He contributed regularly to the Protestant churches, "for sentiment's sake," as he said with a flourish of the hand. He came from a town in Iowa where there were a great many Swedes, and could speak a little Swedish, which gave him a great advantage with the early Scandinavian settlers.

In every frontier settlement there are men who have come there to escape restraint. Cutter was one of the "fast set" of Black Hawk business men. He was an <u>inveterate</u> gambler, though a poor loser. When we saw a light burning in his office late at night, we knew that a game of poker was going on. Cutter boasted that he never drank anything stronger than sherry, and he said he got his start in life by saving the money that other young men spent for cigars. He was full of moral <u>maxims</u> for boys. When he came to our house on business, he quoted *Poor Richard's Almanack*[1] to me, and told me he was delighted to find a town boy who could milk a cow. He was particularly affable to grandmother, and whenever they met he would begin at once to talk about "the good old times" and simple living. I detested his pink, bald head, and his yellow whiskers, always soft and glistening. It was said he brushed them every night, as a woman does her hair. His white teeth looked factory-made. His skin was red and rough, as if from perpetual sunburn; he often went away to hot springs to take mud baths. He was notoriously <u>dissolute</u> with women. Two Swedish girls who had lived in his house were the worse for the experience. One of them he had taken to Omaha and established in the business for which he had fitted her. He still visited her.

◄ *What is Wick Cutter's relationship with women?*

---

1. ***Poor Richard's Almanack.*** Collection of wise sayings by Benjamin Franklin

---

words for everyday use

in • ve • ter • ate (in ve′ tə rət) adj., habitual. *An <u>inveterate</u> liar often tells the truth so infrequently that he loses track of what the truth is.*

max • im (mak′ səm) n., a saying of a proverbial nature. *Hsuan lived by the <u>maxim</u>*

"To have friends, you have to be a friend."

dis • so • lute (di sə lüt′) adj., lacking restraint, marked by indulgence in things deemed vices. *After the divorce, he became <u>dissolute</u>, often gambling and mismanaging his money.*

Cutter lived in a state of perpetual warfare with his wife, and yet, apparently, they never thought of separating. They dwelt in a fussy, scroll-work house, painted white and buried in thick evergreens, with a fussy white fence and barn. Cutter thought he knew a great deal about horses, and usually had a colt which he was training for the track. On Sunday mornings one could see him out at the fair grounds, speeding around the race-course in his trotting-buggy, wearing yellow gloves and a black-and-white-check traveling cap, his whiskers blowing back in the breeze. If there were any boys about, Cutter would offer one of them a quarter to hold the stop-watch, and then drive off, saying he had no change and would "fix it up next time." No one could cut his lawn or wash his buggy to suit him. He was so <u>fastidious</u> and prim about his place that a boy would go to a good deal of trouble to throw a dead cat into his back yard, or to dump a sackful of tin cans in his alley. It was a peculiar combination of old-maidishness and <u>licentiousness</u> that made Cutter seem so despicable.

He had certainly met his match when he married Mrs. Cutter. She was a terrifying-looking person; almost a giantess in height, raw-boned, with iron-gray hair, a face always flushed, and prominent, hysterical eyes. When she meant to be entertaining and agreeable, she nodded her head incessantly and snapped her eyes at one. Her teeth were long and curved, like a horse's; people said babies always cried if she smiled at them. Her face had a kind of fascination for me: it was the very color and shape of anger. There was a gleam of something akin to insanity in her full, intense eyes. She was formal in manner, and made calls in rustling, steel-gray brocades and a tall bonnet with bristling aigrettes.

Mrs. Cutter painted china so assiduously that even her washbowls and pitchers, and her husband's shaving-mug, were covered with violets and lilies. Once when Cutter was exhibiting some of his wife's china to a caller, he dropped a piece. Mrs. Cutter put her handkerchief to her lips as if she were going to faint and said grandly: "Mr. Cutter, you have broken all the Commandments—spare the finger-bowls!"

▶ What fascinates Jim about Mrs. Cutter's face?

words for everyday use

fas • tid • i • ous (fa sti′ dē əs) adj., showing or demanding excessive delicacy or care. *My roommate was so <u>fastidious</u> about housecleaning that she would take the trash directly out to the trash can rather than putting it in the waste basket inside.*

li • cen • tious • ness (lī sen′ shəs nəs) n., lack of legal or moral restraint, especially disregard of sexual restraint. *Because he was known for <u>licentiousness</u>, he was not allowed to be around the young women.*

They quarreled from the moment Cutter came into the house until they went to bed at night, and their hired girls reported these scenes to the town at large. Mrs. Cutter had several times cut paragraphs about unfaithful husbands out of the newspapers and mailed them to Cutter in a disguised handwriting. Cutter would come home at noon, find the mutilated journal in the paper-rack, and triumphantly fit the clipping into the space from which it had been cut. Those two could quarrel all morning about whether he ought to put on his heavy or his light underwear, and all evening about whether he had taken cold or not.

The Cutters had major as well as minor subjects for dispute. The chief of these was the question of inheritance: Mrs. Cutter told her husband it was plainly his fault they had no children. He insisted that Mrs. Cutter had purposely remained childless, with the determination to outlive him and to share his property with her "people," whom he detested. To this she would reply that unless he changed his mode of life, she would certainly outlive him. After listening to her <u>insinuations</u> about his physical soundness, Cutter would resume his dumb-bell practice for a month, or rise daily at the hour when his wife most liked to sleep, dress noisily, and drive out to the track with his trotting-horse.

Once when they had quarreled about household expenses, Mrs. Cutter put on her brocade and went among their friends soliciting orders for painted china, saying that Mr. Cutter had compelled her "to live by her brush." Cutter wasn't shamed as she had expected; he was delighted!

Cutter often threatened to chop down the cedar trees which half-buried the house. His wife declared she would leave him if she were stripped of the "privacy" which she felt these trees <u>afforded</u> her. That was his opportunity, surely; but he never cut down the trees. The Cutters seemed to find their relations to each other interesting and stimulating, and certainly the rest of us found them so. Wick Cutter was different from any other rascal I have ever known, but I have found Mrs. Cutters all over the world; sometimes founding new religions, sometimes being forcibly fed—easily recognizable, even when superficially tamed.

◀ Why, according to Jim, do the Cutters stay married?

words for everyday use

in • sin • u • a • tions (in sin yə wā′ shənz) n., something communicated by indirect means. *I'm not sure exactly what he meant, but his insinuations suggest that he thought the others were lying.*

af • ford (ə fōrd′) vt., to provide naturally or inevitably. *The lunch break afforded the students a chance to relax before the afternoon classes.*

Chapter 12

After Ántonia went to live with the Cutters, she seemed to care about nothing but picnics and parties and having a good time. When she was not going to a dance, she sewed until midnight. Her new clothes were the subject of <u>caustic</u> comment. Under Lena's direction she copied Mrs. Gardener's new party dress and Mrs. Smith's street costume so ingeniously in cheap materials that those ladies were greatly annoyed, and Mrs. Cutter, who was jealous of them, was secretly pleased.

Tony wore gloves now, and high-heeled shoes and feathered bonnets, and she went downtown nearly every afternoon with Tiny and Lena and the Marshalls' Norwegian Anna. We High-School boys used to linger on the playground at the afternoon recess to watch them as they came tripping down the hill along the board sidewalk, two and two. They were growing prettier every day, but as they passed us, I used to think with pride that Ántonia, like Snow-White in the fairy tale, was still "fairest of them all."

▶ Who, according to Jim, is the prettiest of the hired girls?

Being a Senior now, I got away from school early. Sometimes I overtook the girls downtown and coaxed them into the ice-cream parlor, where they would sit chattering and laughing, telling me all the news from the country. I remember how angry Tiny Soderball made me one afternoon. She declared she had heard grandmother was going to make a Baptist preacher of me. "I guess you'll have to stop dancing and wear a white necktie then. Won't he look funny, girls?"

Lena laughed. "You'll have to hurry up, Jim. If you're going to be a preacher, I want you to marry me. You must promise to marry us all, and then baptize the babies."

Norwegian Anna, always dignified, looked at her reprovingly.

"Baptists don't believe in christening babies, do they, Jim?"

I told her I didn't know what they believed, and didn't care, and that I certainly wasn't going to be a preacher.

"That's too bad," Tiny simpered. She was in a teasing mood. "You'd make such a good one. You're so studious.

---

words for everyday use

caus • tic (kōs′ tik) adj., marked by cutting sarcasm. *His <u>caustic</u> wit is sometimes engaging, but it can also be hurtful.*

Maybe you'd like to be a professor. You used to teach Tony, didn't you?"

Ántonia broke in. "I've set my heart on Jim being a doctor. You'd be good with sick people, Jim. Your grandmother's trained you up so nice. My papa always said you were an awful smart boy."

I said I was going to be whatever I pleased. "Won't you be surprised, Miss Tiny, if I turn out to be a regular devil of a fellow?"

They laughed until a glance from Norwegian Anna checked them; the High-School Principal had just come into the front part of the shop to buy bread for supper. Anna knew the whisper was going about that I was a sly one. People said there must be something queer about a boy who showed no interest in girls of his own age, but who could be lively enough when he was with Tony and Lena or the three Marys.

The enthusiasm for the dance, which the Vannis had kindled, did not at once die out. After the tent left town, the Euchre Club became the Owl Club, and gave dances in the Masonic Hall once a week. I was invited to join, but declined. I was moody and restless that winter, and tired of the people I saw every day. Charley Harling was already at Annapolis, while I was still sitting in Black Hawk, answering to my name at roll-call every morning, rising from my desk at the sound of a bell and marching out like the grammar-school children. Mrs. Harling was a little cool toward me, because I continued to champion Ántonia. What was there for me to do after supper? Usually I had learned next day's lessons by the time I left the school building, and I couldn't sit still and read forever.

◀ Name several reasons that Jim is moody and restless.

In the evening I used to prowl about, hunting for diversion. There lay the familiar streets, frozen with snow or liquid with mud. They led to the houses of good people who were putting the babies to bed, or simply sitting still before the parlor stove, digesting their supper. Black Hawk had two saloons. One of them was admitted, even by the church people, to be as respectable as a saloon could be. Handsome Anton Jelinek, who had rented his homestead and come to town, was the proprietor. In his saloon there were long tables where the Bohemian and German farmers could eat the lunches they brought from home while they drank their beer. Jelinek kept rye bread on hand and smoked fish and strong imported cheeses to please the foreign palate. I liked to drop into his bar-room and listen to the talk. But one day he overtook me on the street and clapped me on the shoulder.

"Jim," he said, "I am good friends with you and I always like to see you. But you know how the church people think about saloons. Your grandpa has always treated me fine, and I don't like to have you come into my place, because I know he don't like it, and it puts me in bad with him."

So I was shut out of that.

One could hang about the drug-store, and listen to the old men who sat there every evening, talking politics and telling raw stories. One could go to the cigar factory and chat with the old German who raised canaries for sale, and look at his stuffed birds. But whatever you began with him, the talk went back to taxidermy. There was the depot, of course; I often went down to see the night train come in, and afterward sat awhile with the <u>disconsolate</u> telegrapher who was always hoping to be transferred to Omaha or Denver, "where there was some life." He was sure to bring out his pictures of actresses and dancers. He got them with cigarette coupons, and nearly smoked himself to death to possess these desired forms and faces. For a change, one could talk to the station agent; but he was another <u>malcontent</u>; spent all his spare time writing letters to officials requesting a transfer. He wanted to get back to Wyoming where he could go trout-fishing on Sundays. He used to say "there was nothing in life for him but trout streams, ever since he'd lost his twins."

These were the distractions I had to choose from. There were no other lights burning downtown after nine o'clock. On starlight nights I used to pace up and down those long, cold streets, scowling at the little, sleeping houses on either side, with their storm-windows and covered back porches. They were flimsy shelters, most of them poorly built of light wood, with spindle porch-posts horribly mutilated by the turning-lathe. Yet for all their frailness, how much jealousy and envy and unhappiness some of them managed to contain! The life that went on in them seemed to me made up of evasions and negations; shifts to save cooking, to save washing and cleaning, devices to <u>propitiate</u> the tongue of gossip. This guarded mode of existence was like living under a tyranny. People's speech,

▶ What do the telegrapher and the station agent both want?

▶ How does Jim describe the life that goes on in Black Hawk houses?

words for everyday use

dis • con • so • late (dis kän' sə lət) adj., cheerless. *The players were <u>disconsolate</u> after losing the big game.*

mal • con • tent (mal kən tent') n., a discontented person. *Do you think his complaints are valid, or is he just a chronic <u>mal-*

content?

pro • pi • ti • ate (prō pi' shē āt) vt., to gain or regain the favor or goodwill of, appease. *Do you feel like you need to <u>propitiate</u> that man because he's so powerful?*

their voices, their very glances, became furtive and repressed. Every individual taste, every natural appetite, was bridled by caution. The people asleep in those houses, I thought, tried to live like the mice in their own kitchens; to make no noise, to leave no trace, to slip over the surface of things in the dark. The growing piles of ashes and cinders in the back yards were the only evidence that the wasteful, consuming process of life went on at all. On Tuesday nights the Owl Club danced; then there was a little stir in the streets, and here and there one could see a lighted window until midnight. But the next night all was dark again.

After I refused to join "the Owls," as they were called, I made a bold resolve to go to the Saturday night dances at Firemen's Hall. I knew it would be useless to acquaint my elders with any such plan. Grandfather didn't approve of dancing, anyway; he would only say that if I wanted to dance I could go to the Masonic Hall, among "the people we knew." It was just my point that I saw altogether too much of the people we knew.

◀ Why does Jim neglect to tell his grandparents that he is going to the dances at the Firemen's Hall?

My bedroom was on the ground floor, and as I studied there, I had a stove in it. I used to retire to my room early on Saturday night, change my shirt and collar and put on my Sunday coat. I waited until all was quiet and the old people were asleep, then raised my window, climbed out, and went softly through the yard. The first time I deceived my grandparents I felt rather shabby, perhaps even the second time, but I soon ceased to think about it.

The dance at the Firemen's Hall was the one thing I looked forward to all the week. There I met the same people I used to see at the Vannis' tent. Sometimes there were Bohemians from Wilber, or German boys who came down on the afternoon freight from Bismarck. Tony and Lena and Tiny were always there, and the three Bohemian Marys, and the Danish laundry girls.

The four Danish girls lived with the laundryman and his wife in their house behind the laundry, with a big garden where the clothes were hung out to dry. The laundryman was a kind, wise old fellow, who paid his girls well, looked out for them, and gave them a good home. He told me once that his own daughter died just as she was getting old enough to help her mother, and that he had been "trying to make up for it ever since." On summer afternoons he used to sit for hours on the sidewalk in front of his laundry, his newspaper lying on his knee, watching his girls through the big open window while they ironed and talked in Danish. The clouds of white dust that blew up the street, the gusts of hot wind that withered his vegetable garden, never disturbed his calm. His droll expression seemed to say that he had found the secret of contentment. Morning and evening he drove about in his spring wagon, distributing freshly ironed clothes, and collecting bags of linen that cried out for his suds and sunny drying-lines. His girls never looked so pretty at the dances as they did standing by the ironing-board, or over the tubs, washing the fine pieces, their white arms and throats bare, their cheeks bright as the brightest wild roses, their gold hair moist with the steam or the heat and curling in little damp spirals about their ears. They had not learned much English, and were not so ambitious as Tony or Lena; but they were kind, simple girls and they were always happy. When one danced with them, one smelled their clean, freshly ironed clothes that had been put away with rosemary leaves from Mr. Jensen's garden.

There were never girls enough to go round at those dances, but everyone wanted a turn with Tony and Lena. Lena moved without exertion, rather indolently, and her hand often accented the rhythm softly on her partner's shoulder. She smiled if one spoke to her, but seldom answered. The music seemed to put her into a soft, waking dream, and her violet-colored eyes looked sleepily and confidingly at one from under her long lashes. When she sighed she exhaled a heavy perfume of sachet powder. To dance "Home, Sweet Home," with Lena was like coming in with the tide. She danced every dance like a waltz, and it was always the same waltz— the waltz of coming home to something, of inevitable, fated return. After a while one got restless under it, as one does under the heat of a soft, sultry summer day.

▶ How is dancing with Tony different from dancing with Lena?

When you spun out into the floor with Tony, you didn't return to anything. You set out every time upon a new adventure. I liked to schottische with her; she had so much spring and variety, and was always putting in new steps and slides. She taught me to dance against and around the hard-and-fast beat of the music. If, instead of going to the end of the railroad, old Mr. Shimerda had stayed in New York and picked up a living with his fiddle, how different Ántonia's life might have been!

Ántonia often went to the dances with Larry Donovan, a passenger conductor who was a kind of professional ladies' man, as we said. I remember how admiringly all the boys looked at her the night she first wore her velveteen dress, made like Mrs. Gardener's black velvet. She was lovely to see, with her eyes shining, and her lips always a little parted when she danced. That constant, dark color in her cheeks never changed.

One evening when Donovan was out on his run, Ántonia came to the hall with Norwegian Anna and her young man, and that night I took her home. When we were in the Cutters' yard, sheltered by the evergreens, I told her she must kiss me good-night.

"Why, sure, Jim." A moment later she drew her face away and whispered indignantly, "Why, Jim! You know you ain't right to kiss me like that. I'll tell your grandmother on you!"

"Lena Lingard lets me kiss her," I retorted, "and I'm not half as fond of her as I am of you."

"Lena does?" Tony gasped. "If she's up to any of her nonsense with you, I'll scratch her eyes out!" She took my arm again and we walked out of the gate and up and down the sidewalk. "Now, don't you go and be a fool like some of these town boys. You're not going to sit around here and whittle store-boxes and tell stories all your life. You are going away to school and make something of yourself. I'm just awful proud of you. You won't go and get mixed up with the Swedes, will you?"

◀ What does Ántonia urge Jim to do?

"I don't care anything about any of them but you," I said. "And you'll always treat me like a kid, I suppose."

She laughed and threw her arms around me. "I expect I will, but you're a kid I'm awful fond of, anyhow! You can like me all you want to, but if I see you hanging round with Lena much, I'll go to your grandmother, as sure as your name's Jim Burden! Lena's all right, only—well, you know yourself she's soft that way. She can't help it. It's natural to her."

If she was proud of me, I was so proud of her that I carried my head high as I emerged from the dark cedars and shut the Cutters' gate softly behind me. Her warm, sweet face, her kind arms, and the true heart in her; she was, oh, she was still my Ántonia! I looked with contempt at the dark, silent little houses about me as I walked home, and thought of the stupid young men who were asleep in some of them. I knew where the real women were, though I was only a boy; and I would not be afraid of them, either!

I hated to enter the still house when I went home from the dances, and it was long before I could get to sleep. Toward morning I used to have pleasant dreams: sometimes Tony and I were out in the country, sliding down straw stacks as we used to do; climbing up the yellow mountains over and over, and slipping down the smooth sides into soft piles of chaff.

One dream I dreamed a great many times, and it was always the same. I was in a harvest-field full of shocks, and I was lying against one of them. Lena Lingard came across the stubble barefoot, in a short skirt, with a curved reaping-hook in her hand, and she was flushed like the dawn, with a kind of luminous rosiness all about her. She sat down beside me, turned to me with a soft sigh and said, "Now they are all gone, and I can kiss you as much as I like."

I used to wish I could have this flattering dream about Ántonia, but I never did.

Chapter 13

I noticed one afternoon that grandmother had been crying. Her feet seemed to drag as she moved about the house, and I got up from the table where I was studying and went to her, asking if she didn't feel well, and if I couldn't help her with her work.

"No, thank you, Jim. I'm troubled, but I guess I'm well enough. Getting a little rusty in the bones, maybe," she added bitterly.

I stood hesitating. "What are you fretting about, grandmother? Has grandfather lost any money?"

"No, it ain't money. I wish it was. But I've heard things. You must 'a' known it would come back to me sometime." She dropped into a chair, and, covering her face with her apron, began to cry. "Jim," she said, "I was never one that claimed old folks could bring up their grandchildren. But it came about so; there wasn't any other way for you, it seemed like."

I put my arms around her. I couldn't bear to see her cry.

"What is it, grandmother? Is it the Firemen's dances?" She nodded.

◀ Why is Jim's grandmother crying?

"I'm sorry I sneaked off like that. But there's nothing wrong about the dances, and I haven't done anything wrong. I like all those country girls, and I like to dance with them. That's all there is to it."

"But it ain't right to deceive us, son, and it brings blame on us. People say you are growing up to be a bad boy, and that ain't just to us."

"I don't care what they say about me, but if it hurts you, that settles it. I won't go to the Firemen's Hall again."

I kept my promise, of course, but I found the spring months dull enough. I sat at home with the old people in the evenings now, reading Latin that was not in our High-School course. I had made up my mind to do a lot of college requirement work in the summer, and to enter the freshman class at the university without conditions[1] in the fall. I wanted to get away as soon as possible.

◀ How does Jim spend spring evenings, and why?

<u>Disapprobation</u> hurt me, I found,—even that of people whom I did not admire. As the spring came on, I grew

---

1. **without conditions.** Without having to take remedial courses to make up work

---

words for everyday use

dis • ap • pro • ba • tion (di sa prə bā′ shən) n., disapproval, condemnation. *By failing to follow through on her campaign promises, the mayor earned the <u>disapprobation</u> of the city.*

more and more lonely, and fell back on the telegrapher and the cigar-maker and his canaries for companionship. I remember I took a melancholy pleasure in hanging a May-basket for Nina Harling that spring. I bought the flowers from an old German woman who always had more window plants than anyone else, and spent an afternoon trimming a little work-basket. When dusk came on, and the new moon hung in the sky, I went quietly to the Harlings' front door with my offering, rang the bell, and then ran away as was the custom. Through the willow hedge I could hear Nina's cries of delight, and I felt comforted.

On those warm, soft spring evenings I often lingered downtown to walk home with Frances, and talked to her about my plans and about the reading I was doing. One evening she said she thought Mrs. Harling was not seriously offended with me.

"Mama is as broad-minded as mothers ever are, I guess. But you know she was hurt about Ántonia, and she can't understand why you like to be with Tiny and Lena better than with the girls of your own set."

"Can you?" I asked bluntly.

Frances laughed. "Yes, I think I can. You knew them in the country, and you like to take sides. In some ways you're older than boys of your age. It will be all right with mama after you pass your college examinations and she sees you're in earnest."

"If you were a boy," I persisted, "you wouldn't belong to the Owl Club, either. You'd be just like me."

She shook her head. "I would and I wouldn't. I expect I know the country girls better than you do. You always put a kind of glamor over them. The trouble with you, Jim, is that you're romantic. Mama's going to your Commencement. She asked me the other day if I knew what your oration is to be about. She wants you to do well."

I thought my oration very good. It stated with fervor a great many things I had lately discovered. Mrs. Harling came to the Opera House to hear the Commencement exercises, and I looked at her most of the time while I made my speech. Her keen, intelligent eyes never left my face. Afterward she came back to the dressing-room where we stood, with our diplomas in our hands, walked up to me, and said heartily: "You surprised me, Jim. I didn't believe you could do as well as that. You didn't get that speech out of books." Among my graduation presents there was a silk umbrella from Mrs. Harling, with my name on the handle.

▶ What observation does Frances make about Jim's character?

I walked home from the Opera House alone. As I passed the Methodist Church, I saw three white figures ahead of me, pacing up and down under the arching maple trees, where the moonlight filtered through the lush June foliage. They hurried toward me; they were waiting for me—Lena and Tony and Anna Hansen.

"Oh, Jim, it was splendid!" Tony was breathing hard, as she always did when her feelings outran her language. "There ain't a lawyer in Black Hawk could make a speech like that. I just stopped your grandpa and said so to him. He won't tell you, but he told us he was awful surprised himself, didn't he, girls?"

Lena sidled up to me and said teasingly: "What made you so solemn? I thought you were scared. I was sure you'd forget."

Anna spoke wistfully. "It must make you very happy, Jim, to have fine thoughts like that in your mind all the time, and to have words to put them in. I always wanted to go to school, you know."

"Oh, I just sat there and wished my papa could hear you! Jim"—Ántonia took hold of my coat lapels,—"there was something in your speech that made me think so about my papa!"

"I thought about your papa when I wrote my speech, Tony," I said. "I dedicated it to him."

◀ To whom does Jim dedicate his graduation speech?

She threw her arms around me, and her dear face was all wet with tears.

I stood watching their white dresses glimmer smaller and smaller down the sidewalk as they went away. I have had no other success that pulled at my heartstrings like that one.

Chapter 14

The day after commencement I moved my books and desk upstairs, to an empty room where I should be undisturbed, and I fell to studying in earnest. I worked off a year's trigonometry that summer, and began Virgil alone. Morning after morning I used to pace up and down my sunny little room, looking off at the distant river bluffs and the roll of the blond pastures between, scanning the *Æneid*[1] aloud and committing long passages to memory. Sometimes in the evening Mrs. Harling called to me as I passed her gate, and asked me to come in and let her play for me. She was lonely for Charley, she said, and liked to have a boy about. Whenever my grandparents had misgivings, and began to wonder whether I was not too young to go off to college alone, Mrs. Harling took up my cause vigorously. Grandfather had such respect for her judgment that I knew he would not go against her.

I had only one holiday that summer. It was in July. I met Ántonia downtown on Saturday afternoon, and learned that she and Tiny and Lena were going to the river next day with Anna Hansen—the elder was all in bloom now, and Anna wanted to make elder-blow wine.

"Anna's to drive us down in the Marshalls' delivery wagon, and we'll take a nice lunch and have a picnic. Just us; nobody else. Couldn't you happen along, Jim? It would be like old times."

I considered a moment. "Maybe I can, if I won't be in the way."

On Sunday morning I rose early and got out of Black Hawk while the dew was still heavy on the long meadow grasses. It was the high season for summer flowers. The pink bee-bush stood tall along the sandy roadsides, and the cone-flowers and rose mallow grew everywhere. Across the wire fence, in the long grass, I saw a clump of flaming orange-colored milkweed, rare in that part of the state. I left the road and went around through a stretch of pasture that was always cropped short in summer, where the gaillardia came up year after year and matted over the ground with the deep, velvety red that is in Bokhara carpets. The country was empty and solitary except for the larks that Sunday morning, and it seemed to lift itself up to me and to come very close.

---

1. *Æneid.* A long, epic poem written in Latin by the famous Roman poet Virgil, 70-19 BC

The river was running strong for midsummer; heavy rains to the west of us had kept it full. I crossed the bridge and went upstream along the wooded shore to a pleasant dressing-room I knew among the dogwood bushes, all overgrown with wild grapevines. I began to undress for a swim. The girls would not be along yet. For the first time it occurred to me that I should be homesick for that river after I left it. The sandbars, with their clean white beaches and their little groves of willows and cottonwood seedlings, were a sort of No Man's Land, little newly-created worlds that belonged to the Black Hawk boys. Charley Harling and I had hunted through these woods, fished from the fallen logs, until I knew every inch of the river shores and had a friendly feeling for every bar and shallow.

◀ What occurs to Jim as he gets ready to swim?

After my swim, while I was playing about indolently in the water, I heard the sound of hoofs and wheels on the bridge. I struck downstream and shouted, as the open spring wagon came into view on the middle span. They stopped the horse, and the two girls in the bottom of the cart stood up, steadying themselves by the shoulders of the two in front, so that they could see me better. They were charming up there, huddled together in the cart and peering down at me like curious deer when they come out of the thicket to drink. I found bottom near the bridge and stood up, waving to them.

"How pretty you look!" I called.

"So do you!" they shouted altogether, and broke into peals of laughter. Anna Hansen shook the reins and they drove on, while I zigzagged back to my inlet and clambered up behind an overhanging elm. I dried myself in the sun, and dressed slowly, reluctant to leave that green enclosure where the sunlight flickered so bright through the grapevine leaves and the woodpecker hammered away in the crooked elm that trailed out over the water. As I went along the road back to the bridge, I kept picking off little pieces of scaly chalk from the dried water gullies, and breaking them up in my hands.

When I came upon the Marshalls' delivery horse, tied in the shade, the girls had already taken their baskets and gone down the east road which wound through the sand and scrub. I could hear them calling to each other. The elder bushes did not grow back in the shady ravines between the bluffs, but in the hot, sandy bottoms along the stream, where their roots were always in moisture and their tops in the sun. The blossoms were unusually <u>luxuriant</u> and beautiful that summer.

I followed a cattle path through the thick underbrush until I came to a slope that fell away abruptly to the water's edge. A great chunk of the shore had been bitten out by some spring freshet, and the scar was masked by elder bushes, growing down to the water in flowery terraces. I did not touch them. I was overcome by content and drowsiness and by the warm silence about me. There was no sound but the high, sing-song buzz of wild bees and the sunny gurgle of the water underneath. I peeped over the edge of the bank to see the little stream that made the noise; it flowed along perfectly clear over the sand and gravel, cut off from the muddy main current by a long sandbar. Down there, on the lower shelf of the bank, I saw Ántonia, seated alone under the pagoda-like elders. She looked up when she heard me, and smiled, but I saw that she had been crying. I slid down into the soft sand beside her and asked her what was the matter.

▶ *For what is Ántonia homesick?*

"It makes me homesick, Jimmy, this flower, this smell," she said softly. "We have this flower very much at home, in the old country. It always grew in our yard and my papa had a green bench and a table under the bushes. In summer, when they were in bloom, he used to sit there with his friend that played the trombone. When I was little I used to go down there to hear them talk— beautiful talk, like what I never hear in this country."

"What did they talk about?" I asked her.

She sighed and shook her head. "Oh, I don't know! About music, and the woods, and about God, and when they were young." She turned to me suddenly and looked into my eyes. "You think, Jimmy, that maybe my father's spirit can go back to those old places?"

I told her about the feeling of her father's presence I had on that winter day when my grandparents had gone over to see his dead body and I was left alone in the house. I said I felt sure then that he was on his way back to his own country, and that even now, when I passed his grave, I always thought of him as being among the woods and fields that were so dear to him.

words for everyday use

lux • ur • i • ant (ləg zhür′ ē ənt) adj., characterized by abundant growth, lush. *Many animals found shelter among the plants in the <u>luxuriant</u> forest.*

Ántonia had the most trusting, responsive eyes in the world; love and <u>credulousness</u> seemed to look out of them with open faces. "Why didn't you ever tell me that before? It makes me feel more sure for him." After a while she said: "You know, Jim, my father was different from my mother. He did not have to marry my mother, and all his brothers quarreled with him because he did. I used to hear the old people at home whisper about it. They said he could have paid my mother money, and not married her. But he was older than she was, and he was too kind to treat her like that. He lived in his mother's house, and she was a poor girl come in to do the work. After my father married her, my grandmother never let my mother come into her house again. When I went to my grandmother's funeral was the only time I was ever in my grandmother's house. Don't that seem strange?"

◀ How was Ántonia's father different from her mother?

While she talked, I lay back in the hot sand and looked up at the blue sky between the flat bouquets of elder. I could hear the bees humming and singing, but they stayed up in the sun above the flowers and did not come down into the shadow of the leaves. Ántonia seemed to me that day exactly like the little girl who used to come to our house with Mr. Shimerda.

"Some day, Tony, I am going over to your country, and I am going to the little town where you lived. Do you remember all about it?"

◀ What promise does Jim make to Ántonia?

"Jim," she said earnestly, "if I was put down there in the middle of the night, I could find my way all over that little town; and along the river to the next town, where my grandmother lived. My feet remember all the little paths through the woods, and where the big roots stick out to trip you. I ain't never forgot my own country."

There was a crackling in the branches above us, and Lena Lingard peered down over the edge of the bank.

"You lazy things!" she cried. "All this elder, and you two lying there! Didn't you hear us calling you?" Almost as flushed as she had been in my dream, she leaned over the edge of the bank and began to demolish our flowery pagoda. I had never seen her so energetic; she was panting with zeal, and the perspiration stood in drops on her

---

words for everyday use

cred • u • lous • ness (kre′ jə ləs nəs) n., readiness to believe, even on slight or uncertain evidence. *Some dishonest people will take advantage of the <u>credulousness</u> of the elderly by pretending that they are calling to award them a prize.*

short, yielding upper lip. I sprang to my feet and ran up the bank.

It was noon now, and so hot that the dogwoods and scrub-oaks began to turn up the silvery under-side of their leaves, and all the foliage looked soft and wilted. I carried the lunch-basket to the top of one of the chalk bluffs, where even on the calmest days there was always a breeze. The flat-topped, twisted little oaks threw light shadows on the grass. Below us we could see the windings of the river, and Black Hawk, grouped among its trees, and, beyond, the rolling country, swelling gently until it met the sky. We could recognize familiar farm-houses and windmills. Each of the girls pointed out to me the direction in which her father's farm lay, and told me how many acres were in wheat that year and how many in corn.

"My old folks," said Tiny Soderball, "have put in twenty acres of rye. They get it ground at the mill, and it makes nice bread. It seems like my mother ain't been so home-sick, ever since father's raised rye flour for her."

▶ What does Lena point out about the lives of their mothers?

"It must have been a trial for our mothers," said Lena, "coming out here and having to do everything different. My mother had always lived in town. She says she started behind in farm-work, and never has caught up."

"Yes, a new country's hard on the old ones, sometimes," said Anna thoughtfully. "My grandmother's getting feeble now, and her mind wanders. She's forgot about this country, and thinks she's at home in Norway. She keeps asking mother to take her down to the waterside and the fish market. She craves fish all the time. Whenever I go home I take her canned salmon and mackerel."

"Mercy, it's hot!" Lena yawned. She was supine under a little oak, resting after the fury of her elder-hunting, and had taken off the high-heeled slippers she had been silly enough to wear. "Come here, Jim. You never got the sand out of your hair." She began to draw her fingers slowly through my hair.

Ántonia pushed her away. "You'll never get it out like that," she said sharply. She gave my head a rough touzling and finished me off with something like a box on the ear. "Lena, you oughtn't to try to wear those slippers any more. They're too small for your feet. You'd better give them to me for Yulka."

"All right," said Lena good-naturedly, tucking her white stockings under her skirt. "You get all Yulka's things, don't you? I wish father didn't have such bad luck with his farm machinery; then I could buy more things for my sisters.

I'm going to get Mary a new coat this fall, if the sulky plough's[2] never paid for!"

Tiny asked her why she didn't wait until after Christmas, when coats would be cheaper. "What do you think of poor me?" she added; "with six at home, younger than I am? And they all think I'm rich, because when I go back to the country I'm dressed so fine!" She shrugged her shoulders. "But, you know, my weakness is playthings. I like to buy them playthings better than what they need."

"I know how that is," said Anna. "When we first came here, and I was little, we were too poor to buy toys. I never got over the loss of a doll somebody gave me before we left Norway. A boy on the boat broke her and I still hate him for it."

"I guess after you got here you had plenty of live dolls to nurse, like me!" Lena remarked cynically.

"Yes, the babies came along pretty fast, to be sure. But I never minded. I was fond of them all. The youngest one, that we didn't any of us want, is the one we love best now."

Lena sighed. "Oh, the babies are all right; if only they don't come in winter. Ours nearly always did. I don't see how mother stood it. I tell you what, girls," she sat up with sudden energy; "I'm going to get my mother out of that old sod house where she's lived so many years. The men will never do it. Johnnie, that's my oldest brother, he's wanting to get married now, and build a house for his girl instead of his mother. Mrs. Thomas says she thinks I can move to some other town pretty soon, and go into business for myself. If I don't get into business, I'll maybe marry a rich gambler."

◄ What ambition does Lena express?

"That would be a poor way to get on," said Anna sarcastically. "I wish I could teach school, like Selma Kronn. Just think! She'll be the first Scandinavian girl to get a position in the High School. We ought to be proud of her."

Selma was a studious girl, who had not much tolerance for giddy things like Tiny and Lena; but they always spoke of her with admiration.

Tiny moved about restlessly, fanning herself with her straw hat. "If I was smart like her, I'd be at my books day and night. But she was born smart—and look how her father's trained her! He was something high up in the old country."

---

2. **sulky plough.** Plow outfitted with wheels and designed to be ridden and pulled by horses

"So was my mother's father," murmured Lena, "but that's all the good it does us! My father's father was smart, too, but he was wild. He married a Lapp. I guess that's what's the matter with me; they say Lapp blood will out."

"A real Lapp, Lena?" I exclaimed. "The kind that wear skins?"

"I don't know if she wore skins, but she was a Lapp all right, and his folks felt dreadful about it. He was sent up north on some Government job he had, and fell in with her. He would marry her."

"But I thought Lapland women were fat and ugly, and had squint eyes, like Chinese?" I objected.

"I don't know, maybe. There must be something mighty taking about the Lapp girls, though; mother says the Norwegians up north are always afraid their boys will run after them."

In the afternoon, when the heat was less oppressive, we had a lively game of "Pussy Wants a Corner," on the flat bluff-top, with the little trees for bases. Lena was Pussy so often that she finally said she wouldn't play any more. We threw ourselves down on the grass, out of breath.

▶ What story does Ántonia want Jim to tell the other girls?

"Jim," Ántonia said dreamily, "I want you to tell the girls about how the Spanish first came here, like you and Charley Harling used to talk about. I've tried to tell them, but I leave out so much."

They sat under a little oak, Tony resting against the trunk and the other girls leaning against her and each other, and listened to the little I was able to tell them about Coronado[3] and his search for the Seven Golden Cities. At school we were taught that he had not got so far north as Nebraska, but had given up his quest and turned back somewhere in Kansas. But Charley Harling and I had a strong belief that he had been along this very river. A farmer in the county north of ours, when he was breaking sod, had turned up a metal stirrup of fine workmanship, and a sword with a Spanish inscription on the blade. He lent these relics to Mr. Harling, who brought them home with him. Charley and I scoured them, and they were on exhibition in the Harling office all summer. Father Kelly, the priest, had found the name of the Spanish maker on the sword and an abbreviation that stood for the city of Cordova.

---

3. **Coronado.** Spanish explorer (1510–1554) who came as far north as Kansas in his futile search for the rumored Seven Cities of Gold. Cornado is credited with discovering the territories that now make up New Mexico, Texas, Oklahoma, and Kansas.

"And that I saw with my own eyes," Ántonia put in triumphantly. "So Jim and Charley were right, and the teachers were wrong!"

The girls began to wonder among themselves. Why had the Spaniards come so far? What must this country have been like, then? Why had Coronado never gone back to Spain, to his riches and his castles and his king? I couldn't tell them. I only knew the schoolbooks said he "died in the wilderness, of a broken heart."

"More than him has done that," said Ántonia sadly, and the girls murmured assent.

◀ What does Ántonia say about "dying of a broken heart"?

We sat looking off across the country, watching the sun go down. The curly grass about us was on fire now. The bark of the oaks turned red as copper. There was a shimmer of gold on the brown river. Out in the stream the sandbars glittered like glass, and the light trembled in the willow thickets as if little flames were leaping among them. The breeze sank to stillness. In the ravine a ringdove mourned plaintively, and somewhere off in the bushes an owl hooted. The girls sat listless, leaning against each other. The long fingers of the sun touched their foreheads.

Presently we saw a curious thing: There were no clouds, the sun was going down in a <u>limpid</u>, gold-washed sky. Just as the lower edge of the red disk rested on the high fields against the horizon, a great black figure suddenly appeared on the face of the sun. We sprang to our feet, straining our eyes toward it. In a moment we realized what it was. On some upland farm, a plough had been left standing in the field. The sun was sinking just behind it. Magnified across the distance by the horizontal light, it stood out against the sun, was exactly contained within the circle of the disk; the handles, the tongue, the share—black against the molten red. There it was, heroic in size, a picture writing on the sun.

◀ What curious thing do they see as the sun is setting?

Even while we whispered about it, our vision disappeared; the ball dropped and dropped until the red tip went beneath the earth. The fields below us were dark, the sky was growing pale, and that forgotten plough had sunk back to its own littleness somewhere on the prairie.

words for everyday use
lim • pid (lim' pəd) adj., absolutely serene and untroubled. *The father loved watching the <u>limpid</u> faces of his children when they were sleeping.*

Chapter 15

Late in August the Cutters went to Omaha for a few days, leaving Ántonia in charge of the house. Since the scandal about the Swedish girl, Wick Cutter could never get his wife to stir out of Black Hawk without him.

The day after the Cutters left, Ántonia came over to see us. Grandmother noticed that she seemed troubled and distracted. "You've got something on your mind, Ántonia," she said anxiously.

"Yes, Mrs. Burden. I couldn't sleep much last night." She hesitated, and then told us how strangely Mr. Cutter had behaved before he went away. He put all the silver in a basket and placed it under her bed, and with it a box of papers which he told her were valuable. He made her promise that she would not sleep away from the house, or be out late in the evening, while he was gone. He strictly forbade her to ask any of the girls she knew to stay with her at night. She would be perfectly safe, he said, as he had just put a new Yale lock on the front door.

Cutter had been so insistent in regard to these details that now she felt uncomfortable about staying there alone. She hadn't liked the way he kept coming into the kitchen to instruct her, or the way he looked at her. "I feel as if he is up to some of his tricks again, and is going to try to scare me, somehow."

Grandmother was apprehensive at once. "I don't think it's right for you to stay there, feeling that way. I suppose it wouldn't be right for you to leave the place alone, either, after giving your word. Maybe Jim would be willing to go over there and sleep, and you could come here nights. I'd feel safer, knowing you were under my own roof. I guess Jim could take care of their silver and old usury notes as well as you could."

Ántonia turned to me eagerly. "Oh, would you, Jim? I'd make up my bed nice and fresh for you. It's a real cool room, and the bed's right next the window. I was afraid to leave the window open last night."

I liked my own room, and I didn't like the Cutters' house under any circumstances; but Tony looked so troubled that I consented to try this arrangement. I found that I slept there as well as anywhere, and when I got home in the morning, Tony had a good breakfast waiting for me. After prayers she sat down at the table with us, and it was like old times in the country.

The third night I spent at the Cutters', I awoke suddenly with the impression that I had heard a door open and shut.

▶ What promises does Mr. Cutter ask Ántonia to make before he leaves for his trip?

▶ How do these arrangements make Ántonia feel?

▶ What solution does Mrs. Burden suggest?

Everything was still, however, and I must have gone to sleep again immediately.

The next thing I knew, I felt someone sit down on the edge of the bed. I was only half awake, but I decided that he might take the Cutters' silver, whoever he was. Perhaps if I did not move, he would find it and get out without troubling me. I held my breath and lay absolutely still. A hand closed softly on my shoulder, and at the same moment I felt something hairy and cologne-scented brushing my face. If the room had suddenly been flooded with electric light, I couldn't have seen more clearly the detestable bearded countenance that I knew was bending over me. I caught a handful of whiskers and pulled, shouting something. The hand that held my shoulder was instantly at my throat. The man became insane; he stood over me, choking me with one fist and beating me in the face with the other, hissing and chuckling and letting out a flood of abuse.

◀ Who has come into Ántonia's room?

"So this is what she's up to when I'm away, is it? Where is she, you nasty whelp, where is she? Under the bed, are you, hussy? I know your tricks! Wait till I get at you! I'll fix this rat you've got in here. He's caught, all right!"

So long as Cutter had me by the throat, there was no chance for me at all. I got hold of his thumb and bent it back, until he let go with a yell. In a bound, I was on my feet, and easily sent him sprawling to the floor. Then I made a dive for the open window, struck the wire screen, knocked it out, and tumbled after it into the yard.

Suddenly I found myself running across the north end of Black Hawk in my nightshirt, just as one sometimes finds one's self behaving in bad dreams. When I got home, I climbed in at the kitchen window. I was covered with blood from my nose and lip, but I was too sick to do anything about it. I found a shawl and an overcoat on the hatrack, lay down on the parlor sofa, and in spite of my hurts, went to sleep.

Grandmother found me there in the morning. Her cry of fright awakened me. Truly, I was a battered object. As she helped me to my room, I caught a glimpse of myself in the mirror. My lip was cut and stood out like a snout. My nose looked like a big blue plum, and one eye was swollen shut and hideously discolored. Grandmother said we must have the doctor at once, but I <u>implored</u> her, as I had never begged for anything before, not to send for him. I could stand anything, I told her, so long as nobody saw me or knew what had happened to me. I entreated her not to let grandfather, even, come into my room. She seemed to understand, though I was too faint and miserable to go into explanations. When she took off my nightshirt, she found such bruises on my chest and shoulders that she began to cry. She spent the whole morning bathing and poulticing me, and rubbing me with arnica. I heard Ántonia sobbing outside my door, but I asked grandmother to send her away. I felt that I never wanted to see her again. I hated her almost as much as I hated Cutter. She had let me in for all this disgustingness. Grandmother kept saying how thankful we ought to be that I had been there instead of Ántonia. But I lay with my disfigured face to the wall and felt no particular gratitude. My one concern was that grandmother should keep every one away from me. If the story once got abroad, I would never hear the last of it. I could well imagine what the old men down at the drug-store would do with such a theme.

▶ How does Jim feel about Ántonia after the ordeal at the Cutters'?

While grandmother was trying to make me comfortable, grandfather went to the depot and learned that Wick Cutter had come home on the night express from the east, and had left again on the six o'clock train for Denver that morning. The agent said his face was striped with court-plaster, and he carried his left hand in a sling. He looked so used up, that the agent asked him what had happened to him since ten o'clock the night before; whereat Cutter began to swear at him and said he would have him discharged for <u>incivility</u>.

That afternoon, while I was asleep, Ántonia took grandmother with her, and went over to the Cutters' to pack her trunk. They found the place locked up, and they had to break the window to get into Ántonia's bedroom. There everything was in shocking disorder. Her clothes had been taken out of her closet, thrown into the middle of the room, and trampled and torn. My own garments had been treated so badly that I never saw them again; grandmother burned them in the Cutters' kitchen range.

While Ántonia was packing her trunk and putting her room in order, to leave it, the front doorbell rang violently.

words for everyday use

in • ci • vil • i • ty (in sə vi' lə tē) n., rudeness, lack of courtesy. *Your absolute lack of interest in our guests borders on <u>incivility</u>.*

There stood Mrs. Cutter,— locked out, for she had no key to the new lock—her head trembling with rage. "I advised her to control herself, or she would have a stroke," grandmother said afterwards.

Grandmother would not let her see Ántonia at all, but made her sit down in the parlor while she related to her just what had occurred the night before. Ántonia was frightened, and was going home to stay for a while, she told Mrs. Cutter; it would be useless to interrogate the girl, for she knew nothing of what had happened.

Then Mrs. Cutter told her story. She and her husband had started home from Omaha together the morning before. They had to stop over several hours at Waymore Junction to catch the Black Hawk train. During the wait, Cutter left her at the depot and went to the Waymore bank to attend to some business. When he returned, he told her that he would have to stay overnight there, but she could go on home. He bought her ticket and put her on the train. She saw him slip a twenty-dollar bill into her handbag with her ticket. That bill, she said, should have aroused her suspicions at once—but did not.

The trains are never called at little junction towns; everybody knows when they come in. Mr. Cutter showed his wife's ticket to the conductor, and settled her in her seat before the train moved off. It was not until nearly nightfall that she discovered she was on the express bound for Kansas City, that her ticket was made out to that point, and that Cutter must have planned it so. The conductor told her the Black Hawk train was due at Waymore twelve minutes after the Kansas City train left. She saw at once that her husband had played this trick in order to get back to Black Hawk without her. She had no choice but to go on to Kansas City and take the first fast train for home.

◀ What trick did Mr. Cutter play on Mrs. Cutter, and why?

Cutter could have got home a day earlier than his wife by any one of a dozen simpler devices; he could have left her in the Omaha hotel, and said he was going on to Chicago for a few days. But apparently it was part of his fun to outrage her feelings as much as possible.

◀ Why, according to Jim, didn't Mr. Cutter keep Mrs. Cutter away in some easier way?

"Mr. Cutter will pay for this, Mrs. Burden. He will pay!" Mrs. Cutter avouched, nodding her horselike head and rolling her eyes.

---

words for everyday use

a • vouch (ə vauch') vt., to declare as a matter of fact, affirm. *Can you avouch that your brother was home with you last Saturday night?*

Grandmother said she hadn't a doubt of it.

Certainly Cutter liked to have his wife think him a devil. In some way he depended upon the excitement he could arouse in her hysterical nature. Perhaps he got the feeling of being a <u>rake</u> more from his wife's rage and amazement than from any experiences of his own. His zest in debauchery might wane, but never Mrs. Cutter's belief in it. The reckoning with his wife at the end of an escapade was something he counted on—like the last powerful liqueur after a long dinner. The one excitement he really couldn't do without was quarreling with Mrs. Cutter!

words for everyday use

rake (rāk) n., a person who is unrestrained by morality or convention. *Would you consider Hank a <u>rake</u> or just a free spirit?*

Respond to the Selection

What do you think of the people of Black Hawk? Would you want to live there? Why, or why not?

Investigate, Inquire, and Imagine

Recall: GATHERING FACTS

1a. Who are the "hired girls"? Name several places the hired girls work. What happens the night Mrs. Gardener, the hotel owner, is out of town and d'Arnault is in town?

2a. The summer the Vannis come to town is described as the "summer that changed everything." Who are the Vannis, and what activity did they bring to Black Hawk?

3a. To whom does Jim dedicate his graduation speech?

4a. After their picnic, what do Jim, Ántonia, and the other "hired girls" see outlined against the setting sun? How does the image change as the sun continues to set?

5a. What happens to Jim when he is staying at Wick Cutter's house?

Interpret: FINDING MEANING

➤ 1b. How do the hired girls feel about moving into town to work? How does Tiny's place of employment open up new worlds to Jim and the hired girls? Why do you think this world is so appealing to them? What rules are broken when Mrs. Gardener is out of town? Why are Jim and Ántonia so excited after they leave the hotel?

➤ 2b. How does this activity "change everything"? What relationship between the town boys and the hired girls is illustrated by this activity?

➤ 3b. Why did he dedicate his speech to this person?

➤ 4b. With what do Jim and the girls associate this object? How does it make them feel? What is significant about how it changes?

➤ 5b. Why is Jim so angry with Ántonia after this incident?

Analyze: TAKING THINGS APART

6a. When the Burdens move into town, Jim says, "I was quite another boy, or thought I was." Compare and contrast the boy he was with the boy he has become in town. What does he learn from the other boys? How does he feel about Black Hawk? What does he love about the area? What qualities of the town make him restless? How do his feelings now compare to those he had for the prairie when he first arrived? What has Jim gained as he has grown up, and what has he lost?

Synthesize: BRINGING THINGS TOGETHER

➤ 6b. In book 1, Jim and Ántonia defied gender roles in several ways. Do they continue to break the rules in this book? Give evidence for your answer, and explain why you think this happens.

Evaluate: MAKING JUDGMENTS

7a. Cather was writing at a time when stereotypes about African Americans and others of different races went largely unquestioned. Examine the description of Samson d'Arnault on pages 119–123. What stereotypes can you discern in the description of his life and work?

Extend: CONNECTING IDEAS

➤ 7b. Retell the story of Samson's childhood encounter with the piano from his perspective. How do you think his childhood was like Jim's or Ántonia's? How was it different?

Understanding Literature

Simile. A **simile** is a type of metaphor using *like* or *as*. A **metaphor** is a figure of speech in which one thing is spoken or written about as if it were another. Metaphors, and more specifically similes, invite the reader to make a comparison between the two things. Cather uses a simile to describe the sound of the thunder over the prairie: "The thunder was loud and metallic, like the rattle of sheet iron…" Similes, like all metaphors, consist of two parts, the *tenor*, or the writer's actual subject, and the *vehicle*, or the thing to which the actual subject is likened. In the example above, the tenor is "the thunder," and the vehicle is "the rattle of sheet metal." Copy the chart below on your own paper. Then, in the first column, copy three additional similes from the first two books of *My Ántonia*. Finally, in the second and third columns, identify the tenor and the vehicle of each simile.

Simile	Tenor	Vehicle
The thunder was loud and metallic, like the rattle of sheet iron...	thunder	rattle of sheet iron

Personification. Personification is a figure of speech in which an idea, animal, or thing is described as if it were a person. Willa Cather personifies many elements of nature in *My Ántonia*. For example, the sun is personified on page 157: "The long fingers of the sun touched their foreheads." What does this image suggest about the nature of the sun? Find at least one other example of personification in books 1 or 2 of *My Ántonia*. What does your example suggest about the narrator's view of life on the prairie?

Subplot. A **subplot** is a subordinate story told in addition to the major story in a work of fiction. Often a subplot mirrors or contrasts with the primary plot. *My Ántonia* contains many subplots, including the story Ántonia tells about the man who threw himself into the threshing machine. What does this story have to do with the larger plot of the novel? What other subplots or mini-stories can you identify from books 1 and 2? What does each add to the novel?

BOOK III

Lena Lingard

Chapter 1

At the university I had the good fortune to come immediately under the influence of a brilliant and inspiring young scholar. Gaston Cleric had arrived in Lincoln only a few weeks earlier than I, to begin his work as head of the Latin Department. He came West at the suggestion of his physicians, his health having been <u>enfeebled</u> by a long illness in Italy. When I took my entrance examinations he was my examiner, and my course was arranged under his supervision.

I did not go home for my first summer vacation, but stayed in Lincoln, working off a year's Greek, which had been my only condition on entering the Freshman class. Cleric's doctor advised against his going back to New England, and except for a few weeks in Colorado, he, too, was in Lincoln all that summer. We played tennis, read, and took long walks together. I shall always look back on that time of mental awakening as one of the happiest in my life. Gaston Cleric introduced me to the world of ideas; when one first enters that world everything else fades for a time, and all that went before is as if it had not been. Yet I found curious survivals; some of the figures of my old life seemed to be waiting for me in the new.

In those days there were many serious young men among the students who had come up to the University from the farms and the little towns scattered over the thinly settled state. Some of those boys came straight from the cornfields with only a summer's wages in their pockets, hung on through the four years, shabby and underfed, and completed the course by really heroic self-sacrifice. Our instructors were oddly assorted; wandering pioneer schoolteachers, stranded ministers of the Gospel, a few enthusiastic young men just out of graduate schools. There was an atmosphere of endeavor, of expectancy and bright hopefulness about the young college that had lifted its head from the prairie only a few years before.

◄ What words does Jim use to describe the atmosphere of the University of Nebraska?

Our personal life was as free as that of our instructors. There were no college dormitories; we lived where we could and as we could. I took rooms with an old couple, early settlers in Lincoln, who had married off their children and now lived quietly in their house at the edge of

---

words for everyday use   en • feeb • led (in fē′ bəld) adj., deprived of strength, weakened. *The old woman was* <u>*enfeebled*</u> *by age as much as by illness.*

town, near the open country. The house was inconveniently situated for students, and on that account I got two rooms for the price of one. My bedroom, originally a linen closet, was unheated and was barely large enough to contain my cot bed, but it enabled me to call the other room my study. The dresser, and the great walnut wardrobe which held all my clothes, even my hats and shoes, I had pushed out of the way, and I considered them non-existent, as children eliminate <u>incongruous</u> objects when they are playing house. I worked at a <u>commodious</u> green-topped table placed directly in front of the west window which looked out over the prairie. In the corner at my right were all my books, in shelves I had made and painted myself. On the blank wall at my left the dark, old-fashioned wall-paper was covered by a large map of ancient Rome, the work of some German scholar. Cleric had ordered it for me when he was sending for books from abroad. Over the bookcase hung a photograph of the Tragic Theater at Pompeii, which he had given me from his collection.

When I sat at work I half faced a deep, upholstered chair which stood at the end of my table, its high back against the wall. I had bought it with great care. My instructor sometimes looked in upon me when he was out for an evening tramp, and I noticed that he was more likely to linger and become talkative if I had a comfortable chair for him to sit in, and if he found a bottle of Bénédictine and plenty of the kind of cigarettes he liked, at his elbow. He was, I had discovered, <u>parsimonious</u> about small expenditures— a trait absolutely inconsistent with his general character. Sometimes when he came he was silent and moody, and after a few sarcastic remarks went away again, to tramp the streets of Lincoln, which were almost as quiet and oppressively domestic as those of Black Hawk. Again, he would sit until nearly midnight, talking about Latin and English poetry, or telling me about his long stay in Italy.

I can give no idea of the peculiar charm and vividness of his talk. In a crowd he was nearly always silent. Even

▶ *What two items hang on Jim's walls?*

for his classroom he had no <u>platitudes</u>, no stock of professorial anecdotes. When he was tired, his lectures were clouded, obscure, <u>elliptical</u>; but when he was interested they were wonderful. I believe that Gaston Cleric narrowly missed being a great poet, and I have sometimes thought that his bursts of imaginative talk were fatal to his poetic gift. He squandered too much in the heat of personal communication. How often I have seen him draw his dark brows together, fix his eyes upon some object on the wall or a figure in the carpet, and then flash into the lamplight the very image that was in his brain. He could bring the drama of antique life before one out of the shadows— white figures against blue backgrounds. I shall never forget his face as it looked one night when he told me about the solitary day he spent among the sea temples at Paestum: the soft wind blowing through the roofless columns, the birds flying low over the flowering marsh grasses, the changing lights on the silver, cloud-hung mountains. He had willfully stayed the short summer night there, wrapped in his coat and rug, watching the constellations on their path down the sky until "the bride of old Tithonus"[1] rose out of the sea, and the mountains stood sharp in the dawn. It was there he caught the fever which held him back on the eve of his departure for Greece and of which he lay ill so long in Naples. He was still, indeed, doing penance for it.

◀ What, according to Jim, killed Gaston Cleric's poetic career?

◀ How did Gaston Cleric come down with the illness with which he still struggles?

I remember vividly another evening, when something led us to talk of Dante's veneration for Virgil. Cleric went through canto after canto of the *Commedia*, repeating the discourse between Dante and his "sweet teacher,"[2] while his cigarette burned itself out unheeded between his long fingers. I can hear him now, speaking the lines of the poet Statius, who spoke for Dante: *"I was famous on earth with the name which endures longest and honors most. The seeds of my ardor were the sparks from that divine flame whereby more*

---

1. **"The bride of old Tithonus."** Aurora, goddess of the dawn, who married the mortal Tithonus

2. his **"sweet teacher."** Virgil, who is Dante's guide and teacher through Hell, Purgatory, and Heaven in Dante's famous trilogy, the *Divine Comedy*, which includes the *Inferno*, the *Purgatorio*, and the *Paradiso*

words for everyday use

pla • ti • tude (pla' tə tüd) n., an overused, trite, or stale remark. *Sometimes when people don't know what to say at a funeral, they resort to <u>platitudes</u>.*

el • lip • ti • cal (i lip' ti kəl) adj., of or relating to deliberate obscurity. *The candidate's speech was so <u>elliptical</u> that I still don't know where she stands on the issues most important to me.*

than a thousand have kindled; I speak of the Æneid, mother to me and nurse to me in poetry."

Although I admired scholarship so much in Cleric, I was not deceived about myself; I knew that I should never be a scholar. I could never lose myself for long among impersonal things. Mental excitement was apt to send me with a rush back to my own naked land and the figures scattered upon it. While I was in the very act of yearning toward the new forms that Cleric brought up before me, my mind plunged away from me, and I suddenly found myself thinking of the places and people of my own infinitesimal past. They stood out strengthened and simplified now, like the image of the plough against the sun. They were all I had for an answer to the new appeal. I begrudged the room that Jake and Otto and Russian Peter took up in my memory, which I wanted to crowd with other things. But whenever my consciousness was quickened, all those early friends were quickened within it, and in some strange way they accompanied me through all my new experiences. They were so much alive in me that I scarcely stopped to wonder whether they were alive anywhere else, or how.

▶ *What thoughts crowd Jim's mind when he gets excited about what he's studying?*

Chapter 2

One March evening in my Sophomore year I was sitting alone in my room after supper. There had been a warm thaw all day, with mushy yards and little streams of dark water gurgling cheerfully into the streets out of old snow-banks. My window was open, and the earthy wind blowing through made me indolent. On the edge of the prairie, where the sun had gone down, the sky was turquoise blue, like a lake, with gold light throbbing in it. Higher up, in the utter clarity of the western slope, the evening star hung like a lamp suspended by silver chains—like the lamp engraved upon the title-page of old Latin texts, which is always appearing in new heavens, and waking new desires in men. It reminded me, at any rate, to shut my window and light my wick in answer. I did so regretfully, and the dim objects in the room emerged from the shadows and took their place about me with the helpfulness which custom breeds.

I propped my book open and stared listlessly at the page of the *Georgics*[1] where tomorrow's lesson began. It opened with the melancholy reflection that, in the lives of mortals the best days are the first to flee. *"Optima dies . . . prima fugit."* I turned back to the beginning of the third book, which we had read in class that morning. *"Primus ego in patriam mecum . . . deducam Musas";* "for I shall be the first, if I live, to bring the Muse[2] into my country." Cleric had explained to us that "patria" here meant, not a nation or even a province, but the little rural neighborhood on the Mincio where the poet was born. This was not a boast, but a hope, at once bold and devoutly humble, that he might bring the Muse (but lately come to Italy from her cloudy Grecian mountains), not to the capital, the *palatia Romana,*[3] but to his own little "country"; to his father's fields, "sloping down to the river and to the old beech trees with broken tops."

◀ What was Virgil's goal as a writer?

Cleric said he thought Virgil, when he was dying at Brindisi, must have remembered that passage. After he had faced the bitter fact that he was to leave the *Æneid* unfinished, and had decreed that the great canvas, crowded with figures of gods and men, should be burned rather than survive him unperfected, then his mind must have

---

1. the *Georgics*. Another epic poem by Virgil
2. the **Muse**. Any one of the nine sister goddesses of the arts in Greek mythology
3. *palatia Romana.* Palaces of Rome

gone back to the perfect utterance of the *Georgics*, where the pen was fitted to the matter as the plough is to the furrow; and he must have said to himself, with the thankfulness of a good man, "I was the first to bring the Muse into my country."

We left the classroom quietly, conscious that we had been brushed by the wing of a great feeling, though perhaps I alone knew Cleric intimately enough to guess what that feeling was. In the evening, as I sat staring at my book, the fervor of his voice stirred through the quantities on the page before me. I was wondering whether that particular rocky strip of New England coast about which he had so often told me was Cleric's *patria*. Before I had got far with my reading, I was disturbed by a knock. I hurried to the door and when I opened it saw a woman standing in the dark hall.

▶ What does Jim wonder about as he tries to study?

"I expect you hardly know me, Jim."

The voice seemed familiar, but I did not recognize her until she stepped into the light of my doorway and I beheld—Lena Lingard! She was so quietly conventionalized by city clothes that I might have passed her on the street without seeing her. Her black suit fitted her figure smoothly, and a black lace hat, with pale-blue forget-me-nots, sat demurely on her yellow hair.

I led her toward Cleric's chair, the only comfortable one I had, questioning her confusedly.

She was not disconcerted by my embarrassment. She looked about her with the naïve curiosity I remembered so well. "You are quite comfortable here, aren't you? I live in Lincoln now, too, Jim. I'm in business for myself. I have a dressmaking shop in the Raleigh Block, out on O Street. I've made a real good start."

▶ What is Lena doing in Lincoln?

"But, Lena, when did you come?"

"Oh, I've been here all winter. Didn't your grandmother ever write you? I've thought about looking you up lots of times. But we've all heard what a studious young man you've got to be, and I felt bashful. I didn't know whether you'd be glad to see me." She laughed her mellow, easy laugh, that was either very <u>artless</u> or very comprehending, one never quite knew which. "You seem the same,

---

words for everyday use

art • less (ärt' ləs) adj., sincerely simple, natural. *His thanks were so <u>artless</u> that everyone knew he was sincere.*

---

though,—except you're a young man, now, of course. Do you think I've changed?"

"Maybe you're prettier—though you were always pretty enough. Perhaps it's your clothes that make a difference."

"You like my new suit? I have to dress pretty well in my business." She took off her jacket and sat more at ease in her blouse, of some soft, flimsy silk. She was already at home in my place, had slipped quietly into it, as she did into everything. She told me her business was going well, and she had saved a little money.

"This summer I'm going to build the house for mother I've talked about so long. I won't be able to pay up on it at first, but I want her to have it before she is too old to enjoy it. Next summer I'll take her down new furniture and carpets, so she'll have something to look forward to all winter."

I watched Lena sitting there so smooth and sunny and well cared-for, and thought of how she used to run barefoot over the prairie until after the snow began to fly, and how Crazy Mary chased her round and round the cornfields. It seemed to me wonderful that she should have got on so well in the world. Certainly she had no one but herself to thank for it.

◀ *What comparison does Jim make as he watches Lena?*

"You must feel proud of yourself, Lena," I said heartily. "Look at me; I've never earned a dollar, and I don't know that I'll ever be able to."

"Tony says you're going to be richer than Mr. Harling some day. She's always bragging about you, you know."

"Tell me, how *is* Tony?"

"She's fine. She works for Mrs. Gardener at the hotel now. She's housekeeper. Mrs. Gardener's health isn't what it was, and she can't see after everything like she used to. She has great confidence in Tony. Tony's made it up with the Harlings, too. Little Nina is so fond of her that Mrs. Harling kind of overlooked things."

"Is she still going with Larry Donovan?"

"Oh, that's on, worse than ever! I guess they're engaged. Tony talks about him like he was president of the railroad. Everybody laughs about it, because she was never a girl to be soft. She won't hear a word against him. She's so sort of innocent."

I said I didn't like Larry, and never would.

Lena's face dimpled. "Some of us could tell her things, but it wouldn't do any good. She'd always believe him. That's Ántonia's failing, you know; if she once likes people, she won't hear anything against them."

◀ *What does Lena identify as Ántonia's failing?*

"I think I'd better go home and look after Ántonia," I said.

"I think you had." Lena looked up at me in frank amusement. "It's a good thing the Harlings are friendly with her again. Larry's afraid of them. They ship so much grain, they have influence with the railroad people. What are you studying?" She leaned her elbows on the table and drew my book toward her. I caught a faint odor of violet sachet. "So that's Latin, is it? It looks hard. You do go to the theater sometimes, though, for I've seen you there. Don't you just love a good play, Jim? I can't stay at home in the evening if there's one in town. I'd be willing to work like a slave, it seems to me, to live in a place where there are theaters."

"Let's go to a show together sometime. You are going to let me come to see you, aren't you?"

"Would you like to? I'd be ever so pleased. I'm never busy after six o'clock, and I let my sewing girls go at half-past five. I board, to save time, but sometimes I cook a chop for myself, and I'd be glad to cook one for you. Well,"—she began to put on her white gloves,—"it's been awful good to see you, Jim."

"You needn't hurry, need you? You've hardly told me anything yet."

"We can talk when you come to see me. I expect you don't often have lady visitors. The old woman downstairs didn't want to let me come up very much. I told her I was from your home town, and had promised your grandmother to come and see you. How surprised Mrs. Burden would be!" Lena laughed softly as she rose.

When I caught up my hat she shook her head. "No, I don't want you to go with me. I'm to meet some Swedes at the drug-store. You wouldn't care for them. I wanted to see your room so I could write Tony all about it, but I must tell her how I left you right here with your books. She's always so afraid someone will run off with you!" Lena slipped her silk sleeves into the jacket I held for her, smoothed it over her person, and buttoned it slowly. I walked with her to the door. "Come and see me sometimes when you're lonesome. But maybe you have all the friends you want. Have you?" She turned her soft cheek to me. "Have you?" she whispered teasingly in my ear. In a moment I watched her fade down the dusky stairway.

When I turned back to my room the place seemed much pleasanter than before. Lena had left something warm and friendly in the lamplight. How I loved to hear her laugh again! It was so soft and unexcited and appreciative—gave a favorable interpretation to everything. When I closed my eyes I could hear them all laughing—the Danish laundry girls and the three Bohemian Marys. Lena had brought them all back to me. It came over me, as it had never done before, the relation between girls like those and the poetry of Virgil. If there were no girls like them in the world, there would be no poetry. I understood that clearly, for the first time. This revelation seemed to me inestimably precious. I clung to it as if it might suddenly vanish.

◄ What is the relationship between the hired girls and poetry?

As I sat down to my book at last, my old dream about Lena coming across the harvest field in her short skirt seemed to me like the memory of an actual experience. It floated before me on the page like a picture, and underneath it stood the mournful line: *Optima dies . . . prima fugit.*

◄ What old dream about Lena does Jim remember? What line does Jim associate with this old dream? What does it mean in English?

Chapter 3

In Lincoln the best part of the theatrical season came late, when the good companies stopped off there for one-night stands, after their long runs in New York and Chicago. That spring Lena went with me to see Joseph Jefferson in "Rip Van Winkle," and to a war play called "Shenandoah." She was inflexible about paying for her own seat; said she was in business now, and she wouldn't have a schoolboy spending his money on her. I liked to watch a play with Lena; everything was wonderful to her, and everything was true. It was like going to revival meetings with someone who was always being converted. She handed her feelings over to the actors with a kind of fatalistic resignation. Accessories of costume and scene meant much more to her than to me. She sat entranced through "Robin Hood" and hung upon the lips of the contralto who sang, "Oh, Promise Me!"

Toward the end of April, the billboards, which I watched anxiously in those days, bloomed out one morning with gleaming white posters on which two names were impressively printed in blue Gothic letters: the name of an actress of whom I had often heard, and the name *Camille*.[1]

I called at the Raleigh Block for Lena on Saturday evening, and we walked down to the theater. The weather was warm and sultry and put us both in a holiday humor. We arrived early, because Lena liked to watch the people come in. There was a note on the program, saying that the "incidental music" would be from the opera *Traviata*,[2] which was made from the same story as the play. We had neither of us read the play, and we did not know what it was about—though I seemed to remember having heard it was a piece in which great actresses shone. *The Count of Monte Cristo*, which I had seen James O'Neill play that winter, was by the only Alexandre Dumas I knew. This play, I saw, was by his son, and I expected a family resemblance. A couple of jack-rabbits, run in off the prairie, could not have been more innocent of what awaited them than were Lena and I.

Our excitement began with the rise of the curtain, when the moody Varville, seated before the fire, interrogated

▶ Why does Jim like to see plays with Lena?

---

1. *Camille*. Play based on a novel by Alexandre Dumas about a transforming love affair between Marguerite, a courtesan in Paris, and the stubborn Armand

2. *Traviata*. La Traviata, a well-known opera by Verdi that tells the same story as the play "Camille"

Nanine. Decidedly, there was a new tang about this dialogue. I had never heard in the theater lines that were alive, that presupposed and took for granted, like those which passed between Varville and Marguerite in the brief encounter before her friends entered. This introduced the most brilliant, worldly, the most enchantingly gay scene I had ever looked upon. I had never seen champagne bottles opened on the stage before— indeed, I had never seen them opened anywhere. The memory of that supper makes me hungry now; the sight of it then, when I had only a students' boarding-house dinner behind me, was delicate torment. I seem to remember gilded chairs and tables (arranged hurriedly by footmen in white gloves and stockings), linen of dazzling whiteness, glittering glass, silver dishes, a great bowl of fruit, and the reddest of roses. The room was invaded by beautiful women and dashing young men, laughing and talking together. The men were dressed more or less after the period in which the play was written; the women were not. I saw no inconsistency. Their talk seemed to open to one the brilliant world in which they lived; every sentence made one older and wiser, every pleasantry enlarged one's horizon. One could experience excess and satiety without the inconvenience of learning what to do with one's hands in a drawing-room! When the characters all spoke at once and I missed some of the phrases they flashed at each other, I was in misery. I strained my ears and eyes to catch every exclamation.

The actress who played Marguerite was even then old-fashioned, though historic. She had been a member of Daly's famous New York company, and afterward a "star" under his direction. She was a woman who could not be taught, it is said, though she had a crude natural force which carried with people whose feelings were accessible and whose taste was not squeamish. She was already old, with a ravaged countenance and a physique curiously hard and stiff. She moved with difficulty— I think she was lame—I seem to remember some story about a malady of the spine. Her Armand was disproportionately young and slight, a handsome youth, perplexed in the extreme. But what did it matter? I believed devoutly in her power to fascinate him, in her dazzling loveliness. I believed her young, ardent, reckless, disillusioned, under sentence, feverish, avid of pleasure. I wanted to cross the footlights and help the slim-waisted Armand in the frilled shirt to convince her that there was still loyalty and devotion in the world. Her sudden illness, when the gaiety was at its height, her pallor, the handkerchief she crushed against her lips, the cough she smothered under the laughter while Gaston kept playing the piano lightly—it all wrung my heart. But not so much as her <u>cynicism</u> in the long dialogue with her lover which followed. How far was I from questioning her unbelief! While the charmingly sincere young man pleaded with her— accompanied by the orchestra in the old *Traviata* duet, *"misterioso, misterios' altero!"*—she maintained her bitter <u>skepticism</u>, and the curtain fell on her dancing recklessly with the others, after Armand had been sent away with his flower.

Between the acts we had no time to forget. The orchestra kept sawing away at the *Traviata* music, so joyous and sad, so thin and far-away, so clap-trap and yet so heart-breaking. After the second act I left Lena in tearful contemplation of the ceiling, and went out into the lobby to smoke. As I walked about there I congratulated myself that I had not brought some Lincoln girl who would talk during the waits about the junior dances, or whether the cadets would camp at Plattsmouth. Lena was at least a woman, and I was a man.

Through the scene between Marguerite and the elder Duval, Lena wept unceasingly, and I sat helpless to prevent the closing of that chapter of <u>idyllic</u> love, dreading the return of the young man whose ineffable happiness was only to be the measure of his fall.

I suppose no woman could have been further in person, voice, and temperament from Dumas' appealing heroine than the veteran actress who first acquainted me with her. Her conception of the character was as heavy and uncompromising as her diction; she bore hard on the idea and on the consonants. At all times she was highly tragic, devoured by remorse. Lightness of stress or behavior was far from her. Her voice was heavy and deep: "Ar-r-r-mond!" she would begin, as if she were summoning him to the bar of Judgment. But the lines were enough. She had only to utter them. They created the character in spite of her.

The heartless world which Marguerite re-entered with Varville had never been so glittering and reckless as on the

▶ What affects Jim most in the first part of the play?

▶ What criticisms does Jim have of the actress, and how does the play succeed anyway?

words for everyday use

cyn • i • cis • m (si' nə si zəm) n., distrust of human nature or motives. *His cynicism about politics comes from having witnessed so many bad decisions.*

skep • ti • cis • m (skep' tə si zəm) n., doubt or disbelief. *She expressed skepticism about how accurate the news coverage was.*

i • dyl • lic (ī di' lik) adj., charmingly or simply poetic. *The night, with its perfectly clear sky and warm breeze, was idyllic.*

night when it gathered in Olympe's salon for the fourth act. There were chandeliers hung from the ceiling, I remember, many servants in livery, gaming-tables where the men played with piles of gold, and a staircase down which the guests made their entrance. After all the others had gathered round the card tables, and young Duval had been warned by Prudence, Marguerite descended the staircase with Varville; such a cloak, such a fan, such jewels—and her face! One knew at a glance how it was with her. When Armand, with the terrible words, "Look, all of you, I owe this woman nothing!" flung the gold and bank notes at the half-swooning Marguerite, Lena cowered beside me and covered her face with her hands.

The curtain rose on the bedroom scene. By this time there wasn't a nerve in me that hadn't been twisted. Nanine alone could have made me cry. I loved Nanine tenderly; and Gaston, how one clung to that good fellow! The New Year's presents were not too much; nothing could be too much now. I wept unrestrainedly. Even the handkerchief in my breast-pocket, worn for elegance and not at all for use, was wet through by the time that moribund woman sank for the last time into the arms of her lover.

When we reached the door of the theater, the streets were shining with rain. I had prudently brought along Mrs. Harling's useful Commencement present, and I took Lena home under its shelter. After leaving her, I walked slowly out into the country part of the town where I lived. The lilacs were all blooming in the yards, and the smell of them after the rain, of the new leaves and the blossoms together, blew into my face with a sort of bitter sweetness. I tramped through the puddles and under the showery trees, mourning for Marguerite Gautier as if she had died only yesterday, sighing with the spirit of 1840, which had sighed so much, and which had reached me only that night, across long years and several languages, through the person of an infirm old actress. The idea is one that no circumstances can frustrate. Wherever and whenever that piece is put on, it is April.

Chapter 4

How well I remember the stiff little parlor where I used to wait for Lena: the hard horsehair furniture, bought at some auction sale, the long mirror, the fashion-plates on the wall. If I sat down even for a moment, I was sure to find threads and bits of colored silk clinging to my clothes after I went away. Lena's success puzzled me. She was so easy-going; had none of the push and self-assertiveness that get people ahead in business. She had come to Lincoln, a country girl, with no introductions except to some cousins of Mrs. Thomas who lived there, and she was already making clothes for the women of "the young married set." Evidently she had great natural aptitude for her work. She knew, as she said, "what people looked well in." She never tired of poring over fashion books. Sometimes in the evening I would find her alone in her work-room, draping folds of satin on a wire figure, with a quite blissful expression of countenance. I couldn't help thinking that the years when Lena literally hadn't enough clothes to cover herself might have something to do with her untiring interest in dressing the human figure. Her clients said that Lena "had style," and overlooked her habitual inaccuracies. She never, I discovered, finished anything by the time she had promised, and she frequently spent more money on materials than her customer had authorized. Once, when I arrived at six o'clock, Lena was ushering out a fidgety mother and her awkward, overgrown daughter. The woman <u>detained</u> Lena at the door to say apologetically:—

"You'll try to keep it under fifty for me, won't you, Miss Lingard? You see, she's really too young to come to an expensive dressmaker, but I knew you could do more with her than anybody else."

"Oh, that will be all right, Mrs. Herron. I think we'll manage to get a good effect," Lena replied blandly.

I thought her manner with her customers very good, and wondered where she had learned such <u>self-possession</u>.

Sometimes after my morning classes were over, I used to

▶ What explanation does Jim offer for Lena's interest in dressmaking?

▶ In what ways was Lena's dressmaking inaccurate?

---

words for everyday use

de • tain (di tān') vt., stop, restrain from proceeding. *Mrs. Berring <u>detained</u> each student at the door until they recited the quotes they were supposed to have memorized.*

self-pos • ses • sion (self pə zə' shən) n., control of one's emotions or reactions, especially under stress. *Without great <u>self-possession</u>, the coach could have let his emotions get out of control during the academic fraud investigation.*

encounter Lena downtown, in her velvet suit and a little black hat, with a veil tied smoothly over her face, looking as fresh as the spring morning. Maybe she would be carrying home a bunch of jonquils or a hyacinth plant. When we passed a candy store her footsteps would hesitate and linger. "Don't let me go in," she would murmur. "Get me by if you can." She was very fond of sweets, and was afraid of growing too plump.

We had delightful Sunday breakfasts together at Lena's. At the back of her long work-room was a bay-window, large enough to hold a box-couch and a reading-table. We breakfasted in this recess, after drawing the curtains that shut out the long room, with cutting-tables and wire women and sheet-draped garments on the walls. The sunlight poured in, making everything on the table shine and glitter and the flame of the alcohol lamp disappear altogether. Lena's curly black water-spaniel, Prince, breakfasted with us. He sat beside her on the couch and behaved very well until the Polish violin-teacher across the hall began to practice, when Prince would growl and sniff the air with disgust. Lena's landlord, old Colonel Raleigh, had given her the dog, and at first she was not at all pleased. She had spent too much of her life taking care of animals to have much <u>sentiment</u> about them. But Prince was a knowing little beast, and she grew fond of him. After breakfast I made him do his lessons; play dead dog, shake hands, stand up like a soldier. We used to put my cadet cap on his head—I had to take military drill at the University— and give him a yard-measure to hold with his front leg. His gravity made us laugh <u>immoderately</u>.

Lena's talk always amused me. Ántonia had never talked like the people about her. Even after she learned to speak English readily, there was always something impulsive and foreign in her speech. But Lena had picked up all the conventional expressions she heard at Mrs. Thomas's dressmaking shop. Those formal phrases, the very flower of small-town proprieties, and the flat commonplaces, nearly all hypocritical in their origin, became very funny, very engaging, when they were uttered in Lena's soft voice,

---

words for everyday use

sen • ti • ment (sen' tə mənt) n., a romantic or nostalgic feeling verging on excess emotion. *In matters about which you care deeply, it's easy to allow <u>sentiment</u> to cloud your rationale judgment.*

im • mod • er • ate • ly (i mä' də rət lē) adv., in a way that exceeds normal bounds, excessively. *Nothing is more likely to make me eat <u>immoderately</u> than a box of maple cake doughnuts.*

with her caressing intonation and arch <u>naïveté</u>. Nothing could be more diverting than to hear Lena, who was almost as candid as Nature, call a leg a "limb" or a house a "home."

We used to linger a long while over our coffee in that sunny corner. Lena was never so pretty as in the morning; she wakened fresh with the world every day, and her eyes had a deeper color then, like the blue flowers that are never so blue as when they first open. I could sit idle all through a Sunday morning and look at her. Ole Benson's behavior was now no mystery to me.

▶ How does Lena feel about Ole's attentions to her?

"There was never any harm in Ole," she said once. "People needn't have troubled themselves. He just liked to come over and sit on the draw-side and forget about his bad luck. I liked to have him. Any company's welcome when you're off with cattle all the time."

"But wasn't he always glum?" I asked. "People said he never talked at all."

"Sure he talked, in Norwegian. He'd been a sailor on an English boat and had seen lots of queer places. He had wonderful tattoos. We used to sit and look at them for hours; there wasn't much to look at out there. He was like a picture book. He had a ship and a strawberry girl on one arm, and on the other a girl standing before a little house, with a fence and gate and all, waiting for her sweetheart. Farther up his arm, her sailor had come back and was kissing her. 'The Sailor's Return,' he called it."

I admitted it was no wonder Ole liked to look at a pretty girl once in a while, with such a fright at home.

▶ According to Lena, why had Ole married Crazy Mary?

"You know," Lena said confidentially, "he married Mary because he thought she was strong-minded and would keep him straight. He never could keep straight on shore. The last time he landed in Liverpool he'd been out on a two years' voyage. He was paid off one morning, and by the next he hadn't a cent left, and his watch and compass were gone. He'd got with some women, and they'd taken everything. He worked his way to this country on a little passenger boat. Mary was a stewardess, and she tried to convert him on the way over. He thought she was just the one to keep him steady. Poor Ole! He used to bring me

<hr>

words for everyday use

na • ïve • té (nä ēv tā′) n., genuine simplicity. *Revealing her <u>naïveté</u>, Larissa expressed shock that anyone would question a politician's judgment.*

candy from town, hidden in his feed-bag. He couldn't refuse anything to a girl. He'd have given away his tattoos long ago, if he could. He's one of the people I'm sorriest for."

If I happened to spend an evening with Lena and stayed late, the Polish violin-teacher across the hall used to come out and watch me descend the stairs, muttering so threateningly that it would have been easy to fall into a quarrel with him. Lena had told him once that she liked to hear him practice, so he always left his door open, and watched who came and went.

There was a coolness between the Pole and Lena's landlord on her account. Old Colonel Raleigh had come to Lincoln from Kentucky and invested an inherited fortune in real estate, at the time of inflated prices. Now he sat day after day in his office in the Raleigh Block, trying to discover where his money had gone and how he could get some of it back. He was a widower, and found very little <u>congenial</u> companionship in this casual Western city. Lena's good looks and gentle manners appealed to him. He said her voice reminded him of Southern voices, and he found as many opportunities of hearing it as possible. He painted and papered her rooms for her that spring, and put in a porcelain bathtub in place of the tin one that had satisfied the former tenant. While these repairs were being made, the old gentleman often dropped in to consult Lena's preferences. She told me with amusement how Ordinsky, the Pole, had presented himself at her door one evening, and said that if the landlord was annoying her by his attentions, he would promptly put a stop to it.

"I don't exactly know what to do about him," she said, shaking her head, "he's so sort of wild all the time. I wouldn't like to have him say anything rough to that nice old man. The colonel is long-winded, but then I expect he's lonesome. I don't think he cares much for Ordinsky, either. He said once that if I had any complaints to make of my neighbors, I mustn't hesitate."

One Saturday evening when I was having supper with Lena, we heard a knock at her parlor door, and there stood the Pole, coatless, in a dress shirt and collar. Prince

words
for
everyday
use

con • ge • ni • al (kən jē′ nē əl) adj., sociable. *Kamisha's <u>congenial</u> personality made her an ideal person to welcome parents as they came through the school doors.*

dropped on his paws and began to growl like a mastiff,[1] while the visitor apologized, saying that he could not possibly come in thus attired, but he begged Lena to lend him some safety pins.

"Oh, you'll have to come in, Mr. Ordinsky, and let me see what's the matter." She closed the door behind him. "Jim, won't you make Prince behave?"

I rapped Prince on the nose, while Ordinsky explained that he had not had his dress clothes on for a long time, and tonight, when he was going to play for a concert, his waistcoat had split down the back. He thought he could pin it together until he got it to a tailor.

Lena took him by the elbow and turned him round. She laughed when she saw the long gap in the satin. "You could never pin that, Mr. Ordinsky. You've kept it folded too long, and the goods is all gone along the crease. Take it off. I can put a new piece of lining-silk in there for you in ten minutes." She disappeared into her work-room with the vest, leaving me to confront the Pole, who stood against the door like a wooden figure. He folded his arms and glared at me with his excitable, slanting brown eyes. His head was the shape of a chocolate drop, and was covered with dry, straw-colored hair that fuzzed up about his pointed crown. He had never done more than mutter at me as I passed him, and I was surprised when he now addressed me. "Miss Lingard," he said haughtily, "is a young woman for whom I have the <u>utmost</u>, the utmost respect."

"So have I," I said coldly.

He paid no heed to my remark, but began to do rapid finger-exercises on his shirt-sleeves, as he stood with tightly folded arms.

▶ What criticism does the Polish violinist make of Lincoln and those who live there?

"Kindness of heart," he went on, staring at the ceiling, "sentiment, are not understood in a place like this. The noblest qualities are ridiculed. Grinning college boys, ignorant and conceited, what do they know of delicacy!²"

I controlled my features and tried to speak seriously.

"If you mean me, Mr. Ordinsky, I have known Miss

---

1. **mastiff.** A large, heavy dog standing at least thirty inches tall
2. **delicacy.** Refined behavior, or behavior that is free of coarseness or vulgarity

---

words for everyday use ut • most (ət' mōst) adj., the most possible, the highest attainable degree. *It took the* <u>utmost</u> *courage for Royce, who is afraid of heights, to skydive.*

Lingard a long time, and I think I appreciate her kindness. We come from the same town, and we grew up together."

His gaze traveled slowly down from the ceiling and rested on me. "Am I to understand that you have this young woman's interests at heart? That you do not wish to compromise her?"

"That's a word we don't use much here, Mr. Ordinsky. A girl who makes her own living can ask a college boy to supper without being talked about. We take some things for granted."

"Then I have misjudged you, and I ask your pardon,"— he bowed gravely. "Miss Lingard," he went on, "is an absolutely trustful heart. She has not learned the hard lessons of life. As for you and me, *noblesse oblige*,[3]"—he watched me narrowly.

Lena returned with the vest. "Come in and let us look at you as you go out, Mr. Ordinsky. I've never seen you in your dress suit," she said as she opened the door for him.

A few moments later he reappeared with his violin case—a heavy muffler about his neck and thick woolen gloves on his bony hands. Lena spoke encouragingly to him, and he went off with such an important professional air that we fell to laughing as soon as we had shut the door. "Poor fellow," Lena said indulgently, "he takes everything so hard."

After that Ordinsky was friendly to me, and behaved as if there were some deep understanding between us. He wrote a furious article, attacking the musical taste of the town, and asked me to do him a great service by taking it to the editor of the morning paper. If the editor refused to print it, I was to tell him that he would be answerable to Ordinsky "in person." He declared that he would never retract one word, and that he was quite prepared to lose all his pupils. In spite of the fact that nobody ever mentioned his article to him after it appeared—full of typographical errors which he thought intentional— he got a certain satisfaction from believing that the citizens of Lincoln had

---

3. *noblesse oblige*. The duty of high-ranking or upper-class people to behave nobly

words for everyday use

com • pro • mise (käm' prə mīz) vt., expose to suspicion, dishonor, or mischief. *I know you would never compromise a friend by involving him in something illegal.*

re • tract (ri trakt') vt., take back, withdraw. *After talking to his lawyer, the suspect wished he could retract his confession.*

meekly accepted the <u>epithet</u> "coarse barbarians." "You see how it is," he said to me, "where there is no <u>chivalry</u>, there is no *amour propre.*[4]" When I met him on his rounds now, I thought he carried his head more disdainfully than ever, and strode up the steps of front porches and rang doorbells with more assurance. He told Lena he would never forget how I had stood by him when he was "under fire."

All this time, of course, I was drifting. Lena had broken up my serious mood. I wasn't interested in my classes. I played with Lena and Prince, I played with the Pole, I went buggy-riding with the old Colonel, who had taken a fancy to me and used to talk to me about Lena and the "great beauties" he had known in his youth. We were all three in love with Lena.

Before the first of June, Gaston Cleric was offered an instructorship at Harvard College, and accepted it. He suggested that I should follow him in the fall, and complete my course at Harvard. He had found out about Lena—not from me— and he talked to me seriously.

"You won't do anything here now. You should either quit school and go to work, or change your college and begin again in earnest. You won't recover yourself while you are playing about with this handsome Norwegian. Yes, I've seen her with you at the theater. She's very pretty, and perfectly irresponsible, I should judge."

Cleric wrote my grandfather that he would like to take me East with him. To my astonishment, grandfather replied that I might go if I wished. I was both glad and sorry on the day when the letter came. I stayed in my room all evening and thought things over. I even tried to persuade myself that I was standing in Lena's way— it is so necessary to be a little noble!—and that if she had not me to play with, she would probably marry and secure her future.

The next evening I went to call on Lena. I found her propped up on the couch in her bay window, with her foot in a big slipper. An awkward little Russian girl whom she had taken into her work-room had dropped a flat-iron on Lena's toe. On the table beside her there was a basket of

> ▶ In what ways is Jim drifting now that Lena has come to town?

> ▶ What does Gaston Cleric suggest Jim do in the fall?

---

4. *amour propre.* Self-esteem or self-respect

words for everyday use

e • pi • thet (e′ pə thet) n., a disparaging or abusive word or phrase. *Tom was reprimanded for calling his younger brother "blockhead" and shouting other <u>epithets</u>.*

chi • val • ry (shi′ vəl rē) n., the customs of medieval knighthood, including honor, generosity, and courtesy. *Stepping back and allowing others to pass before you into a room is a practice of <u>chivalry</u> that has survived into the modern era.*

early summer flowers which the Pole had left after he heard of the accident. He always managed to know what went on in Lena's apartment.

Lena was telling me some amusing piece of gossip about one of her clients, when I interrupted her and picked up the flower basket.

"This old chap will be proposing to you some day, Lena."

"Oh, he has—often!" she murmured.

"What! After you've refused him?"

"He doesn't mind that. It seems to cheer him to mention the subject. Old men are like that, you know. It makes them feel important to think they're in love with somebody."

"The Colonel would marry you in a minute. I hope you won't marry some old fellow; not even a rich one."

Lena shifted her pillows and looked up at me in surprise. "Why, I'm not going to marry anybody. Didn't you know that?"

"Nonsense, Lena. That's what girls say, but you know better. Every handsome girl like you marries, of course."

She shook her head. "Not me."

"But why not? What makes you say that?" I persisted.

Lena laughed. "Well, it's mainly because I don't want a husband. Men are all right for friends, but as soon as you marry them they turn into cranky old fathers, even the wild ones. They begin to tell you what's sensible and what's foolish, and want you to stick at home all the time. I prefer to be foolish when I feel like it, and be accountable to nobody." ◀ *Why doesn't Lena want a husband?*

"But you'll be lonesome. You'll get tired of this sort of life, and you'll want a family."

"Not me. I like to be lonesome. When I went to work for Mrs. Thomas I was nineteen years old, and I had never slept a night in my life when there weren't three in the bed. I never had a minute to myself except when I was off with the cattle."

Usually, when Lena referred to her life in the country at all, she dismissed it with a single remark, humorous or mildly cynical. But to-night her mind seemed to dwell on those early years. She told me she couldn't remember a time when she was so little that she wasn't lugging a heavy baby about, helping to wash for babies, trying to keep their little chapped hands and faces clean. She remembered home as a place where there were always too many children, a cross man, and work piling up around a sick woman. ◀ *What associations does Lena have with her childhood home?*

▶ How has Lena
always felt about
Jim?

"It wasn't mother's fault. She would have made us comfortable if she could. But that was no life for a girl! After I began to herd and milk, I could never get the smell of the cattle off me. The few underclothes I had I kept in a cracker box. On Saturday nights, after everybody was in bed, then I could take a bath if I wasn't too tired. I could make two trips to the windmill to carry water, and heat it in the wash-boiler on the stove. While the water was heating, I could bring in a washtub out of the cave, and take my bath in the kitchen. Then I could put on a clean night-gown and get into bed with two others, who likely hadn't had a bath unless I'd given it to them. You can't tell me anything about family life. I've had plenty to last me."

"But it's not all like that," I objected.

"Near enough. It's all being under somebody's thumb. What's on your mind, Jim? Are you afraid I'll want you to marry me some day?"

Then I told her I was going away.

"What makes you want to go away, Jim? Haven't I been nice to you?"

"You've been just awfully good to me, Lena," I blurted. "I don't think about much else. I never shall think about much else while I'm with you. I'll never settle down and grind if I stay here. You know that." I dropped down beside her and sat looking at the floor. I seemed to have forgotten all my reasonable explanations.

Lena drew close to me, and the little hesitation in her voice that had hurt me was not there when she spoke again.

"I oughtn't to have begun it, ought I?" she murmured. "I oughtn't to have gone to see you that first time. But I did want to. I guess I've always been a little foolish about you. I don't know what first put it into my head, unless it was Ántonia, always telling me I mustn't be up to any of my nonsense with you. I let you alone for a long while, though, didn't I?"

She was a sweet creature to those she loved, that Lena Lingard!

At last she sent me away with her soft, slow, <u>renunciatory</u> kiss. "You aren't sorry I came to see you that time?" she whispered. "It seemed so natural. I used to think I'd

---

**words
for
everyday
use** re • nun • ci • a • tor • y (ri nən′ sē ə tŏr ē) adj., relating to giving up or pushing away, often with regret. *Trying to stay true to her commitment to cut down on sugar, she pushed the cake away with a <u>renunciatory</u> sigh.*

like to be your first sweetheart. You were such a funny kid!" She always kissed one as if she were sadly and wisely sending one away forever.

We said many good-byes before I left Lincoln, but she never tried to hinder me or hold me back. "You are going, but you haven't gone yet, have you?" she used to say.

My Lincoln chapter closed abruptly. I went home to my grandparents for a few weeks, and afterward visited my relatives in Virginia until I joined Cleric in Boston. I was then nineteen years old.

BOOK IV

The Pioneer Woman's Story

Chapter 1

Two years after I left Lincoln I completed my academic course at Harvard. Before I entered the Law School I went home for the summer vacation. On the night of my arrival, Mrs. Harling and Frances and Sally came over to greet me. Everything seemed just as it used to be. My grandparents looked very little older. Frances Harling was married now, and she and her husband managed the Harling interests in Black Hawk. When we gathered in grandmother's parlor, I could hardly believe that I had been away at all. One subject, however, we avoided all evening.

When I was walking home with Frances, after we had left Mrs. Harling at her gate, she said simply, "You know, of course, about poor Ántonia."

Poor Ántonia! Everyone would be saying that now, I thought bitterly. I replied that grandmother had written me how Ántonia went away to marry Larry Donovan at some place where he was working; that he had deserted her, and that there was now a baby. This was all I knew.

◀ Why is everyone referring to Ántonia as "poor Ántonia"?

"He never married her," Frances said. "I haven't seen her since she came back. She lives at home, on the farm, and almost never comes to town. She brought the baby in to show it to mama once. I'm afraid she's settled down to be Ambrosch's drudge for good."

I tried to shut Ántonia out of my mind. I was bitterly disappointed in her. I could not forgive her for becoming an object of pity, while Lena Lingard, for whom people had always foretold trouble, was now the leading dress-maker of Lincoln, much respected in Black Hawk. Lena gave her heart away when she felt like it, but she kept her head for her business and had got on in the world.

◀ How does Jim feel toward Ántonia?

Just then it was the fashion to speak indulgently of Lena and severely of Tiny Soderball, who had quietly gone West to try her fortune the year before. A Black Hawk boy, just back from Seattle, brought the news that Tiny had not gone to the coast on a venture, as she had allowed people to think, but with very definite plans. One of the roving promoters that used to stop at Mrs. Gardener's hotel owned idle property along the waterfront in Seattle, and he had offered to set Tiny up in business in one of his empty buildings. She was now conducting a sailors' lodging-house. This, everyone said, would be the end of Tiny. Even if she had begun by running a decent place, she couldn't keep it up; all sailors' boarding-houses were alike.

When I thought about it, I discovered that I had never known Tiny as well as I knew the other girls. I remembered her tripping briskly about the dining-room on her high heels, carrying a big tray full of dishes, glancing rather pertly at the spruce traveling men, and contemptuously at the scrubby ones— who were so afraid of her that they didn't dare to ask for two kinds of pie. Now it occurred to me that perhaps the sailors, too, might be afraid of Tiny. How astonished we would have been, as we sat talking about her on Frances Harling's front porch, if we could have known what her future was really to be! Of all the girls and boys who grew up together in Black Hawk, Tiny Soderball was to lead the most adventurous life and to achieve the most solid worldly success.

This is what actually happened to Tiny: While she was running her lodging-house in Seattle, gold was discovered in Alaska. Miners and sailors came back from the North with wonderful stories and pouches of gold. Tiny saw it and weighed it in her hands. That daring which nobody had ever suspected in her, awoke. She sold her business and set out for Circle City, in company with a carpenter and his wife whom she had persuaded to go along with her. They reached Skaguay in a snowstorm, went in dog sledges over the Chilkoot Pass, and shot the Yukon in flatboats. They reached Circle City on the very day when some Siwash Indians came into the settlement with the report that there had been a rich gold strike farther up the river, on a certain Klondike Creek. Two days later Tiny and her friends, and nearly everyone else in Circle City, started for the Klondike fields on the last steamer that went up the Yukon before it froze for the winter. That boatload of people founded Dawson City. Within a few weeks there were fifteen hundred homeless men in camp. Tiny and the carpenter's wife began to cook for them, in a tent. The miners gave her a building lot, and the carpenter put up a log hotel for her. There she sometimes fed a hundred and fifty men a day. Miners came in on snowshoes from their placer claims twenty miles away to buy fresh bread from her, and paid for it in gold.

That winter Tiny kept in her hotel a Swede whose legs had been frozen one night in a storm when he was trying to find his way back to his cabin. The poor fellow thought it great good fortune to be cared for by a woman, and a woman who spoke his own tongue. When he was told that his feet must be amputated, he said he hoped he would not get well; what could a working-man do in this hard world

▶ *Where has Tiny run a hotel?*

without feet? He did, in fact, die from the operation, but not before he had deeded Tiny Soderball his claim on Hunker Creek. Tiny sold her hotel, invested half her money in Dawson building lots, and with the rest she developed her claim. She went off into the wilds and lived on the claim. She bought other claims from discouraged miners, traded or sold them on percentages.

◀ How has Tiny made her fortune?

After nearly ten years in the Klondike, Tiny returned, with a considerable fortune, to live in San Francisco. I met her in Salt Lake City in 1908. She was a thin, hard-faced woman, very well-dressed, very reserved in manner. Curiously enough, she reminded me of Mrs. Gardener, for whom she had worked in Black Hawk so long ago. She told me about some of the desperate chances she had taken in the gold country, but the thrill of them was quite gone. She said frankly that nothing interested her much now but making money. The only two human beings of whom she spoke with any feeling were the Swede, Johnson, who had given her his claim, and Lena Lingard. She had persuaded Lena to come to San Francisco and go into business there.

"Lincoln was never any place for her," Tiny remarked. "In a town of that size Lena would always be gossiped about. Frisco's the right field for her. She has a fine class of trade. Oh, she's just the same as she always was! She's careless, but she's level-headed. She's the only person I know who never gets any older. It's fine for me to have her there; somebody who enjoys things like that. She keeps an eye on me and won't let me be shabby. When she thinks I need a new dress, she makes it and sends it home—with a bill that's long enough, I can tell you!"

Tiny limped slightly when she walked. The claim on Hunker Creek took toll from its possessors. Tiny had been caught in a sudden turn of weather, like poor Johnson. She lost three toes from one of those pretty little feet that used to trip about Black Hawk in pointed slippers and striped stockings. Tiny mentioned this mutilation quite casually—didn't seem sensitive about it. She was satisfied with her success, but not elated. She was like someone in whom the faculty of becoming interested is worn out.

◀ How does Jim describe Tiny's personality change as a result of her adventurous life?

Chapter 2

Soon after I got home that summer, I persuaded my grandparents to have their photographs taken, and one morning I went into the photographer's shop to arrange for sittings. While I was waiting for him to come out of his developing-room, I walked about trying to recognize the likenesses on his walls: girls in Commencement dresses, country brides and grooms holding hands, family groups of three generations. I noticed, in a heavy frame, one of those depressing "crayon enlargements"[1] often seen in farmhouse parlors, the subject being a round-eyed baby in short dresses. The photographer came out and gave a constrained, apologetic laugh.

"That's Tony Shimerda's baby. You remember her; she used to be the Harlings' Tony. Too bad! She seems proud of the baby, though; wouldn't hear to a cheap frame for the picture. I expect her brother will be in for it Saturday."

I went away feeling that I must see Ántonia again. Another girl would have kept her baby out of sight, but Tony, of course, must have its picture on exhibition at the town photographer's, in a great gilt frame. How like her! I could forgive her, I told myself, if she hadn't thrown herself away on such a cheap sort of fellow.

Larry Donovan was a passenger conductor, one of those train-crew aristocrats who are always afraid that someone may ask them to put up a car-window, and who, if requested to perform such a <u>menial</u> service, silently point to the button that calls the porter. Larry wore this air of official aloofness even on the street, where there were no car-windows to compromise his dignity. At the end of his run he stepped indifferently from the train along with the passengers, his street hat on his head and his conductor's cap in an alligator-skin bag, went directly into the station and changed his clothes. It was a matter of the utmost importance to him never to be seen in his blue trousers away from his train. He was usually cold and distant with men, but with all women he had a silent, grave familiarity, a special handshake, accompanied by a significant, delib-

---

1. "**crayon enlargements.**" Crayon tracings of photographic images

---

words for everyday use   men • i • al (mē' nē əl) adj., of or relating to servants, lowly. *Jobs considered by many to be <u>menial</u>—cooking, cleaning, doing laundry—are also the most important to keeping any family running.*

erate look. He took women, married or single, into his confidence; walked them up and down in the moonlight, telling them what a mistake he had made by not entering the office branch of the service, and how much better fitted he was to fill the post of General Passenger Agent in Denver than the roughshod man who then bore that title. His unappreciated worth was the tender secret Larry shared with his sweethearts, and he was always able to make some foolish heart ache over it.

◀ What tactic does Larry Donovan use to attract women?

As I drew near home that morning, I saw Mrs. Harling out in her yard, digging round her mountain-ash tree. It was a dry summer, and she had now no boy to help her. Charley was off in his battleship, cruising somewhere on the Caribbean sea. I turned in at the gate—it was with a feeling of pleasure that I opened and shut that gate in those days; I liked the feel of it under my hand. I took the spade away from Mrs. Harling, and while I loosened the earth around the tree, she sat down on the steps and talked about the oriole family that had a nest in its branches.

"Mrs. Harling," I said presently, "I wish I could find out exactly how Ántonia's marriage fell through."

"Why don't you go out and see your grandfather's tenant, the Widow Steavens? She knows more about it than anybody else. She helped Ántonia get ready to be married, and she was there when Ántonia came back. She took care of her when the baby was born. She could tell you everything. Besides, the Widow Steavens is a good talker, and she has a remarkable memory."

◀ What is Jim's purpose in going to see the Widow Steavens?

Chapter 3

On the first or second day of August I got a horse and cart and set out for the high country, to visit the Widow Steavens. The wheat harvest was over, and here and there along the horizon I could see black puffs of smoke from the steam threshing-machines. The old pasture land was now being broken up into wheatfields and cornfields, the red grass was disappearing, and the whole face of the country was changing. There were wooden houses where the old sod dwellings used to be, and little orchards, and big red barns; all this meant happy children, contented women, and men who saw their lives coming to a fortunate issue. The windy springs and the blazing summers, one after another, had enriched and mellowed that flat tableland; all the human effort that had gone into it was coming back in long, sweeping lines of fertility. The changes seemed beautiful and harmonious to me; it was like watching the growth of a great man or of a great idea. I recognized every tree and sandbank and rugged draw. I found that I remembered the <u>conformation</u> of the land as one remembers the modeling of human faces.

When I drew up to our old windmill, the Widow Steavens came out to meet me. She was brown as an Indian woman, tall, and very strong. When I was little, her massive head had always seemed to me like a Roman senator's. I told her at once why I had come.

"You'll stay the night with us, Jimmy? I'll talk to you after supper. I can take more interest when my work is off my mind. You've no prejudice against hot biscuit for supper? Some have, these days."

While I was putting my horse away I heard a rooster squawking. I looked at my watch and sighed; it was three o'clock, and I knew that I must eat him at six.

After supper Mrs. Steavens and I went upstairs to the old sitting-room, while her grave, silent brother remained in the basement to read his farm papers. All the windows were open. The white summer moon was shining outside, the windmill was pumping lazily in the light breeze. My hostess put the lamp on a stand in the corner, and turned it low because of the heat. She sat down in her favorite

> ▶ How has the landscape changed while Jim has been away at Harvard, and how does Jim judge those changes?

---

rocking-chair and settled a little stool comfortably under her tired feet. "I'm troubled with calluses, Jim; getting old," she sighed cheerfully. She crossed her hands in her lap and sat as if she were at a meeting of some kind.

"Now, it's about that dear Ántonia you want to know? Well, you've come to the right person. I've watched her like she'd been my own daughter.

"When she came home to do her sewing that summer before she was to be married, she was over here about every day. They've never had a sewing machine at the Shimerdas', and she made all her things here. I taught her hemstitching, and I helped her to cut and fit. She used to sit there at that machine by the window, pedaling the life out of it— she was so strong—and always singing them queer Bohemian songs, like she was the happiest thing in the world.

"'Ántonia,' I used to say, 'don't run that machine so fast. You won't hasten the day none that way.'

"Then she'd laugh and slow down for a little, but she'd soon forget and begin to pedal and sing again. I never saw a girl work harder to go to housekeeping right and well-prepared. Lovely table linen the Harlings had given her, and Lena Lingard had sent her nice things from Lincoln. We hemstitched all the tablecloths and pillow-cases, and some of the sheets. Old Mrs. Shimerda knit yards and yards of lace for her underclothes. Tony told me just how she meant to have everything in her house. She'd even bought silver spoons and forks, and kept them in her trunk. She was always coaxing brother to go to the post-office. Her young man did write her real often, from the different towns along his run.

"The first thing that troubled her was when he wrote that his run had been changed, and they would likely have to live in Denver. 'I'm a country girl,' she said, 'and I doubt if I'll be able to manage so well for him in a city. I was counting on keeping chickens, and maybe a cow.' She soon cheered up, though.

◀ What first troubled Ántonia about her wedding plans?

"At last she got the letter telling her when to come. She was shaken by it; she broke the seal and read it in this room. I suspected then that she'd begun to get faint-hearted, waiting; though she'd never let me see it.

"Then there was a great time of packing. It was in March, if I remember rightly, and a terrible muddy, raw spell, with the roads bad for hauling her things to town. And here let me say, Ambrosch did the right thing. He went to Black Hawk and bought her a set of plated silver in a purple velvet box, good enough for her station. He gave her three hundred dollars in money; I saw the check. He'd collected her wages all those first years she worked out, and it was but right. I shook him by the hand in this room. 'You're behaving like a man, Ambrosch,' I said, 'and I'm glad to see it, son.'

"'Twas a cold, raw day he drove her and her three trunks into Black Hawk to take the night train for Denver—the boxes had been shipped before. He stopped the wagon here, and she ran in to tell me good-bye. She threw her arms around me and kissed me, and thanked me for all I'd done for her. She was so happy she was crying and laughing at the same time, and her red cheeks was all wet with rain.

"'You're surely handsome enough for any man,' I said, looking her over.

"She laughed kind of flighty like, and whispered, 'Good-bye, dear house!' and then ran out to the wagon. I expect she meant that for you and your grandmother, as much as for me, so I'm particular to tell you. This house had always been a refuge to her.

"Well, in a few days we had a letter saying she got to Denver safe, and he was there to meet her. They were to be married in a few days. He was trying to get his promotion before he married, she said. I didn't like that, but I said nothing. The next week Yulka got a postal card, saying she was 'well and happy.' After that we heard nothing. A month went by, and old Mrs. Shimerda began to get fretful. Ambrosch was as sulky with me as if I'd picked out the man and arranged the match.

"One night brother William came in and said that on his way back from the fields he had passed a livery team from town, driving fast out the west road. There was a trunk on the front seat with the driver, and another behind. In the back seat there was a woman all bundled up; but for all her veils, he thought 'twas Ántonia Shimerda, or Ántonia Donovan, as her name ought now to be.

"The next morning I got brother to drive me over. I can walk still, but my feet ain't what they used to be, and I try to save myself. The lines outside the Shimerdas' house was full of washing, though it was the middle of the week. As we got nearer, I saw a sight that made my heart sink—all those underclothes we'd put so much work on, out there swinging in the wind. Yulka came bringing a dishpanful of wrung clothes, but she darted back into the house like she

▶ What news didn't Mrs. Steavens like?

was loath to see us. When I went in, Ántonia was standing over the tubs, just finishing up a big washing. Mrs. Shimerda was going about her work, talking and scolding to herself. She didn't so much as raise her eyes. Tony wiped her hand on her apron and held it out to me, looking at me steady but mournful. When I took her in my arms she drew away. 'Don't, Mrs. Steavens,' she says, 'you'll make me cry, and I don't want to.'

"I whispered and asked her to come out of doors with me. I knew she couldn't talk free before her mother. She went out with me, bareheaded, and we walked up toward the garden.

"'I'm not married, Mrs. Steavens,' she says to me very quiet and natural-like, 'and I ought to be.'

"'Oh, my child,' says I, 'what's happened to you? Don't be afraid to tell me!'

"She sat down on the draw-side, out of sight of the house. 'He's run away from me,' she said. 'I don't know if he ever meant to marry me.'

"'You mean he's thrown up his job and quit the country?' says I.

"'He didn't have any job. He'd been fired; blacklisted for knocking down fares. I didn't know. I thought he hadn't been treated right. He was sick when I got there. He'd just come out of the hospital. He lived with me till my money gave out, and afterward I found he hadn't really been hunting work at all. Then he just didn't come back. One nice fellow at the station told me, when I kept going to look for him, to give it up. He said he was afraid Larry'd gone bad and wouldn't come back any more. I guess he's gone to Old Mexico. The conductors get rich down there, collecting half-fares off the natives and robbing the company. He was always talking about fellows who had got ahead that way.'

◀ What did Ántonia find out about Larry when she got to Denver?

"I asked her, of course, why she didn't insist on a civil marriage at once— that would have given her some hold on him. She leaned her head on her hands, poor child, and said, 'I just don't know, Mrs. Steavens. I guess my patience was wore out, waiting so long. I thought if he saw how well I could do for him, he'd want to stay with me.'

"Jimmy, I sat right down on that bank beside her and made lament. I cried like a young thing. I couldn't help it. I was just about heart-broke. It was one of them lovely warm May days, and the wind was blowing and the colts jumping around in the pastures; but I felt bowed with despair. My Ántonia, that had so much good in her, had come home disgraced. And that Lena Lingard, that was always a bad one, say what you will, had turned out so well, and was coming home here every summer in her silks and her satins, and doing so much for her mother. I give credit where credit is due, but you know well enough, Jim Burden, there is a great difference in the principles of those two girls. And here it was the good one that had come to grief! I was poor comfort to her. I marveled at her calm. As we went back to the house, she stopped to feel of her clothes to see if they was drying well, and seemed to take pride in their whiteness—she said she'd been living in a brick block, where she didn't have proper conveniences to wash them.

"The next time I saw Ántonia, she was out in the fields ploughing corn. All that spring and summer she did the work of a man on the farm; it seemed to be an understood thing. Ambrosch didn't get any other hand to help him. Poor Marek had got violent and been sent away to an institution a good while back. We never even saw any of Tony's pretty dresses. She didn't take them out of her trunks. She was quiet and steady. Folks respected her industry and tried to treat her as if nothing had happened. They talked, to be sure; but not like they would if she'd put on airs. She was so crushed and quiet that nobody seemed to want to humble her. She never went anywhere. All that summer she never once came to see me. At first I was hurt, but I got to feel that it was because this house reminded her of too much. I went over there when I could, but the times when she was in from the fields were the times when I was

▶ On what does Ántonia's talk focus now?

▶ Why won't she go to the dentist in Black Hawk?

busiest here. She talked about the grain and the weather as if she'd never had another interest, and if I went over at night she always looked dead weary. She was afflicted with toothache; one tooth after another ulcerated, and she went about with her face swollen half the time. She wouldn't go to Black Hawk to a dentist for fear of meeting people she knew. Ambrosch had got over his good spell long ago, and was always surly. Once I told him he ought not to let Ántonia work so hard and pull herself down. He said, 'If you put that in her head, you better stay home.' And after that I did.

"Ántonia worked on through harvest and threshing, though she was too modest to go out threshing for the neighbors, like when she was young and free. I didn't see much of her until late that fall when she begun to herd Ambrosch's cattle in the open ground north of here, up toward the big dog town. Sometimes she used to bring them over the west hill, there, and I would run to meet her and walk north a piece with her. She had thirty cattle in her bunch; it had been dry, and the pasture was short, or she wouldn't have brought them so far.

"It was a fine open fall, and she liked to be alone. While the steers grazed, she used to sit on them grassy banks along the draws and sun herself for hours. Sometimes I slipped up to visit with her, when she hadn't gone too far.

"'It does seem like I ought to make lace, or knit like Lena used to,' she said one day, 'but if I start to work, I look around and forget to go on. It seems such a little while ago when Jim Burden and I was playing all over this country. Up here I can pick out the very places where my father used to stand. Sometimes I feel like I'm not going to live very long, so I'm just enjoying every day of this fall.'

"After the winter begun she wore a man's long overcoat and boots, and a man's felt hat with a wide brim. I used to watch her coming and going, and I could see that her steps were getting heavier. One day in December, the snow began to fall. Late in the afternoon I saw Ántonia driving her cattle homeward across the hill. The snow was flying round her and she bent to face it, looking more lonesome-like to me than usual. 'Deary me,' I says to myself, 'the girl's stayed out too late. It'll be dark before she gets them cattle put into the corral.' I seemed to sense she'd been feeling too miserable to get up and drive them.

"That very night, it happened. She got her cattle home, turned them into the corral, and went into the house, into her room behind the kitchen, and shut the door. There, without calling to anybody, without a groan, she lay down on the bed and bore her child.

"I was lifting supper when old Mrs. Shimerda came running down the basement stairs, out of breath and screeching:—

"'Baby come, baby come!' she says. 'Ambrosch much like devil!'

"Brother William is surely a patient man. He was just ready to sit down to a hot supper after a long day in the fields. Without a word he rose and went down to the barn and hooked up his team. He got us over there as quick as it was humanly possible. I went right in, and began to do for Ántonia; but she laid there with her eyes shut and took no account of me. The old woman got a tubful of warm water to wash the baby. I overlooked what she was doing and I said out loud:—

"'Mrs. Shimerda, don't you put that strong yellow soap near that baby. You'll blister its little skin.' I was indignant.

"'Mrs. Steavens,' Ántonia said from the bed, 'if you'll look in the top tray of my trunk, you'll see some fine soap.' That was the first word she spoke.

"After I'd dressed the baby, I took it out to show it to Ambrosch. He was muttering behind the stove and wouldn't look at it.

"'You'd better put it out in the rain-barrel,' he says.

"'Now, see here, Ambrosch,' says I, 'there's a law in this land, don't forget that. I stand here a witness that this baby has come into the world sound and strong, and I intend to keep an eye on what befalls it.' I pride myself I cowed him.

"Well I expect you're not much interested in babies, but Ántonia's got on fine. She loved it from the first as dearly as if she'd had a ring on her finger, and was never ashamed of it. It's a year and eight months old now, and no baby was ever better cared-for. Ántonia is a natural-born mother. I wish she could marry and raise a family, but I don't know as there's much chance now."

I slept that night in the room I used to have when I was a little boy, with the summer wind blowing in at the windows, bringing the smell of the ripe fields. I lay awake and watched the moonlight shining over the barn and the stacks and the pond, and the windmill making its old dark shadow against the blue sky.

▶ What does Ambrosch tell Mrs. Steavens to do with the baby? How does Mrs. Steavens respond?

Chapter 4

The next afternoon I walked over to the Shimerdas'. Yulka showed me the baby and told me that Ántonia was shocking wheat on the southwest quarter. I went down across the fields, and Tony saw me from a long way off. She stood still by her shocks, leaning on her pitchfork, watching me as I came. We met like the people in the old song[1], in silence, if not in tears. Her warm hand clasped mine.

"I thought you'd come, Jim. I heard you were at Mrs. Steavens's last night. I've been looking for you all day."

She was thinner than I had ever seen her, and looked as Mrs. Steavens said, "worked down," but there was a new kind of strength in the gravity of her face, and her color still gave her that look of deep-seated health and ardor. Still? Why, it flashed across me that though so much had happened in her life and in mine, she was barely twenty-four years old.

Ántonia stuck her fork in the ground, and instinctively we walked toward that unploughed patch at the crossing of the roads as the fittest place to talk to each other. We sat down outside the sagging wire fence that shut Mr. Shimerda's plot off from the rest of the world. The tall red grass had never been cut there. It had died down in winter and come up again in the spring until it was as thick and shrubby as some tropical garden-grass. I found myself telling her everything: why I had decided to study law and to go into the law office of one of my mother's relatives in New York City; about Gaston Cleric's death from pneumonia last winter, and the difference it had made in my life. She wanted to know about my friends, and my way of living, and my dearest hopes.

"Of course it means you are going away from us for good," she said with a sigh. "But that don't mean I'll lose you. Look at my papa here; he's been dead all these years, and yet he is more real to me than almost anybody else. He never goes out of my life. I talk to him and consult him all the time. The older I grow, the better I know him and the more I understand him."

She asked me whether I had learned to like big cities. "I'd always be miserable in a city. I'd die of lonesomeness. I like to be where I know every stack and tree, and where all the ground is friendly. I want to live and die here.

---

1. **the old song.** Reference to Byron's poem, "When we two parted," the last lines of which read "If I should meet thee/After long years/How should I greet thee/In silence and tears"

▶ For what does Ántonia believe she was put in this world?

▶ How has Ántonia impacted Jim's life?

Father Kelly says everybody's put into this world for something, and I know what I've got to do. I'm going to see that my little girl has a better chance than ever I had. I'm going to take care of that girl, Jim."

I told her I knew she would. "Do you know, Ántonia, since I've been away, I think of you more often than of anyone else in this part of the world. I'd have liked to have you for a sweetheart, or a wife, or my mother or my sister—anything that a woman can be to a man. The idea of you is a part of my mind; you influence my likes and dislikes, all my tastes, hundreds of times when I don't realize it. You really are a part of me."

She turned her bright, believing eyes to me, and the tears came up in them slowly. "How can it be like that, when you know so many people, and when I've disappointed you so? Ain't it wonderful, Jim, how much people can mean to each other? I'm so glad we had each other when we were little. I can't wait till my little girl's old enough to tell her about all the things we used to do. You'll always remember me when you think about old times, won't you? And I guess everybody thinks about old times, even the happiest people."

As we walked homeward across the fields, the sun dropped and lay like a great golden globe in the low west. While it hung there, the moon rose in the east, as big as a cartwheel, pale silver and streaked with rose color, thin as a bubble or a ghost-moon. For five, perhaps ten minutes, the two luminaries confronted each other across the level land, resting on opposite edges of the world. In that singular light every little tree and shock of wheat, every sunflower stalk and clump of snow-on-the-mountain, drew itself up high and pointed; the very clods and furrows in the fields seemed to stand up sharply. I felt the old pull of the earth, the solemn magic that comes out of those fields at nightfall. I wished I could be a little boy again, and that my way could end there.

▶ What pull does Jim feel, and what magic?

We reached the edge of the field, where our ways parted. I took her hands and held them against my breast, feeling once more how strong and warm and good they were, those brown hands, and remembering how many kind things they had done for me. I held them now a long while, over my heart. About us it was growing darker and darker, and I had to look hard to see her face, which I meant always to carry with me; the closest, realest face, under all the shadows of women's faces, at the very bottom of my memory.

▶ What does Jim intend to carry at the bottom of his memory?

"I'll come back," I said earnestly, through the soft, intrusive darkness.

"Perhaps you will"—I felt rather than saw her smile. "But even if you don't, you're here, like my father. So I won't be lonesome."

As I went back alone over that familiar road, I could almost believe that a boy and girl ran along beside me, as our shadows used to do, laughing and whispering to each other in the grass.

◀ What does Jim "almost believe"?

Respond to the Selection

If you were Ántonia at this point in her life, how would you feel about being back in Black Hawk? How would you feel about seeing Jim again after everything that has happened?

Investigate, Inquire, and Imagine

Recall: GATHERING FACTS

1a. What does Jim learn is Virgil's great hope? How does this hope apply also to Gaston Cleric? What line from Virgil (in English) does Jim associate with his old dream about Lena?

2a. Who comes to visit Jim in Lincoln?

3a. By the end of book 3, Jim is neglecting his studies at the University of Nebraska. What has distracted him? About whom does he think when he gets excited by what he is learning? What does Gaston Cleric suggest Jim do, and what is Jim's response?

4a. What has happened to Ántonia in Colorado? How does Jim say he felt about Ántonia when he first heard this story? What does Ántonia say is her purpose in life?

5a. What happens to Tiny Soderball? Where does Lena end up living?

Interpret: FINDING MEANING

→ 1b. How does Virgil's goal relate to Jim's memoirs? to Cather's novels? What is the significance of this line for the novel?

→ 2b. What significance does this visit have for Jim?

→ 3b. Why is this distraction so compelling for Jim? Why does he think about those people so much? How does Jim feel about Gaston Cleric's suggestion? What larger choice would agreeing to Cleric's suggestion force Jim to make?

→ 4b. Why does Jim feel this way about Ántonia at this point? What does Ántonia's response to her situation tell you about her character?

→ 5b. How does Jim feel about the way Tiny has lived? How can you tell?

Analyze: TAKING THINGS APART

6a. Ántonia and Lena have both played significant roles in the novel so far. In what ways are these two young women alike and different? How does each of them feel about the past? How does Jim feel about each of them? Of which is he more approving?

Synthesize: BRINGING THINGS TOGETHER

➤ 6b. If My Ántonia is supposedly about Ántonia, why did Cather devote an entire section of the novel to Lena Lingard? What does Lena enable readers to see about Ántonia?

Evaluate: MAKING JUDGMENTS

7a. Jim says, of the people and places of his past, "They stood out strengthened and simplified now, like the image of the plough against the sun." Based on this statement, describe the qualities of Jim's memories in your own words. Do you think his impressions of the "hired girls" are realistic and balanced? Why, or why not? What does he mean when he says, "They were so much alive in me that I scarcely stopped to wonder whether they were alive anywhere else, or how"?

Extend: CONNECTING IDEAS

➤ 7b. Why do you think Jim's memories have taken on these qualities? How do memories change over time?

Understanding Literature

Allusion. An **allusion** is a rhetorical technique in which reference is made to a person, event, object, or work from history or literature. The epigraph, or quote at the beginning of the novel, alludes to Virgil: "The best days are the first to pass." How is this allusion appropriate to the novel?

On your own paper, make a chart like the one below. Use the page numbers listed to find the allusion to each of the lines given from the Bible. Then copy the passage that makes the allusion. Finally, indicate what you think each allusion adds to the narrative.

Biblical Verse	Page	Passage	Purpose of Allusion
"And the angel of the Lord appeared unto him in a flame of fire out of the midst of a bush: and he looked, and behold, the bush burned with fire, and the bush was not consumed." Exodus 3:2	28		
"And the Lord God said unto the woman, What is this that thou hast done? And the woman said, The serpent beguiled me, and I did eat. And the Lord God said unto the serpent, Because thou hast done this, thou art cursed above all cattle, and above every beast of the field; upon thy belly shalt thou go, and dust shalt thou eat all the days of thy life: And I will put enmity between thee and the woman, and between thy seed and her seed, it shall bruise thy head, and thou shalt bruise his heel." Genesis 3:13–15	32		
"And out of the ground made the Lord God to grow every tree that is pleasant to the sight, and good for food; the tree of life also in the midst of the garden, and the tree of knowledge of good and evil." Genesis 2:9	54		
"The Philistines seized [Samson, leader of the Israelites], gouged out his eyes, took him down to Gaza, bound him in bronze chains, and put him to grind-ing in the prison." Judges 16:21	118–125		

Image and Imagery. Imagery is the set of images in a literary work. An **image** is language that creates a concrete representation of an object or an experience. An image is also the vivid mental picture created in the reader's mind by that language. What images do you remember most vividly from the first four books of the novel? Why do you think Cather uses sun imagery so frequently?

Foil. A **foil** is a character whose attributes, or characteristics, contrast with, and therefore throw into relief, the attributes of another character. Lena, with her rejection of farm and family life, is a foil for Ántonia, who embraces that lifestyle. In what sense might Mr. Harling be considered a foil for Mr. Shimerda?

BOOK V

Cuzak's Boys

Chapter 1

I told Ántonia I would come back, but life intervened, and it was twenty years before I kept my promise. I heard of her from time to time; that she married, very soon after I last saw her, a young Bohemian, a cousin of Anton Jelinek; that they were poor, and had a large family. Once when I was abroad I went into Bohemia, and from Prague I sent Ántonia some photographs of her native village. Months afterward came a letter from her, telling me the names and ages of her many children, but little else; signed, "Your old friend, Ántonia Cuzak." When I met Tiny Soderball in Salt Lake, she told me that Ántonia had not "done very well"; that her husband was not a man of much force, and she had had a hard life. Perhaps it was cowardice that kept me away so long. My business took me West several times every year, and it was always in the back of my mind that I would stop in Nebraska some day and go to see Ántonia. But I kept putting it off until the next trip. I did not want to find her aged and broken; I really dreaded it. In the course of twenty crowded years one parts with many illusions. I did not wish to lose the early ones. Some memories are realities, and are better than anything that can ever happen to one again.

◀ Why does Jim dread going to see Ántonia?

I owe it to Lena Lingard that I went to see Ántonia at last. I was in San Francisco two summers ago when both Lena and Tiny Soderball were in town. Tiny lives in a house of her own, and Lena's shop is in an apartment house just around the corner. It interested me, after so many years, to see the two women together. Tiny audits Lena's accounts occasionally, and invests her money for her; and Lena, apparently, takes care that Tiny doesn't grow too miserly. "If there's anything I can't stand," she said to me in Tiny's presence, "it's a shabby rich woman." Tiny smiled grimly and assured me that Lena would never be either shabby or rich. "And I don't want to be," the other agreed complacently.

Lena gave me a cheerful account of Ántonia and urged me to make her a visit.

"You really ought to go, Jim. It would be such a satisfaction to her. Never mind what Tiny says. There's nothing the matter with Cuzak. You'd like him. He isn't a hustler, but a rough man would never have suited Tony. Tony has nice children—ten or eleven of them by this time, I guess. I shouldn't care for a family of that size myself, but somehow it's just right for Tony. She'd love to show them to you."

◀ Would Lena want a family the size of Ántonia's? What does she think about Ántonia's having so many children?

On my way East I broke my journey at Hastings, in Nebraska, and set off with an open buggy and a fairly good livery team to find the Cuzak farm. At a little past midday, I knew I must be nearing my destination. Set back on a swell of land at my right, I saw a wide farmhouse, with a red barn and an ash grove, and cattle yards in front that sloped down to the highroad. I drew up my horses and was wondering whether I should drive in here, when I heard low voices. Ahead of me, in a plum thicket beside the road, I saw two boys bending over a dead dog. The little one, not more than four or five, was on his knees, his hands folded, and his close-clipped, bare head drooping forward in deep <u>dejection</u>. The other stood beside him, a hand on his shoulder, and was comforting him in a language I had not heard for a long while. When I stopped my horses opposite them, the older boy took his brother by the hand and came toward me. He, too, looked grave. This was evidently a sad afternoon for them.

"Are you Mrs. Cuzak's boys?" I asked.

▶ Whom does Jim meet on the way to Ántonia's house?

The younger one did not look up; he was submerged in his own feelings, but his brother met me with intelligent gray eyes. "Yes, sir."

"Does she live up there on the hill? I am going to see her. Get in and ride up with me."

He glanced at his reluctant little brother. "I guess we'd better walk. But we'll open the gate for you."

I drove along the side-road and they followed slowly behind. When I pulled up at the windmill, another boy, barefooted and curly-headed, ran out of the barn to tie my team for me. He was a handsome one, this chap, fair-skinned and freckled, with red cheeks and a ruddy pelt as thick as a lamb's wool, growing down on his neck in little tufts. He tied my team with two flourishes of his hands, and nodded when I asked him if his mother was at home. As he glanced at me, his face dimpled with a seizure of irrelevant merriment, and he shot up the windmill tower with a lightness that struck me as disdainful. I knew he was peering down at me as I walked toward the house.

Ducks and geese ran quacking across my path. White cats were sunning themselves among yellow pumpkins on the porch steps. I looked through the wire screen into a

---

words for everyday use   **de • jec • tion** (di jek' shən) n., lowness of spirits. *As much as everyone tried to keep their spirits up at the election results party for the losing candidate, the dejection in the room was evident.*

---

big, light kitchen with a white floor. I saw a long table, rows of wooden chairs against the wall, and a shining range in one corner. Two girls were washing dishes at the sink, laughing and chattering, and a little one, in a short pinafore, sat on a stool playing with a rag baby. When I asked for their mother, one of the girls dropped her towel, ran across the floor with noiseless bare feet, and disappeared. The older one, who wore shoes and stockings, came to the door to admit me. She was a buxom girl with dark hair and eyes, calm and self-possessed.

"Won't you come in? Mother will be here in a minute."

Before I could sit down in the chair she offered me, the miracle happened; one of those quiet moments that clutch the heart, and take more courage than the noisy, excited passages in life. Ántonia came in and stood before me; a stalwart, brown woman, flat-chested, her curly brown hair a little <u>grizzled</u>. It was a shock, of course. It always is, to meet people after long years, especially if they have lived as much and as hard as this woman had. We stood looking at each other. The eyes that peered anxiously at me were— simply Ántonia's eyes. I had seen no others like them since I looked into them last, though I had looked at so many thousands of human faces. As I confronted her, the changes grew less apparent to me, her identity stronger. She was there, in the full vigor of her personality, battered but not diminished, looking at me, speaking to me in the husky, breathy voice I remembered so well.

◀ How does Jim describe the moment Ántonia enters the room?

"My husband's not at home, sir. Can I do anything?"

"Don't you remember me, Ántonia? Have I changed so much?"

She frowned into the slanting sunlight that made her brown hair look redder than it was. Suddenly her eyes widened, her whole face seemed to grow broader. She caught her breath and put out two hard-worked hands.

"Why, it's Jim! Anna, Yulka, it's Jim Burden!" She had no sooner caught my hands than she looked alarmed. "What's happened? Is anybody dead?"

I patted her arm. "No. I didn't come to a funeral this time. I got off the train at Hastings and drove down to see you and your family."

She dropped my hand and began rushing about.

---

words for everyday use griz • zled (griz′ zəld) adj., sprinkled or streaked with gray. *The man's beard had grown more <u>grizzled</u> with age.*

"Anton, Yulka, Nina, where are you all? Run, Anna, and hunt for the boys. They're off looking for that dog, somewhere. And call Leo. Where is that Leo!" She pulled them out of corners and came bringing them like a mother cat bringing in her kittens. "You don't have to go right off, Jim? My oldest boy's not here. He's gone with papa to the street fair at Wilber. I won't let you go! You've got to stay and see Rudolph and our papa." She looked at me imploringly, panting with excitement.

While I reassured her and told her there would be plenty of time, the barefooted boys from outside were slipping into the kitchen and gathering about her.

"Now, tell me their names, and how old they are."

As she told them off in turn, she made several mistakes about ages, and they roared with laughter. When she came to my light-footed friend of the windmill, she said, "This is Leo, and he's old enough to be better than he is."

He ran up to her and butted her playfully with his curly head, like a little ram, but his voice was quite desperate. "You've forgot! You always forget mine. It's mean! Please tell him, mother!" He clenched his fists in vexation and looked up at her <u>impetuously</u>.

She wound her forefinger in his yellow fleece and pulled it, watching him. "Well, how old are you?"

"I'm twelve," he panted, looking not at me but at her; "I'm twelve years old, and I was born on Easter Day!"

She nodded to me. "It's true. He was an Easter baby."

The children all looked at me, as if they expected me to exhibit astonishment or delight at this information. Clearly, they were proud of each other, and of being so many. When they had all been introduced, Anna, the eldest daughter, who had met me at the door, scattered them gently, and came bringing a white apron which she tied round her mother's waist.

"Now, mother, sit down and talk to Mr. Burden. We'll finish the dishes quietly and not disturb you."

Ántonia looked about, quite distracted. "Yes, child, but why don't we take him into the parlor, now that we've got a nice parlor for company?"

The daughter laughed indulgently, and took my hat from me. "Well, you're here, now, mother, and if you talk here, Yulka and I can listen, too. You can show him the parlor after while." She smiled at me, and went back to the dishes, with her sister. The little girl with the rag doll found a place on the bottom step of an enclosed back stairway, and sat with her toes curled up, looking out at us expectantly.

"She's Nina, after Nina Harling," Ántonia explained. "Ain't her eyes like Nina's? I declare, Jim, I loved you children almost as much as I love my own. These children know all about you and Charley and Sally, like as if they'd grown up with you. I can't think of what I want to say, you've got me so stirred up. And then, I've forgot my English so. I don't often talk it any more. I tell the children I used to speak real well." She said they always spoke Bohemian at home. The little ones could not speak English at all—didn't learn it until they went to school.

"I can't believe it's you, sitting here, in my own kitchen. You wouldn't have known me, would you, Jim? You've kept so young, yourself. But it's easier for a man. I can't see how my Anton looks any older than the day I married him. His teeth have kept so nice. I haven't got many left. But I feel just as young as I used to, and I can do as much work. Oh, we don't have to work so hard now! We've got plenty to help us, papa and me. And how many have you got, Jim?"

When I told her I had no children, she seemed embarrassed. "Oh, ain't that too bad! Maybe you could take one of my bad ones, now? That Leo; he's the worst of all." She leaned toward me with a smile. "And I love him the best," she whispered.

"Mother!" the two girls murmured reproachfully from the dishes.

Ántonia threw up her head and laughed. "I can't help it. You know I do. Maybe it's because he came on Easter Day, I don't know. And he's never out of mischief one minute!"

I was thinking, as I watched her, how little it mattered—about her teeth, for instance. I know so many women who have kept all the things that she had lost, but whose inner glow has faded. Whatever else was gone, Ántonia had not lost the fire of life. Her skin, so brown and hardened, had not that look of flabbiness, as if the sap beneath it had been secretly drawn away.

◀ What has Ántonia not lost?

While we were talking, the little boy whom they called Jan came in and sat down on the step beside Nina, under the hood of the stairway. He wore a funny long gingham apron, like a smock, over his trousers, and his hair was clipped so short that his head looked white and naked. He watched us out of his big, sorrowful gray eyes.

"He wants to tell you about the dog, mother. They found it dead," Anna said, as she passed us on her way to the cupboard.

Ántonia beckoned the boy to her. He stood by her chair, leaning his elbows on her knees and twisting her apron strings in his slender fingers, while he told her his story softly in Bohemian, and the tears brimmed over and hung on his long lashes. His mother listened, spoke soothingly to him and in a whisper promised him something that made him give her a quick, teary smile. He slipped away and whispered his secret to Nina, sitting close to her and talking behind his hand.

When Anna finished her work and had washed her hands, she came and stood behind her mother's chair. "Why don't we show Mr. Burden our new fruit cave?" she asked.

We started off across the yard with the children at our heels. The boys were standing by the windmill, talking about the dog; some of them ran ahead to open the cellar door. When we descended, they all came down after us, and seemed quite as proud of the cave as the girls were. Ambrosch, the thoughtful-looking one who had directed me down by the plum bushes, called my attention to the stout brick walls and the cement floor. "Yes, it is a good way from the house," he admitted. "But, you see, in winter there are nearly always some of us around to come out and get things."

Anna and Yulka showed me three small barrels; one full of dill pickles, one full of chopped pickles, and one full of pickled watermelon rinds.

"You wouldn't believe, Jim, what it takes to feed them all!" their mother exclaimed. "You ought to see the bread we bake on Wednesdays and Saturdays! It's no wonder their poor papa can't get rich, he has to buy so much sugar for us to preserve with. We have our own wheat ground for flour,—but then there's that much less to sell."

Nina and Jan, and a little girl named Lucie, kept shyly pointing out to me the shelves of glass jars. They said nothing, but, glancing at me, traced on the glass with their finger-tips the outline of the cherries and strawberries and crab-apples within, trying by a blissful expression of countenance to give me some idea of their deliciousness.

"Show him the spiced plums, mother. Americans don't have those," said one of the older boys. "Mother uses them to make *kolaches*,[1]" he added.

Leo, in a low voice, tossed off some scornful remark in Bohemian.

◀ Why is Leo initially scornful of Jim?

I turned to him. "You think I don't know what kolaches are, eh? You're mistaken, young man. I've eaten your mother's kolaches long before that Easter Day when you were born."

"Always too fresh, Leo," Ambrosch remarked with a shrug.

Leo dived behind his mother and grinned out at me.

We turned to leave the cave; Ántonia and I went up the stairs first, and the children waited. We were standing outside talking, when they all came running up the steps together, big and little, tow heads and gold heads and brown, and flashing little naked legs; a <u>veritable</u> explosion of life out of the dark cave into the sunlight. It made me dizzy for a moment.

The boys escorted us to the front of the house, which I hadn't yet seen; in farmhouses, somehow, life comes and goes by the back door. The roof was so steep that the eaves were not much above the forest of tall hollyhocks, now brown and in seed. Through July, Ántonia said, the house was buried in them; the Bohemians, I remembered, always planted hollyhocks. The front yard was enclosed by a thorny locust hedge, and at the gate grew two silvery, mothlike trees of the mimosa family. From here one looked down over the cattle yards, with their two long ponds, and over a wide stretch of stubble which they told me was a rye-field in summer.

At some distance behind the house were an ash grove and two orchards; a cherry orchard, with gooseberry and currant bushes between the rows, and an apple orchard, sheltered by a high hedge from the hot winds. The older children turned back when we reached the hedge, but Jan and Nina and Lucie crept through it by a hole known only to themselves and hid under the low-branching mulberry bushes.

---

1. *kolaches*. Pastries from Bohemia, typically filled with fruit

words for everyday use

ver • i • ta • ble (ver′ ə tə bəl) adj., true, actual. *She has a <u>veritable</u> mountain of home-work to do, and it would take her the whole weekend to climb through it.*

▶ How does Ántonia feel about the trees in the orchards?

As we walked through the apple orchard, grown up in tall bluegrass, Ántonia kept stopping to tell me about one tree and another. "I love them as if they were people," she said, rubbing her hand over the bark. "There wasn't a tree here when we first came. We planted every one, and used to carry water for them, too—after we'd been working in the fields all day. Anton, he was a city man, and he used to get discouraged. But I couldn't feel so tired that I wouldn't fret about these trees when there was a dry time. They were on my mind like children. Many a night after he was asleep I've got up and come out and carried water to the poor things. And now, you see, we have the good of them. My man worked in the orange groves in Florida, and he knows all about grafting. There ain't one of our neighbors has an orchard that bears like ours."

In the middle of the orchard we came upon a grape arbor, with seats built along the sides and a warped plank table. The three children were waiting for us there. They looked up at me bashfully and made some request of their mother.

"They want me to tell you how the teacher has the school picnic here every year. These don't go to school yet, so they think it's all like the picnic."

After I had admired the arbor sufficiently, the youngsters ran away to an open place where there was a rough jungle of French pinks, and squatted down among them, crawling about and measuring with a string. "Jan wants to bury his dog there," Ántonia explained. "I had to tell him he could. He's kind of like Nina Harling; you remember how hard she used to take little things? He has funny notions, like her."

We sat down and watched them. Ántonia leaned her elbows on the table. There was the deepest peace in that orchard. It was surrounded by a triple enclosure; the wire fence, then the hedge of thorny locusts, then the mulberry hedge which kept out the hot winds of summer and held fast to the protecting snows of winter. The hedges were so tall that we could see nothing but the blue sky above them, neither the barn roof nor the windmill. The afternoon sun poured down on us through the drying grape leaves. The orchard seemed full of sun, like a cup, and we could smell the ripe apples on the trees. The crabs hung on the branches as thick as beads on a string, purple-red, with a thin silvery glaze over them. Some hens and ducks had crept through the hedge and were pecking at the fallen apples. The drakes were handsome fellows, with pinkish gray bodies, their heads and necks covered with iridescent green feathers which grew close and full, changing to blue like a peacock's neck. Ántonia said they always reminded her of soldiers—some uniform she had seen in the old country, when she was a child.

"Are there any quail left now?" I asked. I reminded her how she used to go hunting with me the last summer before we moved to town. "You weren't a bad shot, Tony. Do you remember how you used to want to run away and go for ducks with Charley Harling and me?"

"I know, but I'm afraid to look at a gun now." She picked up one of the drakes and ruffled his green capote[2] with her fingers. "Ever since I've had children, I don't like to kill anything. It makes me kind of faint to wring an old goose's neck. Ain't that strange, Jim?"

◀ How has having children changed Ántonia's feelings about guns?

"I don't know. The young Queen of Italy said the same thing once, to a friend of mine. She used to be a great huntswoman, but now she feels as you do, and only shoots clay pigeons."

"Then I'm sure she's a good mother," Ántonia said warmly.

She told me how she and her husband had come out to this new country when the farm land was cheap and could be had on easy payments. The first ten years were a hard struggle. Her husband knew very little about farming and often grew discouraged. "We'd never have got through if I hadn't been so strong. I've always had good health, thank God, and I was able to help him in the fields until right up to the time before my babies came. Our children were good about taking care of each other. Martha, the one you saw when she was a baby, was such a help to me, and she trained Anna to be just like her. My Martha's married now, and has a baby of her own. Think of that, Jim!

"No, I never got down-hearted. Anton's a good man, and I loved my children and always believed they would turn out well. I belong on a farm. I'm never lonesome here like I used to be in town. You remember what sad spells I used to have, when I didn't know what was the matter with me? I've never had them out here. And I don't mind work a bit, if I don't have to put up with sadness." She leaned her chin on her hand and looked down through the orchard, where the sunlight was growing more and more golden.

◀ Where does Ántonia feel she belongs?

---

2. **capote.** Iridescent green feathers on the duck's head

"You ought never to have gone to town, Tony," I said, wondering at her.

▶ What makes her glad she went to live in town for a while?

She turned to me eagerly. "Oh, I'm glad I went! I'd never have known anything about cooking or housekeeping if I hadn't. I learned nice ways at the Harlings', and I've been able to bring my children up so much better. Don't you think they are pretty well-behaved for country children? If it hadn't been for what Mrs. Harling taught me, I expect I'd have brought them up like wild rabbits. No, I'm glad I had a chance to learn; but I'm thankful none of my daughters will ever have to work out. The trouble with me was, Jim, I never could believe harm of anybody I loved."

While we were talking, Ántonia assured me that she could keep me for the night. "We've plenty of room. Two of the boys sleep in the haymow till cold weather comes, but there's no need for it. Leo always begs to sleep there, and Ambrosch goes along to look after him."

I told her I would like to sleep in the haymow, with the boys.

"You can do just as you want to. The chest is full of clean blankets, put away for winter. Now I must go, or my girls will be doing all the work, and I want to cook your supper myself."

As we went toward the house, we met Ambrosch and Anton, starting off with their milking-pails to hunt the cows. I joined them, and Leo accompanied us at some distance, running ahead and starting up at us out of clumps of ironweed, calling, "I'm a jack rabbit," or, "I'm a big bull-snake."

▶ How does Jim feel, walking across the land with Ántonia's sons?

I walked between the two older boys—straight, well-made fellows, with good heads and clear eyes. They talked about their school and the new teacher, told me about the crops and the harvest, and how many steers they would feed that winter. They were easy and confidential with me, as if I were an old friend of the family— and not too old. I felt like a boy in their company, and all manner of forgotten interests revived in me. It seemed, after all, so natural to be walking along a barbed-wire fence beside the sunset, toward a red pond, and to see my shadow moving along at my right, over the close-cropped grass.

"Has mother shown you the pictures you sent her from the old country?" Ambrosch asked. "We've had them framed and they're hung up in the parlor. She was so glad to get them. I don't believe I ever saw her so pleased about anything." There was a note of simple gratitude in his voice that made me wish I had given more occasion for it.

I put my hand on his shoulder. "Your mother, you know, was very much loved by all of us. She was a beautiful girl."

"Oh, we know!" They both spoke together; seemed a little surprised that I should think it necessary to mention this. "Everybody liked her, didn't they? The Harlings and your grandmother, and all the town people."

"Sometimes," I ventured, "it doesn't occur to boys that their mother was ever young and pretty."

"Oh, we know!" they said again, warmly. "She's not very old now," Ambrosch added. "Not much older than you."

"Well," I said, "if you weren't nice to her, I think I'd take a club and go for the whole lot of you. I couldn't stand it if you boys were inconsiderate, or thought of her as if she were just somebody who looked after you. You see I was very much in love with your mother once, and I know there's nobody like her."

◀ What does Jim confess to the boys?

The boys laughed and seemed pleased and embarrassed.

"She never told us that," said Anton. "But she's always talked lots about you, and about what good times you used to have. She has a picture of you that she cut out of the Chicago paper once, and Leo says he recognized you when you drove up to the windmill. You can't tell about Leo, though; sometimes he likes to be smart."

We brought the cows home to the corner nearest the barn, and the boys milked them while night came on. Everything was as it should be: the strong smell of sunflowers and ironweed in the dew, the clear blue and gold of the sky, the evening star, the purr of the milk into the pails, the grunts and squeals of the pigs fighting over their supper. I began to feel the loneliness of the farm-boy at evening, when the chores seem everlastingly the same, and the world so far away.

◀ How does Jim explain "the loneliness of the farm-boy"?

What a tableful we were at supper; two long rows of restless heads in the lamplight, and so many eyes fastened excitedly upon Ántonia as she sat at the head of the table, filling the plates and starting the dishes on their way. The children were seated according to a system; a little one next an older one, who was to watch over his behavior and to see that he got his food. Anna and Yulka left their chairs from time to time to bring fresh plates of *kolaches* and pitchers of milk.

After supper we went into the parlor, so that Yulka and Leo could play for me. Ántonia went first, carrying the lamp. There were not nearly chairs enough to go round, so the younger children sat down on the bare floor. Little

▶ *Whose violin does Leo play?*

Lucie whispered to me that they were going to have a parlor carpet if they got ninety cents for their wheat. Leo, with a good deal of fussing, got out his violin. It was old Mr. Shimerda's instrument, which Ántonia had always kept, and it was too big for him. But he played very well for a self-taught boy. Poor Yulka's efforts were not so successful. While they were playing, little Nina got up from her corner, came out into the middle of the floor, and began to do a pretty little dance on the boards with her bare feet. No one paid the least attention to her, and when she was through she stole back and sat down by her brother.

Ántonia spoke to Leo in Bohemian. He frowned and wrinkled up his face. He seemed to be trying to pout, but his attempt only brought out dimples in unusual places. After twisting and screwing the keys, he played some Bohemian airs, without the organ to hold him back, and that went better. The boy was so restless that I had not had a chance to look at his face before. My first impression was right; he really was faun-like. He hadn't much head behind his ears, and his tawny fleece grew down thick to the back of his neck. His eyes were not frank and wide apart like those of the other boys, but were deep-set, gold-green in color, and seemed sensitive to the light. His mother said he got hurt oftener than all the others put together. He was always trying to ride the colts before they were broken, teasing the turkey gobbler, seeing just how much red the bull would stand for, or how sharp the new axe was.

After the concert was over, Ántonia brought out a big boxful of photographs: she and Anton in their wedding clothes, holding hands; her brother Ambrosch and his very fat wife, who had a farm of her own, and who bossed her husband, I was delighted to hear; the three Bohemian Marys and their large families.

"You wouldn't believe how steady those girls have turned out," Ántonia remarked. "Mary Svoboda's the best butter-maker in all this country, and a fine manager. Her children will have a grand chance."

As Ántonia turned over the pictures the young Cuzaks stood behind her chair, looking over her shoulder with interested faces. Nina and Jan, after trying to see round the taller ones, quietly brought a chair, climbed up on it, and stood close together, looking. The little boy forgot his shyness and grinned delightedly when familiar faces came into view. In the group about Ántonia I was conscious of a kind of physical harmony. They leaned this way and that, and were not afraid to touch each other. They contemplated the photographs with pleased recognition; looked at some admiringly, as if these characters in their mother's girlhood had been remarkable people. The little children, who could not speak English, murmured comments to each other in their rich old language.

Ántonia held out a photograph of Lena that had come from San Francisco last Christmas. "Does she still look like that? She hasn't been home for six years now." Yes, it was exactly like Lena, I told her; a comely woman, a trifle too plump, in a hat a trifle too large, but with the old lazy eyes, and the old dimpled ingenuousness still lurking at the corners of her mouth.

There was a picture of Frances Harling in a befrogged riding costume that I remembered well. "Isn't she fine!" the girls murmured. They all assented. One could see that Frances had come down as a heroine in the family legend. Only Leo was unmoved.

"And there's Mr. Harling, in his grand fur coat. He was awfully rich, wasn't he, mother?"

"He wasn't any Rockefeller," put in Master Leo, in a very low tone, which reminded me of the way in which Mrs. Shimerda had once said that my grandfather "wasn't Jesus." His habitual skepticism was like a direct inheritance from that old woman.

◀ From whom does Leo get his skepticism?

"None of your smart speeches," said Ambrosch severely.

Leo poked out a supple red tongue at him, but a moment later broke into a giggle at a tintype of two men, uncomfortably seated, with an awkward-looking boy in baggy clothes standing between them: Jake and Otto and I! We had it taken, I remembered, when we went to Black Hawk on the first Fourth of July I spent in Nebraska. I was glad to see Jake's grin again, and Otto's ferocious moustaches. The young Cuzaks knew all about them.

"He made grandfather's coffin, didn't he?" Anton asked.

"Wasn't they good fellows, Jim?" Ántonia's eyes filled. "To this day I'm ashamed because I quarreled with Jake that way. I was saucy and <u>impertinent</u> to him, Leo, like you are with people sometimes, and I wish somebody had made me behave."

"We aren't through with you, yet," they warned me. They produced a photograph taken just before I went away

---

words for everyday use

im • per • ti • nent (im pər′ tən ənt) adj., rude. *I understand that you are angry, but I don't appreciate your <u>impertinent</u> comments.*

to college; a tall youth in striped trousers and a straw hat, trying to look easy and <u>jaunty</u>.

"Tell us, Mr. Burden," said Charley, "about the rattler you killed at the dog town. How long was he? Sometimes mother says six feet and sometimes she says five."

These children seemed to be upon very much the same terms with Ántonia as the Harling children had been so many years before. They seemed to feel the same pride in her, and to look to her for stories and entertainment as we used to do.

It was eleven o'clock when I at last took my bag and some blankets and started for the barn with the boys. Their mother came to the door with us, and we <u>tarried</u> for a moment to look out at the white slope of the corral and the two ponds asleep in the moonlight, and the long sweep of the pasture under the star-sprinkled sky.

The boys told me to choose my own place in the hay-mow, and I lay down before a big window, left open in warm weather, that looked out into the stars. Ambrosch and Leo cuddled up in a hay-cave, back under the eaves, and lay giggling and whispering. They tickled each other and tossed and tumbled in the hay; and then, all at once, as if they had been shot, they were still. There was hardly a minute between giggles and bland slumber.

▶ What does Jim think about before falling asleep?

I lay awake for a long while, until the slow-moving moon passed my window on its way up the heavens. I was thinking about Ántonia and her children; about Anna's solicitude for her, Ambrosch's grave affection, Leo's jealous, animal little love. That moment, when they all came tumbling out of the cave into the light, was a sight any man might have come far to see. Ántonia had always been one to leave images in the mind that did not fade—that grew stronger with time. In my memory there was a succession of such pictures, fixed there like the old woodcuts of one's first primer: Ántonia kicking her bare legs against the sides of my pony when we came home in triumph with our snake; Ántonia in her black shawl and fur cap, as she stood by her father's grave in the snowstorm; Ántonia coming in with her work-team along the evening sky-line. She lent herself to immemorial human attitudes which we

words for everyday use

jaun • ty (jon′ tē) adj., stylish. *She preferred to wear the hat at a jaunty angle rather than directly over the crown of her head.*

tar • ry (tar′ ē) vi., linger, wait. *Tom tarried in the hallway, hoping to see Julie at her locker.*

recognize by instinct as universal and true. I had not been mistaken. She was a battered woman now, not a lovely girl; but she still had that something which fires the imagination, could still stop one's breath for a moment by a look or gesture that somehow revealed the meaning in common things. She had only to stand in the orchard, to put her hand on a little crab tree and look up at the apples, to make you feel the goodness of planting and tending and harvesting at last. All the strong things of her heart came out in her body, that had been so tireless in serving generous emotions.

◄ What unusual quality does Ántonia still possess?

It was no wonder that her sons stood tall and straight. She was a rich mine of life, like the founders of early races.

◄ To what two things does Jim compare Ántonia?

Chapter 2

When I awoke in the morning long bands of sunshine were coming in at the window and reaching back under the eaves where the two boys lay. Leo was wide awake and was tickling his brother's leg with a dried cone-flower he had pulled out of the hay. Ambrosch kicked at him and turned over. I closed my eyes and pretended to be asleep. Leo lay on his back, elevated one foot, and began exercising his toes. He picked up dried flowers with his toes and brandished them in the belt of sunlight. After he had amused himself thus for some time, he rose on one elbow and began to look at me, cautiously, then critically, blinking his eyes in the light. His expression was <u>droll</u>; it dismissed me lightly. "This old fellow is no different from other people. He doesn't know my secret." He seemed conscious of possessing a keener power of enjoyment than other people; his quick recognitions made him frantically impatient of deliberate judgments. He always knew what he wanted without thinking.

After dressing in the hay, I washed my face in cold water at the windmill. Breakfast was ready when I entered the kitchen, and Yulka was baking griddle-cakes. The three older boys set off for the fields early. Leo and Yulka were to drive to town to meet their father, who would return from Wilber on the noon train.

"We'll only have a lunch at noon," Ántonia said, "and cook the geese for supper, when our papa will be here. I wish my Martha could come down to see you. They have a Ford car now, and she don't seem so far away from me as she used to. But her husband's crazy about his farm and about having everything just right, and they almost never get away except on Sundays. He's a handsome boy, and he'll be rich some day. Everything he takes hold of turns out well. When they bring that baby in here, and unwrap him, he looks like a little prince; Martha takes care of him so beautiful. I'm reconciled to her being away from me now, but at first I cried like I was putting her into her coffin."

We were alone in the kitchen, except for Anna, who was pouring cream into the churn. She looked up at me. "Yes,

---

words for everyday use

droll (drōl) adj., having a humorous, whimsical, or odd quality. *The cartoons Barbara drew all over her book covers revealed her <u>droll</u> personality.*

she did. We were just ashamed of mother. She went round crying, when Martha was so happy, and the rest of us were all glad. Joe certainly was patient with you, mother."

Ántonia nodded and smiled at herself. "I know it was silly, but I couldn't help it. I wanted her right here. She'd never been away from me a night since she was born. If Anton had made trouble about her when she was a baby, or wanted me to leave her with my mother, I wouldn't have married him. I couldn't. But he always loved her like she was his own."

"I didn't even know Martha wasn't my full sister until after she was engaged to Joe," Anna told me.

Toward the middle of the afternoon the wagon drove in, with the father and the eldest son. I was smoking in the orchard, and as I went out to meet them, Ántonia came running down from the house and hugged the two men as if they had been away for months.

"Papa" interested me, from my first glimpse of him. He was shorter than his older sons; a crumpled little man, with run-over boot heels, and he carried one shoulder higher than the other. But he moved very quickly, and there was an air of jaunty liveliness about him. He had a strong, ruddy color, thick black hair, a little grizzled, a curly moustache, and red lips. His smile showed the strong teeth of which his wife was so proud, and as he saw me his lively, <u>quizzical</u> eyes told me that he knew all about me. He looked like a humorous philosopher who had hitched up one shoulder under the burdens of life, and gone on his way having a good time when he could. He advanced to meet me and gave me a hard hand, burned red on the back and heavily coated with hair. He wore his Sunday clothes, very thick and hot for the weather, an unstarched white shirt, and a blue necktie with big white dots, like a little boy's, tied in a flowing bow. Cuzak began at once to talk about his holiday—from politeness he spoke in English.

"Mama, I wish you had see the lady dance on the slack-wire in the street at night. They throw a bright light on her and she float through the air something beautiful, like a bird! They have a dancing bear, like in the old country, and two three merry-go-around, and people in balloons, and what you call the big wheel, Rudolph?"

words for everyday use

quiz • zi • cal (kwi' zi kəl) adj., expressive of curiosity. *As if puzzled by my behavior, the woman gave me a quizzical look.*

"A Ferris wheel," Rudolph entered the conversation in a deep baritone voice. He was six foot two, and had a chest like a young blacksmith. "We went to the big dance in the hall behind the saloon last night, mother, and I danced with all the girls, and so did father. I never saw so many pretty girls. It was a Bohunk crowd, for sure. We didn't hear a word of English on the street, except from the show people, did we, papa?"

Cuzak nodded. "And very many send word to you, Ántonia. You will excuse"—turning to me—"if I tell her." While we walked toward the house he related incidents and delivered messages in the tongue he spoke fluently, and I dropped a little behind, curious to know what their relations had become—or remained. The two seemed to be on terms of easy friendliness, touched with humor. Clearly, she was the impulse, and he the corrective. As they went up the hill he kept glancing at her sidewise, to see whether she got his point, or how she received it. I noticed later that he always looked at people sidewise, as a work-horse does at its yoke-mate. Even when he sat opposite me in the kitchen, talking, he would turn his head a little toward the clock or the stove and look at me from the side, but with frankness and good-nature. This trick did not suggest <u>duplicity</u> or secretiveness, but merely long habit, as with the horse.

He had brought a tintype of himself and Rudolph for Ántonia's collection, and several paper bags of candy for the children. He looked a little disappointed when his wife showed him a big box of candy I had got in Denver—she hadn't let the children touch it the night before. He put his candy away in the cupboard, "for when she rains," and glanced at the box, chuckling. "I guess you must have hear about how my family ain't so small," he said.

Cuzak sat down behind the stove and watched his women-folk and the little children with equal amusement. He thought they were nice, and he thought they were funny, evidently. He had been off dancing with the girls and forgetting that he was an old fellow, and now his family rather surprised him; he seemed to think it a joke that all these children should belong to him. As the younger ones slipped up to him in his retreat, he kept taking things

▶ What seems to disappoint Cuzak?

---

words for everyday use

du • pli • ci • ty (du pli′ sə tē) n., contradictory doubleness of thought, speech, or action. *You say she "talks out of both sides of her mouth"; do you mean to accuse her of <u>duplicity</u>?*

out of his pockets; penny dolls, a wooden clown, a balloon pig that was inflated by a whistle. He beckoned to the little boy they called Jan, whispered to him, and presented him with a paper snake, gently, so as not to startle him. Looking over the boy's head he said to me, "This one is bashful. He gets left."

Cuzak had brought home with him a roll of illustrated Bohemian papers. He opened them and began to tell his wife the news, much of which seemed to relate to one person. I heard the name Vasakova, Vasakova, repeated several times with lively interest, and presently I asked him whether he were talking about the singer, Maria Vasak[1].

"You know? You have heard, maybe?" he asked incredulously. When I assured him that I had heard her, he pointed out her picture and told me that Vasak had broken her leg, climbing in the Austrian Alps, and would not be able to fill her engagements. He seemed delighted to find that I had heard her sing in London and in Vienna; got out his pipe and lit it to enjoy our talk the better. She came from his part of Prague. His father used to mend her shoes for her when she was a student. Cuzak questioned me about her looks, her popularity, her voice; but he particularly wanted to know whether I had noticed her tiny feet, and whether I thought she had saved much money. She was extravagant, of course, but he hoped she wouldn't squander everything, and have nothing left when she was old. As a young man, working in *Wien*[2], he had seen a good many artists who were old and poor, making one glass of beer last all evening, and "it was not very nice, that."

When the boys came in from milking and feeding, the long table was laid, and two brown geese, stuffed with apples, were put down sizzling before Ántonia. She began to carve, and Rudolph, who sat next his mother, started the plates on their way. When everybody was served, he looked across the table at me.

"Have you been to Black Hawk lately, Mr. Burden? Then I wonder if you've heard about the Cutters?"

---

1. **Maria Vasak.** Name Cather appears to have made up to refer to the Czech opera singer Emmy Destinn, also known as Destinnova

2. *Wien.* German spelling of Vienna, the culturally sophisticated city in Austria that was home to the Hapsburg ruling family, which governed Bohemia

---

words for everyday use

squan • der (skwän′ dər) vt., to spend extravagantly or foolishly. *It's sometimes tempting to squander one's paycheck on entertainment rather than saving for the future.*

No, I had heard nothing at all about them.

"Then you must tell him, son, though it's a terrible thing to talk about at supper. Now, all you children be quiet, Rudolph is going to tell about the murder."

"Hurrah! The murder!" the children murmured, looking pleased and interested.

Rudolph told his story in great detail, with occasional promptings from his mother or father.

Wick Cutter and his wife had gone on living in the house that Ántonia and I knew so well, and in the way we knew so well. They grew to be very old people. He shriveled up, Ántonia said, until he looked like a little old yellow monkey, for his beard and his fringe of hair never changed color. Mrs. Cutter remained flushed and wild-eyed as we had known her, but as the years passed she became afflicted with a shaking palsy which made her nervous nod continuous instead of occasional. Her hands were so uncertain that she could no longer disfigure china, poor woman! As the couple grew older, they quarreled more and more often about the ultimate <u>disposition</u> of their "property." A new law was passed in the state, securing the surviving wife a third of her husband's estate under all conditions. Cutter was tormented by the fear that Mrs. Cutter would live longer than he, and that eventually her "people," whom he had always hated so violently, would inherit. Their quarrels on this subject passed the boundary of the close-growing cedars, and were heard in the street by whoever wished to loiter and listen.

▶ *What did Cutter buy at the hardware store?*

One morning, two years ago, Cutter went into the hardware store and bought a pistol, saying he was going to shoot a dog, and adding that he "thought he would take a shot at an old cat while he was about it." (Here the children interrupted Rudolph's narrative by smothered giggles.)

Cutter went out behind the hardware store, put up a target, practiced for an hour or so, and then went home. At six o'clock that evening, when several men were passing the Cutter house on their way home to supper, they heard a pistol shot. They paused and were looking doubtfully at one another, when another shot came crashing through an upstairs window. They ran into the house and found Wick

words for everyday use
dis • po • si • tion (dis pə zi' shən) n., transfer to the care or possession of another. *The woman made a will in which she carefully outlined the <u>disposition</u> of her belongings.*

Cutter lying on a sofa in his upstairs bedroom, with his throat torn open, bleeding on a roll of sheets he had placed beside his head.

"Walk in, gentlemen," he said weakly. "I am alive, you see, and competent. You are witnesses that I have survived my wife. You will find her in her own room. Please make your examination at once, so that there will be no mistake."

◄ What did Cutter want the men to witness?

One of the neighbors telephoned for a doctor, while the others went into Mrs. Cutter's room. She was lying on her bed, in her nightgown and wrapper, shot through the heart. Her husband must have come in while she was taking her afternoon nap and shot her, holding the revolver near her breast. Her nightgown was burned from the powder.

The horrified neighbors rushed back to Cutter. He opened his eyes and said distinctly, "Mrs. Cutter is quite dead, gentlemen, and I am conscious. My affairs are in order." Then, Rudolph said, "he let go and died."

On his desk the coroner found a letter, dated at five o'clock that afternoon. It stated that he had just shot his wife; that any will she might secretly have made would be invalid, as he survived her. He meant to shoot himself at six o'clock and would, if he had strength, fire a shot through the window in the hope that passersby might come in and see him "before life was extinct," as he wrote.

◄ What was Cutter's plan?

"Now, would you have thought that man had such a cruel heart?" Ántonia turned to me after the story was told. "To go and do that poor woman out of any comfort she might have from his money after he was gone!"

"Did you ever hear of anybody else that killed himself for spite, Mr. Burden?" asked Rudolph.

I admitted that I hadn't. Every lawyer learns over and over how strong a motive hate can be, but in my collection of legal anecdotes I had nothing to match this one. When I asked how much the estate amounted to, Rudolph said it was a little over a hundred thousand dollars.

Cuzak gave me a twinkling, sidelong glance. "The lawyers, they got a good deal of it, sure," he said merrily.

A hundred thousand dollars; so that was the fortune that had been scraped together by such hard dealing, and that Cutter himself had died for in the end!

After supper Cuzak and I took a stroll in the orchard and sat down by the windmill to smoke. He told me his story as if it were my business to know it.

His father was a shoemaker, his uncle a furrier, and he, being a younger son, was apprenticed to the latter's trade. You never got anywhere working for your relatives, he said, so when he was a journeyman he went to Vienna and worked in a big fur shop, earning good money. But a young fellow who liked a good time didn't save anything in Vienna; there were too many pleasant ways of spending every night what he'd made in the day. After three years there, he came to New York. He was badly advised and went to work on furs during a strike, when the factories were offering big wages. The strikers won, and Cuzak was blacklisted. As he had a few hundred dollars ahead, he decided to go to Florida and raise oranges. He had always thought he would like to raise oranges! The second year a hard frost killed his young grove, and he fell ill with malaria. He came to Nebraska to visit his cousin, Anton Jelinek, and to look about. When he began to look about, he saw Ántonia, and she was exactly the kind of girl he had always been hunting for. They were married at once, though he had to borrow money from his cousin to buy the wedding-ring.

"It was a pretty hard job, breaking up this place and making the first crops grow," he said, pushing back his hat and scratching his grizzled hair. "Sometimes I git awful sore on this place and want to quit, but my wife she always say we better stick it out. The babies come along pretty fast, so it look like it be hard to move, anyhow. I guess she was right, all right. We got this place clear now. We pay only twenty dollars an acre then, and I been offered a hundred. We bought another quarter ten years ago, and we got it most paid for. We got plenty boys; we can work a lot of land. Yes, she is a good wife for a poor man. She ain't always so strict with me, neither. Sometimes maybe I drink a little too much beer in town, and when I come home she don't say nothing. She don't ask me no questions. We always get along fine, her and me, like at first. The children don't make trouble between us, like sometimes happens." He lit another pipe and pulled on it contentedly.

I found Cuzak a most companionable fellow. He asked me a great many questions about my trip through Bohemia, about Vienna and the Ringstrasse and the theaters.

"Gee! I like to go back there once, when the boys is big enough to farm the place. Sometimes when I read the papers from the old country, I pretty near run away," he confessed with a little laugh. "I never did think how I would be a settled man like this."

▶ What advice did Ántonia give Cuzak regarding the land, and how did it turn out?

He was still, as Ántonia said, a city man. He liked theaters and lighted streets and music and a game of dominoes after the day's work was over. His sociability was stronger than his acquisitive instinct. He liked to live day by day and night by night, sharing in the excitement of the crowd.—Yet his wife had managed to hold him here on a farm, in one of the loneliest countries in the world.

I could see the little chap, sitting here every evening by the windmill, nursing his pipe and listening to the silence; the wheeze of the pump, the grunting of the pigs, an occasional squawking when the hens were disturbed by a rat. It did rather seem to me that Cuzak had been made the instrument of Ántonia's special mission. This was a fine life, certainly, but it wasn't the kind of life he had wanted to live. I wondered whether the life that was right for one was ever right for two!

I asked Cuzak if he didn't find it hard to do without the gay company he had always been used to. He knocked out his pipe against an upright, sighed, and dropped it into his pocket.

"At first I near go crazy with lonesomeness," he said frankly, "but my woman is got such a warm heart. She always make it as good for me as she could. Now it ain't so bad; I can begin to have some fun with my boys, already!"

As we walked toward the house, Cuzak cocked his hat jauntily over one ear and looked up at the moon. "Gee!" he said in a hushed voice, as if he had just wakened up, "it don't seem like I am away from there twenty-six year!"

◀ How is Cuzak's life different than he expected? What keeps him living this way?

◀ How did Cuzak feel about rural life at first, and how has that changed now?

Chapter 3

After dinner the next day I said good-bye and drove back to Hastings to take the train for Black Hawk. Ántonia and her children gathered round my buggy before I started, and even the little ones looked up at me with friendly faces. Leo and Ambrosch ran ahead to open the lane gate. When I reached the bottom of the hill, I glanced back. The group was still there by the windmill. Ántonia was waving her apron.

At the gate Ambrosch lingered beside my buggy, resting his arm on the wheel-rim. Leo slipped through the fence and ran off into the pasture.

"That's like him," his brother said with a shrug. "He's a crazy kid. Maybe he's sorry to have you go, and maybe he's jealous. He's jealous of anybody mother makes a fuss over, even the priest."

I found I hated to leave this boy, with his pleasant voice and his fine head and eyes. He looked very manly as he stood there without a hat, the wind rippling his shirt about his brown neck and shoulders.

▶ What offer has Jim made Rudolph and Ambrosch?

"Don't forget that you and Rudolph are going hunting with me up on the Niobrara next summer," I said. "Your father's agreed to let you off after harvest."

He smiled. "I won't likely forget. I've never had such a nice thing offered to me before. I don't know what makes you so nice to us boys," he added, blushing.

"Oh, yes, you do!" I said, gathering up my reins.

He made no answer to this, except to smile at me with unabashed pleasure and affection as I drove away.

▶ Why is Jim's day in Black Hawk disappointing?

My day in Black Hawk was disappointing. Most of my old friends were dead or had moved away. Strange children, who meant nothing to me, were playing in the Harlings' big yard when I passed; the mountain ash had been cut down, and only a sprouting stump was left of the tall Lombardy poplar that used to guard the gate. I hurried on. The rest of the morning I spent with Anton Jelinek, under a shady cottonwood tree in the yard behind his saloon. While I was having my midday dinner at the hotel, I met one of the old lawyers who was still in practice, and he took me up to his office and talked over the Cutter case with me. After that, I scarcely knew how to put in the time until the night express was due.

▶ Where does Jim again feel at home?

I took a long walk north of the town, out into the pastures where the land was so rough that it had never been ploughed up, and the long red grass of early times still grew shaggy over the draws and hillocks. Out there I felt at home again. Overhead the sky was that indescribable blue of autumn; bright and shadowless, hard as enamel. To the south I could see the dun-shaded river bluffs that used to look so big to me, and all about stretched drying corn-fields, of the pale-gold color, I remembered so well. Russian thistles were blowing across the uplands and piling against the wire fences like barricades. Along the cattle paths the plumes of goldenrod were already fading into sun-warmed velvet, gray with gold threads in it. I had escaped from the curious depression that hangs over little towns, and my mind was full of pleasant things; trips I meant to take with the Cuzak boys, in the Bad Lands and up on the Stinking Water. There were enough Cuzaks to play with for a long while yet. Even after the boys grew up, there would always be Cuzak himself! I meant to tramp along a few miles of lighted streets with Cuzak.

◀ What pleasant thoughts does Jim have as he wanders the prairie?

As I wandered over those rough pastures, I had the good luck to stumble upon a bit of the first road that went from Black Hawk out to the north country; to my grandfather's farm, then on to the Shimerdas' and to the Norwegian set-tlement. Everywhere else it had been ploughed under when the highways were surveyed; this half-mile or so within the pasture fence was all that was left of that old road which used to run like a wild thing across the open prairie, clinging to the high places and circling and dou-bling like a rabbit before the hounds. On the level land the tracks had almost disappeared—were mere shadings in the grass, and a stranger would not have noticed them. But wherever the road had crossed a draw, it was easy to find. The rains had made channels of the wheel-ruts and washed them so deeply that the sod had never healed over them. They looked like gashes torn by a grizzly's claws, on the slopes where the farm wagons used to lurch up out of the hollows with a pull that brought curling muscles on the smooth hips of the horses. I sat down and watched the haystacks turn rosy in the slanting sunlight.

◀ What remnant of the past does Jim find?

This was the road over which Ántonia and I came on that night when we got off the train at Black Hawk and were bedded down in the straw, wondering children, being taken we knew not whither. I had only to close my eyes to hear the rumbling of the wagons in the dark, and to be again overcome by that obliterating strangeness. The feel-ings of that night were so near that I could reach out and touch them with my hand. I had the sense of coming home to myself, and of having found out what a little circle man's experience is. For Ántonia and for me, this had been the road of Destiny; had taken us to those early accidents of fortune which predetermined for us all that we can ever be. Now I understood that the same road was to bring us together again. Whatever we had missed, we possessed together the precious, the incommunicable past.

▶ *What would Jim and Ántonia always share?*

THE END

Respond to the Selection

Which life is more appealing to you: Jim's busy, adventurous life of travel, or Ántonia's quiet life connected to the land? Why?

Investigate, Inquire, and Imagine

Recall: GATHERING FACTS

1a. How long does Jim go without seeing Ántonia after he visits with her and the baby? Describe some of the details that strike Jim about the Cuzak family when he does visit them.

2a. What language do the Cuzaks speak? How do they know who Jim is?

3a. When the orchard trees were young, how did Ántonia feel about them?

4a. How is Anton Cuzak's life with Ántonia different than the life he expected to live?

5a. What remnant of the past does Jim find as he is wandering the prairie before leaving Black Hawk?

Interpret: FINDING MEANING

→ 1b. Why does he stay away so long? Why is he so powerfully affected by his visit to Ántonia's family?

→ 2b. Why do you think Ántonia speaks that language with them? In what ways has Ántonia kept the past alive even in the present?

→ 3b. How does her feeling for the trees relate to Jim's feelings in his childhood?

→ 4b. How does Anton Cuzak feel about how his life is turning out? How do his feelings about prairie life compare to Mr. Shimerda's?

→ 5b. Of what does this finding remind him? In what way does it bring the novel full circle?

Analyze: TAKING THINGS APART

6a. Look back over the passages where Jim talks about what Ántonia means to him. To what things does he compare her? With what things is she associated? What values does Ántonia represent in this novel?

Synthesize: BRINGING THINGS TOGETHER

→ 6b. Why is Ántonia so important to Jim? How does Jim feel about the values she represents? How do you think Cather feels about them?

Evaluate: MAKING JUDGMENTS

7a. One of the central conflicts in *My Ántonia* is between movement (adventure, excitement) and staying in one place, connected to one's past. Do you think Jim was wrong to leave his hometown? Why, or why not? Should he have kept in closer touch with Ántonia? Why, or why not? Which kind of life appeals to you more: the quiet, rural life immersed in family, or the busy, traveling life of a city businessperson? Why? Do you think the values of one life are superior to the values of the other? Explain your answer.

Extend: CONNECTING IDEAS

→ 7b. *My Ántonia*, which was published just as World War I was ending, is sometimes read as an elegy to, or lament for, a value system that was shattered by that war. What contemporary books, movies, or TV shows best epitomize the values of our time? What shifts in values do you think the country is undergoing now? How are your values different from your parents'? What is causing this shift? Do you think the shift is positive or negative, and why?

Understanding Literature

Symbol. A **symbol** is a thing that stands for or represents both itself and something else. To figure out what a symbol represents, you need to think about the associations most people have with the object, but you also need to look closely at the part of the text in which the symbol appears. How is the object described? Does it appear once, or several times? How does it change, if at all? Is it associated with a particular emotion, character, or occurrence? Symbols in *My Ántonia* include the snake Jim kills, the small insect he and Ántonia find while playing, the plow outlined against the sun, the old overgrown road Jim finds at the end of the novel, and many more. Pick one of these symbols or one you have identified, and explain what it might represent.

Archetype. An **archetype** is an inherited, often unconscious, ancestral memory or motif that recurs throughout history and literature. The notion of the archetype derives from the psychology of Carl Jung, who described archetypes as symbols from humanity's "collective unconscious." The term is often used, more generally, to refer to any element that recurs throughout the literature of the world. In *My Ántonia*, Ántonia is related to the archetype of the earth mother, or the woman intimately connected to the cycles of the earth and its fertility. What aspects of Ántonia's character and lifestyle reflect the earth mother archetype? Do you think Ántonia is a realistic character? Why, or why not?

Theme. A **theme** is a central idea in a literary work. One theme of *My Ántonia* can be found in the epigraph. What is this theme, and how is it woven throughout the book? How does it impact each of the following characters: Jim, Mr. Shimerda, Ántonia, Lena? Are there any disadvantages to dwelling in memory as much as Jim does? What do you think Cather wanted to say about the value of the past? Do you agree with her? Why, or why not?

Plot Analysis of
My Ántonia

A **plot** is a series of events related to a **central conflict**, or struggle. The following plot pyramid illustrates the main parts of a plot.

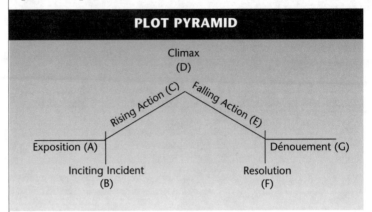

PLOT PYRAMID

Climax (D)

Rising Action (C)

Falling Action (E)

Exposition (A)

Inciting Incident (B)

Dénouement (G)

Resolution (F)

The parts of a plot are as follows:

The **exposition** is the part of a plot that provides the background information, often about the characters, setting, or conflict.

The **inciting incident** is the event that introduces the central conflict.

The **rising action**, or complication, develops the conflict to a high point of intensity.

The **climax** is the high point of interest or suspense in the plot.

The **falling action** is all the events that follow the climax.

The **resolution** is the point at which the central conflict is ended, or resolved.

The **dénouement** is any material that follows the resolution and that ties up any loose ends.

Exposition (A)

The reader first encounters Jim as he is traveling by train to Nebraska, where he will live on his grandparents' farm. Upon arriving on the prairie, Jim is struck by the emptiness of the country. Lying in the garden, he feels himself absorbed into the landscape, a part of "something complete and great." He soon meets Ántonia Shimerda, the fourteen-year-old daughter in a family that has just immigrated from Bohemia, and the two become friends, exploring the prairie together. Jim is simultaneously intrigued and puzzled by Mr. Shimerda, Ántonia's father, whose longing for a cultured, European life comes through as a great sadness and seriousness.

Inciting Incident (B)

Mr. Shimerda is found dead in his barn in what appears to be a suicide. Jim is convinced that the old man has died of homesickness and that his spirit will now travel back to Bohemia. Alone in the house, Jim identifies with Mr. Shimerda, reliving the Bohemian man's memories as if they were his own. In this process, Jim experiences for the first time the tension between complete identification with prairie life and the culture and education that more developed parts of the United States and Europe can offer. Neighbors help the Shimerda family bury Mr. Shimerda in the corner of the property, just where the crossroads will meet. The friendship between Jim and Ántonia is tested as Ántonia takes on more heavy farm work and Jim starts school.

Rising Action (C)

Jim moves with his grandparents into town, figuratively moving further from union with the rugged prairie landscape and closer to "civilization." From the other boys in town, Jim learns gender-appropriate behavior. His friendship with Ántonia continues, and he also comes to admire the other "hired girls" for the hardships they have overcome. Still, because he is absorbed in school, he is more distant from Ántonia than he had been during the first year of their friendship. He is also growing restless with life in Black Hawk and critical of townspeople he sees as small-minded. Through his connections to one of the girls who works at the town's only hotel, Jim comes into contact with the larger world in the form of traveling businessmen and an occasional artist. After graduating from high school, Jim leaves Black Hawk for the University of Nebraska in Lincoln. At the university, he is exposed to classical literature as well as to culture in the form of theater productions in the city. He is torn between his interest in these subjects and his passionate attachment to Ántonia, Lena, and the personal past they represent. When Lena moves to Lincoln as a dressmaker, she tempts him to neglect his studies, sharpening the tension between Jim's aspirations toward education and his loyalty to his past.

Climax, Crisis/Turning Point (D)

Seeing that Jim's focus on school is wavering, Gaston Cleric, one of Jim's professors, suggests that Jim accompany him to Harvard the following year. With the advice of his grandparents, Jim must choose between staying in Nebraska with Lena, seeking to recapture the past he loved, and following his interest in learning to the East coast, the most cultured part of the United States at this time. At the end of book 3, Jim chooses to go east and study at Harvard.

Falling Action (E)

Jim completes his degree at Harvard and returns to Nebraska to visit his grandparents, having heard that Ántonia has suffered a misfortune. While he is in Nebraska, he goes out to visit the Widow Steavens, who is living in his grandparents' old house in the country. She tells him that Ántonia went to Denver to meet Larry Donovan, the man she was engaged to marry. When she arrived in Denver, she discovered that Larry had lost his job. After he depleted her savings, he disappeared. She returned to the Nebraska Divide pregnant and humiliated. By moving to the East coast, Jim has moved far from the values that informed his friendship with Ántonia, and he initially feels scornful of her and her situation. Eventually, though, he decides to visit her. The two talk at Mr. Shimerda's grave. Ántonia tells Jim that she feels closer now than ever to her father, and Jim, in turn, confesses that he thinks of Ántonia more than anyone else in his life. For a short time, Jim feels reconnected to his past through Ántonia, but he gets caught up once again in his very different life.

Resolution (F)

Finally, after twenty years, Jim goes to see Ántonia again. She has remarried and borne many more children, and her family, farm, and orchard are all thriving. She seems to Jim weathered but stronger than ever, and while he visits her, he recaptures a happiness he thought he had lost. Her connection to her past—apparent in her use of the Bohemian language with her family and in her children's evident knowledge of her life story—inspires him. Jim affirms to himself his commitment to spend time with Ántonia and her family.

Dénouement (G)

Before he leaves Black Hawk, Jim wanders around out on the prairie. In his wanderings, he comes across the old road that leads out to his grandparents' house and beyond, to the spot where Mr. Shimerda is buried. While Jim regrets the fact that the past is irretrievable, he feels he has come full circle and that a shared past joins him to Ántonia in a way that cannot be broken.

Introduction to the 1926 Edition
of *My Ántonia*
by Willa Cather

ABOUT THE RELATED READING

The introduction included in the text of this edition of *My Ántonia* is the one Cather wrote for the first edition in 1918. In 1926, she revised the introduction, shortening it by several pages. The shorter version appears below.

Introduction

Last summer, in a season of intense heat, Jim Burden and I happened to be crossing Iowa on the same train. He and I are old friends, we grew up together in the same Nebraska town, and we had a great deal to say to each other. While the train flashed through never-ending miles of ripe wheat, by country towns and bright-flowered pastures and oak groves wilting in the sun, we sat in the observation car, where the woodwork was hot to the touch and red dust lay deep over everything. The dust and heat, the burning wind, reminded us of many things. We were talking about what it is like to spend one's childhood in little towns like these, buried in wheat and corn, under stimulating extremes of climate: burning summers when the world lies green and billowy beneath a brilliant sky, when one is fairly stifled in vegetation, in the colour and smell of strong weeds and heavy harvests; blustery winters with little snow, when the whole country is stripped bare and grey as sheet-iron. We agreed that no one who had not grown up in a little prairie town could know anything about it. It was a kind of freemasonry, we said.

Although Jim Burden and I both live in New York, I do not see much of him there. He is legal counsel for one of the great Western railways and is often away from his office for weeks together. That is one reason why we seldom meet. Another is that I do not like his wife. She is handsome, energetic, executive, but to me seems unimpressionable and temperamentally incapable of enthusiasm. Her husband's quiet tastes irritate her, I think, and she finds it worth while to play the patroness to a group of young poets and painters of advanced ideas and mediocre ability. She has her own fortune and lives her own life. For some reason, she wishes to remain Mrs. James Burden.

As for Jim, disappointments have not changed him. The romantic disposition which often made him seem very funny as a boy, has been one of the strongest elements of his success. He loves with a personal passion the great country through which his railway runs and branches. His faith in it and his knowledge of it have played an important part in its development.

During that burning day when we were crossing Iowa, our talk kept returning to a central figure, a Bohemian girl whom we had both known long ago. More than any other person we remembered, this girl seemed to mean to us the country, the conditions, the whole adventure of our childhood. I had lost sight of her altogether, but Jim had found her again after long years, and had renewed a friendship that meant a great deal to him. His mind was full of her that day. He made me see her again, feel her presence, revived all my old affection for her.

◀ How does Jim amuse himself on long train rides?

"From time to time I've been writing down what I remember about Ántonia," he told me. "On my long trips across the country, I amuse myself like that, in my stateroom."

◀ What would the narrator like to do?

When I told him that I would like to read his account of her, he said I should certainly see it—if it were ever finished.

Months afterward, Jim called at my apartment one stormy winter afternoon, carrying a legal portfolio. He brought it into the sitting-room with him, and said, as he stood warming his hands,

"Here is the thing about Ántonia. Do you still want to read it? I finished it last night. I didn't take time to arrange it; I simply wrote down pretty much all that her name recalls to me. I suppose it hasn't any form. It hasn't any title, either." He went into the next room, sat down at my desk and wrote across the face of the portfolio the word "Ántonia." He frowned at this a moment, then prefixed another word, making it "My Ántonia." That seemed to satisfy him.

Critical Thinking

1. Cather chose to italicize this version of the introduction. What is the effect of the italics?

2. This introduction does not specify what happens to Jim's manuscript after he gives it to the narrator. What is the reader supposed to infer about what happened to the manuscript?

3. Compare and contrast the original introduction with this one. Name at least four pieces of information Cather included in the first version but cut from this one. Explain why she might have chosen to cut each.

4. Which version of the introduction do you think is more effective, and why?

Letter to Frances Samlund
by Anna Pavelka

ABOUT THE RELATED READING

Anna Pavelka, whose maiden name was Anna Sadilek, is the woman on whom the character of Ántonia is based. Willa Cather and Anna Sadilek knew each other in the late 1880s, when Willa was attending school in Red Cloud and Anna was working for the Miner family who lived down the street from the Cathers. After a failed engagement with a railroad man, Anna married John Pavelka, who is the basis for Anton Cuzak in *My Ántonia* and for Anton Rosicky in Cather's late short story, "Neighbor Rosicky."

In this letter to a student at Benson High School in Omaha, Nebraska, Anna, now eighty-six years old, tells the real story of her first year in Nebraska. The letter is reprinted exactly as Anna wrote it.

Letter to Frances Samlund

Bladen [Nebraska] February 24–1955

Dear Frantiska

recieved your nice and wellcome letter few days ago, thought I would please you and answer your queastions about our coming to this country from Bohemia 75 years ago last November the 5. we started from our vilage Mzizovice[?] 16th of October 1880 and got to Red Cloud in November 5 we were on the water 11 days, there was another Bohemia family came with us, rest on the ship were pollish, my father wanted to bring us to this country so we would have it better here as he used to hear how good it was hear as he had letters from here how wonderfull it was out here that there were beutifull houses lots of trees and so on, but how disapointed he was when he saw them pretty houses duged in the banks of the deep draws. You couldnt see them untill you came rite to the door Just steel chimmeny in the roof. there were no roads Just tracks from wagon wheels peaple cut acros land to get anywhere at all well we came to Joe Polnickys by hiring a man at Red Cloud, and from there Mr Polnicky tok us out to Charlie Krecek thats the one wrote so nice about Nebraska and

▶ *What disappointed Anna's father?*

behold our surprise in sieng such beuttiful building and our first meal there was corn meal mush ana molasses that was what the peaple lived on and wild fowls and rabbits well my father boght 10060 acker farm, there was nothing on it exept sod shack it had Just a board bed and 4 lid stove, no well Just 5 aikers of land broken that much the first homesteder had to owe [?] when he didnt live there all time Just so many months so he could realy own it but the folks didnt live there they moved in with some Jerman family. and that was a bad winter lots of snow not much to cook nothing to burn no place to go nothing to read peaple had to burn corn stalk sunflowers and cow chips it was lucky mother brought feather beds as we had to sleep on the dirt floors with hay for mattres, that was hard on father in the old country he had weaver when it was cold and in the evenings he would sit and make linens and any kind of wearing material allways and was allways Joking and happy he was a man in a million allways had lots of friend I was allways with when there was anything to do allways called me naminka, and mother maminka he never swore or used dirty words like other men nor he never drank or play cards he was a clean man in everyway. then one nice afternoon it was 15 of feb he told mother he was going to hunt rabbits he brought a shot gun from the old country he never used it there nobody dared to shoot there that was all rich peaples property when he didnt return by fiveo clock mother older brother and the man we lived with went to look for him it was dark when they found him half siting in that old house aback of the bed shot in the head and allready cold nearly frozen. the sherif said it was a suiside there no cemetery or nothing one of the near neghbors had to make a wooden box and they had to make his grave in the corner of our farm but my brother him moved and him and my mother and brother are sleeping in Red Cloud cemetery and they have a tumb stone I hope they are restting sweetly. most of all is true that you read in the Book thoug most of the names are changed, our name was Sadilek, Lena Lidgard was Mary Dusek Kid Clutter was Willa's cousin. and was a good look-ing cowboy my friend guess I will close for this time I hope this will help you in anyway.

Your friend
Mrs Pavelka

◀ Why, according to Anna, was the first winter bad?

◀ What had Anna's father done in the evenings in the old country?

◀ What happened to Anna's father the day he said he was going hunting for rabbits?

◀ Where was her father initially buried? Where is he buried now?

Critical Thinking

1. **Verbal Irony.** A statement that says one thing but means the opposite is an example of verbal irony. For example, if someone pushes to the front of a line, and a bystander says, "What polite behavior," that statement expresses verbal irony. Anna includes two examples of verbal irony in describing the discrepancy between what her family expected to see in Nebraska and what they actually saw. What are those two examples?
2. How did the Sadileks feel about their new home?
3. Describe Anna's father's personality.
4. How does Anna's version of her father's suicide differ from Cather's version? How do you account for those differences?
5. Does reading Anna's letter change how you feel about *My Ántonia* in any way? If so, how?

from *History of the State of Nebraska*
by William G. Cutler and A. T. Andreas

ABOUT THE RELATED READING

The following excerpt comes from the first known history of Nebraska ever written. Published in 1882 by the Western Historical Company, this history bears the following full title: *HISTORY of the State of Nebraska; containing A FULL ACCOUNT OF ITS GROWTH FROM AN UNINHABITED TERRITORY TO A WEALTHY AND IMPORTANT STATE; OF ITS EARLY SETTLEMENTS; ITS RAPID INCREASE IN POPULATION, AND THE MARVELLOUS DEVELOPMENT OF ITS GREAT NATURAL RESOURCES. ALSO AN EXTENDED DESCRIPTION OF ITS COUNTIES, CITIES, TOWN AND VILLAGES, THEIR ADVANTAGES, INDUSTRIES, MANUFACTURES AND COMMERCE; BIOGRAPHICAL SKETCHES, PORTRAITS OF PROMINENT MEN AND EARLY SETTLERS; VIEWS OF RESIDENCES AND BUSINESS BLOCKS, CITIES AND TOWNS.* In the preface of the history, the publisher declares this work to be "the most elaborate and perfect history of a State ever written."

Publisher A. T. Andreas contracted with historian William G. Cutter and writers from various Nebraska counties to complete the history. To capture the histories of individual towns like Red Cloud, the writer interviewed residents and then asked other prominent citizens to read the findings and vouch for their accuracy. In the preface, Andreas and Cutter warn of the unique challenges of creating a history that includes information about people who are still living or people whose relatives are still living. Their concern is that inaccurate memories, prejudices, "and a thousand other frailties and weaknesses of human nature" could distort the stories of what happened.

This excerpt is the part of Andreas and Cutter's history covering Red Cloud, Nebraska, the town where Willa Cather spent her teenage years from 1884 to 1890. Red Cloud is the model for the town of Black Hawk in *My Ántonia*.

from *History of the State of Nebraska*

RED CLOUD

This is the county seat and largest town of Webster County, and is situated on the Burlington & Missouri River Railroad in Nebraska. The location is a very pleasant one on level terrace, on the north side of the Republican River, and about midway between that stream and the bluffs that ascend to the upland prairie. The elevation of the town-site is about twenty-five feet above the river level. It derives its name from the famous Sioux Chief Red Cloud[1], who up to the time of settlement by the white people, held his war councils on what is now the town site.

▶ *Where does Red Cloud get its name?*

EARLY HISTORY

The history of Red Cloud begins with the settlement of Capt. Silas Garber[2], and others, in 1870. The site of the town was entered under the homestead laws on July 17th, 1870. In August a stockade[3] was built, that the settlers might protect themselves against the Indians. Among the first settlers were ex-Governor Silas Garber, Dr. Peter Head, Albert Lathrop, George M. Taylor, W. E. Jackson, James Calvert, Dr. T. B. Williams, Wheeler Wicks, A. H. Roat, D. Hefflebower, Ed. and John Parks, and L. F. Munsel. The first white women in the settlement were Mrs. W. E. Jackson and Mrs. James Calvert, who arrived with their husbands, on August 9, 1870.

▶ *What was the first building in Red Cloud?*

After the stockade the first building was by Silas Garber, and constructed by digging a hole in the ground, then laying a few logs around the banks, and putting on a dirt roof. This dug-out became of historic importance. Mr. Garber was a widower and lived there alone doing his own cooking. Whenever public meetings were to be held that was the place selected. Meetings to take measures to organize the county were held there, and so was the first county election. For some months afterward it was occupied as the court house. The dug-out was on the bank of a small draw[4],

---

1. **Red Cloud.** Chief of the Oglala Sioux who fought during the 1860s and 1870s to preserve sacred grounds in present-day South Dakota and Montana
2. **Capt. Silas Garber.** A captain in the Civil War who became the second person to settle in Webster County. He served as governor of Nebraska from 1874–1878
3. **stockade.** Fort or wall providing protection for those inside it
4. **draw.** Gully shallower than a ravine

west of the magnificent residence[5] of ex-Governor Garber, and on the east side of the street, leading from the business part of Red Cloud to the depot.

At the election of April 19, 1871, the county seat was located on the homestead of Mr. Garber, on the east half of the northeast quarter of Section 2, Town 1, Range 11, west, upon which a portion of it was at once laid out as a town-site, by Silas Garber. This was not platted[6] and filed in the office of the county clerk until November 12, 1872. Since that time several additions[7] have been made. The first of these were, one on the northeast by T. B. Williams in November, 1873, another in October, 1873, by W. N. Richardson on the north of the old town; another in March, 1874, still farther north, by Ed. Smith and Levi Moore, which in extent was nearly as large as the original town-site. Sometime afterward Jas. LeDuc laid out an addition on the northwest. Since that time additions have been laid out as the growth of the town required.

The first store in Red Cloud was opened in the spring of 1871, by Smith Brothers, and in a short time sold to Fennemore & Penny, who sold to Silas Garber in November, 1871.

In the spring of 1871, G. M. Taylor built a log house, just in the rear of where Dr. R. R. Sherer's store now is, and occupied it as a hotel.

The first physicians were T. B. Williams and Peter Head, who were among the settlers of 1870.

The first school in Red Cloud was taught by Miss Fannie Barber, now Mrs. Edward McCune. The term of school began June 3, 1871, and the wages paid were $12 per month.

◄ *How much money was Miss Fannie Barber paid to teach at the school?*

The first child born was Frances, daughter of G. M. and Carrie Taylor, in the year 1871.

The first attorney to locate in the new town was J. R. Willcox, from Brownville, Nebraska, who settled in July, 1871. He was soon followed by H. S. Kaley.

In the fall of 1871 David Lutz started a drug store.

In March, 1872, the first blacksmith shop was started in Red Cloud by Ira Sleeper, who removed from his homestead about a mile east of town where he had a small shop for about a year before.

---

5. **magnificent residence.** Silas Garber's residence at the time this history was written. He had lived in the dugout before becoming governor
6. **platted.** Officially plotted, drawn, or mapped
7. **additions.** Expansions of the town limits

During the summer of 1872 J. Q. and J. Potter opened a saw mill in the southern part of town.

In the spring of 1872 Silas Garber built the stone store now occupied by Samuel Garber & Bros.

In November, 1872, John Parks built a small shoe shop.

The above <u>comprises</u> nearly all the improvements made in 1872. The next year, however, the town began to grow quite rapidly, and continued to progress until the summer of 1874, when the grasshoppers came.

During the fall of 1874, and the year 1875, business was dull, and the town grew but very little. But during the year 1876 there was an increased immigration to the county and Red Cloud began again to improve and steadily progressed until the year 1878, when the prospects for an early completion of the line of railroad, brought settlers to Red Cloud in large numbers. During the years 1878 and 1879 there was a grand rush of business and professional men and mechanics to this town. So fast did the town settle during those two years that the population numbered over 600.

Ever since that time the town has continued to improve steadily, and the population will now number about 800. There are many very fine buildings, neat in design, that give the town an attractive appearance. Besides this, many of the residence lots have been planted with shade trees, which have already attained considerable size and add much to the beauty of the town.

THE GREAT STORM

In the history of Red Cloud there have been but few exciting events. There was, however, a storm in the summer of 1879 that came near destroying the town. About seven o'clock of the evening of June 10th a heavy, black cloud was seen in the west. As it steadily came up it assumed a terrible <u>aspect</u>, rolling and tumbling along. About eight o'clock the storm burst upon Red Cloud, and lasted about three-quarters of an hour. The rain fell in torrents, and the wind blew a hurricane, <u>eddying</u> and whirling about, blowing down some buildings and unroofing others. A great

▶ *What happened to slow growth in 1874?*

▶ *What brought a large number of settlers to Red Cloud in 1878 and 1879?*

▶ *What things contribute to the attractiveness of the town?*

words for everyday use

com • prise (kəm prīz′) vt., include, be made up of. *The west end of the school <u>comprises</u> the science classrooms, the guidance counselors' offices, and the teachers' lounge.*

as • pect (as′ pəkt) n., appearance to the eye or mind. *The sea horse at the aquarium presents a gentle <u>aspect</u>.*

ed • dy (e′ dē) vi., move in a circular direction or against the current. *The water in the tidepool <u>eddied</u> constantly.*

many people were blown and tumbled about until quite badly bruised, while about twenty received severe and dangerous injuries. A great many buildings were leveled to the ground, and the only way their occupants were saved was by flying to their cellars. Altogether more than $10,000 damage was done. The Methodist church was blown down; Mrs. Brigg's house blown away; Joseph Warner's livery stable[8] torn to pieces; the Red Cloud hotel unroofed; the front of Sherer's store blown out; the front of Putnam's store blown out and the building wrecked; the front and roof torn from the jewelry and clothing store; the Boy's Home livery barn unroofed; the windows broken from the *Argus* office; the front of J. G. Potter's store torn out; Mr. Gibb's house blown away; Smith's carpenter shop in ruins; C. W. Springer's house demolished; the *Chief* office badly racked and several hundred pounds of type pied[9]; the roof torn from Mr. Miner's residence; Sherer's house blown from the foundation; Mr. Smith's house ruined; Reed's furniture store badly damaged; Sleeper's paint shop blown down; portions of the roof of the Boy's Home Hotel and Carr's billiard hall unroofed; Beekman's and Jackson's houses badly blown around; Perin's house blown from foundation; Joseph Garber's house badly damaged; the front of McFarland's store torn out; the plow factory torn down; Dr. Tulleys' house and granaries badly blown around; Mr. Crook's house carried away; the livery stable and a number of buildings around the depot blown away. Besides the above mentioned, all the smaller buildings in the town were overturned or demolished, and nearly all the chimneys blown down. It was the most terrible storm ever known in the Republican Valley.

◄ *How many people were seriously injured in the great storm?*

LOCAL MATTERS

Manufactures.—The Red Cloud flouring and grist mill was built in 1874 by Potter & Sayre. This mill has four run of buhrs and an excellent quality of flour is made. There is a saw mill attached.

The Red Cloud Brewery was established in 1875, by Berenzen & Co. A large quantity of beer is made.

Banks.—Smith Bros.' Bank was organized in 1879, and has always had a very large general banking and collection business. It is a branch of the First National Bank of

---

8. **livery stable.** A barn where horses are boarded or kept for hire
9. **pi.** Mix together, reduce to a state of confusion

Beatrice, of which Smith Bros. are the principal members.

The Webster County Bank was established in the fall of 1881. Though just beginning with the enterprise at Red Cloud, this bank has already a large and paying patronage. It does a general loan and collection business.

Hotels.—Besides the boarding houses and restaurants, the hotels are five in number. They are the Holland House, the Boys' Home, the Valley House, the Commercial House, and the Kirby House. The two first named are first class hotels, while all are very good houses.

▶ What are the two first class hotels in Red Cloud?

Churches.—The religious element is well represented in Red Cloud. A number of the different denominations have organized societies, but the only ones having church <u>edifices</u> are the Methodist Episcopal and Congregational, who have large and comfortable buildings, well furnished.

Schools.—From the date of the first settlement, the school has been the pride of the village, and has always been well sustained by the public spirited citizens. The old school house has proved too small; and another one is now in process of erection, which will, when completed, cost about $6,000. The school is now divided in four departments but another is soon to be added.

***

NEWSPAPERS

▶ What was the first newspaper in Red Cloud?

The Webster County Argus was established in August, 1878, by A. J. Kenney. *The Argus* is Republican in politics, and is an able newspaper. In size the paper is an eight column folio[10]. It has a large circulation. The office is well fitted up with news and job material.

The Red Cloud Chief was established in July, 1873, by C. L. Mather, who published it until July 1, 1875, when he sold it to M. Warner, who continued its publication until October 19, 1876; he sold it to M. L. Thomas. After publishing it until November, 1877, Thomas sold it to Borin & Springer, but bought it back again on February 18, 1879, and still continues to publish it. The *Chief* is ably con-

---

10. **folio**. Sheet of paper folded once

words for everyday use   e • di • fice (e' də fəs) n., large building. *The art museum in Chicago just moved into a new and impressive <u>edifice</u> downtown.*

ducted, is Republican in politics, and has a good circulation. It is printed on a Washington hand press on which the oldest paper in Nebraska, the Brownville *Advertiser*, was first published in 1856. It is said that the first issue of the Lincoln *Daily State Journal* was printed on the same press.

Critical Thinking

1. When, according to this writer, did the history of Red Cloud begin? What went on in Red Cloud before this date?
2. Who is excluded from "history" if history didn't begin until this date?
3. History is often considered to be an objective report on past events. How objective is this history? What statements of opinion can you find in the text?
4. What do you think are the purposes of this history? Why was it written?
5. Could *My Ántonia* also be read as a history of Red Cloud? If so, in what sense? If you want to learn about a place, would you rather read fiction or non-fiction? Why?

"The Fir Tree"
by Hans Christian Andersen

ABOUT THE RELATED READING

Danish writer Hans Christian Andersen (1805–1875) is best known for fairy tales like "The Little Mermaid," "The Ugly Duckling," and "The Emperor's New Clothes," although he also wrote six novels for adults and many plays, operas, poems, and travel narratives. Andersen was also a skilled visual artist, and his visual abilities are evident in the vivid descriptions in his stories.

"The Fir Tree" was written in 1845. Like most of Andersen's tales, it combines elements of fantasy appealing to children with a message of significance to adults.

The Fir Tree

▶ *Why was the fir tree unhappy?*

Far down in the forest, where the warm sun and the fresh air made a sweet resting-place, grew a pretty little fir-tree; and yet it was not happy, it wished so much to be tall like its companions— the pines and firs which grew around it. The sun shone, and the soft air fluttered its leaves, and the little peasant children passed by, prattling merrily, but the fir-tree heeded them not. Sometimes the children would bring a large basket of raspberries or strawberries, wreathed on a straw, and seat themselves near the fir-tree, and say, "Is it not a pretty little tree?" which made it feel more unhappy than before. And yet all this while the tree grew a notch or joint taller every year; for by the number of joints in the stem of a fir-tree we can discover its age. Still, as it grew, it complained, "Oh! how I wish I were as tall as the other trees, then I would spread out my branches on every side, and my top would over-look the wide world. I should have the birds building their nests on my boughs, and when the wind blew, I should bow with stately dignity like my tall companions." The tree was so discontented, that it took no pleasure in the warm sunshine, the birds, or the rosy clouds that floated over it morning and evening. Sometimes, in winter, when the snow lay white and glittering on the ground, a hare would come springing along, and jump right over the little tree;

and then how <u>mortified</u> it would feel! Two winters passed, and when the third arrived, the tree had grown so tall that the hare was obliged to run round it. Yet it remained unsatisfied, and would exclaim, "Oh, if I could but keep on growing tall and old! There is nothing else worth caring for in the world!" In the autumn, as usual, the wood-cutters came and cut down several of the tallest trees, and the young fir-tree, which was now grown to its full height, shuddered as the noble trees fell to the earth with a crash. After the branches were lopped off, the trunks looked so slender and bare, that they could scarcely be recognized. Then they were placed upon wagons, and drawn by horses out of the forest. "Where were they going? What would become of them?" The young fir-tree wished very much to know; so in the spring, when the swallows and the storks came, it asked, "Do you know where those trees were taken? Did you meet them?"

The swallows knew nothing, but the stork, after a little reflection, nodded his head, and said, "Yes, I think I do. I met several new ships when I flew from Egypt, and they had fine masts that smelt like fir. I think these must have been the trees; I assure you they were stately, very stately."

"Oh, how I wish I were tall enough to go on the sea," said the fir-tree. "What is the sea, and what does it look like?"

"It would take too much time to explain," said the stork, flying quickly away.

"Rejoice in thy youth," said the sunbeam; "rejoice in thy fresh growth, and the young life that is in thee."

◀ What does the sunbeam urge the tree to do?

And the wind kissed the tree, and the dew watered it with tears; but the fir-tree regarded them not.

Christmas-time drew near, and many young trees were cut down, some even smaller and younger than the fir-tree who enjoyed neither rest nor peace with longing to leave its forest home. These young trees, which were chosen for their beauty, kept their branches, and were also laid on wagons and drawn by horses out of the forest.

"Where are they going?" asked the fir-tree. "They are not taller than I am: indeed, one is much less; and why are the branches not cut off? Where are they going?"

"We know, we know," sang the sparrows; "we have

▶ What happens to the smaller trees that leave the forest with their branches still attached?

looked in at the windows of the houses in the town, and we know what is done with them. They are dressed up in the most splendid manner. We have seen them standing in the middle of a warm room, and adorned with all sorts of beautiful things,—honey cakes, <u>gilded</u> apples, playthings, and many hundreds of wax <u>tapers</u>."

"And then," asked the fir-tree, trembling through all its branches, "and then what happens?"

"We did not see any more," said the sparrows; "but this was enough for us."

"I wonder whether anything so brilliant will ever happen to me," thought the fir-tree. "It would be much better than crossing the sea. I long for it almost with pain. Oh! when will Christmas be here? I am now as tall and well grown as those which were taken away last year. Oh! that I were now laid on the wagon, or standing in the warm room, with all that brightness and splendor around me! Something better and more beautiful is to come after, or the trees would not be so decked out. Yes, what follows will be grander and more splendid. What can it be? I am weary with longing. I scarcely know how I feel."

▶ What does the fir tree think the decorations indicate about the trees' futures?

"Rejoice with us," said the air and the sunlight. "Enjoy thine own bright life in the fresh air."

But the tree would not rejoice, though it grew taller every day; and, winter and summer, its dark-green foliage might be seen in the forest, while passers by would say, "What a beautiful tree!"

A short time before Christmas, the discontented fir-tree was the first to fall. As the axe cut through the stem, and divided the pith[1], the tree fell with a groan to the earth, conscious of pain and faintness, and forgetting all its anticipations of happiness, in sorrow at leaving its home in the forest. It knew that it should never again see its dear old companions, the trees, nor the little bushes and many-colored flowers that had grown by its side; perhaps not even the birds. Neither was the journey at all pleasant. The tree first recovered itself while being unpacked in the courtyard of a house, with several other trees; and it heard a man say, "We only want one, and this is the prettiest."

---

1. **pith.** The continuous central strand of spongy tissue in plant stems

| **words for everyday use** | **gild** (gild) vt., overlay with a thin covering of gold. *Some thought the <u>gilded</u> bathroom fixtures looked classy, but others thought they were gaudy.* | **ta • per** (tā′ pər) n., slender candle. *This candle holder is intended to hold a <u>taper</u>, not a votive candle.* |

Then came two servants in grand livery[2], and carried the fir-tree into a large and beautiful apartment. On the walls hung pictures, and near the great stove stood great china vases, with lions on the lids. There were rocking chairs, silken sofas, large tables, covered with pictures, books, and playthings, worth a great deal of money,—at least, the children said so. Then the fir-tree was placed in a large tub, full of sand; but green baize [3] hung all around it, so that no one could see it was a tub, and it stood on a very handsome carpet. How the fir-tree trembled! "What was going to happen to him now?" Some young ladies came, and the servants helped them to adorn the tree. On one branch they hung little bags cut out of colored paper, and each bag was filled with sweetmeats; from other branches hung gilded apples and walnuts, as if they had grown there; and above, and all round, were hundreds of red, blue, and white tapers, which were fastened on the branches. Dolls, exactly like real babies, were placed under the green leaves,—the tree had never seen such things before,—and at the very top was fastened a glittering star, made of tinsel. Oh, it was very beautiful!

"This evening," they all exclaimed, "how bright it will be!" "Oh, that the evening were come," thought the tree, "and the tapers lighted! then I shall know what else is going to happen. Will the trees of the forest come to see me? I wonder if the sparrows will peep in at the windows as they fly? shall I grow faster here, and keep on all these ornaments summer and winter?" But guessing was of very little use; it made his bark ache, and this pain is as bad for a slender fir-tree, as headache is for us. At last the tapers were lighted, and then what a glistening blaze of light the tree presented! It trembled so with joy in all its branches, that one of the candles fell among the green leaves and burnt some of them. "Help! help!" exclaimed the young ladies, but there was no danger, for they quickly extinguished the fire. After this, the tree tried not to tremble at all, though the fire frightened him; he was so anxious not to hurt any of the beautiful ornaments, even while their brilliancy dazzled him. And now the folding doors were thrown open, and a troop of children rushed in as if they intended to upset the tree; they were followed more silently by their elders. For a moment the little ones stood silent with astonishment, and then they shouted for joy,

◀ What does the tree think it will know when evening comes and the tapers are lit?

---

2. **livery.** Uniforms or distinctive clothing
3. **baize.** A coarse, woolen or cotton fabric made to imitate felt

till the room rang, and they danced merrily round the tree, while one present after another was taken from it.

"What are they doing? What will happen next?" thought the fir. At last the candles burnt down to the branches and were put out. Then the children received permission to plunder the tree.

Oh, how they rushed upon it, till the branches cracked, and had it not been fastened with the glistening star to the ceiling, it must have been thrown down. The children then danced about with their pretty toys, and no one noticed the tree, except the children's maid who came and peeped among the branches to see if an apple or a fig had been forgotten.

▶ What do the children request of the little man?

"A story, a story," cried the children, pulling a little fat man towards the tree.

"Now we shall be in the green shade," said the man, as he seated himself under it, "and the tree will have the pleasure of hearing also, but I shall only relate one story; what shall it be? Ivede-Avede, or Humpty Dumpty, who fell down stairs, but soon got up again, and at last married a princess."

"Ivede-Avede," cried some. "Humpty Dumpty," cried others, and there was a fine shouting and crying out. But the fir-tree remained quite still, and thought to himself, "Shall I have anything to do with all this?" but he had already amused them as much as they wished. Then the old man told them the story of Humpty Dumpty, how he fell down stairs, and was raised up again, and married a princess. And the children clapped their hands and cried, "Tell another, tell another," for they wanted to hear the story of "Ivede-Avede;" but they only had "Humpty Dumpty." After this the fir-tree became quite silent and thoughtful; never had the birds in the forest told such tales as "Humpty Dumpty," who fell down stairs, and yet married a princess.

▶ To what does the fir tree look forward?

"Ah! yes, so it happens in the world," thought the fir-tree; he believed it all, because it was related by such a nice man. "Ah! well," he thought, "who knows? perhaps I may fall down too, and marry a princess;" and he looked forward joyfully to the next evening, expecting to be again decked out with lights and playthings, gold and fruit. "To-morrow I will not tremble," thought he; "I will enjoy all my splendor, and I shall hear the story of Humpty Dumpty again, and perhaps Ivede-Avede." And the tree remained quiet and thoughtful all night. In the morning the servants and the housemaid came in. "Now," thought the fir, "all my splendor is going to begin again." But they dragged him out of the room and up stairs to the <u>garret</u>, and threw him on the floor, in a dark corner, where no daylight shone, and there they left him. "What does this mean?" thought the tree, "what am I to do here? I can hear nothing in a place like this," and he had time enough to think, for days and nights passed and no one came near him, and when at last somebody did come, it was only to put away large boxes in a corner. So the tree was completely hidden from sight as if it had never existed. "It is winter now," thought the tree, "the ground is hard and covered with snow, so that people cannot plant me. I shall be sheltered here, I dare say, until spring comes. How thoughtful and kind everybody is to me! Still I wish this place were not so dark, as well as lonely, with not even a little hare to look at. How pleasant it was out in the forest while the snow lay on the ground, when the hare would run by, yes, and jump over me too, although I did not like it then. Oh! it is terrible lonely here."

◀ How does the fir tree feel about the forest now?

"Squeak, squeak," said a little mouse, creeping cautiously towards the tree; then came another; and they both sniffed at the fir-tree and crept between the branches.

"Oh, it is very cold," said the little mouse, "or else we should be so comfortable here, shouldn't we, you old fir-tree?"

"I am not old," said the fir-tree, "there are many who are older than I am."

"Where do you come from? and what do you know?" asked the mice, who were full of curiosity. "Have you seen the most beautiful places in the world, and can you tell us all about them? and have you been in the storeroom, where cheeses lie on the shelf, and hams hang from the ceiling? One can run about on tallow[4] candles there, and go in thin and come out fat."

"I know nothing of that place," said the fir-tree, "but I know the wood where the sun shines and the birds sing." And then the tree told the little mice all about its youth. They had never heard such an account in their lives; and after they had listened to it attentively, they said, "What a

---

4. **tallow.** A solid white fat obtained from cattle and sheep and used in soap, candles, and lubricants

---

words for everyday use

gar • ret (gar' ət) n., room or unfinished part of the house just under the roof. *She used to dream of moving her bed up to the garret, where she would have a view of the whole neighborhood.*

▶ What assessment
of the tree's life do
the mice make?

number of things you have seen? you must have been very
happy."

"Happy!" exclaimed the fir-tree, and then as he reflected
upon what he had been telling them, he said, "Ah, yes!
after all those were happy days." But when he went on and
related all about Christmas-eve, and how he had been
dressed up with cakes and lights, the mice said, "How
happy you must have been, you old fir-tree."

"I am not old at all," replied the tree, "I only came from
the forest this winter, I am now checked in my growth."

"What splendid stories you can relate," said the little
mice. And the next night four other mice came with them
to hear what the tree had to tell. The more he talked the
more he remembered, and then he thought to himself,
"Those were happy days, but they may come again.
Humpty Dumpty fell down stairs, and yet he married the
princess; perhaps I may marry a princess too." And the fir-
tree thought of the pretty little birch-tree that grew in the
forest, which was to him a real beautiful princess.

▶ What hope for the
future does the fir
tree maintain?

"Who is Humpty Dumpty?" asked the little mice. And
then the tree related the whole story; he could remember
every single word, and the little mice was so delighted with
it, that they were ready to jump to the top of the tree. The
next night a great many more mice made their appearance,
and on Sunday two rats came with them; but they said, it
was not a pretty story at all, and the little mice were very
sorry, for it made them also think less of it.

"Do you know only one story?" asked the rats.

"Only one," replied the fir-tree; "I heard it on the happiest evening of my life; but I did not know I was so happy
at the time."

"We think it is a very miserable story," said the rats.
"Don't you know any story about bacon, or tallow in the
storeroom."

"No," replied the tree.

"Many thanks to you then," replied the rats, and they
marched off.

The little mice also kept away after this, and the tree
sighed, and said, "It was very pleasant when the merry little mice sat round me and listened while I talked. Now that
is all passed too. However, I shall consider myself happy
when some one comes to take me out of this place." But
would this ever happen? Yes; one morning people came to
clear out the garret, the boxes were packed away, and the
tree was pulled out of the corner, and thrown roughly on
the garret floor; then the servant dragged it out upon the

staircase where the daylight shone. "Now life is beginning again," said the tree, rejoicing in the sunshine and fresh air. Then it was carried down stairs and taken into the courtyard so quickly, that it forgot to think of itself, and could only look about, there was so much to be seen. The court was close to a garden, where everything looked blooming. Fresh and fragrant roses hung over the little palings[5]. The linden-trees were in blossom; while the swallows flew here and there, crying, "Twit, twit, twit, my mate is coming,"—but it was not the fir-tree they meant. "Now I shall live," cried the tree, joyfully spreading out its branches; but alas! they were all withered and yellow, and it lay in a corner amongst weeds and nettles. The star of gold paper still stuck in the top of the tree and glittered in the sunshine. In the same courtyard two of the merry children were playing who had danced round the tree at Christmas, and had been so happy. The youngest saw the gilded star, and ran and pulled it off the tree. "Look what is sticking to the ugly old fir-tree," said the child, treading on the branches till they crackled under his boots. And the tree saw all the fresh bright flowers in the garden, and then looked at itself, and wished it had remained in the dark corner of the garret. It thought of its fresh youth in the forest, of the merry Christmas evening, and of the little mice who had listened to the story of "Humpty Dumpty." "Past! past!" said the old tree; "Oh, had I but enjoyed myself while I could have done so! but now it is too late." Then a lad came and chopped the tree into small pieces, till a large bundle lay in a heap on the ground. The pieces were placed in a fire under the copper, and they quickly blazed up brightly, while the tree sighed so deeply that each sigh was like a pistol-shot. Then the children, who were at play, came and seated themselves in front of the fire, and looked at it and cried, "Pop, pop." But at each "pop," which was a deep sigh, the tree was thinking of a summer day in the forest; and of Christmas evening, and of "Humpty Dumpty," the only story it had ever heard or knew how to relate, till at last it was consumed. The boys still played in the garden, and the youngest wore the golden star on his breast, with which the tree had been adorned during the happiest evening of its existence. Now all was past; the tree's life was past, and the story also,—for all stories must come to an end at last.

◀ What three things does the fir tree remember as it is burning?

---

5. **palings.** Fence pickets

Critical Thinking

1. What regret does the fir tree express at the end of its life?
2. Many children's stories involve morals designed to teach a lesson. Does this story have a moral? If so, what is it?
3. What is the significance of the fact that the young boy wears the gold star from the tree at the end of the story?
4. What is the role of stories in this tale? What stories does the tree hear? What stories does it tell? What purposes do these various stories serve?
5. When have stories served any of these purposes for you? What other purposes have stories served in your life?
6. What does Cather's allusion to the "talking tree of the fairy tale" on page 53 add to *My Ántonia*? Do you see any similarities between "The Fir Tree" and that novel? Consider the epigraph to *My Ántonia* as well as the text of the novel.

"Riding into California"
by Shirley Geok-lin Lim

ABOUT THE RELATED READING

Shirley Geok-lin Lim (1944–) grew up in Malacca, a coastal city in western Malaysia and an area heavily influenced by Chinese culture. At the age of twenty-four, Lim moved from Malaysia to Massachusetts to pursue her Ph.D. in English and American literature.

Lim's writing grapples with issues from her life: coming to terms with the difference between the real America and the glamorized image of the U.S. overseas, fitting into a new culture, bringing together the self she is now with the person she was in Malaysia. Her poetry expresses the loneliness of being Asian in America: "There are many ways in which America tells you you don't belong."

In the poem "Riding into California," the speaker notes the challenge of coming "to a land with no ancestors to bless you." In Chinese culture, dead ancestors, sometimes called ghosts, are believed to watch over their living family members and keep them safe.

Riding into California

If you come to a land with no ancestors
to bless you, you have to be your own
ancestor. The veterans in the mobile home
park don't want to be there. It isn't easy.
Oil rigs litter the land like giant frozen birds.
Ghosts welcome us to a new life, and
an immigrant without home ghosts
cannot believe the land is real. So you're
grateful for familiarity, and Bruce Lee[1]
becomes your hero. Coming into Fullerton[2],
everyone waiting at the station is white.
The good thing about being Chinese on Amtrak[3]
is no one sits next to you. The bad thing is
you sit alone all the way to Irvine[4].

◄What do you have to do if you have no ancestors in a new land?

◄What is the good thing about being Chinese on Amtrak? What is the bad thing about it?

1. **Bruce Lee.** Chinese-American best known as an actor in martial arts movies and the television show *The Green Hornet*. Lee (1940–1973) also founded and taught *Jeet Kune Do*, a form of martial art, and wrote a book on Chinese Gung Fu
2. **Fullerton.** Small city in Southern California, twenty-two miles southeast of Los Angeles
3. **Amtrak.** A transnational train service
4. **Irvine.** A larger city about twenty miles southeast of Fullerton

Critical Thinking

1. What might it mean to "be your own ancestor"?
2. What might being one's own ancestor have to do with Bruce Lee?
3. What images of America does this poem present? What sort of mood do these images create?
4. What challenges does the speaker of this poem face as a Chinese person riding into California?
5. How do these challenges compare to those the Shimerdas faced as they rode into Nebraska? What other connections can you find between this poem and *My Ántonia* or the other related readings?

"Mint Snowball"
by Naomi Shihab Nye

ABOUT THE RELATED READING

Naomi Shihab Nye (1959–), the daughter of a Palestinian father and an American mother, is the author of six books of poems, several children's books, and two collections of essays. She has also edited a number of poetry and prose collections.

The selection "Mint Snowball" appears in a collection of the same name. Naomi Shihab Nye describes the pieces in this collection as "simple paragraphs rather than prose poems…. The paragraph, standing by itself, has a lovely pocket-sized quality. It garnishes the page, as mint garnishes a plate. Many people say (foolishly, of course), they don't like poetry, but I've never heard anyone say that they don't like paragraphs. It would be like disliking five-minute increments on the clock."

Mint Snowball

My great-grandfather on my mother's side ran a drugstore in a small town in central Illinois. He sold pills and rubbing alcohol from behind the big cash register and creamy ice cream from the soda fountain. My mother remembers the counter's long polished sweep, its shining face. She twirled on the stools. Dreamy fans. Wide summer afternoons. Clink of nickels in anybody's hand. He sold milkshakes, cherry cokes, old fashioned sandwiches. What did an old fashioned sandwich look like? Dark wooden shelves. Silver spigots on chocolate dispensers.

My great grandfather had one specialty: a Mint Snowball which he invented. Some people drove all the way in from Decatur just to taste it. First he stirred fresh mint leaves with sugar and secret ingredients in a small pot on the stove for a very long time. He concocted a <u>flamboyant</u> <u>elixir</u> of mint. Its scent clung to his fingers even

---

words for everyday use

flam • boy • ant (flam bȯiʹ ənt) adj., strikingly elaborate or colorful. *Today she is dressed <u>flamboyantly</u> in a feather boa and a hat loaded with fruit.*

e • lix • ir (i likʹ sər) n., a sweetened liquid used for its medicinal properties or its flavor. *This cherry-flavored <u>elixir</u> is used to treat a cough.*

after he washed his hands. Then he shaved ice into tiny particles and served it mounded in a glass dish. <u>Permeated</u> with mint syrup. Scoops of rich vanilla ice cream to each side. My mother took a bite of minty ice and ice cream mixed together. The Mint Snowball tasted like winter. She closed her eyes to see the Swiss village my great-grandfather's parents came from. Snow frosting the roofs. Glistening, dangling spokes of ice.

Before my great-grandfather died, he sold the recipe for the mint syrup to someone in town for one hundred dollars. This hurt my grandfather's feelings. My grandfather thought he should have inherited it to carry on the tradition. As far as the family knew, the person who bought the recipe never used it. At least not in public. My mother had watched my grandfather make the syrup so often she thought she could replicate it. But what did he have in those little unmarked bottles. She experimented. Once she came close. She wrote down what she did. Now she has lost the paper.

Perhaps the clue to my entire personality connects to the lost Mint Snowball. I have always felt out-of-step with my environment, disjointed in the modern world. The crisp flush of cities makes me weep. Strip centers, Poodle grooming and Take-out Thai. I am angry over lost department stores, wistful for something I have never tasted or seen.

Although I know how to do everything one needs to know—change airplanes, find my exit off the interstate, charge gas, send a fax—there is something missing. Perhaps the stoop of my great-grandfather over the pan, the slow patient swish of his spoon. The spin of my mother on the high stool with her whole life in front of her, something fine and fragrant still to happen. When I breathe a handful of mint, even pathetic sprigs from my sunbaked Texas earth, I close my eyes. Little chips of ice on the tongue, their cool slide down. Can we follow the long river of the word "refreshment" back to its spring? Is there another land for me? Can I find any lasting <u>solace</u> in the color green?

> ▶ What did the narrator's mother see when she ate a mint snowball?

> ▶ What happened to the mint snowball recipe?

> ▶ How has the narrator always felt?

> ▶ What four things does the narrator think might be the "something missing"?

Critical Thinking

1. For what was the narrator's great-grandfather famous?
2. What did this concoction mean to the narrator's mother?
3. What, based on this essay, would it mean to "follow the long river of the word 'refreshment' back to its spring"? What is missing for the narrator, and where might it be found?
4. In what way might the mint snowball be the clue to the narrator's whole personality?
5. In what ways is this narrator's view of the past like Jim Burden's view of the past in *My Ántonia*?

"The Prairie Grass Dividing"
by Walt Whitman

ABOUT THE RELATED READING

Walt Whitman (1819–1892) is considered by many to be the greatest of all American poets, and *Leaves of Grass*, his life's work, is probably the most influential volume of poetry in the history of American literature. Whitman's poetry was revolutionary in both its form and its content. Its long lines, infrequent rhyme, and common language all departed from poetic tradition, and its subjects—working class people, everyday objects, and the poet's own pleasures—were deemed by many to be inappropriate for poetry.

Willa Cather had a mixed reaction to Whitman's poetry. In a review of his work, she criticized his tendency to throw every random object he saw into a poem and compared him to a "joyous elephant" who cared about nothing but his own pleasure. Still, she appreciated his celebration of the common person and even named her novel *O Pioneers!* after Whitman's poem, "Pioneers! O Pioneers!"

"The Prairie Grass Dividing" belongs to a group of poems called the "Calamus" poems in *Leaves of Grass*. Calamus is a particularly hardy form of grass that grows approximately three feet high, is common in the Great Plains states, and gives off a strong, pleasant odor.

The Prairie Grass Dividing

The prairie-grass dividing, its special odor breathing,
I demand of it the spiritual corresponding,
Demand the most <u>copious</u> and close companionship of men,
Demand the blades to rise of words, acts, beings,
Those of the open atmosphere, coarse, sunlit, fresh, nutritious,

▶ What adjectives does the speaker use to describe the men whose close companionship he demands?

words for everyday use

co • pi • ous (kō′ pē əs) adj., profuse or exuberant. *Tom is such a <u>copious</u> talker that there is no such thing as a brief conversation with him.*

Those that go their own <u>gait</u>, erect, stepping with freedom and command, leading not following,
Those with a never-<u>quell'd</u> <u>audacity</u>, those with sweet and lusty flesh clear of taint,
Those that look carelessly in the faces of Presidents and governors, as to say *Who are you?*
Those of earth-born passion, simple, never constrain'd, never obedient,
Those of inland America.

◀ *Where do the speaker's desired companions live?*

Critical Thinking

1. What does the speaker of this poem want?
2. What question do the looks of the men in the poem ask of presidents and governors?
3. What quality of these men is revealed by the fact that their looks ask this question?
4. Based on the details of the poem, describe the people of "inland America." What does the speaker find appealing about these people?
5. Why is this poem called "The Prairie Grass Dividing"?
6. What qualities does Ántonia share with Whitman's "people of inland America"?

words for everyday use

gait (gāit) n., a way of walking or moving on foot. *The horse's gait seemed clumsy, so the trainer examined its hooves.*

quell (kwel) vt., reduce to submission or passivity. *Despite the government's commitment of additional troops, the rebellion could not be quelled.*

au • da • ci • ty (ō da' sə tē) n., bold or arrogant disregard of normal limits. *He couldn't believe the protesters had the audacity to stop traffic on one of the busiest streets in town.*

Creative Writing Activities

Conveying Landscape and Mood

One of the hallmarks of Willa Cather's writing is a strong sense of place. Her descriptions of the landscape not only enable readers to imagine the place vividly, but they also evoke a particular mood. Think of a landscape that has special meaning or powerful associations for you. You might choose a town where your family has vacationed, a place in your neighborhood where something important happened to you or someone you know, or any place that makes you feel a particular way. Use the chart below to list sensory details about the place you have chosen. The details you choose should help to evoke the mood you want to convey.

Sensory Detail Chart				
Sight	Hearing	Touch	Taste	Smell

Then use these details to write a description of your landscape. Use vivid language to allow your reader to experience the place you have chosen. You might also include metaphors, similes, personification, or other kinds of figurative language to make your writing more interesting.

Representing a Time Period

My Ántonia gives modern readers valuable insight into late nineteenth-century life on the prairie. What events or aspects of life today are likely to interest people a hundred or more years from now? Make a list of these events and activities. Choose one item from your list, and write a short story, scene from a play, or poem that illustrates it. For example, you might write a scene illustrating a current event that has impacted your life, a poem about connecting with someone over e-mail, or a story that captures details about your school day.

Illustrating Character

In *My Ántonia*, Jim Burden describes a woman who made

a huge impression on him. He reveals Ántonia's character and values by describing her, but also by letting the reader see and hear Ántonia as she interacts with people. Think about people who have been important in your life so far, people who have somehow captured your interest or impacted your decisions. Pick one of those people, and write a scene that illustrates something about the person's values, personality, or manner through his or her actions or conversation. Concentrate on *showing* the reader who this person is rather than *telling* the reader about him or her. You might begin by making a list of details about the person you have chosen. What qualities are important to who this person is? What details can you use to convey those qualities? For example, if the person you are describing is particularly generous, you could show him giving someone something significant. Your scene should tell a brief story while conveying what the person is like.

Altering Point of View

Most of the events in *My Ántonia* are told from Jim's point of view, and all of them are filtered through his voice as narrator. How would these events look if someone else in the story told about them? Pick one scene from the novel and rewrite it from the point of view of a character other than Jim. For example, you might choose to rewrite Jim's arrival in Nebraska from Mrs. Burden's point of view, Lena's first visit to Jim's room in Lincoln from Lena's point of view, or Jim's last visit with Ántonia from Ántonia's point of view. Try to get inside the head of the character you have chosen, and write about the events as he or she would have experienced them.

Writing a Personal Narrative

My Ántonia records the events from Jim's life that are most prominent in his memory. Each memory is told in the form of a miniature story. Select an event from your life, and write a narrative, or miniature story, about that event. The occurrence you choose to relate doesn't have to be earth-shattering; the important thing is that it meant something to you. If you are having trouble identifying a topic, start with a cluster chart like the one below. In the middle, write "Memories." Then write down your memories as they occur to you. Don't stop to judge them yet; just try to get as many ideas down as you can.

Memories

Now pick a memory that especially interests you, and write about what happened. To help you get started, you might want to create a second cluster chart like the one above. This time, put the memory you have chosen in the center oval, and fill in the peripheral ovals with details about that memory. Use these details to write a first draft in which you concentrate on getting the story down on paper. Then go back and revise the essay using the most vivid, interesting language you can find. You might want to add dialogue to your narrative to make the people in it come to life.

Critical Writing Activities

The following topics are suitable for short critical essays on *My Ántonia*. An essay on any one of these topics should begin with an introductory paragraph that introduces the topic and states the thesis, or main idea, of the essay. This introduction should be followed by several paragraphs that support the thesis using examples from the novel. The last paragraph of the essay should be a conclusion that restates the thesis of the essay in different words. The conclusion should also bring a sense of closure to the essay.

Comparing and Contrasting Two Characters

Write a comparison-and-contrast essay about one of the following pairs of characters:

Ántonia (Shimerda) Cuzak and Genevieve Burden
Mr. Shimerda and Anton Cuzak
Mr. Shimerda and Josiah Burden
Ántonia (Shimerda) Cuzak and Lena Lingard

On your own paper, draw a Venn diagram like the one shown below. In the center of each of the two ovals, write the names of the two characters you are examining. Record similarities between the two characters in the overlapping part of the ovals and differences in the parts of the ovals that do not overlap.

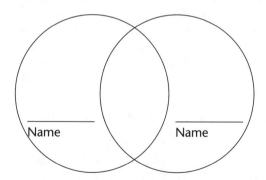

Use the points from your graphic organizer to draft your essay. You will need to decide whether to use point-by-point or block organization. In **point-by-point organiza-tion**, you discuss one topic as it applies to the first charac-ter, and then discuss the same topic in relation to the second character. Throughout the essay, you move back and forth between the two characters. If you choose this organizational method, be sure to start a new paragraph every time you switch characters. In **block organization**, you discuss all aspects of one character and then discuss all aspects of the other character. Usually, block organization works best if you will focus on one major point of comparison, and point-by-point organization works best if you have several important points of comparison.

As you develop your essay, be sure to include specific examples from the book. Direct quotations from the text, with page references, will also make your essay more persuasive.

In your conclusion, you might suggest how the similarities and differences between the two characters you have chosen relate to the meaning of the novel as a whole.

Exploring the Theme of Exile

Exile means the state of being away from one's home, either through force or by choice. Think about how many characters in *My Ántonia* leave home at some point. Many of these characters are shaped in powerful ways by the fact that they have lost their original homes. Select three of the following characters and discuss how each is affected by being in exile: Jim, Ántonia, Mr. Shimerda, Mrs. Shimerda, Lena, Anton, Peter, and Pavel. For each character, identify the home they have lost and what has happened to them after leaving that home. Then discuss how they are affected by having left home. Use events and quotations from the text to support your ideas. In your introduction and/or conclusion, you might consider how the theme of exile is related to Cather's residence in New York City as an adult.

Defining the Freemasonry of Nebraska Childhood

In the introduction, Jim and the unnamed narrator discuss growing up in small prairie towns, suggesting that it is "a kind of freemasonry." What does this statement mean, and in what sense is it true? What, if anything, does this statement have to do with why Ántonia is so important to Jim? Write an essay that uses evidence from the novel to answer these questions. You might begin by defining freemasonry in your introduction. Your thesis statement should relate the idea of freemasonry to the novel. Then draft several paragraphs that use examples and quotations from the text to support your thesis. Finally, in your conclusion, summarize your answer to the questions. You might also evaluate the importance of freemasonry to the novel as a whole.

Analyzing Point of View

Everything we know about Ántonia and the other characters in the novel has been filtered through Jim's point of view. Write an essay in which you analyze his point of view. What is his motive in telling this story? (Consider his stated motive, but also any other motives he might have.) How reliable is Jim as a narrator? In what ways do you think his perceptions of Ántonia are accurate or inaccurate? How would this story be different if it had been told by Ántonia herself? What are the advantages or disadvantages of having Jim rather than Ántonia tell the story? Be sure to formulate a thesis that expresses the main idea you want to convey about Jim's point of view. Every paragraph in your essay should support that thesis.

Tracing Sun Symbolism

Images of the sun occur throughout the novel. Why is this image so central? What does it symbolize? Locate as many sun passages as you can in the novel. Also find passages that are about nightfall and the absence of the sun. Then write an essay in which you trace the use of sun imagery throughout the book. Your introduction should contain a thesis in which you suggest what the sun symbolizes. Each body paragraph should use quotations and other evidence from the novel to support this thesis. In your conclusion, you might want to connect the meaning of the sun symbolism to the overall themes of the novel.

Projects

Presenting Local Histories

In her Nebraska novels, Willa Cather captured aspects of Nebraska history, providing modern readers valuable insight into what it was like to live on the frontier in the late nineteenth century. In small groups, research various historical aspects of your community. One group might focus on the history of Native American presence in your area, and another on the immigrant groups that first settled in the region. Other groups might focus on the role your area played in the Revolutionary War, the Civil War, the World Wars, the Civil Rights Movement, or some other important period in American history. Still others could research the history of women's roles or racial relations in your area. Use your school library, the public library, any local visitors' bureaus, and other city, town, and county resources to locate information.

Once your group has collected information, create a multimedia presentation on your aspect of local history. Use audio and visual elements to make history real for your audience. Share your presentation with your class. You might also consider inviting parents and community members to an evening of historical presentations.

Creating a Scrapbook for Ántonia

Readers of *My Ántonia* learn a lot about Ántonia Shimerda Cuzak's life. Use your knowledge of her experiences and interests to create a scrapbook commemorating important events in her life. Include items that signify events from her birth up until a few years before her death. You will need to use your imagination to fill in the gaps in the story and to guess at how her life continues beyond the point where the novel ends. Include in the scrapbook images and/or headlines from magazines and newspapers, small objects like those that might have had significance for Ántonia, and any other items you think are appropriate. Feel free to use your own artistic talents to create portraits, maps, or other replicas of items from Ántonia's life.

In the front of the scrapbook, include a written reflection in which you explain the significance of the items you've chosen to include.

Surveying Willa Cather Web Pages

A number of websites contain information on Willa Cather. Create a Willa Cather Web Research Guide in which you evaluate the information available on at least five of these web pages. You can use the following three websites as a starting point:

- http://www.willacather.org/
- http://www.libfind.unl.edu/Cather/cather.htm
- http://icg.harvard.edu/~cather/home.html.

For each web page you review, answer the following list of questions:

1. Who created the website? Who is responsible for its content?
2. How much do you trust this person or organization to provide accurate information? What credentials make this person or organization a reliable source of information?
3. Does the site provide contact information for the creator or webmaster? (The most reliable sites generally provide a means through which researchers can ask questions or make comments.)
4. How recently was the site updated?
5. What kinds of information are provided?
6. How detailed is the information?
7. How easy is it to navigate the site? How many dead links did you find?
8. Would you recommend this site to students researching Cather? Why, or why not?

Use your answers to write a one- or two-paragraph review of each site, and collect these reviews in your Willa Cather Web Research Guide. You should also develop a rating system so that readers can see at a glance what your impression of each site is. For example, you might designate an outstanding site with a rating of four stars and a poor site with only one star. You can design your own rating system; just be sure to explain it somewhere in your Research Guide.

Make copies of your Willa Cather Web Research Guide for your teacher, any interested classmates, and for your classroom or school library.

Recording A Soundtrack

Imagine that a movie studio is working on a new movie adaptation of *My Ántonia* and that you have been asked to create the soundtrack. Record on audiotape or burn on CD a collection of at least ten songs or pieces appropriate to various scenes from the novel. Consider using music from a variety of different genres, and pay special attention to the way music sets a mood for the scene.

In addition to recording the soundtrack, create a list of the tracks on the tape or CD, and provide for the movie producer a written rationale for each track you've chosen. Explain which scene the piece accompanies, why you chose that piece, and how it is appropriate to the scene.

Finally, design appropriate audiotape or CD packaging for the soundtrack.

Glossary

VOWEL SOUNDS

a	hat	ō	go	u̇	book, put
ā	play	ȯ	paw, born		blue, stew
ä	star	oi	boy	ə	extra
e	then	ou	wow		under
ē	me	u	up		civil
i	sit	ʉ	burn		honor
ī	my				bogus

CONSONANT SOUNDS

b	but	l	lip	t	sit
ch	watch	m	money	th	with
d	do	n	on	v	valley
f	fudge	ŋ	song, sink	w	work
g	go	p	pop	y	yell
h	hot	r	rod	z	pleasure
j	jump	s	see		
k	brick	sh	she		

a • bom • in • a • ble (e bäm′ nə bəl) adj., worthy of disgust or hatred, detestable.

a • cquit (ə kwit′) vt., to conduct oneself, behave.

af • fab • le (a′ fə bəl) adj., characterized by ease and friendliness.

af • flic • tion (ə flik′ shən) n., the cause of persistent pain or distress.

af • ford (ə fōrd′) vt., to provide naturally or inevitably.

am • i • a • ble (ā′ mē ə bəl) adj., friendly, sociable, and congenial.

an • ar • chist (a′ nər kist) n., one who rebels against any authority, established order, or ruling power.

an • tag • o • nist (an ta′ gə nist) n., adversary, opponent.

ap • pease (ə pēz′) vt., bring to a state of peace or quiet, calm.

arch • ly (ärch′ lē) adv., mischievously.

ar • roy • o (ə roi′ ō) n., a water-carved gully or channel.

art • less (ärt′ ləs) adj., sincerely simple, natural.

as • pect (as′ pəkt) n., appearance to the eye or mind.

au • da • ci • ty (ō da′ sə tē) n., bold or arrogant disregard of normal limits.

a • vouch (ə vauch′) vt., to declare as a matter of fact, affirm.

ban • ter • ing (ban′ tər iŋ) adj., speaking in a playful, teasing manner.

bar • bar • ous • ly (bär′ bə rəs lē) adv., in a way lacking culture or refinement.

be • ne • fi • cent (bə ne′ fə sənt) adj., doing or producing good.

bois • ter • ous • ly (boi′ strəs lē) adv., noisily, rowdily.

bran • dish • ing (bran′ dish iŋ) v., shaking or waving menacingly or aggressively.

ca • per (kā′ pər) vi., leap or prance about in a playful manner.

caus • tic (kōs′ tik) adj., marked by cutting sarcasm.

chi • val • ry (shi′ vəl rē) n., the customs of medieval knighthood, including honor, generosity, and courtesy.

cle • men • cy (kle′ mən sē) n., desire to be merciful or lenient.

co • pi • ous (kō′ pē əs) adj., profuse or exuberant.

com • prise (kəm prīz′) vt., include, be made up of.

com • mo • di • ous (kə mō′ dē əs) adj., roomy, spacious.

com • pro • mise (käm′ prə mīz) vt., expose to suspicion, dishonor, or mischief.

con • fer (kən fər′) vt., bestow, grant.

con • fi • dence (kän′ fə dəns) n., relationship of trust or intimacy.

con • for • ma • tion (kän for mā′ shən) n., the shape or dimensions of something, structure.

con • ge • ni • al (kən jē′ nē əl) adj., sociable.

con • sci • en • tious • ly (kän shē en' shəs lē) adv., meticulously, carefully.

con • temp • tu • ous (kən tem' chə wəs) adj., manifesting, expressing, or feeling disdain.

cor • dial • ly (korj' lē) adv., sincerely, warmly.

coun • te • nance (kaun' tən əns) n., face.

co • vet (kə' vət) vt., wish for enviously, desire inordinately.

cred • i • tab • ly (kre' di tə blē) adv., sufficiently well to bring esteem or praise.

cred • u • lous • ness (kre' jə ləs nəs) n., readiness to believe, even on slight or uncertain evidence.

cul • tiv • a • tion (kəl tə vā' shən) n., culture, refinement.

cyn • i • cis • m (si' nə si zəm) n., distrust of human nature or motives.

de • cor • um (di kōr' əm) n., conventions of polite behavior.

de • fer (di fər') vt., submit to another's wishes, opinion, or governance.

de • gra • ded (di grād' əd) adj., reduced far below ordinary standards of civilized life.

de • jec • tion (di jek' shən) n., lowness of spirits. *A*

de • mon • stra • tive (di män' strə' tiv) adj., inclined to display feelings openly.

de • mure (di myur') adj., reserved, modest.

der • i • sion (di ri' zhən) n., the use of ridicule or scorn to show contempt.

de • so • late (de' sə lət) adj., barren, lifeless.

de • spoiled (di spoild') adj., stripped of belongings, possessions, or value.

de • tain (di tān') vt., stop, restrain from proceeding.

dis • ap • pro • ba • tion (di sa prə bā' shən) n., disapproval, condemnation. .

dis • con • cert • ed (dis kən sərt' id) adj., disturbed, bothered.

dis • con • so • late (dis kän' sə lət) adj., cheerless.

dis • po • si • tion (dis pə zi' shən) n., character, personality.

dis • po • si • tion (dis pə zi' shən) n., transfer to the care or possession of another.

dis • so • lute (di sə lüt') adj., lacking restraint, marked by indulgence in things deemed vices.

dis • suade (di swād') vt., advise a person against something.

do • cile (dä' səl) adj., easily led or managed.

dole • ful (dōl' fəl) adj., expressing grief.

do • mes • tic (də mes' tik) adj., relating to the household or family.

droll (drōl) adj., having a humorous, whimsical, or odd quality.

du • pli • ci • ty (du pli' sə tē) n., contradictory doubleness of thought, speech, or action.

e • di • fice (e' də fəs) n., large building.

e • lix • ir (i lik' sər) n., a sweetened liquid used for its medicinal properties or its flavor.

ed • dy (e' dē) vi., move in a circular direction or against the current.

el • lip • ti • cal (i lip' ti kəl) adj., of or relating to deliberate obscurity.

e • ma • ci • a • ted (i mā' shē āt əd) adj., wasted away physically, enfeebled.

en • cum • bered (in kəm' bərd) adj., weighed down, burdened.

en • feeb • led (in fē' bəld) adj., deprived of strength, weakened.

en • ter • pri • sing (en' tər prī zin) adj., independent, energetic, spirit and by ready to undertake or experiment.

en • treat (in trēt') vt., make an earnest request, plead.

e • pi • thet (e' pə thet) n., a disparaging or abusive word or phrase.

e • va • sive • ly (i vā' siv lē) adv., in a way intended to avoid answering directly.

ex • ec • u • tive (ig ze' k[y]ə tiv) adj., designed for carrying into effect.

ex • em • plar • y (ig zem' plə rē) adj., deserving imitation, commendable.

ex • or • bi • tant (ig zȯr' bə tənt) adj., excessive, exceeding the customary limits.

ex • ul • ta • tion (ek səl tā' shən) n., a state of being filled with great joy. *hallways.*

fa • mished (fa' misht) adj., intensely hungry.

fas • tid • i • ous (fa sti' dē əs) adj., showing or demanding excessive delicacy or care.

fe • tid (fe' təd), adj., having a heavy, offensive smell.

flam • boy • ant (flam bȯi' ənt) adj., strikingly elaborate or colorful.

fore • stall (fōr stol') vt., prevent, hinder.

fra • ter • nal (frə tər' nəl) adj., belonging to a society or brotherhood.

fur • tive (fər' tiv) adj., expressive of stealth, sly.

fu • tur • i • ty (fu̇ tur' ə tē) n., the quality or state of being in the future.

gait (gāit) n., a way of walking or moving on foot.

gar • ret (gar' ət) n., room or unfinished part of the house just under the roof.

gau • di • ly (gȯ' dōl ē) adv., Showily, tastelessly.

gaunt (gȯnt) adj., barren, desolate.

gen • teel (jen tēl') adj., free from vulgarity or rudeness, polite.

ges • tic • u • la • tions (je sti kyə la' shənz) n., gestures.

gild (gild) vt., overlay with a thin covering of gold.

gorg • ing (gorj iŋ) vi., to eat greedily.

griz • zled (gri' zəld) adj., sprinkled or streaked with gray.

gul • ly (gu̇' lē) n., a trench created by running water.

hec • tor • ing • ly (hək' tə riŋ lē) adv., in a manner intended to intimidate or harass by bluster or personal pressure.

i • dyl • lic (ī di′ lik) adj., charmingly or simply poetic.

im • mod • er • ate • ly (i mä′ də rət lē) adv., in a way that exceeds normal bounds, excessively.

im • per • i • al (im pir′ ē əl) adj., befitting an emperor.

im • per • ti • nent (im pər′ tən ənt) adj., rude.

im • pet • u • ous • ly (im pech′ wəs lē) adv., in a manner marked by impulsive passion.

im • plore (im plōr′) vt., request urgently, beg.

in • ces • sant • ly (in se′ sənt lē) adv., without interruption, continually.

in • ci • vil • i • ty (in sə vi′ lə tē) n., rudeness, lack of courtesy.

in • con • gru • ous (in kän′ grə wəs) adj., not fitting, unsuitable.

in • do • lence (in′ də ləns) n., laziness, sloth.

in • fir • mi • ty (in fər′ mə tē) n., disease, malady.

in • gen • u • ous • ness (in jen′ yə wəs nəs) n., quality of innocent or childlike simplicity and candidness.

in • qui • si • tion (in kwə zi′ shən) n., an official, often severe inquiry.

in • sen • si • ble (in sen′ sə bəl) adj., lacking sensory perception or ability to react.

in • sin • u • a • ting (in sin′ yə wāt iŋ) adj., subtly causing doubt or distrust.

in • sin • u • a • tion (in sin yə wā′ shən) n., something communicated by indirect means.

in • ter • ces • sor (in tər se′ sər) n., one who prays, petitions, or entreats in favor of another.

in • ter • min • ab • le (in tərm′ nə bəl) adj., seeming to have no end.

in • ter • val (in′ tər vəl) n., space of time between events or states.

in • ve • ter • ate (in ve′ tə rət) adj., habitual.

jaun • ty (jon′ tē) adj., stylish.

jo • vi • al • i • ty (jō vē a′ lə tē) n., good humor.

jur • is • dic • tion (jŭr əs dik′ shən) n., the limits within which authority may be exercised.

la • con • i • cal • ly (lə kä′ nik lē) adv., concisely, even to the point of being rude.

las • si • tude (la′ sə tüd) n., lethargy, listlessness.

li • a • bil • i • ty (lī ə bi′ lə tē) n., something for which one is financially responsible, debt.

li • cen • tious • ness (lī sen′ shəs nəs) n., lack of legal or moral restraint, especially disregard of sexual restraint.

lim • pid (lim′ pəd) adj., absolutely serene and untroubled.

loath (lōth) adj., reluctant, unwilling to do something contrary to one's way of thinking.

loath • some (lōth′ səm) adj., giving rise to dislike, disgust, or hatred.

lu • mi • nous (lu′ mə nəs) adj., emitting or reflecting steady, suffused, or glowing light.

lux • ur • i • ant (ləg zhür′ ē ənt) adj., characterized by abundant growth, lush.

mal • con • tent (mal kən tent′) n., a discontented person.

max • im (mak′ səm) n., a saying of a proverbial nature.

me • di • o • cre (mē dē ō′ kər) adj., average or low.

men • i • al (mē′ nē əl) adj., of or relating to servants, lowly.

mer • i • tor • i • ous (mer ə tōr′ ē əs) adj., deserving of honor or esteem.

met • tle (me′ təl) n., vigor or strength of spirit or temperament.

mol • li • fied (mä′ lə fid) adj., soothed in temper or disposition, appeased.

mor • ti • fy (mȯr′ tə fī) vt., subject to severe embarrassment, shame.

na • ïve • té (nä ēv tā′) n., genuine simplicity.

no • tor • i • et • y (nō tə rī′ ə tē) n., a state of being widely and unfavorably known.

ob • lit • e • rate (ə bli′ tə rāt) vt., destroy utterly all trace, indication, or significance of.

o • ra • cu • lar (o ra′ kye lər) adj., wise and authoritative.

par • si • mon • i • ous (pär sə mō′ nē əs) adj., frugal to the point of stinginess.

per • me • ate (pər′ mē āt) vt., spread through.

per • func • tor • y (pər fəŋ′ tə rē) adj., routine, superficial, mechanical.

pet • u • lant • ly (pe′ chə lənt lē), adv., with temporary ill humor, peevishly.

pi • quant (pē′ kənt) adj., having a lively, mischievous charm.

pla • ti • tude (pla′ tə tüd) n., an overused, trite, or stale remark.

pri • me • val (prī mē′vəl) adj., of or relating to the earliest ages, ancient, primitive.

pro • pi • ti • ate (prō pi′ shē āt) vt., to gain or regain the favor or goodwill of, appease.

pro • pi • ti • a • tory (prō pi′ shē ə tor ē) adj., intended to appease or satisfy.

quay (kē) n., a structure built parallel to a waterway and used as a landing place.

quell (kwel) vt., reduce to submission or passivity.

quiz • zi • cal (kwi′ zi kəl) adj., expressive of curiosity.

rake (rāk) n., a person who is unrestrained by morality or convention.

re • con • cil • i • a • tion (re kən si lē ā′ shən) n., restoration of friendship or harmony.

re • nun • ci • a • tor • y (ri nən′ sē ə tōr ē) adj., relating to giving up or pushing away, often with regret.

re • pose (ri pōz′) n., a state of resting after exertion or strain.

re • prove (ri prüv′) vt., to scold or correct, usually gently or with kindly intent.

re • ti • cent (re′ tə sənt) adj., inclined to be silent or uncommunicative in speech, reserved.

re • tract (ri trakt′) vt., take back, withdraw.

rout (raut) vt., dispel, drive out.

score (skōr) n., twenty.

self-pos • ses • sion (self pə zə' shən) n., control of one's emotions or reactions, especially under stress.

sen • ti • ment (sen' tə mənt) n., a romantic or nostalgic feeling verging on excess emotion.

shrewd (shrüd) adj., clever, discerning.

sin • gu • lar (siŋ' gyə lər) adj., unusual, out of the ordinary.

skep • ti • cis • m (skep' tə si zəm) n., a doubt or disbelief.

slav • ish • ly (slā' vish lē) adj., like a slave, basely or abjectly servile.

so • lace (sä' ləs) n., consolation, relief from grief or anxiety.

so • li • ci • tous (sə li' sə təs) adj., full of concerns or fears, apprehensive.

sol • i • dar • i • ty (sä lə dar' ə tē) n., unity based on community interests, objectives, or values.

spry (sprī) adj., nimble, quick and light in motion.

squan • der (skwän' dər) vt., to spend extravagantly or foolishly.

stark (stärk) adj., utter, sheer.

stout • ly (staut' lē) adv., firmly, with determination.

stu • pe • fy (stü' pə fī) vt., to make stupid, groggy, or insensible.

sub • se • quent (səb' si kw[a]nt) adj., following in time, order, or place.

sub • ser • vi • ence (səb sər' vē əns) n., assumption of a lower position.

sub • ter • ra • nean (səb tə rā' nē ən) adj., underground.

sup • er • cil • i • ous (sü pər si' le əs) adj., coolly and patronizingly haughty, proud.

sur • ly (sər' le) adj., irritably sullen and difficult in mood.

tac • i • turn (ta′ sə tərn) adj., temperamentally disinclined to talk, quiet.

ta • per (tā′ pər) n., slender candle.

tar • ry (tar′ ē) vi., linger, wait.

tem • per • a • men • tal • ly (tem prə men′ təl ē) adv., as a result of personality.

tor • por (tor′ pər) n., a state of extreme sluggishness or stagnation, lethargy.

trans • fig • ur • a • tion (trans fi gyə rā′ shən) n., an exalting, glorifying, or spiritual change.

un • couth (ən küth′) adj., awkward, unrefined.

un • mol • li • fied (ən mäl′ lə fīd) adj., not soothed.

un • scrup • u • lous (ən skrü′ pyə ləs) adj., lacking in morality, unprincipled.

ut • most (ət′ mōst) adj., the most possible, the highest attainable degree.

ver • i • ta • ble (ver′ ə tə bəl) adj., true, actual.

ver • mil • ion (vər mil′ yən) adj., bright reddish-orange.

vin • dic • tive (vin dik′ tiv) adj., spiteful, intended to cause anguish or hurt.

vi • tal • i • ty (vī ta′ lə tē), n., the peculiarity distinguishing the living from the nonliving.

vi • tal • ize (vī′ təl īz) vt., endow with life, animate.

Handbook of Literary Terms

Allusion. An **allusion** is a rhetorical technique in which reference is made to a person, event, object, or work from history or literature. The epigraph, or quote at the beginning of the novel, alludes to Virgil: "The best days are the first to pass."

Archetype. An **archetype** is an inherited, often unconscious, ancestral memory or motif that recurs throughout history and literature. The notion of the archetype derives from the psychology of Carl Jung, who described archetypes as symbols from humanity's "collective unconscious." The term is often used, more generally, to refer to any element that recurs throughout the literature of the world. In *My Ántonia*, Ántonia is related to the archetype of the earth mother, or the woman intimately connected to the cycles of the earth and its fertility.

Conflict. A **conflict** is a struggle between two forces in a literary work. A *plot* involves the introduction, development, and eventual resolution of a conflict. One side of the central conflict in a story or drama is usually taken by the main character. That character may struggle against another character, against the forces of nature, against society or social norms, against fate, or against some element within himself or herself. A struggle that takes place between a character and some outside force is called an *external conflict*. A struggle that takes place within a character is called an *internal conflict*.

Foil. A **foil** is a character whose attributes, or characteristics, contrast with, and therefore throw into relief, the attributes of another character.

Frame narrative. A **frame narrative** is a narrative, or story, that provides a vehicle for telling another story. *My Ántonia* begins with a frame narrative in which an unnamed narrator meets Jim Burden on a train.

Image. An **image** is language that creates a concrete representation of an object or an experience. An image is also the vivid mental picture created in the reader's mind by that language. The images in a literary work are referred to, collectively, as the work's *imagery*.

Imagery. See *image*.

Metaphor. A **metaphor** is a figure of speech in which one thing is spoken or written about as if it were another. Metaphors invite the reader to make a comparison between the two things. The assertion that "Tom is a real clown" is an example of a metaphor. Metaphors consist of two parts, the *tenor*, or the writer's actual subject, and the *vehicle*, or the thing to which the actual subject is likened. In the example above, the tenor is "Tom" and the vehicle is "a real clown." They can be compared because they share some quality, in this case, being entertaining and silly.

Narrator. A **narrator** is one who tells a story. Works of fiction always have a narrator, unless they consist entirely of dialogue without tag lines, in which case they cease to be fictions and become closet dramas, drama meant to be read aloud but not performed. The narrator in a work of fiction may be a central or minor character or simply someone who witnessed or heard about the events being related. Writers achieve a wide variety of ends by varying the characteristics of the narrator chosen for a particular work. Of primary importance is the choice of the narrator's *point of view*. Will the narrator be *omniscient*, knowing all things, including the internal workings of the minds or the characters in the story, or will the narrator be *limited* in his or her knowledge? Will the narrator participate in the action of the story or stand outside that action and comment on it? Will the narrator be reliable or unreliable? That is, will the reader be able to trust the narrator's statements? These are all questions that a writer must answer when developing a narrator.

Personification. Personification is a figure of speech in which an idea, animal, or thing is described as if it were a person. Willa Cather personifies many elements of nature in *My Ántonia*. For example, the sun is personified on page 157: "The long fingers of the sun touched their foreheads."

Plot. A **plot** is a series of events related to a central *conflict,* or struggle. A typical plot involves the introduction of a conflict, its development, and its eventual resolution. Terms used to describe elements of plot include the following:

- The **exposition** is the part of a plot that provides the background information, often about the characters, setting, or conflict.
- The **inciting incident** is the event that introduces the central conflict.

- The **rising action**, or complication, develops the conflict to a high point of intensity.
- The **climax** is the high point of interest or suspense in the plot.
- The **falling action** is all the events that follow the climax.
- The **resolution** is the point at which the central conflict is ended, or resolved.
- The **dénouement** is any material that follows the resolution and that ties up any loose ends.

Setting. The **setting** of a literary work is the time and place in which it occurs, together with all the details used to create a sense of a particular time and place. Writers create settings by various means. In fiction, setting is most often revealed by means of description of such elements as landscape, scenery, buildings, furniture, clothing, the weather, and the season. It can also be revealed by how characters talk and behave. In its widest sense, setting includes the general social, political, moral, and psychological conditions in which characters find themselves.

Simile. A **simile** is a type of *metaphor* using *like* or *as*. Similes invite the reader to make a comparison between two things. Cather uses a simile to describe the sound of the thunder over the prairie: "The thunder was loud and metallic, like the rattle of sheet iron..." Similes, like all metaphors, consist of two parts, the *tenor*, or the writer's actual subject, and the *vehicle*, or the thing to which the actual subject is likened. In the example above, the tenor is "the thunder," and the vehicle is "the rattle of sheet metal." They can be compared because they share some quality, in this case, a loud, booming sound.

Subplot. A **subplot** is a subordinate story told in addition to the major story in a work of fiction. Often a subplot mirrors or provides a *foil* for the primary plot. *My Ántonia* contains many subplots, including the story Ántonia tells about the man who threw himself into the threshing machine.

Symbol. A **symbol** is a thing that stands for or represents both itself and something else. Writers use two types of symbols—conventional, and personal or idiosyncratic. A conventional symbol is one with traditional, widely recognized associations. Such symbols include doves for peace; laurel wreaths for heroism or poetic excellence; the color green for jealousy; the color purple for royalty; the color red for anger; morning or spring for youth; winter, evening, or night for old age; wind for change or inspiration; rainbows for hope; roses for beauty; the moon for fickleness or inconstancy; roads or paths for the journey through life; woods or darkness for moral or spiritual confusion; thorns for troubles or pain; stars for unchangeableness or constancy; mirrors for vanity or introspection; snakes for evil or duplicity; and owls for wisdom. A personal or idiosyncratic symbol is one that assumes its secondary meaning because of the special use to which it is put by a writer. In "The Prairie Grass Dividing," Walt Whitman uses the prairie grass as a personal symbol for heartiness and independence.

Theme. A **theme** is a central idea in a literary work.

Acknowledgments

Anhinga Press. "Mint Snowball" by Naomi Shihab Nye, published in *Mint Snowball*, (2001) Anhinga Press, PO Box 10595, Tallahassee, Florida, 32302.

Shirley Geok-lin Lim. "Riding into California" from *What The Fortune Teller Didn't Say* (1998) by Shirley Geok-lin Lim. Copyright ©Shirley Geok-lin Lim. Reprinted by permission of the author.

Nebraska State Historical Society. Letter written by Anna Pavelka to Frances Samland on February 24, 1955, from the Willa Cather Pioneer Memorial and Educational Foundation Collection, provided courtesy of the Nebraska State Historical Society.